THE SHADOW OF GODS

THE GODLING CHRONICLES

THE SHADOW OF GODS

BRIAN D. ANDERSON

4 Horsemen
Publications, Inc.

DEDICATION

For Helen and "K." Their devotion to each other is a constant source of inspiration.

CONTENTS

PROLOGUE

Theopolou and Eftichis sat quietly by the small fire. Over the past three days, the makeshift camp had become a divided scene. Theopolou had convinced more than half of the remaining elders to join together against the armies of Angrääl, but Bellisia still held fast to her convictions. Her influence was the only thing preventing Theopolou from turning the tide completely.

"She is a stubborn one," mused Eftichis.

"She believes in what she says," said Theopolou. He looked out over the camp. Noble elves were wandering around in tattered and ripped clothing. The stench of burned-out tents and the decay of the wounded made him want to retch. "And I must admit, her arguments are compelling. There have been times I have doubted my own resolve because of her words."

Eftichis nodded in agreement. "She has passion. There is no doubt about that. But we have pledged our houses to Gewey, and I, for one, will honor that pledge."

"As will I," said Theopolou. "But I cannot deny that my heart has been swayed to the brink. I only hope that my words have had a similar impact on her."

Eftichis nodded. "As do I. The others are sure to join our cause if she relents."

Theopolou stood up and rubbed the back of his neck. "True. And we will need them if we are to have any hope of succeeding."

"Perhaps you should simply try to focus their attention on the elves of the Steppes," Eftichis offered. "It would end the debate. At least for now. We all know that they must be dealt with."

Theopolou shook his head. "No. We must deal with all of the forces arrayed against us at the same time. I believe that one cannot be conquered without the other. They are intertwined." He felt old and weary. "This may break our people. But we have no other choice."

"But Gewey..." said Eftichis, an edge of desperation creeping into his voice. "He can help us remain whole, can he not?"

Theopolou sighed. "Gewey may be a god, but he is not the Creator. As powerful as he is—and will become still—he struggles as well. Gewey does not, and never will, have the power to restore our people. Can he save us from annihilation? Perhaps. But we cannot look to him for our salvation."

"But he opened the Book of Souls," Eftichis contended. "Surely..."

"And what of it?" asked Theopolou, cutting him off. "Did you hear what he said when he read the title?" His eyes gazed into the fire. "It is a true history. A true history."

"Yes, and..." Eftichis began, but the sight of Theopolou's sadness halted him.

"I am the eldest of the elders," said Theopolou in a half-whisper. "I lived through the Great War. But unlike the others, I am old enough to have seen what we were before. We were a broken people, even then. Arrogant and selfish. We were so convinced that humans were inferior."

"But they are," said Eftichis. "They are fragile and weak. They grovel in the mud and live in squalor. How could we not see them as a lesser people?"

"Yes," Theopolou laughed sardonically. "But are we so much better? We have lost, while the humans continue to gain. They build, while we gaze at our former glories." His hand shot out, pointing to the Chamber of the Maker silhouetted against the fading light. "Can we claim to be the same people who built this? Look at us. Are we so different than they?"

"Do you see hope for us?" Eftichis asked, sorrow in his eyes.

"I don't know," Theopolou replied. "I hope so. But whatever hope we have will arise from us, not from Gewey. He may be the instrument of our survival, but in the end, we must determine our own fate. If we live through the coming storm, it will be up to us." He forced a smile. "However, I do have faith in our people. I believe there is still a spark of grace within us."

Just then, Bellisia approached, dressed in a soft, cream linen robe. Her eyes showed fatigue, yet she managed to walk straight and tall with graceful strides. Eftichis and the others rose to their feet and bowed.

"You have been tending the wounded," said Theopolou. "You should rest. Our debate can continue tomorrow."

"I am in no mood for debate," said Bellisia. "I am weary, as you have noticed. I only wish to join you by the fire."

Theopolou offered her a place beside him, which she gratefully accepted.

"Have you eaten?" asked Eftichis.

"I am not hungry," she replied. "Just tired. My heart breaks when I look at what our own kind has done."

"I understand," said Theopolou. "I hoped I would never see such a thing happen again. I have already seen far too much elf blood spilled in my life."

"Do you really believe Angrääl is responsible?" she asked, closing her eyes while contemplating the truth. "Do you think his power is that great?"

"I cannot say for sure," Theopolou admitted. "But I see no other way for this to have happened. Long have our brothers and sisters on the Steppes lived alongside Angrääl. If the Reborn King has the key to heaven, and I believe he does, then it is very possible he could have bent our kin to his will."

"The elves of the Steppes are a strong people," said Eftichis. "If they have indeed been corrupted, then what resistance can we hope to offer? Already we have been betrayed from within our own ranks."

"I do not know what hope there is," said Theopolou. "Only that there is hope. And the elves of the Steppes have been close to the influence of Angrääl from the moment the Reborn King seized power. We have been far removed by comparison. If things had been different, who knows what would have become of us."

"I agree," said Bellisia. "And they are still our kin, regardless of what they have done. I, for one, will not abandon the idea that they can be redeemed. So, if we are to follow the example that you have set before us Theopolou, forgiveness must be in our hearts." Her eyes drifted over the camp. "Though, I admit, it will be difficult. I have not seen so many elves slain since the Great War. I was only twenty-five during the First Split, but the memories are still fresh in my mind."

"It is so for all of us who lived through it," said Theopolou. "And we have passed that memory to our children—along with our hatred and fear. It is a cycle that must end."

A sudden disturbance near the healing pavilion drew everyone's attention. Theopolou and all the others gathered around the fire immediately reached for their weapons. From the direction of the commotion, Marinos appeared. He came half-running toward them.

"What is it?" asked Theopolou as soon as Marinos was within earshot.

"Red sails," he replied. His voice cracked. "Red sails on the horizon."

Theopolou stiffened. "Are you certain?"

"There is no question," he replied.

The others looked confused.

"Red sails? What does that mean?" asked Eftichis

Theopolou lowered his head and took a deep breath. "It means the elves are coming."

CHAPTER 1

Kaylia drifted in and out of consciousness. She knew she had been bound and slung, face down, across the back of a horse. But each time her thoughts came into focus, an unseen force pressed against her and the world would go black again. Finally, she was able to resist long enough to hear voices. Elven voices.

"This does not sit well with me," said a deep male voice. "It is one thing to bring traitors to justice. But I was not told that these creatures would be among us."

"Nor was I," replied another. "Though it is far too late to turn back. Once we are home, then we can consult the elders. Until that time, we must endure their company."

Kaylia felt a hand grab her hair and lift her head. Though she was not blindfolded, she dared not open her eyes.

"Is she awake?" asked the first voice.

"I can't tell," replied the second. "The beast has blocked all connection to the flow. I cannot sense anything."

The first voice grumbled and cursed, but made no other response.

Hours passed before they came to a halt. Kaylia was still feigning unconsciousness when she felt the hair on the back of her neck stand up. Suddenly, the air carried the foul stench of death and she sensed the approach of ... of something?

"She is not asleep," came a rasping voice. "Are you, elf?"

Kaylia felt her bonds being cut. As she slid down from the horse, her legs nearly gave out, but strong arms in rough leathers steadied her. She jerked herself free for a moment while her eyes focused. It was well after nightfall, and a small campfire was being built in a clearing a few yards away. She could make out about twenty elves, but that was not what caught her attention. It was the thing standing in front of her: a Vrykol, tall and slender, adorned in a sleek, hooded black robe and carrying a long, vicious-looking curved blade. It reeked of decay, and its foul breath wheezed and gurgled.

Kaylia glared at the creature. "So, this is what our people have become? Murderers of their own kind, and slaves to the darkness of this world?" Her tone was proud and defiant.

"Mind your tongue," warned the elf holding her. "We are the bringers of justice. It is you who have betrayed our people."

Kaylia threw her head back in harsh laughter. "You travel with the Vrykol. You attack elves on sacred ground. How dare you name me traitor?"

"Enough of this," screeched the Vrykol. The sound pierced the air, causing Kaylia to wince. "You are to remain silent unless spoken to." He turned to the elf at her back. "As for you—your comrades grow restless. Calm them." His black hands reached out and grasped Kaylia's arm in an iron grip. "I can manage this one."

The elf grunted and strode off in the direction of the others.

"I will make you pay for what you have done to my people," seethed Kaylia. "And I will make your master pay as well."

Before she could measure the moment, the Vrykol's fist crashed into Kaylia's jaw, sending her sprawling to the ground.

"I told you to be silent." The Vrykol lowered his blade, pressing the tip against Kaylia's throat. "My master has insisted that you be kept alive. But he said nothing about your condition."

Even though Kaylia's face throbbed from the impact, she glared unflinchingly.

"That's better," growled the Vrykol. "Remain still and silent."

A few minutes had passed when the tall elf returned. He looked down at Kaylia, then back at the Vrykol.

"She was to be left unharmed," he grumbled angrily. "That was the agreement. No elf is to be injured by your hands." He looked back at the group of elves gathering around the crackling fire. "If you do not uphold your end of the bargain, you will find yourself quickly surrounded by enemies."

The Vrykol let out a vile laugh. "As you wish." He removed the blade from Kaylia's throat. "But see to it that she is well tended. Should she escape, it will be you who pays the price." With that, he spun around and disappeared into the darkness.

The tall elf held out his hand. "I am Freistal. Do not try to escape. The elves you see here are not the only ones I have with me. The forest is filled with my kin. I would hate to see you harmed before you can be brought to justice."

Kaylia sneered and struggled to her feet. "We will see who is brought to justice."

Freistal pulled her roughly to his side. "Perhaps you think your human mate will save you? Or perhaps Linis and his seekers? Let me assure you that they have been dealt with. And even if they have somehow survived, they will not be able to save you."

Kaylia forced a malicious laugh. "Let me assure you that Gewey and Linis would not fall to the likes of you or your rabble. And when they find you, you will wish you had never left your lands. If you think to look to the Vrykol for safety, you will find that they can be slain just as easily as you."

Freistal shrugged. "Perhaps. But for now, you will remain with us, and you will not escape. I will allow you to stay unbound. Do not make me regret it, or you certainly will." He motioned for her to go to the fire. "We rest for only a short time. Unless you wish me to strap you back onto the horse, you should eat so that you will have the strength to travel."

Kaylia rubbed her jaw, then made her way to the fire. Freistal followed close behind. Though he held no weapon, she was certain that if she made a wrong move, her body would be filled with arrows before she could take more than a few steps. As she approached the group by the fire, she could feel everyone's eyes upon her. She stiffened her back while choosing an empty space a moderate distance away from the others. Freistal knelt beside her and handed her a flask of water and a handful of jerky.

"I suggest you hold your tongue," he whispered. "Things are a bit tense. And your comments will not be welcome."

"I take it they are not pleased with your traveling companion," she mocked. "I cannot say that I blame them."

"That is putting it mildly," Freistal replied. "But your presence is just as unwelcome to us. So mind that you give them no excuse to take their frustrations out on you."

"So I am to be beaten if I speak?" Kaylia sneered. "You will behave as the Vrykol?"

"I would not have you harmed," Freistal retorted. "We are not animals. Speak as you will, but be warned. There are those among us that have a deep hatred for your kin—and you in particular."

"Why?" asked Kaylia. "Where does this hatred come from?"

Freistal looked at her sideways. "We know who your kin have allied themselves with. They would make us allies of the very people that destroyed us in the first place. And you..."

He paused. "You bond yourself to a human, seeking to doom us all. Your crimes are beyond forgiveness." He rose to his feet and glared down at her. "I, for one, will not stand idly by while you and your people annihilate what is left of our kind."

"How can you accuse me or my kin of betrayal?" shot back Kaylia. "You have been deceived by the evil that dwells in Angrääl."

"Then you deny that elves and humans are allowed to befriend each other?" he said angrily. "You deny that your elders do nothing to stop it? You deny that you have bonded yourself to a human?"

She glared at him defiantly. "Who I choose to love is my own affair, not yours. And if you are so foolish as to think it shall be the end of our people, then your stupidity knows no bounds."

He met her gaze. "Because of you and others like you, our people will disappear and become nothing more than a distant memory. A mere shadow of what we once were."

"So that is why you have done this?" said Kaylia, loud enough for all to hear. "Because of half-truths and fear?"

"You deny it then?" Freistal asked. "You deny that your kin intends to join with the humans?"

"I do not deny that I have bonded myself to a human," she replied defiantly. "And I do not deny that many of my kin have formed friendships with humans. But we are not destroying our people. We are saving them." She stood to address the entire group, but Freistal caught her arm.

"Do not do this," he warned. "You will not sway us. You will only anger them and put yourself in further danger."

"It seems to me that I can be in no more danger than I am already," said Kaylia, jerking her arm free. "And if you intend to take me back to your people on the Steppes, then you will not harm me until then." She stood straight and proud. And though disheveled from being captured, her fierce gaze gave her a regal appearance.

"Let her speak," came a voice from the crowd. "Her lies will do nothing but strengthen our resolve."

"Very well," sighed Freistal.

Kaylia squared her shoulders and took a step forward. "I know you think me a traitor. I know you believe that your actions are justified." Her tone was imposing. "But ask yourself this—who is it that you serve? Is this the will of the elders? Or is this the will of the King in Angrääl? You are pawns in his game of conquest. Surely, at least some of you sense this."

A few elves stirred, but none said anything as Kaylia continued.

"If this is not so, then why are you traveling with a Vrykol? Do you really believe that this creature will allow you to take me to your elders? It will never let that happen. I am to be used as leverage against the one being who can challenge the power of Angrääl." Tears began to well in her eyes, but her voice remained steady. "You have killed your own kin based on a lie. You have led your brothers and sisters to their death in the process. How many of you died in your attack? Twenty? Thirty?"

Angry murmurs and tearful stares told her that it was far more.

"Fifty-seven," whispered Freistal. "And your deceptions will not make us believe that they died for nothing. You accuse us of being weak. But we are the pawns of no one. Not the Reborn King—and not you. While you and your kin have made alliances with the humans and the gods, we have remained true to our traditions and ways. We have not diluted our blood with that of lesser beings, and we will never do so. The armies you gather against us will fall."

"Armies?" Kaylia cried. "We have raised no armies. It is Angrääl that raises armies. It is this 'Reborn King' who threatens to march. Not us."

"You lie!" shouted Freistal. "I have seen them. Your ships have been spotted many times by my own eyes. And your war council we attacked will no doubt hasten plans now that they know we are aware of their treachery."

"You speak nonsense," said Kaylia. "Your mind has been twisted by the power of the Dark One. Can you not see this? I did not accuse you of weakness before, but I do so now. You have been touched by the power he wields. The Sword of Truth has bent you to his will. But surely some of your own will remains?"

"I told you to keep her silent," hissed the voice of the Vrykol as it appeared from behind the outlying brush. "Her words are poison. She seeks to deceive you."

The Vrykol moved to grab Kaylia, but Freistal stepped between them.

"She is our responsibility now," he said. "You need not concern yourself with her any longer."

"Fool," said the Vrykol. "If I were not here, her mate would have already found you and slaughtered you all like sheep." It took a step forward. "She will remain with me until I am certain we are no longer being pursued."

"You are not master here," said Freistal. "And she remains with me. I have no fear of any human."

Freistal and the Vrykol stood mere inches from each other, but neither made a move to draw a weapon. Though his features were hidden, Kaylia knew that the creature was scowling with fury.

"Very well," relented the Vrykol after a very long moment. "She will remain with you—for now." It spun around and vanished into the forest.

Freistal called two elves to him and commanded them to watch over Kaylia.

"Do not mistake my defense of you as a sign that your words have swayed me," said Freistal. "But I will not see you brought to Angrääl, and I believe you are right about one thing. That creature out there has no intention of allowing you to be delivered to our elders."

As soon as the party had finished their meal, they packed and set out again at an even more desperate pace than before. Kaylia repeatedly tried to reach out to Gewey, but found that her bond with him was somehow being blocked—by the Vrykol, she assumed. She could only hope for a chance to escape.

By midday, Kaylia began to sense further unrest among her captors. The Vrykol made occasional appearances, each time its foul gaze lingering on her before disappearing once again into the forest. She could feel the tension rising with each encounter. Clearly, the elves were finding the presence of such an evil creature increasingly difficult to bear. Several were becoming more vocal in their displeasure.

"Why tolerate this?" Kaylia asked Freistal, who was running just behind her. "Nothing good can come from such a being."

"We are commanded to allow its presence," grumbled Freistal. "And so long as it makes no move against us, we shall obey that command." He shoved her roughly. "So keep moving and mind your tongue."

Just then, the Vrykol appeared a little ahead of the band, motioning for them to halt.

"What is it?" asked Freistal, clearly annoyed. "Why are we stopping?"

"The elf woman's mate is drawing near. She must come with me," the Vrykol hissed. His black hand reached out to grab Kaylia.

Freistal jerked Kaylia behind him, at the same time drawing his long knife. The ringing of Elven steel sliding free could be heard from all directions.

The Vrykol let loose a harsh rasping laugh. "You think to stop me?" It took a step forward, then let out a high, piercing cry. So harsh was the sound that the elves were forced to cover their ears. "Alone I could take her," he said. "But did you really think my master would send only one servant to guard his prize? You are a pitiful fool."

Just then, six more Vrykol stepped into view, each holding a long blade.

"You will not be taking her anywhere, demon," Freistal roared.

Kaylia heard the snap of a bowstring and the whiz of an arrow. The Vrykol hardly had time to react as the arrow buried itself deep into its chest. But the creature merely stepped back, pulling the arrow free and tossing it carelessly to the ground. The air grew cold and still as the Vrykol turned to its comrades and gave a curt nod. With astounding swiftness, it then spun back around and charged at Kaylia. The elves erupted in response, some rushing at the other six Vrykol, others to aid Freistal.

Freistal slashed at the Vrykol's neck; the beast easily blocked the blow with his own blade and brought the hilt up, crashing into the elf's jaw. Freistal staggered back, barely able to keep his feet. Several more arrows pierced the Vrykol's flesh as it brought its blade down, attempting to hew the elf in twain. Freistal raised his knife just in time. Sparks flew as metal clashed on metal.

Kaylia knew this was her chance to flee. Rapidly, she looked at her surroundings. Six Vrykol had engaged the bulk of the company, and though the elves were fighting with ferocity, they were falling one by one to the wicked swords of their foes. Five other elves had joined Freistal in the fight and were driving the solitary Vrykol back, but their blades were useless. Clearly, they did not know how to kill the creature. The arrows had ceased, and the elf archers filed in from the forest, blades drawn.

Without hesitation, Kaylia turned and ran. The last thing she saw of the battle was Freistal clutching desperately at the Vrykol's blade, which had run through his gullet only a moment before.

She felt anger and regret, but there was no time to dwell on it. She needed to get as far away as possible. The Vrykol had said Gewey was near, but she still couldn't feel where he was through their bond. She hoped that if she got far enough away, the Vrykol's influence would wane and she would once again be able to feel Gewey's reassuring presence to guide her. The trees were a blur as she ran faster and faster.

While she was still in full flight, a dark figure appeared a few yards ahead. Kaylia slid to a halt. A Vrykol loomed, sword drawn. Its cloak was shredded from the battle with the elves, but still, she could not make out its form beneath the tattered rags. Instinctively, she reached for her knife, only to realize she was unarmed. She looked around for signs of other Vrykol, but there were none. Her legs tensed for a moment, then burst into action as she ran straight at the creature. Clearly surprised by this unexpected tactic, it sidestepped, slightly lowering its blade. Just as Kaylia was in reach, she ducked and slammed her fist into the Vrykol's knee.

It was like hitting iron. She felt pain shoot through her hand and up her arm, but her blow was enough to part the Vrykol's legs and force it to lean forward. Kaylia immediately thrust her body upward, burying her shoulder into the beast's chest, sending it stumbling back.

Kaylia knew she had no hope of defeating the Vrykol without a blade and trying to disarm it would mean certain death. It was far too strong; her only hope was to outrun the creature. But could she? She had seen how fast they could move. Even with several minutes' head start, this one had managed to catch up with her. Fear gripped her chest, but she fought it back and ran as fast as she could, not even bothering to glance back. She had unbalanced it, but she knew that would only be for a few seconds at best. I must move faster, she told herself.

She had only run a few yards further when something hard struck the back of her head. She tried to keep on her feet but could feel herself losing consciousness and tumbling hard to the ground. The world began to turn dark as she heard the footfalls of the Vrykol approaching and the hiss of its foul breath.

She wanted to cry out, but the light faded from her vision as the blow to her head overcame her.

CHAPTER 2

L inis halted, a confused look on his face.
"What is it?" asked Gewey.

Linis bent down, placing his palm just above the ground and closing his eyes. "Something follows our quarry," he muttered. "Something unclean."

"Vrykol," growled Gewey.

"Yes," agreed Linis. "It must be. Nothing else I can imagine would leave such a scent. It's like ... death."

"Then we have to catch up with Kaylia before they do," said Gewey without hesitation.

Linis opened his eyes and looked straight at Gewey. "Don't worry, my friend. We will."

They continued to race through the forest. Gewey kept a few paces behind Linis, all the while reaching out to Kaylia. He told himself that since he hadn't lost her entirely, that meant they were still going in the right direction. It wasn't until it was fully night that Linis halted again.

"We must slow our pace," he stated.

Gewey's jaw tightened. "If you can't keep going..."

"It is not that I am weary, my friend," said Linis, cutting him off. "But if either the elves or the Vrykol are aware of our pursuit, they may decide to lay in wait. And though I am uncertain of the Vrykol's skill in stealth, I do know that it is unwise to believe the elves are without such ability." He peered into the night. "I can spot a trap in the deepest darkness. But not if I move too quickly."

"I can sense every living being for hundreds of yards," argued Gewey. "There is no way they can hide from me."

Linis thought for a moment. Gewey had been channeling the flow from the moment they left, and there was no doubt he could do as he claimed. "No," he said finally. "Whatever is blocking your connection to Kaylia may also be able to hide itself from you. I would not risk it."

Gewey was silent for several seconds, then nodded sharply.

Linis withdrew a flask from his pocket and drank deeply. "Jawas tea," he said, handing it to Gewey.

Gewey took the flask and drained it. The tea filled his belly and relaxed his limbs. Even the flow felt as if it came with more ease. He drew his sword, taking in more power. Then, from a few hundred yards away, he sensed something. His muscles tensed as he reached out to find the source. He had done this several times before during the pursuit. Usually, it had been a deer or a bear, and once, a fox. In fact, under different circumstances, he would have marveled at being able to touch the mind of a wild animal.

But what Gewey sensed now possessed passion and life in a way no human or elf could understand. It lived for the moment, with no care for anything other than survival. And this time, the mind he had found touched him back. Dark and tortured, it was filled with hate and anger, yet also sorrow and desperation. He recoiled and drew back within himself. He knew he had just touched the mind of a Vrykol. And he knew it had sensed him as well.

"They're here," whispered Gewey. "The Vrykol are here."

It took Linis a moment, but then he felt it as well. "There are eight of them." He drew his knife. "This will not be easy."

Gewey filled his lungs and allowed the flow to saturate him. "Let me handle them. You stay back."

"I will not," Linis said, his face set. "You may be powerful, but we still do not know the extent of these creatures' powers. It could well be that they are the reason you cannot feel your bond with Kaylia. If that is the case, they may be able to do more than we imagine."

"Then what do you think we should do?" asked Gewey.

"They know we are here," said Linis. "But they do not move against us just yet. Perhaps they want us to move against them." He surveyed the area. "We should move past them and put ourselves between them and Kaylia. If I am correct, that will force them to move against us. I would rather them act according to our plan than us to theirs."

Gewey nodded, then followed closely behind as Linis led them in a wide arc around the Vrykol's location. Gewey knew that their movements had been detected. In fact, Linis made certain of it, making just enough noise to draw the Vrykol's attention.

"Now what?" asked Gewey.

Before Linis could answer, he sensed the Vrykol moving. But to his dismay, only two were coming in their direction. The other six were heading west in an apparent attempt to flank them. Gewey faced the direction of the two oncoming creatures while Linis peered into the forest, listening for the others. Just when the two Vrykol were in sight, they stopped and separated to left and right, forcing Linis to turn his attention away from the flanking maneuver.

"We must kill these first two before the others reach us," shouted Linis. "If not, we will be overwhelmed."

Gewey's heart raced. He could feel his sword, hot in his hand. The flow was like a flood raging through him. He turned to Linis with a malicious grin. "They will never have that chance." He took a step forward, focusing on the single Vrykol moving to his left. With a tremendous boom, the earth exploded beneath the creature, sending it flying—limbs flailing. Its screams pierced the air as it slammed into a tall pine and then slid to the forest floor.

"Finish the beast, Linis," Gewey said in a near whisper. "I'll deal with the other one." He focused his mind on the second Vrykol. It had stopped a moment after he'd unleashed the flow on the first. Gewey stretched out again, but this time something stopped him. It felt the same as when trying and failing to reach out to Kaylia. A cold chill seized his chest.

Linis had sped off toward the fallen Vrykol. He saw it leaning against the tree, struggling to rise, its cruel sword still in hand. Linis knew he had only seconds before the beast recovered. He rushed headlong at it, swinging his long knife at the creature's neck. The Vrykol tried to move away, but Linis was too fast. His blade severed its head clean. He glanced over to Gewey for a moment and saw him moving steadily toward the second Vrykol. He then listened out for the sound of the others, but couldn't hear them—not anywhere.

Gewey knew now why he was unable to contact Kaylia. Somehow, the beasts were able to block him. He tried again to explode the earth beneath the Vrykol but with the same result.

The soft hiss of evil laughter seeped from within the hood of the Vrykol's cloak. "That only works once, boy."

"It won't save you," growled Gewey. The flow was still raging within. Maybe he could not use it to destroy this Vrykol directly, but so long as the flow remained with him, he knew that the monster would stand no chance.

"Perhaps not," said the Vrykol. Its voice was thin and raspy, though clearer than others Gewey had encountered. "But then again, I am not the one that needs to be saved."

In a flash, the Vrykol charged, its sword held so low it was almost touching the ground. Gewey stood in a wide stance and steadied himself for the onslaught. His sword was fire in his hand as the Vrykol reached him, swinging its blade upward. Gewey easily dodged the blow and stepped to one side, ready to take the beast's head. Then, from the corner of his eye, he saw a flash as the creature stabbed at his neck with the other hand. Its fingers were wrapped loosely around a small dagger. Gewey turned again, but the tip of the blade found flesh, cutting deep.

A burning pain shot through his body. He stumbled back, slashing wildly, but the Vrykol moved away just out of reach.

"Arrogant fool," the Vrykol taunted, twirling the dagger in its hand. "And you hope to challenge my master?"

Dizziness started to overcome Gewey—his vision was slowly becoming more and more blurred. Struggling to keep his focus on the Vrykol, he waited for it to charge again, but it remained still. He reached up and touched the wound on his neck. Blood poured down, soaking his shoulder. Though the cut was deep, it shouldn't have been bleeding this badly. *Poison*, he thought with disgust.

"So frail," laughed the Vrykol. "So foolish."

The Vrykol feinted left, then right, throwing Gewey off balance. He just managed to bring his sword up in time to deflect a blow that came in a wide arc. He could feel the flow draining from him as the beast pushed forward. Soon, he knew, he would be defenseless. He tried to counter, but his blurred vision was causing him to strike off target each time. A sudden wave of nausea swept through his body. Falling to one knee, Gewey glared up defiantly, jaw clenched tight.

"You see," the Vrykol taunted. "You are not even a match for the servants of the Great Lord." He kicked Gewey's sword from his hand.

Gewey leaned back on his knees and held his head high, readying himself for the final blow. He heard the whip of a blade approach. But the expected slash of steel never came. Instead, the Vrykol let out a mighty roar of anger, a small dagger protruding from his left shoulder. The beast spun to meet his attacker, but Linis was upon him before he could react. His long knife cleaved off the Vrykol's leg just below the hip. It toppled back and fell to the ground. Without missing a step, Linis swung again, this time decapitating his enemy. Thick black blood oozed from the wounds, hissing as it touched the soft forest turf.

Gewey smiled with satisfaction, even though the cut on his neck was now burning with an evil fury. He looked at the head of the slain creature—twisted and scorched, but clearly human. Its skin blackened, just like the others he'd encountered, but not nearly as badly. He thought about how the first Vrykol had looked and sounded. This one was most certainly an advancement on that. Definitely stronger. But why?

These thoughts vanished from his mind as another wave of nausea took him. He emptied his stomach with a groan. Linis was at his side in an instant.

"Poison," Linis spat, examining the cut. "Red Spider Blossom, from the look of it." He smiled. "Nothing to worry about. It is meant to incapacitate, not kill." He reached to his belt and removed his flask.

Gewey drank greedily, nearly draining it dry. The jawas tea was cool and instantly settled his stomach. His wound still throbbed, but the burning slowly subsided. He sighed with relief. "And the other Vrykol?"

"I don't know," Linis admitted. "They seemed to have retreated. Why, I could not say, but I take it as good fortune. We will need to rest for at least a few hours. You cannot continue until the poison wears off."

Gewey shook his head. "We rest only until I can regain my feet, and not a second more." He tried to let the flow pass through him, but it was sluggish and weak.

Linis looked at him disapprovingly. He thought about objecting but could see that Gewey would not be dissuaded. Sighing, he closed his eyes and placed his hands on the wound.

Gewey felt as if a blade of ice had shot through his neck. The sudden shock made him gasp out loud. But then, within a matter of seconds, the intense cold became a pleasant, cool sensation. The cut on his neck ceased to throb and his head began to clear. Linis kept his hands on Gewey for several more minutes before finally removing them. He breathed heavily and opened his eyes.

"You should be ready to travel soon," he said wearily.

"What did you do?" asked Gewey, touching his neck gingerly. The wound was nearly closed. It itched a bit, but the pain was completely gone.

Linis rubbed the bridge of his nose and lowered his head. "I have channeled my flow into you. You are healed, but I am drained." He squeezed his eyes shut.

Gewey placed his hand on Linis's shoulder. "Will you be all right?"

Linis looked up and smiled weakly. He took the flask from Gewey and frowned as he found it empty. He reached in his belt and pulled out another. "I will be. Though I will not be able to travel as fast, or fight as well, for at least a day. But do not fear. I can move fast enough for our purpose, and I'm still more than a match for our prey. Just give me a little time to regain some strength." He crossed his legs and bowed his head. "Go back to the path. I must focus. I will be along shortly."

Gewey sat there for a moment, then struggled to his feet and retrieved his sword. Though still unsteady, his strength was returning, and he slowly made his way back to the path. Nearly an hour had passed by the time Linis rejoined him. Gewey scrutinized the elf for a moment. If he was unable to continue, it didn't show. As for Gewey, much of his strength had already returned. He had been listening for signs of the other Vrykol, but just as Linis had said, they were gone.

"I think we should follow them," said Linis. "I do not believe that this encounter was a coincidence. They will lead us to Kaylia."

Gewey nodded sharply and focused. The trail the Vrykol had left was clear and easy to follow. "I'll lead," he said.

Without another word, the two of them raced off after the Vrykol. Gewey could tell that Linis was struggling to keep pace, but he also knew they could ill afford to slow down. Too much time had already been lost. They continued for more than three hours without pause. For a while, Gewey could still feel the fatigue left over from the poison, but it soon vanished as the flow continued to course through his body. From time to time he reached out for Kaylia, but her mind was still shrouded.

As the sun waned, they had still come no closer to catching the Vrykol or Kaylia. Then, just as desperation was returning, Gewey was flooded with her presence. So suddenly did this happen, it nearly caused him to lose his footing. He ground to a sudden halt.

Linis almost ran into him. "What is it?" he panted, the evidence of his diminished condition obvious in his voice.

Gewey held out his hand to silence the elf. He closed his eyes and concentrated with all his power. "She is near," he whispered almost inaudibly. His eyes widened. "And she's in danger." The sinews of his legs burst into life, propelling him forward with such speed that Linis had no chance of catching him.

The forest was a blur as Gewey ran headlong in Kaylia's direction. She was near, though, heading away from him. But there was something else—a Vrykol was pursuing her. Its velocity was great, and he knew Kaylia would not be able to escape it.

He unsheathed his sword and power exploded within him. This caught the Vrykol's attention. It was only a few hundred yards away and standing between himself and Kaylia. The beast turned to Gewey for an instant, then back around. Gewey could feel the hatred spewing out of the creature. Hatred for everything. The creature raised its sword arm.

It was then that Gewey spotted Kaylia. He knew the Vrykol intended to heave its blade at her, and he knew that he was still too far away. He let out a scream, and with all his might, thrust a burst of power directly at the Vrykol. He feared this one would block him in the same way the other had, but it didn't. The strength of the flow flattened the creature to the ground. But Gewey had not been fast enough. The blade had already flown from its hand. With one last burst, Gewey tried to change the sword's direction, but instead, he only succeeded in pushing it forward even faster.

"No!" His cry shook the ground as the sword struck its target.

Kaylia jerked forward and fell to the ground, the hilt of the blade nearly crushing her skull. Gewey leaped over the flattened body of the Vrykol and was at Kaylia's side without pause. She was face down, blood pouring from the wound on the back of her head. Immediately, he tore the sleeve from his shirt and pressed it tightly over the wound, trying desperately to stop the bleeding.

"I will not lose you," he cried. "Not now."

He closed his eyes and let the flow rage through him. Slowly, he allowed it to pass into Kaylia, focusing his mind on her injury. At first, he wasn't sure that anything was happening. Then he felt it. The wound was closing, and the flow of blood lessened to a trickle. Gewey could feel this draining him, making him weaker, but he didn't care. When the wound had closed completely, he stopped and gently turned her over. It was then he heard Linis approaching. The elf paused beside the Vrykol and beheaded the mangled body.

"She lives?" asked Linis, out of breath.

Gewey nodded, cradling Kaylia in his arms. "She lives." Tears were streaming down his face as he stroked her hair tenderly. "Thank the gods ... she lives."

Linis knelt beside them. He placed his hand on Gewey's shoulder and squeezed. "You did well, my friend."

Nearly ten minutes passed before Kaylia stirred. Her eyes fluttered open as her hands slid up Gewey's chest and wrapped themselves around his neck. "I knew you would come," she whispered. She pulled him close and embraced him tightly.

Gewey could feel the bond between them growing ever stronger and allowed himself to be engulfed by their connection. He hadn't realized just how much a part of himself their bond had become until it had been weakened. And now it had returned. He was happy to bathe in the sensation.

Linis stood, his legs still a bit unsteady. "We cannot stay here." He looked down at Kaylia. "Can you travel?"

Kaylia reluctantly released her hold on Gewey and sat up straight. "I am fine." She noticed the seeker's condition and frowned. "But you are clearly not well."

Linis smiled. "I will be fine once I have had a chance to rest." He peered into the forest for a moment. "For now, I can sense no pursuit. But I would have us far from this place come sundown."

Gewey listened for signs of anyone nearby. "I can't sense anything, either. But I think you're right. We should get as far from here as we can." He looked over at the body of the beheaded Vrykol and his face darkened. He stood, helping Kaylia to her feet.

"No need to coddle me," she scolded playfully. "From the look of you two, I am by far in the best condition." Without another word, she strode away north.

"I take it you will lead," remarked Linis.

Kaylia glanced over her shoulder. "I know these lands very well. Maybe even as well as you, seeker. My captors wasted their time if they thought to confuse me."

A wave of anger shot through her bond with Gewey when she mentioned her captivity. Gewey felt a sudden urge to hunt them all down and make them pay, but quickly pushed it from his thoughts. This was not the time.

Kaylia led them skillfully through the forest until the light of the day waned. By then, they had traveled many miles. Linis managed to keep pace despite his growing fatigue.

"I will scout the area," he said when they finally stopped to make camp.

"No," said Kaylia, firmly. "You are too weak. I will see that the area is unwatched." She turned to Gewey and took his empty flask from his belt. "There is a stream nearby, and possibly some herbs. In the meantime, we will risk a small fire. Attend to it, if you please, Gewey."

Linis tossed her his flask as well. "You may find jawas roots in these parts, or perhaps yellow silisia bulbs."

Kaylia nodded and disappeared into the brush.

Linis offered to help with the fire, but Gewey wouldn't hear of it. "We need you strong again," he said. "You must rest. I can build a fire without help."

Linis smiled and sat down against a nearby tree. He allowed his eyes to fall shut and his mind to drift.

By the time Kaylia returned, Gewey had a small fire crackling cheerfully. Linis was still leaning against the tree, arms folded and eyes closed.

Kaylia handed Gewey his now-filled flask and sat next to him by the fire. "I could not find jawas, but silisia was plentiful."

She withdrew a handful of small yellow flowers from her belt and began tearing them into tiny pieces. The air filled with a sickly sweet odor that reminded Gewey of plum brandy, only stronger. Once she was finished, she opened

Linis's flask and placed the shredded bulbs inside. Tearing a strip of cloth from her sleeve, she tied the flask to a long twig and held it over the fire. "It's not as good as jawas, but it will help." She glanced over at Linis. Her expression was grave.

"What's wrong?" asked Gewey.

"Nothing," she replied. "It is just odd to see someone such as Linis in this state."

"He got that way healing me," explained Gewey. He recounted the fight with the Vrykol.

"Then it is a wonder he was able to make it this far," said Kaylia. "Healing of that sort is not easy, and the cost is great." She touched the back of her head where the sword had struck, then looked deep into Gewey's eyes. She leaned in and kissed him gently. "You are powerful to have healed me the way you did. Such a feat would have incapacitated even the strongest elf."

Gewey flushed bright red. His heart was pounding and he could still feel the warmth of her lips, even though they were no longer on his. It took him a minute to speak. "I honestly don't know how I did it. Since we left the spirit world, it's like I understand the flow in my heart—but I still can't understand it in my mind." His thoughts turned to how the Vrykol had been able to block his abilities. "There's too much I don't understand." He waved it off and smiled. "I wasn't able to reach out to you when the elves held you captive. I think somehow the Vrykol was responsible, but..."

He shook his head and took hold of Kaylia's hands. "Tell me what happened?"

Kaylia told him about her time in captivity. When she was done, she dropped the flask next to the fire and kissed Gewey again, this time long and deep.

"What was that for?" he stammered.

Kaylia smiled. "Because I feared I would never again have the chance. And..."

She grabbed Gewey's collar roughly and met his eyes. Her smile had vanished. "As we are bonded, it is my right."

There was a long pause, then they both burst out laughing. Gewey felt as if a weight had been lifted from his heart. They spent the next hour huddled together in silence, staring into the fire. Their bond made words unnecessary. Kaylia finished the tea and left it to cool.

"It will be ready by daybreak," she said. "Linis should drink most of it, but be certain you have at least a mouthful." She lay down on the forest floor. "Strong as you are, I can tell that healing me has taken its toll on you."

Gewey hadn't noticed until that moment how much his body ached. He lay next to Kaylia and allowed his mind to drift into hers. He felt closer to her than ever before.

A satisfied smile washed over his face as sleep finally took him.

CHAPTER 3

As Millet and Dina neared Sharpstone, Millet's spirits noticeably lifted. When they were only a mile from town, they spurred their horses to a quick trot. Millet looked to and fro, taking in familiar sights and grinning happily. Martha Tredall, one of the village mothers and the wife of Hallis Tredall, the cooper, was the first person they encountered. Martha was a short, sturdy woman with short mouse-brown hair and a cheerful demeanor. She'd had many past dealings with Millet, and he'd built a good rapport with both her and her husband. Nonetheless, as soon as she saw the two riding up, her typical good-natured smile turned to a sour stare.

Millet took a quick glance at his dusty, stained shirt and trousers. Once tan, they were blotched with mud, making him look more like a farmer than a lord. Dina fared a bit better. She had chosen a dark brown blouse and matching pants, which hid the dirt from the long road far better.

"And just where have you been, Master Millet?" Martha asked when they were by her side. "Off making trouble with that Starfinder fellow, I imagine." She looked back down the road they had come along. "I see he's not with you. So much the better. We have enough troubles here without the likes of him around."

"Mind what you say, Martha Tredall," said Millet. "Lee Starfinder has never given you reason to speak ill of him. He's given your husband more than his share of business."

Martha lowered her eyes. "He has, true enough. But that doesn't excuse him for bringing trouble to our town, now does it?"

"What trouble?" asked Millet, steadying in his horse.

Martha looked up at Millet. Her eyes were filled with anger. "Those bloody faithful. They started arriving just after you and Lee made off with young Gewey Stedding." She lowered her voice to a whisper. "Gewey's not coming back, is he?"

"Why do you ask?"

She stepped close. "Because they keep askin' about him— those faithful, I mean. They've asked everyone in town if they know where he is."

Millet suddenly felt very exposed on the road. "And what do you tell them?"

Martha stood up straight and held her head high. "I don't tell them nothin'. I don't care how much gold they throw around. Besides, I don't know nothin' anyway. Last I heard, he went north with Lee. Not that I believed a word of it, but that's what we were told by Lee's servants. From what I hear about those faithful, they're from up north themselves. I figure if Gewey went that way for real, they wouldn't be down here lookin' for him."

Millet thought for a moment. "How many of these faithful are there?"

Martha shrugged. "Not many. Ten or so maybe. But they got lots of gold. They make your master look like a beggar. And they use it, too. They've practically bought the town. There's not a shop or farm in Sharpstone that isn't caught up with them somehow or other."

"Where do they stay?" asked Millet.

"They built themselves a big house just north of town. Not far from your master's place." She took a step back and glanced at Dina. "You and your friend might want to stay away. They ain't hurt no one yet, but they look like they could."

Millet's eye narrowed. "No, my dear. I will not be staying away." He looked down the road toward town. "And just so you know, Lee Starfinder is no longer master. I am." He spurred his horse. Dina followed closely behind.

The way to the manor took them to the outskirts of town. The few people they passed on the way stopped and stared. Some dashed away. When they arrived at the entrance to one of the many roads that led to the house, Millet slowed his horse to a walk.

"I take it this is not the homecoming you were expecting," said Dina.

Millet dropped his head and took a deep breath. "I wasn't certain what to expect. I thought Angrääl might be watching Sharpstone, being that it is Gewey's hometown. But I didn't expect them to set up a base here."

"What are you going to do?"

Millet looked up. Anger burned in his eyes. "I'm going to kick them out of my town."

As they approached the house, Millet caught sight of two servants busy tending the garden. He recognized them as Barty Inglewood and his son, Randson. Lee had hired them five years ago. Originally from Gath, they were as stout and dedicated workers as a person could hope to find. Their faces lit up when they saw Millet.

"I thought you'd left us for good," called Barty. He set down his rake and removed his work gloves, shoving them into his pocket. His son only glanced up and nodded from where he was trimming the hedges, then went back to his work.

"As did I," said Millet.

"Randson," called Barty. "Help Millet and…"

"This is Dina," said Millet. "A friend. This is Barty Inglewood and his son, Randson. They are by far the best gardeners for a hundred miles."

"A friend of Millet's is my friend as well." Barty bowed awkwardly. "And where is Lord Starfinder?"

Millet and Dina dismounted and began unpacking their gear. "Lee will not be coming."

Barty rubbed his chin. "I see. I've never heard you call him Lee before, so I reckon you have news to tell." He began gathering their things. "You'll be wanting to wash up. I'll get Lydia started on your rooms and a bath. Mealtime may have to wait for a couple of hours, though. Most everyone is staying down at the Stedding farm nowadays."

"Lee instructed for the farm to be cared for," said Millet. "But I don't think he intended for his entire staff to move there." He took a quick look around. "Who's left?"

"Me and my boy, of course. Lydia does most of the housework, and Trevor, the old cook Lee hired a couple of years ago, is still here. But he doesn't move around so good anymore, so Lydia helps in the kitchen too." He slung a pack over his shoulder. "No one wants to be around here for too long now. All those newcomers are about. The rest of the staff comes about once a week to see to repairs and the like, but then they're off again. If Lord Starfinder didn't pay so good, they'd all be moved away by now."

Mention of the newcomers brought tension to Millet's face.

"I see you've already heard about them," said Barty. He started toward the house. "Well, don't you worry. They don't come calling here anymore. Me and my boy ran them off."

Millet kept silent as he and Dina followed Barty through the front door. The house was exactly as Millet remembered. The main hall was just beyond the door and furnished with heavy oak couches and chairs covered with soft suede upholstery. The walls were decorated with exotic tapestries that

Lee had acquired during his many travels. A fire crackled in the hearth at the far right end, and two silver lamps glowed dimly against the wall behind the couches. Just next to the fireplace was a door leading to the dining hall and sitting room, while on the near corner was another one that led through to Lee's study and bedrooms. The hardwood floor was covered with a large, blood red rug woven with delicate silver patterns. Lee had purchased it in Dantory when he was not much more than a boy.

Millet moved to the wall to avoid stepping on the rug as he made his way to the near door. It would be a shame to muddy such a beautiful thing. "I will take the master suite," he said.

Barty cocked an eyebrow but said nothing.

On reaching the master bedroom door, he asked Barty to show Dina to a guest room and stepped inside. Barty could see that Millet was now in charge, and obeyed at once. Millet took a long look around. The large bed was built from flame maple, polished and stained to a dark brown, while the green coverings on top were soft and thick. Millet had often envied Lee for such a comfortable sleep. In the corner were two chairs and a small round table where Lee used to take his breakfast. A book of Baltrian poems rested on the table, still open on the last page he had been reading. A large wardrobe in the corner remained ajar from Lee's quick departure, and a bookcase against the wall still bore all the signs of his rummaging through it. Millet took a deep breath and began to unpack. It was his now. All of it. For good or ill, he was lord of the manor.

Randson brought a washbasin and hot water a few minutes later. After he had cleaned and changed, Millet strode back to the main hall. Dina was already waiting for him. She now wore a blue cotton dress and was sat in a chair thumbing through a small leather-bound book.

"Lee certainly liked books," she said. "There must be fifty in my room alone."

Millet smiled and took a seat across from her. "He did indeed." He leaned back and rubbed his neck. "There is much about Lee Starfinder that lives in this house." He began pointing out the tapestries and other various decorations, telling Dina where they came from and how Lee had acquired them. Dina smiled and listened patiently.

After a time, Lydia entered the room. Dressed in a dark brown skirt that reached all the way to the floor and a white cotton shirt, she was tall, lean, and despite her advancing years, looked as if she could labor alongside any man. Her once-black hair was now streaked with gray and wrapped in a tight bun.

Lydia looked disapprovingly at Millet. "What business do you have in Lord Starfinder's chambers?"

"Fetch Barty, Randson, and Trevor," ordered Millet. "I have something to tell you all."

"Trevor's cooking supper," said Lydia.

Millet's faced hardened. "Then tell him to stop."

Lydia glared at Millet for a moment, then stormed off toward the kitchen. A few minutes later she returned, followed by a thinly built old man wearing a tan shirt and trousers. He was covered from head to toe in flour. The old man beamed when he saw Millet.

"Good to see you, old friend," said Trevor. He looked at Dina. "I see your taste in company has improved."

Dina stood and introduced herself. Trevor bowed and started to take a seat on the couch.

"I'll not have you getting flour all over the furniture," shouted Lydia.

"Calm down, woman," said Trevor. "I'll clean it."

"You sit too," Millet said to Lydia.

The front door opened and Barty and his son entered. Millet motioned for them to be seated as well.

Millet retrieved the parchment that Lee had given to him when they parted and handed it to Lydia. She and the others read it for several minutes before returning the document to Millet.

"I don't know who Lee Nal'Thain is," said Lydia. "But if you think for one minute that..."

"You know full well who Lee Nal'Thain is," Millet countered. "As do the rest of you." He stood. "Lee has given me rights to his lands and titles. That includes this estate."

Lydia huffed. "And what do you intend to do with these 'rights', might I ask?"

Millet thought he heard a slight quiver in the woman's voice.

"Before I reveal my intentions, tell me about the faithful."

Lydia took a deep breath. "About a week after you and Lord Starfinder left Sharpstone, three oddly dressed men came to the door inquiring as to your whereabouts, and the whereabouts of master Stedding. They sounded like those folks from Baltria to me, but they wore black cloaks and kept their faces hidden with their hoods. I've never trusted people who won't show their faces. Anyway, I told them you had all left and didn't know where you had gone... or when you'd return. At the time, I didn't think much on it. Lord Starfinder has had odd people call on him before, and he's always taken an interest in young Gewey. But when I went to market a few days later, I noticed they were still around and asking more questions."

She shrugged. "Even so, what could I do? They weren't causing trouble, and no one seemed to mind them. All the same, I told the staff to keep an eye on them." She looked at Barty.

"Ah, yes," said Barty. "When Lydia told me about these characters, I made sure I knew what they were up to. I even had my boy follow them a few times. Like Lydia said, at first, they didn't do anything other than ask questions. And apart from causing rumors to fly, they didn't make trouble. In fact, the way they let their coins pass freely, people actually started to take a liking to them. Especially Mayor Freidly. He had them over at his house almost every night."

Barty's lip curled in anger. "It wasn't long before they started comin' 'round here again, though. And this time, they were more forceful. They insisted that someone here knew where Lord Starfinder was and demanded to know." He puffed out his chest. "Well, my friend, no one bullies me. I snatched up my shovel and ran them off."

"And you were a fool for it," snapped Lydia. "You could have gotten yourself killed."

Barty ignored her comment. "After that, they didn't come back. I'd see them watching people coming in and out, but that was as close as they came. I guess I scared 'em good enough."

"And that's the reason we don't know anything," scolded Lydia. She then turned to Millet. "If you work for Lord Starfinder these days, you had just as well be an elf. No one says a word to us anymore."

"They still talk to me," said Trevor. "One of the advantages to being an old man."

Millet smiled. "What do they say?"

"First, you should know what happened after Barty ran those fellows off." Trevor leaned back in his seat and crossed his legs. "From what I heard, they went and reported him to the mayor. Not much that fat lout could do about it, though. Barty didn't hit them, and they were on Lord Starfinder's property at the time. I guess they decided to find a better way to watch us. It was only a few days later when they bought the land just next to here. They must have spent a fortune, 'cause they had a house built in just over a week. That was about the time their friends started showing up."

"We ran into Martha Tredall on our way here," said Millet. "She told us a little about what's going on, and said that there's about ten of them."

"Sounds about right," said Trevor. "They said they were here to set up a trading business, but no one really believed them. Especially with all their talk about the Reborn King."

This caused Millet and Dina to shift in their seats.

Trevor cocked his head. "I see you've heard about him. Well, that's no surprise if half of what they say is true."

"And what is that?" asked Millet.

"Mostly that he's coming to free us from the gods," said Trevor. "Bring back the old days like before the Great War. Things like that. I thought they were just some new cult. But whatever they are, and whoever this Reborn King is, they sure do have a lot of gold. Not long after the rest of these faithful got here, they paid to have the market rebuilt and started buying out anyone who'd sell. Even the folks who didn't sell took their gold on loan. Almost everyone in Sharpstone owes them something."

"We can barely keep our cupboards stocked," said Lydia. "No one wants to do business with us. They're either working for the faithful or just too scared to cross them."

"That's why most of the staff stays out at the Stedding farm," said Barty. "They leave them alone out there, and they can get supplies. Master Stedding still produces more hay than anyone else in these parts, even if he's not around. People don't have much choice but to sell them what they need." He leaned forward. "But you can bet they're watching everything that happens at that farm, too. They ask as much about Master Stedding as they do Lord Starfinder."

Millet bowed his head in thought. "Trevor, I want you to go into town after our meal. Say that I have returned to settle some business for Lord Starfinder." He looked up and met Trevor's eyes. "Do not say anything else. Only that." He turned to Barty. "I want you to secure the front door and windows, but leave the back open. Then take Trevor, Lydia, and your son to the Stedding farm. Stay there until I send for you."

"I'll not be spirited away," said Lydia, sternly. "If you're fool enough to do what I think you're going to do, then I'll..."

"You will do as I say," snapped Millet. "I cannot do what I must do if I have to worry about your safety."

"And what is it that you must do?" asked Dina.

"I intend to send the faithful a message," Millet replied darkly.

"If that's the case," said Barty, "then you'll need me and my boy." He stood up straight and squared his broad shoulders. "Lydia and Trevor may not be much good in a fight, but I can still swing a sword if need be. I've shown my boy how to take care of himself, too. You may be Lord of the Manor, but you ain't no Lee Starfinder. You're gonna need more than just you and a young woman if the faithful come callin'."

Millet looked at the gardener and his son. Their jaws were tight and their eyes blazed with determination. He sighed. "Very well. But you must do exactly as I say."

"The faithful may not even come here," offered Dina.

"They'll come," said Millet.

"But how can you be sure?" she asked.

"If these are the same lot we ran into in Baltria, then they're likely nobles or maybe merchants," said Millet. "I know how they think. They'll want to dispose of us quickly and quietly before we can get ready for them or flee. By now they will know who I am, and without Lee here as protection, they will not fear me. They'll either try and take me prisoner and torture me for information, or just simply kill me." He shrugged. "Whatever they do, it will not be in the open. They'll come at night."

After the meal, Trevor and Lydia cleaned the dishes before making their way into town. Once they had gone, Millet went over his plan with Dina and then helped Barty and Randson secure the front door and windows, as well as the stables. Dina busied herself with other preparations. Before long, the sun was sinking low in the sky and the chill air made the crackling fire a welcome sight.

"All is ready," said Barty as he, Dina, and Randson entered.

Millet was sitting in a leather chair by the fire, staring intently at the dancing flames. He glanced up and smiled. "Good." He rose from his chair and looked at each of them for a moment. "If you want to go to the Stedding farm, now is the time."

No one replied.

"Then I suppose it's time for bed."

CHAPTER 4

The lanterns burned brightly in the front of Starfinder manor that night, as they did every night. The sound of restless horses in the nearby stables carried on the chill night air, masking the rustle of the approaching footfalls. Two cloaked figures, one tall and thin, the other shorter and almost portly, made their way around the edge of the yard and toward the back of the house.

"Are you certain he's inside?" whispered the short man.

The other brought his finger to the side of his nose and scanned the area. He pointed to the second window from the corner of the house. The short man nodded, then slowly pushed it open. The soft sound of the well-crafted window sliding upward caused both men to wince. They paused and waited to see if they had been heard, but to their relief, no one inside stirred.

The tall man peered inside. All was blackness at first. But then his eyes began to adjust and he could see that the window led to a small pantry. Shelves filled with cans and jars lined the walls; herbs and dried meats hung from small hooks on the ceiling. He looked back at his companion and nodded sharply. Carefully, he pulled himself inside and gently placed his moccasin-covered feet on the floor. The slight squeak of the wooden floor was like a thunderclap, but he ignored it and went on.

Creeping to the door at the far end, he cracked it open. There was no one in sight. He glanced behind him to make sure his companion was following, but to his dismay, he was still alone. The tall man hissed, but there was no response.

"Devon," he whispered angrily. "Get in here." But Devon was silent. His lip curled with anger. He drew his knife and crept to the window. Devon was nowhere to be seen. Coward, he thought. I'll have his hide for this. Devon had been far from his first choice to go with him on this mission. He was fat, clumsy, and not very bright. But his father was rich and had largely funded the efforts of the faithful in Sharpstone. However, rich or not, the faithful would not tolerate a coward.

He tiptoed back to the door. Going on alone was a risk, even if Starfinder wasn't in the house, but there was no backing out now. He knew what would happen to him if he failed. He pushed the door open wider and ever so slowly stepped silently into the kitchen. The room was still warm from an earlier meal, and the air still bore the scent of roast meat and bread. Beads of sweat quickly formed on his brow.

At the far end of the room was a door that he assumed led to the dining hall. From there, he needed to make his way to the sleeping chambers at the other end of the house. One of Starfinder's less-than-loyal servants had given them a good description of the layout, and he had been over it several times. Still, there was always the chance that it was inaccurate. He shifted his knife into his left hand, dried his palm on his trousers, and took a slow, deep breath.

He heard movement behind him coming from the pantry. The coward had regained his nerve. He was almost at the kitchen door when it burst open. A dark figure stood in the doorway, the glint of steel shining through the darkness. He instinctively raised his knife. Then there was a thud and sharp pain to the back of his head. He fell to his knees, his knife falling from his grasp.

"I surrender!" he cried.

The figure in the doorway stepped forward, his face still obscured by darkness. "Again."

Another blow came from behind. This one sent him into unconsciousness.

CHAPTER 5

Millet paced the floor in the main hall while Dina remained in a chair by the fire, calmly reading. Her honey-blond hair was pushed back, revealing her delicate features. Her lips were twisted into a tiny smile as she fingered through the pages of a Baltrian comedy.

Millet finally stopped pacing to look at the two bound and unconscious men in the corner. With the hoods of their black cloaks now thrown back, he could see them clearly. The tall one was dark-haired, with long features and narrow-set eyes. The other, short and plump, had the look of a true aristocrat. Soft pale skin, and well-oiled black hair. Millet wondered why they would send someone like this to kill him. Clearly, they didn't think the task would be difficult. Barty was kneeling next to them, a short sword in hand. On the other side, his son was holding a thick herding club.

"Do you know them?" asked Millet.

Barty nodded. "The fat one is called Devon. The other fellow goes by Sherone. Both are from Baltria, I think. At least, that's what they sound like when they talk, and Devon does most of that. He's a bit of a braggart." He cupped

Devon's chin in his hand. "Goes 'round telling tales of his adventures. Not that anyone believes a word of it, but he's free with his gold, so no one seems to mind."

"Do you recognize them?" Dina asked Millet, without looking up from her book.

"No," he replied. "But it has been many years since I associated with the nobles of Baltria. These two don't look to be old enough for me to have known them when Lee and I lived there."

"What do you intend to do with them?" asked Barty.

Millet's eyes shot to Dina, who gave him a knowing look.

"I cannot ask you or your son to participate in what is about to happen," said Millet.

Barty rose to his feet. His face flushed. "I see." He turned to his son. "Go to the Stedding farm."

Randson glared at his father defiantly, squaring his shoulders.

Barty heaved a sigh. "Not this time, boy." He placed his hand on Randson's arm.

"I will not leave you," said Randson. His voice was deep and powerful.

Dina looked up with raised eyebrows, realizing that this was the first time she had heard Randson speak.

Barty looked at Millet, and then back to his son. "If Lord Millet is going to do what I think he's going to do, then I will not have you a part of this."

"And if you think I am blind to what these people are up to, then you also think me stupid," said Randson. "They have practically enslaved Sharpstone. People are afraid to speak against the faithful out of fear they'll lose all they own. They curse the gods openly, and mock those who refuse to do the same." His knuckles wrapped around the club turned white. "And now they come here to do murder. If Lord Millet decides they should die, then it's no less than they deserve. You taught me right from wrong, father. And we are in the right."

Barty nodded slowly, pride glimmering in his eyes.

"Actually, I need him to do something for me," said Millet. "And he would need to leave now."

"If you think to send me away..." began Randson.

"I do indeed," said Millet, cutting him off. "I need you to protect Dina."

"Protect me from what?" asked Dina.

"I intend to start fighting Angrääl here," explained Millet. "If I'm to do that, I'll need more than just the four of us." He turned to Barty. "I assume there are still some people in town who want to stand up to the faithful?"

"A few," said Barty. "But they're afraid of losing what they have. Practically the whole town is in debt to them. It's all legal, too. Signed by the mayor, then sent to Helenia. If anyone gets out of line, they threaten to go to the king."

"Smart," Millet muttered, rubbing his chin. "In the morning, go to those who you think you can still trust. Tell them that all their debts will be paid tomorrow. Then have them join me here." He looked decisively at Dina. "I need you to go to Helenia to hire men at arms. By the morning, the faithful will likely send for more people. And unless I miss my guess, the next group that arrives in Sharpstone won't be nobles and merchants. We'll need muscle and steel to rid us of this lot."

"I can do better than sell-swords and thugs," said Dina. "If I am to go to Helenia, then I can bring back Knights of Amon Dähl."

Millet's eyes widened. "Really? How many?"

"I can send word for them to come from the temples," Dina told him. "How many, I don't know. But even if only a few were to answer the call, Angrääl would have to send a whole army to match them. And I wager they can be here faster than the faithful will be able to reinforce."

"Then it will be up to us to keep them busy until these fellows get here," said Barty. "You can count on me, and a few others at the Stedding farm as well."

Just then, Devon stirred, groaning.

Millet looked at Barty grimly. "For now, I need you and Randson to go outside and get a wagon ready. Don't come back in until I call for you."

Barty hesitated, then nodded sharply. "Of course."

After Barty and Randson had left, Millet knelt down in front of Devon, who was just starting to open his eyes. In Millet's right hand was a small dagger. Dina stood just behind him, her face expressionless.

Devon turned his head and saw that Sherone was still unconscious. "What do you want with me?"

"First, I want you to see something," said Millet. "Then I'll let you decide what I want with you."

Before Devon could respond, Millet reached out and slit Sherone's throat. Blood spewed forth, pouring down the man's cloak. His eyes opened for a just moment as he gurgled for breath, then slowly closed.

"Gods protect me!" cried Devon. Tears streamed down his plump cheeks as he struggled against his bonds.

Millet laughed mockingly. "Gods? The faithful invoking the gods?" He wiped the bloody dagger on Sherone's cloak. "What would your master say if he heard that, I wonder?"

"I renounce the faithful," said Devon between his sobs. "Please, spare me."

Millet stood and turned his back to Devon. "Did you come here to spare me?"

"My father is rich," cried Devon. "If you let me live, he'll pay you whatever you want."

"And who is your father?" asked Millet.

"Lord Devon Drevaldon, the Second of Baltria."

"I know your father," said Millet. "At least, I know of him through Lee Starfinder. It doesn't surprise me that he has fallen in with Angrääl. But you should know that I am lord of this manor now. And as a Baltrian noble, you know well what it means to attack a lord in his own home."

Devon began to shake uncontrollably. "I swear I didn't know. I only came to ... to ... "

Millet spun around and held up his hand, silencing him. "You came to prove to the rest that you're good for more than just your father's gold." He knelt down. "Now you can prove your worth to me. Would you like that?"

"Yes!" Devon blurted out. "I swear to it!"

"I've asked no oath from you," said Millet. "Nor would I believe any that you could give. So I will swear an oath to you."

He leaned in. "You tell me everything you know, and flee this very night back to Baltria without a word to the rest of the faithful, and I swear that you will not die this night. Should I find out that you have lied, that you have spoken to your friends, or should the sun find you still in Sharpstone in the morning? Regardless of what happens to me, you will die. Do not think you can find safety in Baltria. Or that your father can protect you. And should I die, your death will come more swiftly than you can imagine."

He stood and turned to Dina. "Please explain to the son of Lord Devon Drevaldon the Second who you are, so that he knows what I say is true."

Dina flashed a shocked glance at Millet, then nodded. "I am a member of the Order of Amon Dähl. Does that name hold any meaning for you?"

"I have heard of it," said Devon. "The faithful speak of it often."

"Then you should know that we have people in cities in every kingdom." Her face was stone. "If you do not do as Lord Millet says, then I will send word to all members of my order that your death is of the greatest importance. There will be nowhere to hide. Do you understand?"

Devon nodded slowly.

"Then tell me everything you know about the plans of the faithful," said Millet. "And if anyone in town has joined your cause. And I don't mean people who owe you money. I mean, those who are really with you."

For the next hour, Devon told them what he knew. But as it turned out, it wasn't much they didn't already know. Angrääl didn't seem to hold the faithful in very high regard, relegating them to petty espionage and assassinations. They received most of their orders from agents traveling up and down the Goodbranch River and sent reports of their progress back the same way. Their orders were to take control of Sharpstone and find any information they could on Lee Starfinder and Gewey Stedding. The king had been resisting their efforts to place an ambassador in his court but had been more than willing to accept their gold. Devon said that if the king didn't relent soon, it was likely he would be killed. When exactly this would happen, he didn't know. But he knew they already had people set up in place in Helenia.

Once Millet was satisfied, he called for Barty and Randson. They paused at the sight of the bloody corpse of Sherone. Randson smiled and nodded approvingly.

"I see you let the fat one live," said Barty.

Millet looked down at Devon. "Load his friend's body in the wagon." He reached into his pocket and handed Barty a small bag of gold. "Take this, and Lord Devon, away from Sharpstone. Make certain he has a shovel to dig a grave and give him the gold when he's done. It should be enough to take him wherever he wants to go."

"And where is that?" asked Barty.

Millet leaned down and cut Devon's bonds. "That's up to him. But I daresay ... he should reconsider a return to Baltria." A sinister grin crept over his face. "Though his father may welcome him, I doubt the rest of the faithful will be as understanding of his failure." He shrugged. "The choice is his. I care not."

Barty and Randson lifted the body and carried it away. Devon followed close behind. When they had gone, Millet sat in a chair close to the fireplace and bowed his head in thought. Dina sat across from him and leaned forward.

"Are you all right?" she asked.

Millet looked up and smiled weakly. "I will be." He looked over at where Sherone's blood still stained the floor. "During my travels with Lee, I've been forced to kill. But never like this. I've never before murdered a helpless man."

Dina reached out and placed her hand on Millet's knee. "You did what had to be done."

Millet nodded. "I know. But I didn't want this." He looked around the room; the walls were decorated with a lifetime of adventures. "Any of it. I was never meant to be a lord."

"I don't know," said Dina. "It seems to me that you are a very good lord. To do things against your own character in order to protect those you love is a very noble thing. It's what a lord should be."

Millet rose to his feet and looked at Dina. His face was filled with contempt. Not for her, but for himself. "And I may never forgive myself for it," he said softly. "Or Lee, either." He took out the blade that had ended the life of Sherone and stared at it. "Once I poisoned a man who was conspiring to kill a sword-master Lee was studying under in Dantory. I watched him writhe and twist on the floor until the life left his body. This was a thousand times worse."

"Do you regret your actions?" asked Dina.

"My heart does. But my mind tells me it was foolish to even let Devon live." He put the knife away. "I'm an old man, Dina. I've traveled far and seen many things. But until now, I've always had the luxury of viewing from the outside." He knelt down in front of the bloodstain on the floor. "Now, I'm in the midst of it. Now, it is me who needs to hear the voice of reason. I was that voice for Lee Starfinder. Who will be that voice for me?"

Dina stood beside him. "Let me be that voice." She gently lifted him to his feet. "Though I doubt I am as wise as you."

"Before I was made Lord of the Nal'Thain family, that was possibly true." He turned to her and shook his head. "But now, I am as Lee once was. The responsibility rests with me, and that responsibility can drive away the person you are, in favor of the person you need to be." He took a long, deep breath. "And I know this is only the beginning. More blood is to come."

"True," said Dina. "But for now, we need to wash this blood away." She headed to the kitchen. "Get some rest," she called back. "I will attend to this and leave for Helenia in the morning."

Millet didn't protest. He went to his bedroom and dressed for bed. As he lay in the dark, he could still see the knife sliding across Sherone's throat. He could see his victim's eyes open in terror, then close forever. The vision filled him with anger and sorrow. Millet Gristall was no more. That man had died the moment Sherone gasped his final breath. Lord Millet Nal'Thain had been left in his stead. And that man was at war. With this troubled thought in his mind, he drifted off to sleep.

The next morning, a loud banging sounded on the manor's front door. Millet donned a robe to answer it but could hear Dina had gotten there first. Angry voices echoed through the house from outside. When he finally arrived at the door, Dina was in the center of the doorway, her hands planted firmly on her hips.

"Who is it?" asked Millet.

"Mayor Freidly," came a voice from just outside. "I'm here with members of the faithful. We need to speak with you."

"Show them in, Dina," said Millet. "I need to dress, then I will join you." He turned and headed back to the bedroom. His heart pounded in his chest. He wondered if Barty and Randson had returned. He dressed in a casual pair of white cotton trousers and shirt and slipped on a pair of soft leather shoes. He knew he didn't exactly look like the richest man in Sharpstone, but it would have to do.

When he arrived in the main hall, Mayor Freidly was standing at the far end of the room. His short, round features and wide-set blue eyes were just as Millet remembered. However, he was wearing a red silk waistcoat and fine linen pants and shirt, which was unusual for the mayor, being a man of modest means. Three black-cloaked men stood beside him. Their hoods were pushed back, revealing their dark hair, pale skin, and angry expressions. Millet thought they had the look of Baltrian nobles.

"Mayor Freidly," said Millet, bowing his head ever so slightly. "It's good to see you again. To what do I owe the pleasure of your visit?"

The mayor looked flushed and nervous. "It's good to see you too, Millet. Though I wish it was under better circumstances."

"I don't understand," said Millet, feigning ignorance. "What is the trouble?"

"You know what the trouble is!" roared the faithful farthest from the mayor.

The mayor held up his hand. "Please, Master Troungo. Let me handle this." He turned back to Millet. "These men claim that two of their brethren disappeared last night."

"I'm sorry to hear that," said Millet. "Still, I fail to see why you've come to me. I've only just arrived back in Sharpstone, and have had little time to get to know the newcomers." He looked at each of the faithful in turn. "Though I must admit, their reputation has preceded them. But why would they think to find their friends here?"

"They claim that two of their order came to this house last night to welcome you home and never returned."

"I'm afraid I can't help you," said Millet. "I swear by the gods that no one other than myself, Dina, and those that live here passed through my door last night."

"Enough of this," said the faithful nearest to the mayor. "You know they came here. And you know where they are."

Millet smiled. "And to whom do I have the pleasure of speaking?"

The man glared daggers but did not answer.

The mayor cleared his throat. "This is Toliver Hall, and the men with him are Henris Longshadow, and Alex Troungo."

"Baltrian nobles, from the sound of them," remarked Millet. "They are very far from home, and dressed ... oddly ... for nobles."

"We are the faithful of the Reborn King," said Toliver. "And I'll ask you again. Where are our people?"

"Yes, I know all about the faithful," said Millet. His tone hardened. "And I already know what you've been up to here in Sharpstone. As I said, no one called on me last night." He shrugged. "Perhaps they longed for home and returned to Baltria rather than come here. It would seem a sensible course. I hear that there are plenty of the faithful in Baltria. At least for now."

Toliver's hand began to slip beneath his robe.

"Gentlemen," said the mayor, stepping in front of Toliver. "Clearly, your companions are not here. We should leave."

The front door opened and Barty and Randson entered. On seeing the three faithful, they quickly moved to Millet's side.

"Mayor Freidly, I'm sure you know Barty and his son Randson," said Millet. "They were here last night, and can certainly attest to the fact that no one came to welcome me home."

"Nope," said Barty, his eyes drilling holes through the black-cloaked men. "We saw no one."

Millet grinned at Barty. "Is all in order?"

"Indeed it is," Barty replied.

"Then, if there is nothing further," said Millet, stepping aside to let the men pass. "I have much to attend to."

The mayor herded the faithful to the door, bowing as he passed.

"This isn't over," muttered Toliver. He then turned on his heels and stormed out.

The door slammed shut.

"No, it isn't," whispered Millet. "It's a very long way indeed from being over."

CHAPTER 6

About half an hour before Gewey, Kaylia, and Linis reached the Chamber of the Maker, the sun finally broke through the clouds. Brilliant rays of light pierced pine needles to dance across the forest floor. The sweet song of birds hidden in the treetops echoed, and the earthy scent of pine and moss carried on a gentle breeze. Kaylia insisted they slow their pace to a leisurely stroll. Holding Gewey's hand, she merrily hummed a tune that Linis recognized and soon joined in with, harmonizing in a deep baritone.

"Why the sudden cheer?" asked Gewey. He was loath to interrupt, but could no longer contain his curiosity.

Kaylia gave his hand a squeeze. "We may be at war, and darkness may swallow the world, but never forget to look around and enjoy the wonder of it." She breathed in deeply. "And I suspect that once we reach the Chamber, these things will go unnoticed for quite some time."

Gewey saw a squirrel darting in and out of view among the branches of a nearby pine. It made him think of the woods close to his farm in Sharpstone. As a young child, just before the Long Freeze, he had built a tree house and spent many afternoons up there, reading and having fun until the sun went down. A family of squirrels had built a nest in a nearby tree. He'd watched as the nest filled with babies and laughed at how the mother would bristle every time he climbed up. Come autumn, the babies had grown enough to leave the nest. He remembered feeling sorry for the abandoned mother squirrel. Gewey smiled and shook his head at the silly things children do.

"That was a lovely vision," said Kaylia.

Kaylia's words brought him back to the here and now. He still found it amazing how much of him she could see through their bond. For Gewey, it was different. He felt emotions and impressions, but never visions. He wondered if that would change when their bond was completed.

"I was a boy," said Gewey. "After the Long Freeze, I went back. The tree house was crumbled and rotten, and the nest was empty."

"All things change, my friend," said Linis. "And sometimes, not for the better."

Soon the trail widened and met with the main road leading to the Chamber. At the crossroads, they saw three elves barring their way. Two were elf men wearing shimmering red tunics and breeches, long black coats that reached their thighs, and soft, black leather boots. At their sides hung long, thin swords, the jewels on each hilt sparkling brightly in the sun. Their silver hair fell loosely over their shoulders and down their backs. Even from a distance, Gewey could see their bright green elf eyes staring keenly at him.

The third was an elf woman. Half a head taller than the men, she was adorned in a blood red gown that fitted nicely around her curves. A white sash was tied about her waist, and along with a thin silver belt, a small dagger hung on each hip. Unlike the others, her hair was jet black and decorated with wisps of silver. These peeked out just enough to catch the sun and give her the illusion of possessing an aura.

"Do you know them?" asked Kaylia. Her hand released Gewey's and slid to her knife.

"No," Linis replied. "But stay your hand. We would not want to make friends into foes from our own fears."

Kaylia tightened her jaw and moved her hand to her side.

"Greetings," called Linis, holding his hand high. The elves didn't move. "Who are you, and what is your business?"

The elf woman whispered into the ear of the elf on her left. He nodded slowly. She took a step forward and held up a delicate hand. "Greetings." Her voice was gentle and calm, and though still several yards away, she sounded as if she were right in front of them. "Come and walk with us. It would seem fortune has made our paths as one."

Gewey, Kaylia, and Linis paused for a second, then approached.

Linis bowed. "I am Linis. This is Kaylia and Gewey. Your speech and dress are unfamiliar. From where do you hail?"

The elf woman smiled brightly, and though she bowed to each in the group, her eyes never left Gewey. "I am Aaliyah," she said. "My companions are Mohanisi and Nehrutu." The elf men bowed in turn. Apart from Mohanisi being a shade slighter in build and maybe an inch taller, they were remarkably similar in appearance. "As for our home—that is a question best answered later."

Kaylia stepped forward. That Aaliyah's eyes still rested on Gewey had not escaped her notice. "I think it is a question to be answered now."

"Fierce," said Mohanisi. "Much as we expected."

"Decorum, my friend," scolded Aaliyah, though not too harshly. "They know us not, and have been through much hardship and pain."

"And what do you know of that?" asked Kaylia.

"More than I care to, I'm afraid," Aaliyah replied. Her voice was filled with pity and sorrow. Gewey found himself wanting to weep at the sound as if her words stirred something deep inside him. "My dear Kaylia," she said, taking a small step forward. "We are here to bring glad tidings. We have come to help you after many lifetimes of waiting."

"I don't understand," said Linis. "Where have you come from?"

Aaliyah glanced at her companions, who nodded in turn. "We are from across the sea. We are of the first race of elves to traverse the Great Sureshi and settle these lands. And now we have returned. Though I fear we have returned too late."

Linis's eyes widened in immediate disbelief. "Sureshi? I have not heard that word used since I was a boy. No one who has journeyed across the Great Abyss has ever returned, and yet you claim to be from there?"

"None of your folk who tried to reach our land would have survived," said Nehrutu. "The Great Barrier has barred the way for thousands of years. It has only been nineteen summers since we have been able to get through ourselves. And yes, that is our home. Once, long ago, it was the home of all elves. But now…"

He paused, placing his hand on Aaliyah's shoulder and nodding at her.

"Yes, quite right," she said. "We should go. Your brothers and sisters await your return. I think they would want our tale told to all." She met Gewey's eyes once again. "And I suspect they are especially anxious to see you again."

"You seem to know something about me," said Gewey. He was no longer afraid to reveal himself.

"Oh, indeed I do," Aaliyah replied, with a hint of laughter. "There is not an elf among us that does not know of the coming of Shivis Mol. News of your arrival has caused great rejoicing. You are the herald of a new age and a new way." She stepped forward and placed her ivory hand on Gewey's cheek. "I have dreamed of this day my entire life. As have all of my people."

Gewey's face felt hot at the touch of Aaliyah's hand. He blushed and tried to look away, but her touch held him fast. A flash of rage then flowed through his bond with Kaylia, breaking the spell. He stepped back.

"I see you have bonded to Shivis Mol," said Aaliyah. Her eyes scrutinized Kaylia for a moment. "And yet you have no connection to—what is it you call it? The flow. How unusual." She smiled. "And how fortunate for you. To be coupled with such as he is a great honor, but requires great strength."

"It is I who am honored," said Gewey. He moved close to Kaylia and took hold of her hand.

Aaliyah laughed. It was like bells on the wind. "I am sure that is so. She is clearly a noble elf ... if noble is the word I should use. I apologize, but certain concepts are difficult for us."

"Being noble is a difficult concept?" remarked Kaylia, trying not to allow her anger to seep into her voice.

Nehrutu interjected. "Perhaps it is better to say we have no concept of..." He paused, searching for the right words. "We have no conflict among our people. At least, not in the way you would understand. The idea of not acting noble, in the sense you see it, is unknown to us."

"But enough," said Aaliyah. "There will be time for this when we arrive." Nimble and swift as the wind, she spun around and walked down the road toward the Chamber of the Maker, Nehrutu and Mohanisi following close behind.

Gewey, Kaylia, and Linis looked at each other, then did the same.

As they approached the field where the pavilion had been erected, Aaliyah and her companions dropped back next to Linis. The field was still abuzz with activity as hundreds of elves darted about.

"I believe you should make the introductions," said Aaliyah. "Considering what has happened here, it may be better if your people are greeted by someone more familiar."

Linis nodded in agreement.

Two guards barred their way when they reached the edge of the field. They eyed the strangers for a moment.

"They are not foes," said Linis.

The guards grunted and stepped aside.

"A bit brutish," remarked Mohanisi.

Linis pretended not to hear. All the same, he couldn't help but bristle at the insult. "They must be hard to survive these times. They fought bravely to protect their kin."

"I meant no disrespect," Mohanisi explained. "It is only that you are so different from what we know."

Theopolou, Eftichis, and Bellisia approached from the pavilion. Kaylia ran ahead and embraced her uncle with joy. She held him tightly for nearly a full minute.

"I am so happy to see you are safe," said Theopolou, smiling broadly. "Though I had no doubt Gewey would succeed in your rescue." As the others approached, Theopolou bowed. "Thank you," he said to Gewey and Linis. "I am in your debt."

Gewey bowed in reply. "I wish I could say I freed her. But as it turned out, she managed that on her own."

Theopolou smiled lovingly at Kaylia. "A tale I would love to hear."

"As would I," said Bellisia. "But first, I would like to know who you have brought among us."

Linis introduced the elves and explained how they met, not failing to mention their claim.

"So, you say you are from beyond the Great Western Abyss," said Theopolou. His tone bore no hint of surprise or trepidation. "That would explain the news we received. Reports of red sails on the horizon have caused quite a stir."

Aaliyah stepped forward and took Theopolou's hand. The old elf stiffened and staggered back. In a flash, Linis and Eftichis had their knives drawn and were pulling Theopolou away. Mohanisi and Nehrutu made no move to stop them.

"No," Theopolou cried out. "Stay your weapons. I am not harmed—only dazed."

"What happened?" asked Linis, still holding Theopolou's arm.

"I beg your forgiveness," said Aaliyah. "I thought it would be easier this way. As you are one of the more—how should I say this? Talented among you. That is to say, you can use the flow."

"Yes," said Theopolou. He steadied himself and straightened his shoulders. "But I suggest you refrain from doing that again. At least until you have addressed the others."

"Theopolou..." began Bellisia.

"She is who she says she is," said Theopolou. "She merely communicated it to me in a manner which I am not accustomed. It was just too much at once."

"I would speak to your people," said Aaliyah. "But first, your wounded should be attended." Her companions nodded in agreement. "You could help as well," she said to Gewey.

"Of course," he said.

Linis stepped forward. "I will join you." He could tell that Theopolou and the others had recently been using their powers to heal and were now exhausted, though they hid it well. "The elders should rest until we have done what can be done."

"Of course," said Aaliyah. "They have accomplished all they can." She looked at Kaylia and smiled. "If you would tend to your elders while we do our work..."

"I will go with you as well," said Kaylia.

"Theopolou and the others have greater need of you." Aaliyah's tone was not contentious, yet it held an air of authority that caused Kaylia to stop short.

"Stay," said Theopolou. "You can tell me what happened after you were taken."

Aaliyah didn't wait for a response. She turned gracefully and walked in the direction of the pavilion. Kaylia's eyes followed her closely.

When Gewey and the elves entered the healing pavilion, they saw scores of injured elves lying in row upon row of beds that had been taken from the tents. Even so, there still weren't enough beds for everyone in need of care, so the least injured had been placed on simple bedrolls. Those administering to them were busy distributing food and medicine, and at first, hardly noticed the group's presence. Gewey peered just beyond the pavilion and could see others tending to the dead. His heart ached.

"How could this happen?" muttered Mohanisi. His face flushed with anger. He spun and faced Linis. "How could this happen?" This time, his voice boomed with rage. Everyone in the pavilion stopped and stared.

Aaliyah gently placed her hand on Mohanisi's shoulder. "Calm yourself, my friend. This is not his doing."

Mohanisi's muscles tensed until he trembled, then he closed his eyes. Gasps filled the pavilion as the elf filled himself with the flow. More and more of it rushed into him until the surrounding air glowed with power. Only Gewey could hold so much—or so they thought. After a few seconds, he released it and opened his eyes.

Mohanisi breathed deeply, then smiled apologetically at Linis. "Forgive my anger. Aaliyah is correct. This is not your doing. But I have not seen a sight such as this before. It took me aback for a moment."

Linis bowed. "There is nothing to forgive. You are not wrong to feel anger. We have all allowed this to come to pass. I am as much at fault as any." He could still feel the lingering power of the flow all around him, and everyone's eyes continued to stare in amazement. "But, I must ask. How is it you can channel so much of the flow? Gewey is the only one I have ever seen use so much."

"I doubt I have the power of Shivis Mol," said Mohanisi.

"Your people have forgotten much," Aaliyah interjected. "Once all elves could do as Mohanisi has done. Why you cannot still, I do not know." She squared her shoulders. "But now is a time to heal, not talk. Talk can wait, but the dying cannot."

They all nodded in agreement. Without another word, Aaliyah, Mohanisi, and Nehrutu started off in different directions and immediately began tending to the wounded with the power of the flow. Linis left the more severely injured to Gewey and the other elves, restricting himself to healing those whom he could more readily help. Gewey went from bed to bed for what seemed like an eternity, using every bit of his strength. By the time it was fully dark, he was barely able to stand. Linis was faring no better, nearly losing his feet several times. Aaliyah and her companions seemed far less affected.

"Are you well, Shivis Mol?" Aaliyah asked Gewey as he knelt at the bedside of an elf who had been run through. He only looked up when she touched his shoulder.

"Just tired," said Gewey. "This takes a lot out of me."

"I see." Her tone sounded confused. "We have nearly done all that we can here. Mohanisi, Nehrutu, and I will finish this. You should rest. I am certain Kaylia will tend you well." Her last remark sounded almost sarcastic.

Gewey shook his head and steadied himself. "I'm fine." He placed his hands on the wounded elf, channeling the flow. The wounded elf gasped, and his eyes opened wide. After a few minutes, the wounds began to close, and the elf relaxed.

Gewey staggered to his feet and stumbled to the next bed.

"That is enough," said Aaliyah. "You cannot go on. There are only a few others remaining who we can help. I insist you rest." Her words were commanding, and Gewey could feel himself wanting to obey as she continued. "If you become ill, then I will have to heal you. This will take from those who need more urgent care." She smiled. "Do not be concerned. Soon I will teach you to heal without so much effort."

Gewey's resolve gave way. "I'll go."

Aaliyah took his arm and guided him from the pavilion to where Kaylia, Theopolou, and the others were gathered.

"He needs rest," stated Aaliyah flatly. "Tend to him."

Before Kaylia could speak, Aaliyah released Gewey and turned back to the pavilion. He nearly collapsed the moment her hand let go. Kaylia was quickly at his side and guided him to a waiting bedroll. Eftichis brought him some bread and wine, which he gratefully accepted. Linis arrived a few minutes later and lay down next to him. He didn't speak a word and was asleep within seconds.

"You should sleep as well," suggested Eftichis, who had seated himself a few feet away.

Gewey rubbed his neck and stretched his back until it made a sharp crack. "The others will be finished shortly. I want to be awake when they get here." He yawned, in spite of himself. "If I sleep now, I won't be able to wake up."

Small fires were being lit throughout the camp. The scent of spiced meat and wine wafted on the breeze.

At that moment, Aaliyah and the others appeared from the fading light. "We have healed as many as we could," she told them.

"You have our gratitude," said Bellisia, who had been seated beside Lord Chiron for several hours, talking quietly.

"Indeed," agreed Chiron. "Many more would have died if not for you."

"I only wish we could have done more," remarked Aaliyah, sadly. "Many were beyond our power."

"You should rest," said Gewey. "You must be exhausted."

"We are," admitted Aaliyah. "More so than we have ever been. And I would have strength before I tell our tale." She reached down and placed the back of her hand on Gewey's cheek. Kaylia's anger flashed across their bond, startling Gewey.

"For one so ignorant of his own abilities, you did well," said Aaliyah. Her voice was tender and musical, like the cradlesong for an infant prince. "Though I admit I was confused to see how little you know of yourself." She glanced over to Kaylia, then fixed her eyes on Gewey's. "That will change. I will see to it."

Kaylia moved close to Gewey, her face hot with jealousy.

Aaliyah smiled. "Fierce and protective. Though I must admit, I can understand why." Her hair shimmered in the firelight. She stepped back and sat on a blanket a few feet away. Mohanisi and Nehrutu rested next to her. "In the morning, I shall address the elves."

"I am afraid it will have to wait until after the funeral rites," said Theopolou. "They begin with the sunrise."

"Of course," said Aaliyah. She lay down and pulled the blanket over her shoulders. It was mere moments before sleep took her.

Gewey looked about him. Small groups of elves were gathered around the fires, speaking in hushed whispers. No one had disturbed the newcomers while they were tending the wounded, but news of them had spread like wildfire. Gewey smiled. Only the arrival of these elves could have overshadowed the presence of a god in their midst. And for that, he was grateful. He finished his meal and lay on his back. The stars were peeking out from behind wisps of thin clouds high in the sky. He wished the night was clear. The nights of a new moon were the best time for stargazing. Kaylia lay next to him, her head turned toward Aaliyah.

"She is beautiful," said Kaylia.

Gewey reached over and took her hand. "I didn't notice."

"You do not need to spare my feelings," she said in a halfwhisper. "I am not doubting your feelings for me."

Gewey turned his head and met Kaylia's eyes. "Good. And I'm not sparing your feelings. I really didn't notice. I was too busy in the pavilion to notice such things."

"And now that you are not in the pavilion?"

Gewey pushed himself up and leaned over to her. "And now that I'm not in the pavilion, you're still more beautiful." He kissed her softly.

She smiled. "She wants you." Pulling him to her, she kissed him back. "But she cannot have you. She called me fierce, but she has no idea of how fierce I can really be." She stroked his cheek. "Now sleep."

Gewey lay back down and closed his eyes. The tingle of Kaylia's touch still caressed his lips. As sleep took him, he could feel his spirit drift. He had come to enjoy the sensation. Then he heard a call. Not in words, but a sweet summons, like soft music. *Kaylia,* he thought. A thin mist surrounded him. It was warm and soothing. He allowed it to penetrate him.

"I am here," called a gentle feminine voice.

A figure approached through the mist. Gewey expected to see Kaylia, but as the figure neared, he realized it was not her.

It was Aaliyah.

CHAPTER 7

A bitter chill woke Gewey the next morning. Kaylia and Linis had already risen and were nearby helping the others prepare the morning meal. Bellisia, Chiron, and Theopolou were gathered a few yards away, and were now donned in white robes; Gewey presumed these were for the funeral rites.

Aaliyah's face still burned in his memory, but he could not recall anything beyond the point when she had first appeared. He scanned the area for her and her friends, but they were nowhere to be seen.

Just next to him, lying atop his sword and scabbard, he noticed his pack. Someone must have retrieved his belongings from Theopolou's tent. He rummaged through his things until he found the clothes Theopolou had given to him, then went to look for someplace private to change. He thought perhaps to seek out water for washing but didn't want to miss the ceremony. Looking toward the burned remains of the camp, he could see dozens of funeral pyres that had been erected during the night. He dreaded the sad ceremony that was to come. Finding a hidden spot just beyond the pavilion, between two tents, Gewey changed into his elf clothing.

"You have an interesting mind." It was Aaliyah.

Gewey flushed. "How long were you watching me?"

Aaliyah smiled. "Long enough." She took a step forward.

Gewey may not have noticed her beauty before, but he certainly did now. She had changed into a white silk dress. Though much the same fashion as the one she had worn the previous day, this one flowed with her movements, wrapping itself playfully around her obvious curves as she moved. Her hair was tied in a loose braid, intertwined with thin white strands of shimmering cloth.

"I thought this may be a bit more appropriate," she said. She held her shapely arms wide and spun around. "What would you say?"

He felt his face grow hot with embarrassment. "I..."

"Perhaps not." With a wry smile, she took another step forward. "However, I brought nothing else other than a set of cotton trousers and tunic. The rest of my attire is on my ship."

"How did you...?" he stammered. "I mean ... last night."

"Oh, that was nothing," she replied, stepping closer. "I only wanted to see your mind for myself. A selfish thing, I admit. But I could not resist the chance to connect with Shivis Mol."

"Kaylia. She..."

"Kaylia knows nothing of it," said Aaliyah. "It was simple to occupy her thoughts. I encouraged her to dream of you. It was easy. She loves you deeply."

The mention of Kaylia's love for him steadied his nerves. "And I love her."

"Well, of course you do." She sounded understanding in the way of a mother to a child. "But then you are quite young. And your bond with her makes your feelings infinitely stronger." Slowly, her face saddened. Gewey suddenly wanted to approach her. To comfort her. But he resisted. Aaliyah then added quietly: "I was bonded once. Long ago."

Gewey's heart ached to see her pain. "What happened?"

She sighed deeply. "He died."

"Then how do you still live?" he asked. "I thought that once bonded, your lives are as one."

This shook her out of her melancholy and she laughed softly. "Perhaps that is true for the elves in this world. They have forgotten how to use their power. The bond between mates is strong, but not unbreakable. One need not lose themselves should the other die." She glanced behind her, toward the pavilion. "A pity. The bond makes you stronger. We could have saved more of the wounded if they'd all had a mate's strength to share. But if the risk is death, I suppose it is to be expected that they do not bond." She tilted her head and smiled. "Perhaps that is yet another thing we can teach them."

Gewey saw Kaylia approaching in the distance. "I should go," he said. Without waiting for Aaliyah's response, he edged his way past her. She did not move to ease his passing, forcing their shoulders to touch.

As he neared Kaylia, he could clearly see that she was not pleased.

She placed her hands on her hips. "What did she want?"

"Nothing," Gewey replied. "She asked if what she was wearing was appropriate for the funeral rites."

Kaylia shot a stare at Aaliyah, who was still standing close to where he had left her. "Is that so?" She took Gewey's hand. "Come. We need to eat."

Gewey allowed Kaylia to lead him back to their bedrolls. A bowl of steaming porridge and a cup of new wine had been placed on the ground for him. After he'd finished these, Kaylia, Linis, and Theopolou walked with him to the funeral pyres, where the gathering was already well underway. The pyres had all been encircled by elves in just the same way as

Gewey had seen Linis and his seekers do during the funeral of Berathis. Aaliyah, Nehrutu, and Mohanisi stood beside Kaylia on his right. Linis, Theopolou, and the remaining elders were to his left. Those wounded who were able to do so had also made their way from the pavilion, unwilling to remain in bed during the rites of their dead brethren.

The ceremony was long, lasting well into the afternoon. Elf after elf stood forward to say words about their fallen comrades. After all had spoken, the fires were lit—so many that the heat caused Gewey to break into a sweat. Finally, it was over and the crowd solemnly dispersed. Most eyes were still swollen with tears.

Gewey, Linis, and Kaylia returned to their bedrolls, while Theopolou instructed everyone to gather an hour before sundown to hear Aaliyah and her companions speak.

Gewey spent the next few hours in light conversation with Kaylia. He wondered what had become of Lee, Dina, Millet, and Maybell. He missed his friends, especially Lee. Linis, meanwhile, searched the area for signs of what had become of his seekers but returned disappointed.

When the time came, they made their way across the field in front of the pavilion. Most of the elves had already assembled. Aaliyah, Nehrutu, and Mohanisi, were standing on a small platform with their backs to the pavilion. The beds of those who could be moved had been pulled close to the edge so they could hear.

Aaliyah had changed back into her red dress. She spotted Gewey as he approached and smiled. In spite of himself, he smiled back. Theopolou, Chiron, Bellisia, and the other elders had already positioned themselves just in front of the platform.

"I'd rather stay to the back," said Gewey.

"You can't," said Kaylia. "I have a feeling that whatever they say will concern you."

Gewey opened his mouth to speak, but Kaylia took his hand and half dragged him through the crowd, urging him to stand next to Theopolou. Linis stood just behind him.

The moment he arrived, Aaliyah nodded to her companions and stepped forward. "Brothers and sisters." Her voice echoed over the field with such tremendous volume that the gathering jumped. "By now, you have heard of our arrival and from where we have come. Some may have doubts. Those who do not may question our motives. To this, I can only say that I speak truth and that there is no deception in my words." She paused and looked over the crowd. Her eyes bore the look of sorrow and pity.

"Many lifetimes ago our people journeyed across the Great Sureshi, or what you now know as the Western Abyss, and settled in this land. We lived and prospered for generations, and for generations, we came to see the land as our own. But it was not so. For this land belonged to another people. This land first belonged to the humans."

Her words provoked a loud stirring amongst the elves.

Aaliyah held out her hand to still the crowd. "I know how many of you feel about the humans. And I know that many believe you have reason to hate them. But what you do not know is that it was we who first sinned against them. The humans were already here when we first arrived. But they were not as you know them today. Mere children they were. Savage children, nomadic hunters and gatherers. We brought to them our ways and our learning. We taught them to build, to farm, to live as a community. But in the end, we did these things for our own purposes. In the end, we subjugated the humans. We turned them into little more than a slave race, born to serve our needs."

She stepped down from the platform and stood in front of Gewey, staring deeply into his eyes. "Not until the gods showed us the error of our ways did we realize what we had done. But by then, it was too late."

She broke her gaze to glance back at her friends, then returned to the gathering. "The gods created the Great Barrier and destroyed any hope of contacting our people beyond. Any who tried to cross perished. For thousands of years, we have kept watch, praying for the day we could return to you. Nineteen years ago, the Great Barrier disappeared, and now we have come."

She stepped back onto the platform. "My brothers and I have lived our lives with the knowledge of our people's sins, and the price we have paid—the price you have paid. But now, we are here to help you regain what you have lost, and to undo the wrongs of our forefathers." She closed her eyes and bowed her head. The only sound was a soft breeze stirring the tents and pavilion.

Theopolou was the first to speak. "You say that you have been able to come here for nearly twenty years. Why have you waited so long? Why have you not revealed yourselves before now?"

Aaliyah opened her eyes and sighed. "We could not know what had become of you. The humans had clearly taken control of this land. We sent scouts to gain information. What we found was that you had become different. You had changed from the people you once were. To us, you had become more like the humans. We were uncertain what to do."

This caused angry shouts and curses.

"Then why now?" asked Bellisia.

"Because of him." She pointed dramatically at Gewey. "When we discovered the coming of Shivis Mol, we knew we must act." She said this as though it was an obvious truth. Her eyes fell on the wounded in the pavilion. "But it is clear we should have acted sooner."

"How did you know about Gewey?" asked Theopolou. "We have only just discovered about him ourselves."

"We were given a prophecy when the Great Barrier appeared," Aaliyah replied. "It says that a god bound to earth will come to show us the way to the Creator. He will wash away our sins and reunite us with our people. We knew when the Barrier disappeared that it heralded his coming."

"But how did you know it was me?" asked Gewey.

"Our people have a connection with what you call the flow," she replied. "Though the elves of this land have lost much of their power, we have not. You could never hide what you are from us."

She held out her hand. Before Gewey realized what he was doing, he had taken hold of it and allowed her to pull him onto the platform. "We have learned much about our brethren since we first arrived." She was speaking to the elves, but her eyes were on Gewey. "You despise the gods. You would turn away your one hope for salvation. But you do not understand what that would mean. You have an enemy rising against you. An enemy that will wipe you from the face of this land. An enemy that has corrupted the hearts of your brothers and sisters."

She released Gewey and pointed to the wounded in the pavilion. "This is the result." Her voice was hard and cold as steel. "You have made war with your own kind once before. This we know. And though it caused us great sorrow to think of such a thing, we hoped that you would have learned from your mistakes. We hoped you had not fallen so far that your spirit was lost." The air around Aaliyah stirred as the flow rushed through her. "You asked why we reveal ourselves now. You wonder why we waited." A flame burst to life above her head and shot skyward. The crowd backed away in shock. Gewey stood transfixed. "We waited because you are as different from us as the humans are from you. We feared your own sins would return. We feared you could not regain what you have lost." She released the flow, and the air stilled. Her features softened and a soft smile returned. "But the time for fear is past, and we waited too long."

"What do you intend to do?" asked Theopolou.

"We intend to teach you," she replied. "All of you. Even those who have lost their way. Those who have attacked this place have been warped and controlled by a force they could not resist. The one you know as the Reborn King has unleashed a power beyond your understanding. It is a power you cannot hope to overcome. Even with Shivis Mol at your side, you will need more."

"We have the Book of Souls," said Theopolou.

"I know," she said. "But have you tried to use it?"

"Gewey has opened it," said Chiron.

"We know of the Book of Souls," said Aaliyah. "And such a thing will be needed in the days ahead. But you need weapons. Weapons that can match those brought to bear against you."

"And where shall we acquire such weapons?" asked Theopolou.

Aaliyah looked at Gewey's sword hanging from his belt. "There is a place. It is where the sword Shivis Mol now wields was forged."

Theopolou raised an eyebrow. "And you know where this place is?"

"We know where to look," she answered. "It is in the desert of the east; we have sensed its power."

"It would take months to make such a journey," said Bellisia. "We are already attacked. I fear we have no time."

"My ship can take us there in less than two weeks." She stated this firmly.

Murmurs of doubt spread through the crowd.

"Our fastest ships couldn't cross the distance in twice that," said Bellisia.

Aaliyah laughed softly. "Our shipbuilders are quite skilled. And, as you will learn, the winds can be controlled." She surveyed the crowd for a moment. "Nehrutu and Mohanisi shall remain here. I will find the location where the weapons are held." Nehrutu and Mohanisi stepped forward. "They will help you as best they can to prepare."

"How many are you?" asked Theopolou.

Nehrutu stepped forward. "We set sail with three ships, and are few in number. But we can help you prepare and teach you things your people have forgotten. We will show you how the flow can be used in ways you have never imagined."

"Can you send for more of your people?" asked Bellisia. "Will more not come?"

"It would take many months to make the crossing," he replied. "More to gather and return. You would be destroyed long before then. I will send one ship back to our land but do not expect help from my people. You are on your own— for the present."

"Now I would speak to your elders," said Aaliyah. "And Shivis Mol. We have much to discuss and little time." She addressed the gathering. "You still have many questions, I know. Tonight, Nehrutu and Mohanisi will tell tales of our home and answer those questions."

She stepped down from the platform. Nehrutu and Mohanisi followed. The gathering of elves gave way as they walked toward their bedrolls. She paused to look back. "Shivis Mol, I would have you and the elders join me. I intend to leave with the dawn." Linis and Kaylia stepped beside Gewey, but Aaliyah held out her hand. "Linis should stay with Nehrutu. Only Kaylia may join us."

Gewey could see Linis tense. He placed his hand on the elf's shoulder. "It's fine. I'll tell you what they say."

Linis's eyes never left Aaliyah's retreating figure. "These elves have plans for you, Gewey. Be careful."

"I am with him, Linis," said Kaylia. "They can plan all they wish. But they must still account to me."

This brought a smile to the elf. "I believe they think us savage and ignorant. But I would wager they have not given you full account."

Kaylia flashed a fiendish grin and took Gewey's hand. "And that would be a mistake they would not soon forget."

This brought a round of laughter. Kaylia and Gewey then headed off to speak with Aaliyah. As they neared, they could see Theopolou and the other elders already standing in a circle with her. Gewey noticed Theopolou was holding the Book of Souls. Nehrutu and Mohanisi were nearby gathering together the other elves into two groups.

Aaliyah beamed as they joined the circle. She bowed. "Shivis Mol." She turned to Theopolou. "I see you have brought the Book of Souls. Good."

"Gewey has already opened it once," Theopolou reminded her again.

"Could you read it?" she asked Gewey.

"I read the cover," he replied. "But I didn't try to read the rest. There was no time."

Aaliyah looked at Gewey thoughtfully. "Try it now."

Gewey took the box and opened it. The book glowed and shimmered in the fading light. Handing the empty box back to Theopolou, he slowly opened the Book. The pages glittered with intricate gold writing. Just as when he had read the cover, at first, the words meant nothing. Then, slowly, they changed in his mind. But this time, it was only a few that made sense. He stared intensely at the first page for several minutes. "I only understand some of it," he said finally. "The rest means nothing to me."

"I am not surprised," said Aaliyah. "These pages were meant for a god. Although a god you are, you have not realized your full power yet. You use only power from the earth. There is so much more. And once you learn what I will teach you, then you will be able to read all from these pages."

"I don't understand," said Gewey. "I use what I can feel."

"You only feel what is easy to feel," said Aaliyah. "The powers of water, air, and spirit are more elusive."

Gewey recalled Lee saying that because his father was Saraf, God of the Seas, he could draw power from the water. "How do I learn?" he asked.

"Through me," she replied. "I can teach you what you need to know. But there is a price."

Kaylia stepped forward. "What price?"

She leveled her gaze at Kaylia. "He is to come with me to seek out the weapons in the desert."

"Is that all?" asked Gewey.

"No," she replied flatly. "You must allow me to show you why I am your best choice for a mate."

Kaylia's hand flew to her knife. But before she could pull it free, Aaliyah waved her arm. Heat flashed through the air and Kaylia was thrown back, nearly losing her footing. Theopolou and Gewey jumped in front of her.

"Are you hurt?" asked Gewey.

Kaylia steadied herself, glaring at Aaliyah. "No. She did not hurt me."

"Still your fury," said Aaliyah. "Fierce though you may be, you cannot do me harm."

Gewey looked over his shoulder at Aaliyah. "I am bonded to Kaylia—I love her. And if you do that again, you'll find out just how powerful I really am." He let the flow swell inside him until the ground trembled.

Aaliyah lowered her eyes and stepped back. "Please, Shivis Mol. I meant no offense."

Gewey allowed the power to ebb.

"I do not doubt your love for Kaylia," said Aaliyah. "Nor hers for you. But I was chosen for a reason, and I will not be deterred. You are a living god, bound to this world. Destined to save it. Destined to save us. Should you not choose a mate who can meet such a challenge?" Her eyes met Kaylia's. "Have you not doubted that you are worthy? You are fierce and strong. Perhaps, in time, you could be even stronger. But should Shivis Mol not have the deepest well to draw from? Are you that well? Or am I?"

Kaylia moved Gewey and Theopolou aside. "You speak of Gewey as if he were a tool—a mere object. You do not love him."

"I speak of him as he is," she replied. This time her tone matched Kaylia's ferocity. "A god. You say that I do not love him. And I do not. Not as you love him. But he is Shivis Mol. And we are not children. For him to bond with me would give him even greater strength. Strength he will need if we are to survive. You must look beyond your own selfish desires."

"This is all irrelevant," Theopolou interjected. "Kaylia and Gewey are already bonded. This cannot be undone."

Aaliyah shook her head. "How little you know. Of course, it can be undone. You may have lost the ability, but we have not."

"I don't want it undone," Gewey objected. His voice was cold and menacing. "And if you try..."

"I will do nothing without your consent," said Aaliyah. She looked at Gewey and Kaylia for a long moment. "I offer you this bargain. Allow Shivis Mol to go with me—alone. I will present my case during our journey. If I am rejected, so be it. In return, I will instruct him, and help him to reach his true potential. I am the most powerful among my people. You will find no better teacher."

"I will not be parted from Kaylia," said Gewey. He pulled Kaylia close.

Aaliyah looked into Kaylia's eyes. "If you are meant to be with him, then you have nothing to fear. Your bond shall remain intact unless Shivis Mol decides otherwise."

"I refuse to..." started Gewey, but Kaylia pulled away.

"If it means saving our people, then you must," she said. Her voice was tender and sad. "I fear losing you." She gave Aaliyah a contemptuous glance. "But not to her. Go, and learn what you must to save us from the darkness that comes. I will be waiting."

"You have made a wise decision," said Aaliyah.

Theopolou placed his hands on Gewey and Kaylia. "If this is to be, then you shall complete the bond. You cannot know what perils lay ahead. I would see you as one before you are parted."

Kaylia smiled and took Theopolou's hands. "Thank you." She released him and looked at Gewey. "Assuming you are agreeable?"

Gewey nodded and bowed. "Of course I am." He scanned the area for Linis. "Would someone tell Linis to come here?"

Bellisia stepped forward. "I will find him." She left and returned with Linis a short time later.

Linis grinned and squeezed Gewey's shoulder. "I am happy for you." He glanced at Kaylia. "Both of you."

"Kneel," said Theopolou.

Without another word, Kaylia and Gewey dropped to their knees. Theopolou placed his hands on their heads and began to recite the ritual. Though Gewey couldn't understand the language, the sound of Theopolou's voice caused images to erupt in his head. Colors swirled and danced until he was dizzy. So much so that he needed to reach out to Kaylia to steady himself. The moment he touched her, he could feel their bond growing stronger, taking root within his very soul. Minutes passed until he realized that Theopolou was no longer speaking. He looked across at Kaylia. Her face was aglow with joy. He could feel every fiber of her being. In that moment, he knew just how deeply she cared. It was as if the bond they had shared before was a shadow of what it had now become.

"Normally, the ceremony is a bit more involved," said Theopolou. "But every minute you have left together is precious."

Gewey and Kaylia rose. Aaliyah was expressionless. The rest of the elders bowed and took a step back.

"When shall you depart?" Theopolou asked Aaliyah.

"At dawn," she replied. "My ship is less than two days' journey."

Theopolou turned to Gewey. "Prepare whatever you intend to take with you, then return here." He took Kaylia's hand. "In the meantime, come with me."

Linis smiled. "I envy you, my friend."

"One day, such joy will be yours, Linis," said Gewey. "I just know it."

Linis let out a hearty laugh and slapped Gewey on the back. "I hope so. But for now, this is your time."

The pair of them went off to collect Gewey's pack. He wanted to travel as light as possible, and as he sifted through his belongings, he told Linis what Aaliyah had said, and the bargain he had made with her.

"I will go with you," offered Linis.

"No," said Gewey. "You're needed here. If the elves are going to gather for war, you must help." He looked across the field to where Nehrutu was speaking to the other elves. "You must learn whatever they can teach you. That's why I'm going. To learn what I must."

"Be careful, Gewey," warned Linis. "She is unlike any elf I have known. She may tempt you in ways you cannot imagine."

Gewey smiled. "She can try. But as long as my heart belongs to Kaylia, she will fail."

When Gewey had finished packing, he returned to where the others were still gathered. Theopolou waited. His smile made him seem almost youthful. Kaylia stood just behind him. She had changed into a white silk dress, tied at the waist by a thin gold sash. Her hair fell loosely about her bare shoulders. Gewey's heart raced at the sight of her familiar but breathtaking beauty.

Theopolou took them both by the hand, leading them across the field and past the pavilion. An area had been hastily cleared just out of sight of the camp, and a small tent was newly erected there. Its purpose was obvious.

Kaylia kissed her uncle lightly on the cheek. He smiled the loving smile of a father before carefully placing her hand into Gewey's. He then simply walked away.

Kaylia looked deeply into Gewey's eyes and led him inside.

CHAPTER 8

After taking a riverboat up the Goodbranch River, Lee and Jacob had ridden at an easy pace for two weeks. They could not risk being seen, so waited until they were three days north of Sharpstone before returning to the road. While on board the riverboat, Lee had heard news of the faithful occupying his beloved town. It had taken a lot of willpower to fight the urge to do something about it. But Millet would have to deal with them. It was now the duty of Lord Nal'Thain, not Lee Starfinder, to save Sharpstone. His tasks lay elsewhere.

Jacob had been relatively quiet during the journey. Lee tried many times to engage his son in conversation, but the boy had little to say. On a few occasions, he attempted to teach Jacob sword techniques, and though he learned quickly, Lee could tell that his heart wasn't in it.

"We'll arrive in Klinton by sundown," said Lee. The air was bitter cold, and Jacob was bundled in a small wool blanket. "We should change clothes before we get there."

"Why?" asked Jacob.

"We must blend in with a less-than-savory crowd," Lee explained. "If we're to gather information and not be discovered, we can't march in there as lords of Hazrah. There are towns near the foothills of the Razor Edge Mountains where news of Angrääl can likely be heard. The bandits and mercenaries make it their business to know the comings and goings of the land."

Jacob sniffed. "So? We're still a week away from the foothills."

"Yes," said Lee. "But our deception should be believable. I'm hoping to find someone heading north. We can perhaps pose as sell-swords. Possibly hire on with a merchant. It will go a lot more smoothly if we arrive up north in character."

"And what makes you think that these people will know anything about my mother?"

Lee shrugged. "They may not. But at least they'll know the best way to get into Angrääl unnoticed."

About an hour before they reached Klinton, they stopped and donned clothing Lee had acquired from the deckhands on board the riverboat. Simple brown wool shirts and pants, together with travel-worn boots, would fit in nicely.

"These clothes smell," remarked Jacob with disgust.

Lee smiled. "All the better."

Klinton was little more than a trading post. Miners and trappers used it to peddle their wares, so avoiding the long journey south. Though not as dangerous as the towns near the Razor Edge Mountains, it still attracted a variety of highwaymen and bandits hoping to find merchants foolish enough to travel without an escort.

The street lamps were just being lit when they arrived, and the main avenue was still busy. The taverns would be empty for a while longer yet. Lee hoped to get lodging before the local riff-raff took to drink. He was familiar with this town, though he hadn't been here for many years. The last time he visited, he had gotten himself into a tavern brawl in which Millet was nearly knifed. He chuckled under his breath at the thought of Millet scolding him after the fight. He missed his company, now more than ever.

Lee led the horses down the main avenue, then along a side street to one of two lodging houses. It was by far the most rundown of the pair.

"We're staying here?" asked Jacob. His top lip curled in disgust.

"We'll be staying in far worse than this before it's over," Lee replied. "Compared to where we're going, this is a palace." He dismounted. "Stay with the horses until I get a room and arrange a stable."

Lee entered the lodging house and stood just beyond the doorway. The main hall was sparsely furnished with a few chairs and a wooden bench. An old and blackened brick fireplace in the far left wall burned brightly. Even so, the room was chilly and unpleasant. A fat, balding man wearing a stained tunic was asleep in the corner, a mug of ale precariously balanced on his round belly. The lodge was otherwise empty.

Lee slammed the door shut, startling the innkeeper awake. The mug fell to the floor, shattering and splashing ale over the man's dingy trousers.

"Bloody hell!" cursed the innkeeper. He looked down at his spilled ale and grumbled. When he saw Lee standing there, he frowned. "What do you want?"

"A room, fat man," said Lee. "And be quick. And send someone to stable my horses." He reached in his belt and pulled out two coppers.

This did nothing to change the innkeeper's demeanor. "Do I look like a groom to you?"

"No," Lee replied. "Grooms are cleaner. Now get off your backside and have my horses tended."

The innkeeper snorted, then heaved himself to his feet with a grunt. He walked over to Lee and snatched the coppers from his hand. "Grant!" he bellowed harshly, spittle flying from his mouth. A rustle came from behind the door just on the other side of the counter. A moment later, a bent old man emerged. Smiling a stupid, toothless grin, he moved with surprising speed.

"Yes, sir?" said Grant.

"Go stable the horses outside," growled the innkeeper. "And don't take all night."

Grant spun around and dashed out of the door. Lee followed. After unpacking their belongings, Lee tossed Grant a copper.

"Thank you, kind sir," said Grant, almost groveling.

"Just see that they're well-tended," said Lee.

"Of course, of course," Grant replied. "You can count on me, sir." He bowed low before leading the horses away.

"What a wretched creature," said Jacob.

Lee looked at his son. "I would say pitiful rather than wretched."

The innkeeper showed them to their room and without a word, shuffled off, cursing under his breath. The room had four walls, three cots, and nothing more. A cold draft seeped in from the cracks in the rotten floor timbers, and the only window had been boarded up.

Lee grinned at his son. "I've stayed in far worse." He placed his pack in the far corner. "We'll find a meal elsewhere. I doubt the good innkeeper here will provide one."

Jacob tossed his pack next to Lee's. "I hope the food in this town is better than the lodging."

"Don't count on it." Lee led Jacob from the room and returned to the main hall. The innkeeper was now back in his chair with a new mug of ale in his hand. "If anyone touches our belongings, I'll hold you accountable." Lee tapped the hilt of his sword.

The innkeeper scowled. "Your things will be fine."

The nearest tavern they came across didn't even have a name, merely a sign that read: Tavern.

Lee surveyed the streets. The traffic was now thinning. He suspected that within an hour or two the lodges and taverns would be full—full, he hoped, with people who could be of use. Inside, the place with no name was equally unremarkable and typical for a trading post tavern. Two long tables were positioned to his left, with several small ones surrounding them. To the right, beside a small bar, a fire burned in the hearth. The bartender, a thin waif of a man, was busy arranging rows of clay mugs. The scent of cooked meat filled the air. Lee knew this would be replaced by the stench of ale and unwashed bodies soon enough.

"I suppose you'll be wantin' to eat," called the bartender, not bothering to look up.

Lee approached the bar and slid four coppers to the bartender. "I'll be wanting information as well."

The bartender raised an eyebrow and quickly shoved the coppers into his pocket. "That'll be fine." He looked up. His gaunt, unshaven face bore the lines and pits of too many winters. "And what information will you be wantin'?"

"I'll let you know," Lee replied. "For now, just bring me and my friend some food."

Without another word, the bartender headed to the kitchen. Lee and Jacob took a seat at the table farthest from the door.

"Do you gamble?" asked Lee.

Jacob shrugged. "When the urge strikes."

Lee nodded approvingly. "Good. There will be games, and I want you to join in." He took two silver coins from his purse and gave them to Jacob.

"And what will you be doing?" asked Jacob.

"Watching," Lee replied.

About halfway through their meal, people began arriving. Within two hours, the tavern was full to bursting, and with just the sort Lee had been counting on. Mostly locals lined the long bench tables, but the outer tables were taken by a myriad of tough-looking characters. As Lee had instructed, Jacob joined in a game of dice in the corner by the bar. By midnight, the place was getting rough. Several fights had already broken out. In one, a knife had been pulled and a local man nearly gutted by what looked to be a sell-sword. Luckily, it had been stopped before it got too far out of hand.

Jacob was doing well at dice and had nearly doubled his money. This, naturally, was not sitting well with the regulars, who were accustomed to fleecing newcomers. Lee knew he would need to keep a close eye on the boy. He made certain that a pitcher of ale stayed full and constantly on the table, though he only pretended to drink. He wanted all his wits about him. Jacob, however, was letting the ale flow freely.

Lee took notice of several merchants who were accompanied by stout swordsmen. One particularly fat merchant was allowing his coin to pass too easily, and his tongue wag far too loosely. Before long, he was boasting about his adventures and wealth between long draughts of wine. The guard he had with him looked irritated, and more than a bit on edge. The bartender had told Lee that the merchant had dealings in the north, and always stopped here on his way to Angrääl.

"You accuse me?" Jacob's raised voice snapped Lee to attention.

Jacob and three locals had squared off in the corner, and Jacob's hand was resting on the hilt of his dagger. The locals had already grabbed up bottles; one was brandishing a small knife. Lee leaped to his feet and pushed his way through to the commotion. Lee made it just as Jacob was about to pull his dagger.

"What the hell is going on here?" roared Lee. His eyes looked accusingly at Jacob. "What did I tell you, boy? You'll send us both to the hangman's noose." He stepped in front of Jacob and roughly snatched him by the collar. "Get to the table, whelp!" He pushed Jacob aside, nearly lifting him off his feet.

Jacob glared. "They..."

"I don't care!" Lee pointed to the table. Reluctantly, Jacob walked away.

"Your friend owes us money," growled a short stocky man, a wine bottle in his hand.

Lee faced the man, his eyes dark and dangerous. "So you say."

"W-well..." he stammered. He looked to his friends for support, but they had already recognized Lee as someone not to be trifled with. "Just keep him away from us."

Lee looked the men over, then pushed his way past them. When he arrived back at the table, Jacob was cursing under his breath and draining a mug of ale.

"Did you learn anything?" asked Lee. His tone was not angry now.

Jacob refused to look up. "Never touch me again."

"Calm yourself," said Lee. "I only did that so we wouldn't have to fight those idiots. I have another fight in mind." He nodded toward the fat merchant. "He's been drinking and boasting all night. It's only a matter of time before someone tries to shut his mouth." He reached over and took Jacob's mug. "And if you're going to be of use, you need to stop this. Now, what did you learn from the locals?"

Jacob clenched his jaw, then gradually relaxed. "All I heard was that there's been a lot of people coming through from the north. Whether they're from Angräal, they didn't say. They also mentioned that winter came early, but that's nothing new. Other than that, they spent their time trying to switch dice on me." He pulled his winnings from his pocket and jingled the coins in his hand. "They failed."

Lee slapped him on the back. "Those dice skills may come in handy. If we can't find employment as sell-swords or bodyguards, we're going to run out of coins soon, and I'm rubbish at games."

Jacob smiled in spite of himself.

"Shut your stupid mouth, braggart!" a voice bellowed over the noise of the crowd.

Lee got to his feet. "Watch my back. And try not to spill any blood—unless you have to."

Across the room, two large men were confronting the fat merchant. Both wore swords and were looming over the merchant. His guard was unsure what to do and stood a few feet behind, fingering his sword and shifting nervously.

Lee made his way across the room and positioned himself behind the men. Jacob was on his heels. One of the men had moved to the side and was eying the guard, who clearly had decided to do nothing.

"You say you fought off ten bandits?" growled the largest lout. He pressed his face into the merchant's. "Let's see how you handle me."

The merchant, fueled by too much wine, didn't back down. "You, sir, would be a waste of time and effort." He glanced over his shoulder at his guard. "I'd rather just have my friend here deal with you."

The man roared with laughter. "I think your friend would rather not." He looked at the guard. "I'll give you this one chance to leave." The guard paused, then turned on his heels and left the tavern.

The merchant turned pale. "Well, ummm." He looked around the room. The tavern patrons were clearly enjoying the spectacle.

"What do you have to say now?" demanded the man.

Quickly, Lee stepped around him, placing himself between the aggressor and the merchant. "That's enough. Leave him be." Jacob moved to Lee's left, facing the other man.

The first man sneered at Lee. "Who the hell are you?"

"I'm with…" He turned and looked enquiringly at the merchant.

"D-Darius," the fat man stuttered.

"I'm with Darius," Lee continued. He glanced sideways at the merchant. "I think it's time to call it a night. Don't you?"

"Indeed," Darius eagerly agreed.

"Jasper," Lee said to Jacob. "Escort Darius outside."

Jacob nodded sharply and helped Darius to his feet. The merchant stumbled to the door and into the street, nearly falling on his face.

Lee backed away toward the door, his hand on the hilt of his sword. The two men followed. Once in the street, Lee called to Jacob. "Take him to our room. I'll be along shortly." He smiled fiendishly as the two men came out of the tavern after him and drew their swords.

"Do you need…?" Jacob began.

"I need you to take care of our new employer," said Lee. "Isn't that right, Darius?" The merchant nodded his head vigorously. Lee smiled. "Then these two brutes are mine."

Jacob decided it best not to argue and led Darius away.

"I hope the fat man was worth your life," said the first man.

Lee widened his stance but did not draw his blade. "I'll not dirty my steel with the likes of you." He waved them in. "Come and get me."

The first man charged in like a mad bull, swinging his sword in a wild arc. The second tried to skewer him through the gut. Lee stepped aside, easily dodging both blades and brought his fist down across the first thug's jaw. Blood and teeth went flying as the man spun and tumbled to the ground, unmoving. Stunned, the second man paused, staring at his comrade.

"You should run," advised Lee.

This enraged the second thug. Reaching in his belt, he drew a small dagger and hurled it at Lee's throat. Lee moved aside, allowing the blade to disappear into the darkness.

Still undeterred, the thug raised his sword and charged. Lee almost laughed at the man's clumsy effort. He sidestepped and brought the back of his fist across the man's temple. He stumbled and fell to one knee, his sword falling to the ground and sliding a few feet away. Lee kicked him to the ground and brought his boot down on the man's neck.

"If you or your friend trouble Darius again, you won't walk away," said Lee.

The thug's eyes were now wide with fear. He was only able to nod his head ever so slightly.

With a snort of derision, Lee released him. After taking a moment to view the crowd that had gathered from inside the tavern, he made his way to the lodge. There, he found Darius and Jacob sitting quietly at a table.

Lee took a seat next to Jacob. "They won't be troubling you anymore."

"That coward of a guard abandoned me," muttered Darius. "I'll see him skinned alive." He reached in his belt and pulled out a flask. The sweet scent of brandy filled the air as he opened it.

"He's long gone," said Lee. "But it seems you are in need of protection. My friend and I would be happy to oblige—for the right price."

"What?" He shook himself to his senses. "Oh yes, yes. Of course." He swallowed a mouthful of brandy. "But you may not be so eager once you hear where I'm going."

"And where is that?" asked Lee.

"I go to Whiterun Pass," said Darius. "Just on the other side of the Angrääl border. Not too many want to go there. Especially with all the soldiers gathering." He handed Lee the flask.

Lee took a long swallow and passed it to Jacob. "Then why are you going?"

"War is profitable," said Darius flatly. "I have twenty wagons full of raw cotton, and the Reborn King pays triple what it's worth anywhere else."

Hearing that name set Lee's heart pounding. "I see. Well, it sounds like just the kind of job Jasper and I are looking for." He reached across the table and held out his hand. "I'm Barath, and this is my nephew, Jasper."

Darius shook Lee's hand, then pulled two silver coins from his purse. He tossed Jacob and Lee a coin each before taking another drink. "Then it's good to have you both with me. This is for what you did for me in the tavern. Normally, I pay eight coppers per week for escorts." He paused to study Lee for a moment. "But I think you're worth nine."

"I'd say we're worth twelve," said Jacob.

Darius rubbed his chin. "Done." He stood up. "Grab your gear. My camp is just a mile north, and a sight more comfortable than this place."

Lee instructed the innkeeper to gather their horses while he and Jacob retrieved their belongings. Lee offered his horse to Darius, but the merchant refused.

"I've had far too much to drink to stay on a horse," he said. "It will do me good to walk it off." He patted his round belly. "Besides, I may break the poor beast's back."

This brought a hearty laugh. Once the horses were packed, they slowly made their way to the main avenue north through town. Lee kept a sharp lookout for any sign of the two thugs still being about, but to his relief, they seemed to have decided that they'd had enough for one night. Lee didn't want to spill blood this early in their journey; such things drew too much attention. And even in a dilapidated camp like Klinton, there was still a constable or sheriff. He certainly didn't need to get mixed up with the local law. Not that they would be in any danger of finding themselves in a hangman's noose, but should men die in the streets, explanations would have to be made and coin spent.

The night was cold, but the brandy helped to fight off the chill. When they arrived at Darius's camp, Lee could see twenty large wagons arranged in a wide circle, each one filled to bursting with cotton. In the center, several small fires were burning, surrounded by sleeping men.

Darius grumbled. "Lazy dogs. They're supposed to be guarding the wagons." He straightened his shirt and belt, then stiffened his back, standing as tall as his girth would allow. "That's why I only brought one blasted guard."

"How many swordsmen do you have?" asked Lee.

"Ten, not counting the two of you," Darius replied. "Well, nine since I lost the cur who I had with me tonight."

"Why so many?" asked Jacob.

"The roads south of Angrääl are dangerous," Darius told him. "You may well see some action before we get there."

Lee nodded. "And after?"

Darius chuckled. "No one raids within the borders of the Reborn King. Not unless they wish for death. I'll be glad when they finish whatever war they are getting ready for. At least the roads will be safe. I gotta give them credit—they know how to keep order."

Lee could tell that Jacob wanted to say something but flashed him a glance. Darius noticed.

"And what do you think about it?" the merchant asked. "I see you have an opinion."

"I think..." Jacob paused. Lee's face was like stone. "I think as long as they let people go about their business, I don't care."

Lee relaxed.

Once within the camp, Darius began kicking awake the men who had been left to guard the wagons, threatening to dock their pay. He pointed to a small tent at the far end of the camp. "I sleep there. After tonight, I want you and Jasper to keep your fire and bedrolls nearby. For tonight, find your-selves a place with the others. We leave at dawn."

Lee and Jacob found a spot in the center of the camp and laid out their bedrolls. The other men scarcely looked at them as they settled in.

"It's going to get even colder soon," remarked Lee as he stretched out.

"I'm a northman," said Jacob. "I don't mind the cold."

Lee smiled. His son had done well that night, and he allowed himself to feel proud. He prayed to the gods that the feeling would last.

CHAPTER 9

For the next several days, Lee and Jacob spent most of their time with Darius and learned much about him. Originally from The Silver Isles, a small group of islands just off the coast one hundred miles east of Baltria, he had inherited a cotton plantation on the mainland when his uncle had died twenty years ago. When sober, he wasn't nearly as much of a loud braggart, and Lee found him to be a man of quick wit and good humor.

On the first day, he invited Lee and Jacob to engage in a dice game with a few of the other men. Though Lee politely refused, Jacob took great joy in the distraction, as well as taking coin from Darius, who turned out to be a very unlucky gambler. After a few more games, Darius chose to sit and talk with Lee rather than lose more coin.

At night, after Darius went to bed, which was usually quite early due to an excess of drink, Lee tried to get to know the others among the caravan. The hired swords were mostly from the edge of the eastern desert. They were regarded as a fierce people of few words and quick temper. Fortunately for Lee, he had spent time in Dantory and knew how to approach them. Three of the guards intended to join the armies of Angrääl when they arrived.

"Better to be on the winning side," said Fennio, a short, thin man, one night over a few cups of wine. He was by far the most experienced of the lot and bore the scars to prove it. Unlike the long swords the others carried, he preferred a short sword and small mace. "And I hear they pay thirty coppers a week."

"I'm not servin' in no army," said Santino, one of the youngest of the group, though he had the look of a hardened veteran. "I don't care if they're payin' fifty coppers. If you ask me, they're payin' so good because you're marchin' off to get killed."

"Ha!" scoffed Fennio. "You ain't seen how big the army is. A hundred thousand if it's ten."

"You ain't seen it neither," said Santino. "So shut up."

Fennio took a swallow of wine and wiped his mouth on his sleeve. "Yeah, but I heard about it plain enough. And they say that before long, Angrääl is gonna march. You don't wanna be in their way when they do."

He looked over to Lee, who was feigning disinterest. "What about you Barath? You have the look of a soldier about you. You gonna join up?"

Lee shrugged and forced a smile. "Perhaps. The pay sounds good. Much better than I thought. But up 'til now, me and Jasper had been thinking about heading east if war comes."

Fennio snorted. "East? You won't find nothin' there but sand and ugly women. Why do you think we left in the first place?" The rest of the group burst out in harsh laughter.

"At least Angrääl isn't likely to go there," said Lee.

"You're right about that," agreed Fennio. "They'll be busy with the elves ... unless I miss my guess."

Lee cocked his head. "The elves?"

"Yeah," said Fennio. "I hear this Reborn King fella's gonna get rid of 'em once and for all." He shrugged. "Good riddance, if you ask me. But who knows? I hear some of 'em are fightin' for him, too."

"Either way," Santino interjected. "I ain't fightin' an elf, and I ain't fightin' with 'em. I'd rather go home and marry me an ugly woman and have some even uglier children." This brought more laughter. "Besides, if what those desert dwellers say is true, there's plenty of elves wandering the sand. 'Course, most of those folk are daft." He turned to Lee. "You let me know if you head east. I might come with you."

Lee smiled and got to his feet. "I'll let you know. But I haven't decided what I'm doing for sure yet." He brushed off his trousers and went to find Darius and Jacob.

It was a week into their journey when they first started seeing soldiers from Angrääl. Mostly small groups of six to ten at a time. They didn't bother with the caravan, other than to warn them to be on their guard for bandits.

"Don't worry," one soldier had said. "It won't be long before the roads are safe from here all the way to Baltria."

Lee continued to train Jacob for at least one hour each day. He noticed that, since that night in Klinton, something had changed. His son now appeared to be more focused, and, in spite of current circumstances, happier, too. He even seemed to be enjoying the training. To Lee's delight, he was also improving dramatically.

On the morning of the eighth day, Lee packed their gear and loaded it onto the horses. Darius had taken to walking rather than riding, spending most of their days spinning tales of his adventures. Though Lee could tell the man embellished quite a bit (though not as much as when he had a belly full of wine) it was clear Darius was indeed well-traveled. On several occasions, Lee was asked to tell of his own exploits. At first, he was resistant, afraid he might give something away that would reveal his true identity. But after being pressed by both Darius and Jacob, he eventually relented. Leaving out certain details, he told them about some of the many wondrous places he had seen.

Just before they stopped for the midday meal, Lee sensed something was wrong. He called for the caravan to halt and reached out with his senses. It was only seconds before he found what he was looking for.

"Gather your men," he ordered.

"What's wrong?" asked Darius.

Lee closed his eyes and listened carefully. "Twenty men. Ten on either side of the road." His eyes opened. "They're waiting for us ahead."

Fear showed on Darius's face. "What should we do?"

"Let them wait," Lee replied. "We'll organize the men and set up positions. If they realize we know they're there, they may choose to withdraw."

"We could sneak around and surprise them," offered Jacob.

Lee shook his head. "We're outnumbered two to one. We only have nine trained men. The others aren't swordsmen. If we set them to attack, they'll just get themselves killed." He examined the surrounding area. The trees and brush along the road were sparse and on relatively high ground. Ahead, where the bandits were waiting, the road dipped and was flanked on either side by a slight incline. "We can defend this position if we need to," he stated before striding off to gather the men.

"I still think we could take them," said Jacob, once Lee had returned. The guards were lined up behind him and checking their weapons.

"You got a lot to learn, young Jasper," said Fennio. "The best way to win is to avoid fighting. We're hired guards, not an army. We ain't lookin' to get killed."

"I thought you wanted to be a soldier," teased Santino. "I'm with Jasper. We should take them by surprise. I don't like waitin' to be slaughtered."

"We're not attacking!" barked Lee. "They'll know we're aware of them soon enough. And I doubt we could get behind them in broad daylight, anyway." He drew his sword. "Believe me, if they decide to attack, they're in for a surprise." His tone silenced any further argument. He turned to Darius. "You stay behind me at all times." He then glanced at Jacob, who had moved beside him and also drawn his weapon. "And you, stay by my side."

Jacob nodded sharply, his muscles tense with anticipation.

Lee positioned the men around the wagons, men at arms in front and the rest several feet behind. An hour passed, and the bandits had not yet made a move, but Lee could still hear them. He looked at his son and furrowed his brow. He had known all along that they would likely have to fight, but now that danger was a reality, he was afraid for Jacob's life. He remembered the dangers he'd faced with Gewey not so long ago. He loved Gewey as a son also, but he'd never been this concerned for him. Gewey was a god, after all, and very hard to kill.

Then, down the road, he saw them—twenty bandits filing up the slope at a slow walk, their weapons drawn. The man in front was tall, broad-shouldered, with his head shaved to leave only an inch-wide strip of black hair down the center of his head. In his right hand, he carried a large battleaxe—in his left, a small round shield. They halted about twenty yards away. The leader then took a few steps further forward.

"Whoever your commander is, he's a sharp one," called the bandit. "But then, so am I."

Darius stepped forward. "What do you want?"

The bandit laughed. "Something tells me you're not the one who spotted us, fat man." He shrugged. "Well, I think you know what we want. The question is, are you willing to die for it?"

Darius held his head high. "Are you?" He looked at his guards, pausing when he met Lee's eyes and smiling. "Give way and find an easier target."

The bandit addressed Darius's men. "Listen to me. This fat, rich merchant will see you all to your graves. If you leave now, none of you will be harmed. Is his gold worth your life?"

Lee stepped forward. He focused his strength on making his voice louder. "If all these men run, I will stand. And by the gods, if I fall, you will fall with me."

The bandit shifted uneasily. "I guess I know who the real leader is here." He steadied his feet. "A man like you could go far. Why are you determined to die? Why not live and get rich?"

Lee tightened his grip on his sword. He glanced at Jacob, giving him a sinister smirk. "I don't need you to get rich. And your time is nearly up."

"So be it," said the bandit. He looked back at his men and raised his hand.

Only the nervous breathing of the men and the uneasy shifting of the pack animals disturbed the brief silence that followed. Darius moved to Lee's back, a short sword in his hand.

"Stay near me," Lee whispered to Jacob. "And keep your back to the wagons."

Then the bandit's hand dropped. The attackers charged, screaming wildly as they came. The guards braced themselves. Within seconds, the deafening clatter of steel on steel cut through the air. Lee hoped that the bandit leader would come at him first, but he did not, instead choosing to engage the guards to his left. Two bandits swung their rusty swords at Lee, but their blades found only empty air. Lee cut them both down with blinding speed.

Jacob was dodging blows from a tall, heavyset bandit wielding a thick broadsword. Fear struck Lee's heart as he saw Jacob being pushed back. He moved to take the bandit's head, but Jacob struck first, thrusting his sword through the man's gut and then ripping it free. He flashed a smile at Lee before stepping forward to greet another attacker.

Two more bandits came at Lee, but they were quickly dispatched. Jacob had taken the arm of another, and by now had placed himself in front of Darius.

"I'll protect Darius!" he shouted to Lee. "Kill the leader!"

Lee swelled with pride. He scanned the melee. The guards were holding their ground well, their experience in keeping the wagons at their backs forcing the bandits to take them on only one at a time. The leader was at the far end. He had killed two guards and was beating back a third. Lee pulled the dagger from his belt and hurled it. The blade flew past the leader's neck, narrowly missing instead of burying itself in his throat. With a scowl, the bandit turned to see Lee charging in his direction. He took a few steps forward to meet him.

Lee killed two more attackers before finally reaching the leader. He could see the fear in the man's eyes as he brought his blade down hard and swift. The bandit was only just able to raise his shield in time, but the force of Lee's blow threw him back. Lee stepped in again, this time bringing his sword upward in a tight arc. The tip dug into the bandit's left thigh, tearing its way through to the hip. The bandit grimaced and staggered, swinging his axe frantically. Lee moved deftly away, then slashed deep into the leader's right shoulder. His axe fell to the dirt with a sharp thud. The man's eyes were already closing against the pain as Lee moved in for the finish. One more powerful blow sent his head flying. The body managed to remain erect for a moment, blood squirting rhythmically from its neck, then it crumbled to the ground. It was the decisive moment. Seeing their leader fall, one by one, the remaining bandits began to flee.

"Do not pursue them," Lee shouted, rushing to his son's side. Jacob was breathing heavily from the fight. His shirt and trousers were drenched in blood. Spots of red also dotted his cheeks.

Darius was backed against the wagon, his hands trembling and his face a ghostly pale. When he saw Lee, he forced a weak smile. "Well done indeed." He nodded at Jacob. "Both of you."

"We need to tend the wounded," said Lee. "And see to the dead."

Lee examined the aftermath of the battle. The guards had already begun to treat the wounds of their comrades. Each gave Lee a respectful nod as he passed. In all, three men had been lost, and three more were wounded. But they had managed to hold off the bandits well enough to protect the untrained workmen. Lee checked his pack and retrieved a healing salve he had brought, then set to help with the treating of the men. Two could still travel on their own, but one would need to ride in a wagon.

Darius had the men dig graves for the fallen guards and ordered the bodies of the bandits placed in a row along the roadside. "They can serve as a warning," he said, gazing upon the sight.

A short ceremony was held for the guards. Each of their comrades said a quiet prayer to Dantenos, God of the Dead, asking him to watch over their friends. After this, no one wanted to stay the night in the same place, so they marched another mile before setting up camp.

After building a fire and setting the bedrolls, most sat in silence, the horror of the battle still fresh in their minds. Lee checked the wounded, then joined Jacob and Darius at the edge of the encampment.

"Quite a day," said Darius.

Lee nodded. "Indeed, it was." He tore off a piece of bread that had been laid out for him. "There is a small town, Farice, a day's ride from here. We should reach it before sundown tomorrow. The wounded should be left behind there. They will not heal if they continue."

"I'm familiar with Farice," said Darius. "I'll see the men are paid and tended." He looked Lee in the eye. "I've never seen anyone fight like you. You could have taken the entire raiding party alone, I suspect." His eyes drifted to Jacob. "And I see you have the same spirit in you as well."

Lee shrugged. "I was well trained. And Jasper is a natural."

"Well trained, you say," said Darius. His eyes bore suspicion. He stretched out on his bedroll, his hands folded behind his head. "You know, I have traveled this road six times since the Reborn King came to power. I've seen many soldiers, mercenaries, thugs, bandits, you name it. I've seen many fights, duels, and even one pitched battle when I was young. But I have never seen a man slay so many with such ease as you."

Lee was silent.

Darius chuckled. "Don't worry. Whatever secrets you keep are yours. You and Jasper have saved my life twice. Not to mention keeping my fortune out of the hands of brigands. I'm not so wealthy that I can afford to lose an entire shipment. In any case, I am in your debt." He rolled over to face Lee. "I have a feeling that you will not be in my employ long. You are a man who acts with purpose, and I think that purpose lies in Angrääl."

Lee met Darius's gaze. "What are you trying to say?"

Darius smiled. "Nothing. I just want you to know that, when the time comes, I will help you as best I can." He rolled back over and closed his eyes. "I owe you that much."

Lee looked at his son, then back at Darius. "When the time comes, your help will be most welcome."

CHAPTER 10

Gewey cracked open his eyes. Kaylia lay peacefully beside him, one arm draped across his chest and a tiny smile on her lips. The scent of porridge and bread blew in from outside the tent, causing his stomach to growl.

"They've left a meal for us," said Kaylia, awake though her eyes were still closed.

Gewey reluctantly sat up and reached for his clothes. He dressed and went to the tent entrance. Just as Kaylia had said, two bowls of porridge and a loaf of bread, along with a cup of sweet wine, had been placed immediately outside. Kaylia got dressed, and they enjoyed their meal in silence. Their bond was all the conversation they needed.

They had barely taken the last bite when a voice called out to them. "Hello?" It was Linis.

"Come inside," Kaylia responded.

Linis entered, his face grave.

"What's happened?" asked Gewey.

"We received word that Valshara has fallen."

Gewey and Kaylia sprang to their feet.

"When?" asked Gewey. He reached down and grabbed his sword.

"Not long after we departed," replied Linis. "The High Lady escaped, along with a few others. They have taken refuge in Althetas for now." Linis pushed open the tent flap. "I am truly sorry, but you are needed. Theopolou and the others have gathered to decide what to do."

Gewey took a deep breath and led Kaylia by the hand from the tent. The morning air was cool and moist, with dew still glistening on the grass-covered field. They joined the others not far from where he and Kaylia had completed their bond the night before. Theopolou and the elders were in deep conversation with Aaliyah and her comrades. Only Aaliyah noticed Gewey, Kaylia, and Linis approach. She nodded a greeting at Gewey.

"What's going on?" he asked.

Theopolou held a small piece of parchment in his hand. "Valshara is destroyed. Very few escaped. The High Lady is in Althetas and plans to petition the king to come to their aid." He looked directly at Aaliyah. "I believe Gewey should delay his journey until we can decide on a course of action, but Aaliyah disagrees."

"Any delay only puts you in greater danger," said Aaliyah. "The presence of Shivis Mol will not help you. Besides, your course is clear. Gather as many as you can and strike back before your enemies can establish a foothold. Unless they have an army, you should be able to mount an attack and retake what you have lost. My people will give you all the help they can. They will expect only swords and arrows—we can bring much more than that to bear." She turned to Gewey. "But we must not delay our departure."

Gewey wanted desperately to stay. Every minute more he could have with Kaylia was precious.

"Aaliyah is right," said Kaylia. Feeling Gewey's doubt, she squeezed his hand. "If what she says is true, we need what is hidden in the desert. And Gewey needs to learn to use his power."

"It is probable they will not look to hold Valshara," said Bellisia. "Not so far from reinforcements. More likely, they are striking at Amon Dähl. And if they do try to hold it, we can take it back." She spoke to Theopolou. "You know Valshara better than most. The battle plan shall be yours."

"And if we find we are mistaken?" Theopolou furrowed his brow. "What then? Valshara can be well-defended by only a few. If they brought enough force, they could hold it indefinitely."

"You think in battle terms without taking all of your weapons into account," said Nehrutu. He held out his palm. The air above it swirled and twisted, then burst into a small flame. The light and heat grew until it forced the gathering back. "We have abilities beyond your understanding." The ball of flames shot skyward, then exploded with an ear-shattering blast. "They will not expect you to possess such weapons."

This demonstration drew gazes of awe and murmurs of approval.

"Please, Shivis Mol," said Aaliyah. We must depart. There is nothing for you to do here."

Gewey looked at Kaylia. She nodded slowly, then kissed his cheek. Gewey nearly lost himself as the love flowed freely between their bond. He sighed heavily and forced himself to look away. "We leave as soon as you're ready." He turned to Theopolou. "I'll return as soon as I can."

Aaliyah was already prepared to depart and told Gewey she would await him at the edge of the encampment. Gewey gathered his pack, Kaylia at his side.

"I'll miss you," he said. Tears welled in his eyes.

Kaylia pulled him close and kissed him deeply. "Just be careful and return to me safe." Choking back her tears, she then reluctantly released her embrace and took hold of his hand. "It's time." They made their way to Aaliyah.

Theopolou and Linis were also there. Linis smiled as they approached. He held a small silver flask.

"I made this last night," he said, handing it to Gewey. "If you are to go to the desert, it may be useful. A single sip will keep you strong should you be unable to find water."

"Thank you, my friend." Gewey put the flask in his pack and gave Linis a fond embrace.

Theopolou bowed. "Farewell, Gewey Stedding. My hopes go with you." He looked at Kaylia, then back to Gewey. "You are now a part of my house and my family. Return to us soon."

Gewey bowed in return. "I will." He kissed Kaylia one last time as tears streamed down both of their faces. He wiped his tears and turned to Aaliyah. "I'm ready."

Aaliyah nodded and led Gewey to the trail. He dared not look back for fear his heart would break.

"Are we going alone?" he asked.

"We need no escort," Aaliyah replied. "There is nothing so dangerous as to trouble us."

"How long until we get there?"

"Two days. But if we press our pace and take no respite, we can reach the shore by morning. My ship awaits us." She slowed to walk beside Gewey. "I know it is hard to leave her. But it is for the best. And you may find you are glad that you did."

Gewey was in no mood for flirting. "You told me you were once bonded."

"I was," she affirmed.

"When he died, did you think it was for the best?" He saw a pang of emotion shoot across her face. Immediately, he regretted his words.

"At the time, I did not." Her lips slowly relaxed, and she smiled sweetly. "But now, I think it might have been."

Gewey struggled not to return her smile. Instead, he reached out to Kaylia. Immense sorrow and worry were all he felt at first, then joy and relief as she reached back. Aaliyah quickened their pace.

By nightfall, Gewey was forced to use the flow more and more to keep up his strength. At times they almost ran. He could tell Aaliyah was using only her natural endurance and marveled, though he said nothing about it.

By midnight, the landscape had flattened, and the trees thinned. Patches of grass were separated by large areas of gray sand and red clay. The tall pines were now outnumbered by curved palms and thick brambles, and the musty scent of the forest was mixed with the salty breeze coming in off the Western Abyss.

"Do you need rest?" asked Aaliyah.

Gewey knew that if he released the flow, fatigue would certainly set in. "No, I'm fine," he said.

Aaliyah reached into a pouch on her belt and pulled out a small, orange berry. "Try this." She handed it to Gewey.

Gewey examined it for a moment. It was smooth and shiny, and no larger than a cherry. "What is it?"

"We call them Rain Berries." She pulled out another and popped it in her mouth. Sighing with satisfaction, she motioned for Gewey to eat.

Gewey held it to his nose. It smelled like a plum, only sweeter. He slowly bit down. Sweet juice exploded and a delicious flavor, unlike any other fruit or berry he had ever encountered, filled his mouth and caressed his tongue. "I've never tasted anything like it," he said.

"They are my favorite," Aaliyah told him. "And very hard to come by. I searched many days to find only a small handful."

"I wish they grew here," said Gewey.

"Perhaps one day you will help me to gather them in my homeland."

Gewey noticed how the moonlight silhouetted the curves of her figure. She moved with a fluid grace that was unmatched by anyone he'd ever seen. She looked over just in time to catch his stare and gave him a sly grin. He felt himself flush with embarrassment.

An hour before sunrise, he could hear the surf beating against the shore. Walking became increasingly difficult as the sand deepened and the dunes began to rise ahead. Not that this appeared to hinder Aaliyah. As they crested the last dune, the dim light of dawn broke at his back. The azure of the Western Abyss stretched out before them. Gewey stood transfixed.

"Have you never seen the sea?" asked Aaliyah.

"No," Gewey replied. "I haven't. I only left my small village a short time ago. Even then, we were on the run most of the time." He breathed in the sea air.

"You will see the world soon enough," said Aaliyah. "But I must warn you. The first time on a ship at sea can be disquieting."

Up until now, Gewey had not thought much about spending two weeks aboard a seagoing vessel. He shrugged, not wanting to show his sudden apprehension. "I'll be fine."

"Of course you will." She led Gewey down the beach to a small boat that had been pulled ashore and tied to a large piece of driftwood. "My ship is just over the horizon."

Gewey looked out at the water. The waves were at least three feet high and the sea beyond the breakers was rough. "Is it safe to go such a long way out in this?"

Aaliyah laughed as she untied the boat. "We won't be going that far. My ship is already heading toward us."

"How...?" Gewey began.

"My crew knows I am here because I let them know," she said before he could complete his question. "It is much the same as when you reach out to Kaylia, only we can do so without the bonding. You will learn soon enough."

Gewey grabbed the side of the boat and helped Aaliyah drag it to the water. It was surprisingly light, which made him even more nervous as he eyed the churning seas. As soon as they were in the water and on board, Gewey noticed something missing. Oars. Aaliyah had seated herself at the front and was sitting cross-legged, hands in her lap, palms up. The boat lurched forward. Spray soaked his clothes as the craft cut through the waves and into open water. He could feel the flow coursing through her.

In the distance, he spotted red sails breaking above the horizon. "I see them," he called out.

"Yes," she replied. "We will be aboard soon."

The ship came closer at an alarming rate. In only a few minutes, it loomed above them. It was well over one hundred feet in length, and its two giant masts were nearly the length of the ship itself. Gewey had only seen drawings of seagoing vessels, but could still tell that this ship was much sleeker in design, and looked faster. The sails were swollen full, and at first, Gewey was afraid the ship would ram them. But just as it came within twenty yards, the sails went limp and the vessel slowed dramatically.

Dozens of elves, all of them dressed in tan shirts and red trousers, could be seen looking down at them. One unfurled a rope ladder, as well as two thin ropes. Aaliyah attached the ropes to steel rings on each side of the boat and then led Gewey up the ladder. He could already feel queasiness in his stomach as he climbed. The ship rose and dipped methodically, causing him to nearly fall twice before he reached the top. Once on deck, he reached over and held the side railing to steady himself.

"You will grow accustomed to the movement soon," Aaliyah promised. "For now, stare at the horizon. It will keep your stomach from turning sour."

Gewey looked doubtful but obeyed. He could hear the whispers of the elves behind him. The words Shivis Mol were repeated over and over. After a few minutes, his nausea subsided, and he turned around. The sway of the ship tipped him slightly off balance. As he stumbled forward, a tall, thin elf with dust-brown hair and ice-blue eyes leaped forward to grab his arm.

"I'm fine," said Gewey. "Thank you."

The elf bowed. "It takes time to grow accustomed to the sea." He smiled brightly. "But I suspect Shivis Mol will have little trouble."

Gewey looked out over the deck. At least a dozen elves were busy about the ship. Aaliyah was standing several feet away, speaking to one of the crew. To the aft end, the deck sloped upward, ending at a cabin that stood nearly ten feet tall. A narrow wooden door leading to the cabin interior was flanked on either side by ladders leading up to the poop deck. The main deck was smooth and glistened in the morning sun, yet despite its slick appearance, it gripped the soles of his boots. He examined the various ropes and pulleys hanging from the first mast, marveling at their sheer complexity. The riverboats he had seen were toys by comparison.

Aaliyah motioned for him to join her. "If you wish, you can spend time among the crew. They will be pleased to show you how the ship works."

"I would like that," said Gewey. His stomach growled loudly.

Several elves began to gather around each mast.

"You should watch this," said Aaliyah. "Then you can eat and rest."

The elves closed their eyes and folded their hands in front of them. Gewey could sense the sudden swell of the flow growing around him. He felt the air begin to stir and build until the sails snapped full. The masts groaned and creaked as the ship lurched forward. The elves opened their eyes, and all but one broke the circle and returned to their work.

"He will maintain the wind until midday," said Aaliyah. She pointed to the bow where another elf woman stood, eyes fixed on the horizon. "And she will guide us."

Gewey could scarcely believe what he had seen. "You can teach me this?"

"Of course." She reached out and took his hand. "That is why you are here, is it not? But come, there will be time for that later."

"But how…"

She placed one delicate finger to his lips. "Later. I am strong, but I still need to eat." She led Gewey across the deck and through the door of the cabin. The wooden interior was polished, clean, and superbly varnished. Long tables had been placed to his right, and a narrow door could be seen just beyond these at the back of the cabin. The walls were bare—with the exception of a silver placard hanging above the far table. This displayed an expertly carved relief of a dolphin leaping playfully from a turbulent sea.

Aaliyah took Gewey's pack and motioned for him to sit. "I will take your belongings to your quarters." She disappeared through the narrow door.

Gewey waited patiently. It wasn't long before Aaliyah returned carrying two bowls. Closely following her came a short, elderly elf woman bearing a bottle, two wooden cups, and two spoons. The scent of fresh fish filled the air. After placing everything on the table, the woman bowed and left.

Aaliyah took a seat across from Gewey. "I hope you enjoy our fare."

In the bowl was a thick creamy stew dotted with red, green, and black spices. His mouth watered. "What is it?" He gathered up a spoonful and saw large chunks of fish mixed in with the thick broth.

"It is a stew made from cream, fish, and spices from my homeland." She poured Gewey a cup of wine.

Gewey's eyes grew wide at the first taste. It was almost sweet, yet the spice caused his tongue to tingle. The fish was tender and just salty enough to be a pleasant addition to the overall experience. He smiled and moaned with satisfaction.

"I am pleased you like it," said Aaliyah.

They ate the rest of the meal in silence. When they were finished, she led him through the door at the back of the cabin and down a narrow corridor that split at the end. To their right was an open door leading into a small kitchen; they continued left, and on to a room at the end of the hallway. Inside was surprisingly luxurious. A thick, indigo rug, woven with swirling silver patterns around its borders, covered the floor. A large oak desk littered with maps, charts, and several leather books lay directly ahead. On either side of this were single beds dressed with plush blue quilts and two small but soft-looking round pillows. A large ash chest had been placed at the foot of each bed. The wall was decorated with paintings of various sea creatures—some Gewey was familiar with, while others looked like monsters out of legends. Glowing spheres hung from the ceiling in the corners.

Aaliyah sat on the bed to the right. She nodded toward the one opposite, with Gewey's pack already on it. "You sleep there."

Gewey froze. "You mean you're staying in the same room?"

"Of course," Aaliyah replied, clearly amused. "Space aboard ship is limited, and I will not have Shivis Mol sleep on deck."

"I wouldn't mind." He made no move toward the bed. Knowing her intentions made him feel uneasy, and he knew Kaylia certainly would not approve.

Her laugh rang out like music. "Calm yourself. I can have one of the crew stay with you if you wish."

Gewey suddenly felt very much like a child. Settling his wits, he said: "I wouldn't want to kick you out of your own room. I didn't mean to overreact."

There was a knock at the door and two elf men entered, carrying a small basin filled with water. Their eyes remained fixed on Gewey as they placed the basin gently on the floor and then left.

Aaliyah rose to her feet. "It is time for your first lesson." She knelt in front of the basin. "The water is cold. You shall heat it."

Gewey knelt beside her. "What do I do?"

"The same as you do with power from the earth. Only you must focus your spirit on the air that surrounds the basin."

Gewey cocked his head. "The air? Not the water?"

Aaliyah shook her head. "No. You could heat it that way, but the effort would be much greater." She reached over and took his hand. "You must learn to find the smooth path. Water will resist you, while the air is pliant." She squeezed his hand tightly. "Open your mind to me. Allow me to guide you."

Gewey breathed deeply and closed his eyes. At once he saw Kaylia, her face anguished and lonely. His eyes snapped open.

Aaliyah released her grip and sprang to her feet. "This will not do." Her voice was disapproving and sharp. "If you cannot govern your bond, I must assist you." Grabbing Gewey by the shoulders, she pressed down hard.

"What are you doing?." he demanded. Then it felt as if he had been struck between the eyes. He fell back, reeling.

Aaliyah knelt beside him. "You are not hurt, Shivis Mol."

Gewey opened his eyes. It took him a moment before he managed to sit up and regain his focus. Something was wrong. An overwhelming sadness filled his heart and tears began streaming down his cheeks. He closed his eyes, reaching out to his bond with Kaylia. It was gone! He glared accusingly at Aaliyah. "What have you done?" he roared, sorrow blending with sheer fury.

Aaliyah looked serene and almost satisfied. "Nothing that cannot be undone."

Gewey leaped to his feet. His hand slid to his sword as the flow raged through him. "Then undo it!"

Aaliyah didn't appear intimidated in the slightest as she slowly stood up. "I will not. Not until your lessons are complete." She turned to the door. "You are unable to control your bond with Kaylia. That will hinder our work, and we can ill afford that. The time I have to teach you is short, and I will not allow passion to cripple you." Reaching for the door, she turned her profile to Gewey. "I will leave until you have calmed your storm." With those words, she left the room.

Gewey let out a tortured scream. For more than an hour, he raged, pacing back and forth. Again and again, he tried to reach out to Kaylia but could feel nothing at all. The sensation of pure emptiness had him weeping openly several times. Finally, he slumped down onto the bed, defeated.

The door opened and Aaliyah returned. She sat next to him, her face showing deep concern and sympathy. "When you have the strength, you can overcome what I have done. I have not broken your bond, merely pulled it from your grasp." She placed her hand on Gewey's. "You must trust me."

Gewey roughly pushed her hand away. "You had no right to do this."

"Better for me to face your anger now than to let you face your enemies unprepared." She knelt back down beside the basin of water. "Come."

Gewey stared with seething anger. He remained sitting on the bed for several minutes before finally kneeling beside her. "You had better keep your word. Once you've taught me—undo it."

Aaliyah took his hand. This time, he did not resist. "When I have taught you what you need to know, you will not need me to undo it." Her mouth turned up to the tiniest of smiles. "When that happens, your foes will tremble before you."

Gewey closed his eyes and let Aaliyah enter his mind. Despite his anger, the touch of her thoughts felt soothing and warm.

"Allow yourself to feel as I feel." Her voice lifted away the loneliness.

Gewey let himself drift nearer and nearer until he could no longer separate where his mind ended, and hers began. He had only ever been this close to Kaylia before. Guilt and regret shot through his heart, but somehow Aaliyah pushed these emotions away, replacing them with a feeling of joy and contentment. He felt her spirit reach out to the air that surrounded the basin. At first, it was confusing. It felt so different to when he was drawing power from the earth—so removed and strange that this couldn't possibly be part of the flow. But as Aaliyah began moving and molding it, he began to see how it melded to the actual fabric of the world. Suddenly, everything was so simple. He wondered how he had never seen it before.

"Magic," he whispered.

"Yes," said Aaliyah. "In a way."

The air above and around the basin swirled and compressed, faster and faster, until heat sprang forth from its core. Increasingly hot, it danced and swayed, caressing the surface of the water and sides of the basin. Then, as suddenly as it began, it ended. The water steamed and rippled.

Gewey reached out and touched the basin, burning the tips of his fingers. He scarcely noticed the pain. "How didn't I see it before?"

Aaliyah squeezed his hand and helped him to his feet. "It may still elude you."

Gewey closed his eyes and reached out for Aaliyah once again. This time, she didn't allow him to join with her. "Why...?"

"You must try without my help," she said.

Gewey realized in that moment that he longed to feel her spirit, and instantly felt ashamed. He felt as if he had betrayed Kaylia. "Of course," he said.

Pushing his feelings aside, he tried to recreate what they had done together. But as Aaliyah had warned, he was not able to. After three straight attempts, he threw his hands up in frustration.

"Patience," said Aaliyah. "It will come more easily with time." She turned to the door. "I will leave you to bathe. Then we can rest."

"But it's still morning."

Her voice became soft and seductive. "I prefer the night. And I am weary from our journey."

Gewey blushed under her gaze. The feeling of guilt and betrayal returned to snap back his reason. He was very tired. Now that he had released the flow and his anger had subsided, he was becoming acutely aware of the dull fatigue now washing over his entire body.

After he had washed and changed into the elf clothing given to him by Theopolou, he settled into his bed. The waves rocked him ever so gently until he drifted close to sleep. He was only vaguely aware of Aaliyah's return. For a moment, just before sleep completely took him, he could feel her mind touching his. It was soft and comforting, much like a mother soothing a frightened child. He felt his lips turn to a smile. Then there was only the dark oblivion of a deep, restful sleep.

CHAPTER 11

Gewey awoke to the sound of Aaliyah humming softly. She was sitting at the desk reading a small blue book. He lay there listening for a time before sitting up. He felt refreshed and strong.

"You slept well, I trust?" she asked.

He yawned and stretched. "Yes. I was more tired than I thought."

"You have had quite an eventful few days." She closed the book and placed it in the desk drawer. "I am sorry to say that you will get little rest while on board. We have much to do."

She waited outside for Gewey to change, then led him to the galley, where two plates of eggs and bread awaited them. After breakfast, she took him out on deck. The cool sea air sent a chill down his spine, and as he looked out onto the Western Abyss, he began to envy the sailors such a life. The dark, rolling waves and the endless expanse of the sea calmed him. The sun was just sinking over the horizon, setting the sky ablaze with swirls of orange, blue, and red. Surely, the stories his father had told him of storms and sea monsters couldn't exist in such a marvelous place.

Aaliyah walked to the port railing and leaned her slender figure over the side. The wind wrapped her thin cotton dress around her curves. "Beautiful, is it not?"

Gewey blushed, thankful she could not see his unease. "It is," he replied, joining her. "It's like nothing I've ever seen."

"It is not always so peaceful," she warned. "The sea is more perilous than you can imagine. Storms can rise without warning, and there are beasts that lurk within that are larger than this ship."

Gewey laughed. "Sea monsters?"

"Some," she replied. "Though not all are monsters. Some are gentle and wise."

Gewey cocked his head. "Wise? How can a beast be wise?"

"There is much about the world you have yet to learn," she said. "One is that not all 'beasts' are what they seem." She took his hand. "Come. It is time to begin."

The crew was busy about their work, but each one took a moment to greet them as they passed. Gewey had counted about thirty elves aboard and assumed there were more below. Aaliyah led him to the bow, where the navigator was concentrating on her duties.

"Is she using wind or water?" asked Gewey.

"Both," said Aaliyah. She placed his hand on the navigator's shoulder. "This is Faaliyasi. Join with her."

Gewey obeyed, allowing his mind and spirit to drift outward toward the navigator. Her mind was different from those of Kaylia or Aaliyah. It was hard, cold, and as unyielding as steel. She let Gewey draw close, but only close enough for him to feel as she did. The flow was similar to what he'd experienced that morning, but a million times more complex. The forces intertwined in perfect harmony, dancing and twisting as one.

"Amazing," he whispered. "How can you do this?"

Faaliyasi did not respond.

After several minutes, Aaliyah pulled Gewey away. "She has trained for many years to learn this skill."

"Can you do that?" Gewey asked.

"Yes, but not as well," she admitted. "Our navigators begin learning their craft in childhood. What you saw was just a small thing. Should a storm arise, you will see her true power."

Aaliyah had a small bowl of water brought on deck, and Gewey spent the rest of the evening trying in vain to touch the power of the air to heat it. He soon found Aaliyah to be as severe a taskmaster as Lee had been, though not as harsh in temperament. By morning, he was exhausted and frustrated.

When they returned to their quarters, he found that a basin of wash water had been left. The prospect of joining with Aaliyah excited him. He had not been alone inside himself since he'd first joined with Kaylia, and the loneliness now bothered him considerably. Had he not been so utterly engrossed in his training, he was certain it would be almost unbearable.

"You shall wash with cold water until you can learn to heat it yourself," Aaliyah told him.

Gewey's heart sank, but he tried once again. And this time, he felt it. Unlike the throbbing pulse of the earth, it was an irregular current of energy.

"Yes," said Aaliyah softly. "The air is not a brute like the earth. It is a whimsical child. Let it dance through you."

Gewey drew in the flow of the air for the first time. His fatigue washed away at once, and just like when he used the earth, his senses erupted with awareness. But unlike the earth, it was difficult to control. It scattered and twirled throughout his body as a tempest. It resisted him, threatening to tear him apart.

"Do not use force," Aaliyah instructed. "Use your heart and your soul to have it obey your commands."

"I don't understand," he said. The flow continued to build, rushing through him. Finally, he could no longer contain it. Gewey let out a horrifying scream at the point of release. The air exploded, tossing both him and Aaliyah back, slamming them hard against the wall.

Gewey slid down onto the floor, gasping. Every bit of breath had been forced from his lungs. Only after several moments was he able to regain his senses and catch his breath. It was then that he saw Aaliyah slumped down next to the door. Springing to his feet, he rushed to her side.

"Are you all right?" he asked desperately. "Gods, I'm sorry. I'm so sorry." He took her limp hand in his and reached out to her spirit. The moment he touched it, he felt the keen sense of loneliness vanish. Her spirit seemed to embrace him, pulling him to her.

Slowly, her eyes fluttered open. "I am unhurt." She managed a smile. "You are far stronger than I could have imagined." She sat up straight. "But I should have known Shivis Mol would be."

"I am sorry," he repeated.

"Do not be sorry," she said soothingly. "The fault was mine. I must be aware that I am not training an elf child, but a young godling." Her hand gently touched his cheek. "And in this world you have only just come of age. I must remember that as well."

Gewey stiffened. "I am a man," he insisted. "Even before I came of age, I was my own master."

She giggled, amused at his reaction. "A man need not assert that he is a man. Only a child would do so." Aided by Gewey, she struggled to her feet and smoothed her dress.

Gewey gave no reply. Embarrassed by the truth in her words, he turned and retrieved his elf clothing from the chest. Aaliyah left the room to allow him to wash, returning just as he was climbing into his bed.

She dimmed all the lights and climbed into her own bed. "I am sorry if I upset you," she said, pulling the blanket close. "But compared with me, your years in this world are few. There are many lessons for you still to learn."

"I know," said Gewey. "I just feel..." he sighed. "I suppose I don't like being reminded that I'm so much younger and inexperienced than everyone else around me."

"Yes, you are young." She closed her eyes and sighed. "But you are not without experience. And you are mature for your age. You should think no more on it. I will try to be more delicate with the matter."

Gewey let the ship rock him to sleep. His dreams were fraught with images of battle, blood, and mayhem. They were so vivid that, at first, he feared the Dark Knight had found him again. But to his relief, he did not appear.

Over the next several nights, Gewey and Aaliyah continued their lessons, but Aaliyah thought it better to do so on deck rather than risk damage to the ship. Though there were no further accidents, Gewey struggled for the first few days to control the flow. The more he failed, the more frustrated he became. But then, on the fourth night, it happened.

One of the navigators was on her way to her quarters. Her face was tense, her eyes narrow, and she appeared to be upset. Gewey stopped her.

"Are you all right?" he asked.

"I am fine, Shivis Mol," she replied.

Her name was Drasalisia. Gewey had seen her nearly every evening on his way up to the deck. Usually, he was already involved in his lesson when she passed by, but this evening, Aaliyah had allowed him a little bit of extra sleep. "It's just that you look upset," he remarked.

Drasalisia's face relaxed a little. She managed a polite smile. "No, Shivis Mol, I am not upset. But when you channel power from the air and water, it can leave you emotional. It takes effort to calm myself."

"Emotional?" Gewey rubbed the back of his neck and tilted his head. There were three navigators on board. All women and all seemed to him to be as stoic as priests of Dantenos, God of the Dead. "How do you mean?"

"The water is power and mystery," she replied. "Difficult to understand, but easy to manipulate. The air is another matter. It is passion and fire. It burns and flows with a will of its own. When you control air, it demands that you use your own passion. Otherwise, it will defy you."

"You speak as if it were alive," he remarked.

"Did you ever think it was not?" She huffed a laugh and walked away.

Gewey thought on her words for a time before sitting next to the waiting bowl of water. He closed his eyes and felt the flow of the air around him, drawing it near. He could feel it raging and bursting with power. Then it came to him. The passion. Love, hate, joy, sorrow, all pressing in together, trying to force their way out. It was alive. He drew it inside and let his own feelings surge into the storm. It was in that moment he understood why he couldn't control it before. In his attempt to control, he had withheld the part of himself needed for the air to join with him as one—his heart. All the lessons suddenly came together, and he knew exactly what to do. Within moments, the air around the bowl had heated.

"Perfect." Aaliyah knelt beside him. "Soon it will become effortless. You will be able to create wonders."

Gewey sighed with satisfaction. "It's alive. I can feel it."

"Of course,it is," she replied. "The world is a living thing formed by the Creator. The pulse of the earth is its heart and body. The air its breath. The water its blood." She took his hand, pulling him to his feet. "And when you are ready, you will see its soul."

"Its soul?" Gewey tried to imagine the world as an immense creature atop which all people resided. "I'll be able to see it?"

"Oh, yes," said Aaliyah. "When you have control enough to master the physical powers of the earth, then you shall be ready to join with its spirit. For an elf, there is no greater power. Only a few of us have touched it."

"Have you?" he asked.

"Yes," she replied. "I am one who has achieved such power. Though I admit, only to a small degree. To journey through the unseen world, touching the minds of others wrapped within your own spirit, is a gift we all possess. But to join with the true spirit of creation—that is unlike anything you can imagine. Once you can do this, you will be invincible."

Gewey realized she was still holding his hand and felt his heart race. He quickly withdrew. Aaliyah smiled and let out a soft, contented laugh. She looked into his eyes for a long moment and then stood over him.

"I know what you're trying to do," he said in a half-whisper. "It won't work. I love Kaylia."

"I have made no secret of my intent," she replied. "But I am no trickster. Do not sully our time together with accusations." She motioned for him to resume his lesson.

For the rest of the night, Gewey practiced channeling the flow. By the end of the lesson, Aaliyah had taught him how to create a tiny ball of flame above his hand and send it flying through the air.

From then on, time aboard passed quickly. By the beginning of the second week, Gewey began rising early in order to study the ship and its workings. All the crew members were happy to teach him, and he found himself looking forward to this as much as he did his lessons with Aaliyah. His new friends relished telling him stories from their homeland and were eager to learn of his life, too. Their cheer and good nature reminded him of Linis and his seekers. It was comforting to know that he did not need to convince them to be his allies. Though they did not say it directly, he felt as if they would do anything he asked of them.

But even though he had immersed his mind in his lessons, Kaylia was never far from his mind. The absence of her thoughts and emotions was an open wound that felt as if it would never heal. Several times every day he tried to reach her, but without success. Each time he attempted this, Aaliyah appeared shortly afterward to give him further instruction. Somehow, she knew what he was doing. But worse, she also knew what he was feeling and was able to say just the right thing to send his heart pounding and cheeks blushing. Most of the time, this was followed by heart-wrenching guilt. But she would occasionally catch him off-guard, and he would respond more in the manner of a suitor than a student. This, naturally, caused him even more guilt and torment.

By midway through the second week, the cool evenings had become warm and muggy. Aaliyah told him that they were about a hundred miles from the shores of a large delta city. Gewey assumed this to be Baltria. She explained that, until they neared their destination in four days' time, they would remain far from shore so as to avoid other ships. Gewey marveled that they had traveled so far in such a short time.

Aaliyah told him that he would begin lessons with water on their return journey. This reminded Gewey of why they had actually come. He had heard stories of the desert nomads: fierce and dangerous; they wandered aimlessly, preying on anyone foolish enough to stray too far from the oasis towns. Ravenous beasts supposedly roamed the sands as well. There were tales of wolves the size of a pony hunting at night, devouring entire caravans and leaving only the bones to bleach in the scorching sun. He'd even heard stories of great flying lizards that breathed fire, though these were the things usually told to children at night. His father had occasionally delighted him with desert tales, and the giant lizard stories had always been his favorite.

On the day of their arrival, Gewey gathered his belongings and went on deck to wait for Aaliyah. He had decided to wear his elf clothes. They were cool and might also keep the sun at bay. It was just before nightfall and the air was unusually mild. He had hoped some of the crew would be joining them—the idea of just him and Aaliyah alone braving the desert sands unsettled him—but she had explained that the crew's place was aboard ship. However, should they need help, she could certainly call them.

The small boat they had used at the beginning of their sea crossing had already been lowered into the water. The water was calm with a pale green tint, unlike the deep, rich blues he had seen before. The crew took turns bidding him farewell and good luck. He knew he would miss their good humor in the days to come, especially if what he had heard of the desert was true.

Gewey saw Aaliyah approaching from the main cabin. She was dressed in a pair of loose-fitting tan trousers and tunic, together with a pair of short leather boots. On her belt were two long daggers. Her hair was tied in a tight braid that danced to and fro as she moved. One of the crew followed close behind, carrying her pack.

"Are you prepared?" she asked Gewey, taking her pack and slinging it across her shoulders.

He nodded. After they'd climbed down the ladder into the boat, Aaliyah channeled the flow as before, sending the craft speeding forward. It wasn't long before Gewey could make out the dunes just beyond the shoreline. Even from so far away, he could see that they were massive, and tried not to think about how hard it would be to walk among them. Then they were at the beach edge. The waves lapped curiously against the small boat as the craft slid ashore. They gathered their packs and Gewey checked his sword. There was no driftwood about, so they pulled the boat to the base of the dunes.

"With luck, the tide will not rise this high," said Aaliyah. "Otherwise we may be forced to swim back to the ship."

"What do you...?" he began but stopped when he spotted Aaliyah's mischievous grin. "You're funny." He looked up at the dunes and sighed. "I assume you know where to go from here."

"I know what direction to take," she replied, "but not the exact whereabouts of our destination."

Suddenly, she stiffened, and her hands shot to her daggers.

Gewey instinctively drew in the flow of the earth. At once, he knew what had alarmed her. He could sense at least fifty humans on the other side of the dune. He could feel them creeping up the slope, and hear the sounds of their swords being drawn and arrows being notched. "Nomads," he whispered. "My father told me stories about them."

Aaliyah drew her daggers. "Whoever they are, they intend us harm."

How she could tell that, Gewey had no idea, but he was not about to question her. He freed his sword and let the flow rage through him. He could feel it flowing through Aaliyah as well, but could not tell if she was drawing it from earth or air.

"Pay heed, and do not lose focus," she commanded. This brought Gewey back to attention. "When they crest the dune, follow me."

Gewey crouched ready to spring, his knuckles white around his sword. Then, from a hundred yards to their left, he heard the snap and twang of bowstrings, followed by the thin whistle of arrows flying. He looked skyward, fearing that a shower of arrows was about to rain down on them. But they were not the targets. A dozen nomads screamed out in agony as the arrows struck home. Gewey reached out to find the source but could sense nothing. Another volley zipped through the air, and more men fell.

"What should we do?" asked Gewey.

"We hope that whoever aids us is not doing so to keep the spoils for themselves," she replied. "I cannot tell who or what they are."

He shook his head. "Nor can I."

The nomads were scattering like ants, some dragging the wounded, others in a full run down the dune, completely abandoning the attack. After a few minutes, there was only the sound of the sea and the rustle of the wind.

Aaliyah tapped Gewey's shoulder. "Should we be attacked, drag the boat to the water."

"What will you do?" he asked. He was not about to let her fight alone.

She held out her palm and a tiny ball of flame appeared above it. "I will be showing them that arrows are of little use."

It was then a thin figure appeared atop a dune one hundred yards to their north. In its right hand it held up a bow, and in its left a quiver. Gewey could hardly believe his eyes.

"Elves," he whispered. "Here in the desert." For the first time, Aaliyah looked surprised and uncertain. "You didn't know?" he asked.

"That there were elves here?" She shook her head slowly. "No, I did not. But I am grateful to see them. Unless I am wrong, that is not a gesture of aggression." She raised her hand, returning the greeting. "Still, mind what you say. Do not tell them who I am. Or, more importantly, who you are. If they are like the other elves of this land, you, being human, may be enough on its own to anger them."

The elf made his way deftly down the dune, slinging the quiver over his back as he descended. He was dressed in white trousers and shirt, and high boots made from a material Gewey had never seen. It was like leather in its thickness but clung like cloth, and was just as pliable. At his side hung a long, curved saber attached to a thick tan belt. His cropped blond hair was shaved to the skin on either side of his head. His face was obscured by a thin piece of cloth wrapped just below the tip of his nose and also around his forehead, but Gewey could see that the skin around his eyes was pale white.

"Have you ever seen an elf like this?" asked Gewey.

It took a moment for her to answer. "You have more experience with elves than I. I only know those of my own land, and none are like this one."

He strode up with amazing grace and speed, seemingly unaffected by the deep sand. "How lucky you are," he called when a few yards away. "Had we not been aware that the Soufis were near, you would now be slaves—or worse." He removed his face covering, revealing a broad smile. He looked young, though Gewey knew that when it came to elves, appearances could be deceiving. "I was not aware that elves from the west journeyed to the desert," the newcomer told them. He laughed. "Or that they preferred the company of humans."

Aaliyah stepped forward. "I am Aaliyah. This is Gewey." It was the first time Gewey had heard her use his name. He cracked a smile. "If we have trespassed..."

The elf held up his hand. "One cannot trespass in the desert. They can only step unwisely, as you have done." He turned his head and let out a high-pitched whistle. "But fortune smiles on you. Now you are our guests, rather than Soufis slaves."

Twelve more elves appeared atop the dune.

"We thank you for your assistance," Aaliyah said, bowing. "And are grateful for your hospitality. We have traveled far."

"Though obviously not alone." The elf glanced at their boat. "You did not come here in that. Will the rest not join us? We have never seen elves from the West and would enjoy knowing them. We have heard of their hatred of humans—a tale clearly not true. We would be pleased to have as many of your comrades as care to come."

"You don't hate humans?" asked Gewey.

He threw his head back in laughter. "Hate? We have few dealing with humans. Why would we hate them? They do not trouble us. Most beyond the heart of the desert do not even know we are here. The humans that choose desert life keep to their own ways, and we have respect for one another." He glanced at the dead Soufis. "Well, there are some that we are not so fond of." He placed his hand on his chest. "I am Pali. And I welcome you." He spun around. "Come. The nights are cold and my belly is empty. Our camp is not far." He paused. "That is, unless you would rather brave the night alone."

Without waiting for a reply, Pali strode off in the direction of his companions. Gewey and Aaliyah followed as best they could, but the deep, soft sand hindered their steps. Soon they were many yards behind, but Pali didn't slow his pace. When they finally reached the dunes where Pali and his companions awaited them, Gewey was already dreading their trek. Days of wading through sand was not going to be easy.

The other elves were dressed in the same fashion as Pali, though the three females kept their hair in lengthy braids rather than short and shaved like the men. It struck Gewey that their skin was just as pale as Pali's. How this was possible in such a climate, he couldn't guess. Pali introduced them, and each elf greeted him and Aaliyah in turn. They all had the same cheerful expressions and seemed more than pleased to have them along.

"We can be at our camp in less than an hour," said Pali. "We move fast across the sands, but we will slow our pace, as you are clearly not accustomed to the terrain."

"Thank you," said Gewey.

Pali led them between the dunes, twisting and turning until Gewey was certain he would be lost without their guidance. By now, the sun had nearly disappeared. The soft orange glow of twilight reflected on the yellow sand, making the world seem surreal and unnatural. The elves began singing loudly, and though Gewey didn't recognize the tune, the words and images were easy to understand. Mostly they were about traveling in the desert with friends or living a life free from troubles. Aaliyah remained quiet and expressionless as walked close by Gewey's side.

Just as Pali had said, an hour later, they rounded a large dune and Gewey spotted several palm trees in the distance. He could hear the sound of voices laughing and talking. They arrived not a moment too soon. The temperature was already beginning to plummet uncomfortably.

"Don't worry," said Pali, noticing Gewey rubbing his hands together. "Soon a warm fire and a hot meal will cure your chill."

As they approached the camp, Gewey could see about twenty elves scattered about a small oasis. The scent of campfires mingled with the pleasing aroma of spiced meat. A cacophony of boisterous greetings rang out, followed by murmurs of curiosity as the camp noticed Gewey and Aaliyah.

"These are our new friends from the west," Pali announced. "They will be joining us for as long as it pleases them to do so."

He turned to Gewey and Aaliyah. "Feel free to explore what little there is to see here." He pointed north to an area behind the fire furthest away from them. "There is a small spring just over there. I only ask that you use it sparingly. It's a slow spring and takes several days to replenish itself." He inhaled deeply. "I can tell you are accustomed to bathing. I'm sorry to say that water is too precious in the desert to be used in that way."

Gewey sniffed the air. "You seem clean to me."

Pali laughed. "I didn't mean to say that we don't clean ourselves. Of course, we do. Just not by the same means. If you wish, I can show you."

"Perhaps later," said Aaliyah. "For now, a meal and your company will be sufficient."

"Our meal will be ready soon," said Pali. "Until then, you may find a place by a fire." He stopped a passing elf and whispered in his ear. "I will have wine brought to you right away. But now I must tell our Sand Master about the encounter with the Soufis."

Aaliyah and Gewey found a vacant spot near one of the fires next to six elves. The much-needed warmth lifted Gewey's spirits, and he was quick to introduce himself. Aaliyah was not as forthcoming, at first, choosing only to say her name and nothing more. It was clear to Gewey that something was troubling her. The elves, two women and four men, greeted them both warmly all the same.

"I'm Dreta," said a short, thin, dark-haired woman. "How lucky we are that you chose this fire to warm yourself. We'll be the envy of the camp."

The rest eagerly called out their names in turn—the other female introduced herself as Freda. Then came Hali, Ghenti, Deransil, and Freuli.

"How is it that your people came to live in the desert?" asked Gewey.

"Some legends say that we were exiled thousands of years ago for protecting humans from slavery," said Dreta. "Others claim that we were put here by the gods as punishment for defying their will." She shrugged. "But who knows what the truth really is? Our people belong to the sands now, and this is our home."

"So you never go west?" asked Gewey.

"No," said Dreta. "Why would we? As I said, this is our home and we love it dearly."

Gewey couldn't imagine living in such a desolate place, let alone loving it. "But wouldn't life be so much easier away from the desert?" he asked.

The elves burst into laughter. "I doubt life is easy no matter where you live," said Dreta. "But still, we live a good life. The sands have made us strong, and, through that strength, we have become one with the Creator. No. There is no other life for us."

"And if you could learn the real reason why you are here?" asked Aaliyah. "What then?"

"What does it matter?" Dreta shook her head and grinned. "This is where we are, and this is where we'll stay. You would be hard-pressed to find any among us who desires to leave."

Aaliyah leaned forward. "And if someone did?"

"We do not hold our people captive," Dreta replied. "If anyone wishes to leave, they are free to do so. It has always been our way."

Just then Pali joined them carrying two bottles of wine. "The Sand Master is in a foul mood now." He passed a bottle to Gewey and opened the other himself. "She was hoping the Soufis would stop venturing this far south after what we did to them the last time." He turned up the bottle and then passed it Dreta. "We must have killed fifty of them."

"Why would they come then?" asked Gewey.

"For slaves," he replied.

Aaliyah stiffened. "They take elves as slaves?"

"Of course not," said Pali. "But there are several small human settlements and a few nomadic tribes in this region. They raid these and take what they want."

"And you protect the humans?" asked Aaliyah.

"We try," Pali replied, casting his eyes downward. "But we cannot be everywhere at once. And the Soufis are clever." He looked up and his smile returned. "But enough tragedy. I am curious; why have you journeyed so far?"

"We seek a very special place," said Aaliyah. "A temple of sorts. I know it is in this area, but I'm not sure exactly where. It is urgent that we find it."

Pali thought for a moment. "There is only one place in the southern desert I know of that would hold interest. But I advise you to abandon the idea. It is an unnatural place—evil lurks there."

"What do you mean?" asked Gewey.

"It is a place where the shadows live." He wrapped his arms. "We have not been there in many years. But those who went did not return."

Aaliyah refused the bottle when Gewey offered it. "Can you tell us how to get there?"

"Yes," said Pali. "But it is some distance from here, and you are not accustomed to the desert. I doubt you would make it alone."

"We are stronger than you might think," said Aaliyah.

Pali chuckled lightly and shook his head. "If you mean you can steal life from the earth, that will do you little good."

Gewey could see that Pali's words bothered Aaliyah. "What do you mean—steal?"

"Our people once drew such power to control and dominate," he explained. "Now, though, to us, using it is unthinkable. We believe the sands live, and we would never take life from them for our own selfish needs."

Gewey understood Aaliyah's apprehension. "So you consider it a crime?"

Pali laughed loudly. "A crime, no. We have few laws beyond murder. But it is ... immoral." He grabbed Gewey's shoulder and gave it a fond squeeze. "But don't worry. We do not judge the ways of others, so long as they do not hurt our people or our friends."

"That is good," said Aaliyah. She relaxed noticeably.

"You didn't think we would extend our hospitality only to do you harm, did you?" This brought another round of gay laughter. "You should spend more time among us. That is, if I can convince you not to complete your quest."

"Sadly, it is a matter of great importance," said Aaliyah. "We would not ignore your warnings if it were not so."

Pali sighed heavily. "The Sand Master will not take you there." He put his hands on his knees and pushed himself to his feet. "But I will. Though I can only take you to the edge of your destination, I will not have new friends brave the desert alone." He took one more long drink from the bottle before adding quietly to himself: "And I thought the Sand Master was in a foul mood before." With that, he left.

Gewey watched him walk away. "What is a Sand Master?" he asked the others.

This time it was Ghenti, a broad-shouldered elf with a hawk-like nose and piercing gray eyes, who spoke. "The Sand Masters are our guides in the desert. They know the sands better than anyone. Though we can all navigate our way, the Sand Master is able to find the easiest trail, nearest water, and nearest shade with barely a thought. When an elf turns eleven, the child is blindfolded, taken deep into the desert, and left alone. If the child finds its way home, training begins as a Sand Master."

"What if the child doesn't make it?" asked Gewey, afraid to hear the answer.

Ghenti met Gewey's eyes. "Then the child dies." His tone was harsh and low. He didn't look away for several seconds, then slowly his face broke into a smile. The others began to giggle and smirk. "We bring the child home, of course." He tossed Gewey the bottle, then addressed his comrades. "I do believe the boy thinks us savages." His tone was teasing and light, as were the voices of agreement from the others.

Gewey felt foolish and embarrassed but forced a smile.

Soon after this, the meal was ready. Aaliyah and Gewey ate and talked with their new friends for a few more hours. From time to time, a fresh face appeared by the fireside, eager to meet the strangers from the west. The conversation kept away from serious matters, and though Aaliyah seemed more at ease than before, Gewey could tell that something still bothered her.

Just as they were about to settle down to sleep, a short, stout elf woman with deep brown hair and careworn eyes approached. Unlike the cheerful expressions held by the others, her demeanor was grim. She sat across from Gewey and Aaliyah, crossing her legs and studying them for several minutes before speaking.

"I am Weila, Sand Master," she said finally. "Pali tells me that he is to lead you to the Black Oasis."

"If that is the location of what we seek, then yes," said Aaliyah, "though he did not call it that."

"I assume he has warned you of the dangers?" she asked.

"He has."

"Then you should also know what he does not," she continued. "The Oasis was always a queer place, but in the past few years, a new evil has arrived there."

"I did not know..." said Pali.

"Of course you didn't," snapped Weila, cutting him off. "You only think you know everything." Her stone gaze made Gewey uneasy. This was clearly a woman to be reckoned with. "You are strangers here." Her eyes drifted to Aaliyah. "And though you are an elf, we are not the same. Certainly, you have sensed it. Your kind steals life from the Mother. We do not, and that leaves you blind to our presence."

Aaliyah started to respond, but Weila held up her hand.

"You cannot deny that it has caused you concern," she continued. "I can see it in your face. But our way has kept our people alive and strong for many generations. If you go to the Black Oasis, you will do so alone, and the creatures that now haunt it will know you are coming."

"If you cannot draw power from earth, air, and water, how can you know this?" asked Aaliyah.

Weila sneered. "You think us unaware of these powers simply because we do not use them? You are blind to us, not us to you." She leaned forward. "You will face an enemy there with no fear and no remorse. It will not hesitate to destroy you." Her eyes shot to Pali. "Or anyone with you. I will allow Pali to guide you, but you must swear to me one thing."

"What is that?" asked Aaliyah.

"Once you come to the edge of the Oasis, you cannot allow Pali to continue." Her face became strained. "Swear it! No matter how much he pleads."

"I told you, mother…" Pali protested, but another glance again silenced him.

Aaliyah nodded with understanding. "I swear to you, he shall guide us only as far as the edge, and no farther. And though you may feel my use of the powers is wrong, I also swear that I will use them to keep him safe."

"I do not fear for my son in the open desert," she replied. "But I thank you." She leaned back. "I know I must appear hard and inhospitable to you. But I assure you, I am not."

"You have no need to explain," said Aaliyah. "I too am responsible for the lives of others, and understand the need for caution when it comes to the safety of my people."

Weila's countenance softened. "Then I shall let you rest. Tomorrow you will get proper clothing for your journey."

Aaliyah and Gewey bowed as the Sand Master rose to her feet.

"That went better than I thought," remarked Pali.

"You're lucky to have a mother who cares so much," said Gewey. He thought of his own mother and her absence from his life. "Mine died when I was very young."

"I am sorry to hear it." Pali cocked his head. "You share much with our kind. I see that you are accustomed to the company of elves. That is good to hear. Most of what we have heard about the West are stories of hatred and war."

"The stories are true," said Gewey. "But things are changing."

They sat up for a few more minutes, then bedded down for the night.

CHAPTER 12

Kaylia awoke screaming and crying uncontrollably. Linis and Theopolou were at her side within seconds.

"It's gone!" she cried. "It's gone!"

Theopolou pulled her close. "What's gone?"

It took her a moment to stifle her sobs. "My bond with Gewey. It's gone!"

Theopolou closed his eyes and breathed deeply. He placed his hands on her head. "It is not gone. It has been somehow blocked."

At that moment, Nehrutu approached. "Is everything all right?" His shimmering red pants and shirt, along with his effortless, regal movements, made him easy to recognize. As graceful as the elves of this land were, they appeared awkward by comparison.

Kaylia tried to rise, but Theopolou held her fast. Her eyes burned. "Aaliyah is behind it! I know she is!"

"What has happened?" asked Nehrutu.

"I believe Aaliyah may have somehow blocked the bond between Kaylia and Gewey," Theopolou explained. "At least, that is the only explanation I can imagine."

Nehrutu leaned down and placed his hand on Kaylia's shoulder. His eyes closed for a full minute. "Yes, she has," he confirmed.

"That witch," Kaylia hissed.

"Can you undo what she has done?" asked Theopolou.

"I could—perhaps," Nehrutu replied. "But I will not."

"Why?" Kaylia screamed. "Why will you not help me?"

Nehrutu sighed. "Aaliyah has done this, and she has her reasons. It is not for me to interfere. Take comfort that she did not break your bond completely. She is certainly strong enough."

"But why?" asked Linis. "What purpose does it serve her?"

Nehrutu thought for a moment. "The only reason would be to help Shivis Mol. If the bond hindered his training, she would not hesitate to block it. I would do the same."

Kaylia's anger boiled over. Pulling away from Theopolou, she jumped to her feet and stood only inches away from Nehrutu. "And if you did, even the powers of the Creator would not save you. Nor would they save Aaliyah, if she were here." Tears welled in her eyes as the pain of Gewey's absence grew.

Nehrutu's face was expressionless. He met her eyes unflinchingly. "Then it is both fortunate that I did not do this, and that she is not here to face your wrath."

Linis gently took hold of Kaylia's arm. "There is nothing to be done. I am certain Gewey will find a way to undo this."

Kaylia stepped back and walked away into the darkness. Over and over she tried reaching out, but to no avail. Finally, she collapsed on the ground and wept. The vast emptiness was more than she could bear. The bond with Gewey was a fundamental part of her. It was as if it had always been there, and until that moment, she thought it always would be. For nearly an hour she wept in the darkness. Then she heard footfalls approaching. Expecting to see Linis or Theopolou, she wiped her eyes and stood. But instead, she saw Nehrutu.

"I do not want to speak to you." Her voice seethed with hatred.

"You may change your mind when you hear what I have to say," said Nehrutu.

Kaylia folded her arms and turned away.

"You are aware of Aaliyah's intentions toward Shivis Mol," he said.

"His name is Gewey," she shot back.

"As you say." He took a step closer. "We are not all in harmony with her intentions. Particularly me."

Kaylia turned. "And why is that?"

"Before we became aware of ... Gewey," he replied, "I was Aaliyah's betrothed. We were to be joined."

This took Kaylia aback. "And now?"

"Aaliyah is determined," he said, lowering his eyes. Kaylia could see the pain in his expression. "She truly believes that it is her duty to join with Gewey, and she will not relent. That he loves you is your greatest ally. But Aaliyah is clever and powerful. She will not make it easy for Gewey to refuse."

"What can I do?" she asked desperately. "How can I stop her?"

"You must learn to use the powers that the Creator has provided." He took her hands and looked into her eyes. "I can help you, but only if you let me. I do not want to lose Aaliyah, and I fear I will. But if you show yourself to her as an equal, she may very well step aside."

"How can I do this?" Kaylia's voice cracked. "I am no seeker, nor am I an elder."

"You have the ability inside you," he assured her. "If only you will allow me to show you how, you will discover your true gifts. Then perhaps we can both find peace and contentment."

Kaylia nodded slowly. "I would be grateful for your help." She pulled away and rubbed her arms from the chill night. "How is it she simply abandoned you?"

Nehrutu gave her a sad smile. "You should not judge her harshly. She is dedicated to the well-being of our people. She looks to the needs of others above her own desires. Everything she has done has been for the good of our people—though I often wish it was not so."

Kaylia choked back her tears. "When shall we begin?"

"As soon as possible," Nehrutu replied. "With your fire, we should accomplish much."

They walked back to camp together. Kaylia felt more at ease, though the loss of the bond still wrenched at her heart.

Since Gewey and Aaliyah's departure, preparations to retake Valshara had begun. Mohanisi, through the power of the flow, was able to get word to his ship and send it back to his homeland. Kaylia and Linis both remarked on the huge advantages of such communication.

The elders immediately sent messengers out to muster the elves and to bear news of the recent events at the Chamber of the Maker. Theopolou had one of his guards take a letter to Selena in Althetas, informing her of their intent. They reckoned it would be at least four weeks before they were ready to mount a viable assault and decided to use that time to gather intelligence on the temple occupation.

The first night of Kaylia's training was more frustrating than anything she had ever experienced before. Nehrutu took her away from the camp and sat her on a soft patch of grass.

"The earth will be first," he said. "It is the simplest to achieve. Once you master it, you will be able to do many things that were far out of your reach before."

"I have seen Linis and Theopolou use such power," she said. "I know..."

"You know nothing," he said, cutting her off, though he did not raise his voice. "The elders and your seekers have no idea of how to harness this power. In my land, elf children can do more." He leveled his gaze. "I am at odds with

Mohanisi by my instructing you exclusively. Do not make me regret this by thinking that you know what you do not."

"I am sorry," said Kaylia. "I will listen to your instructions."

"Good," said Nehrutu. "Now close your eyes and reach out with your spirit as you do through your bond. Only this time, touch the world around you."

Kaylia tried but could feel nothing. For hours she concentrated, still with no results. Finally, Nehrutu stood and held out his hand.

"I am sorry," said Kaylia. "I tried."

Nehrutu smiled warmly. "You did well." She took his hand, and he pulled her up. "Most cannot sit so long without breaking their concentration. You are using a power you have forgotten. Should you not use your legs for a hundred years, would you walk the first day?" He offered her a flask of honeyed water, which she gratefully accepted. "You will get stronger very soon. This I promise."

Over the next three days, Kaylia's frustration grew even more, but still, she did not give up. For hour upon hour, she continued to reach out, hoping and striving to feel something—anything.

It was on the fourth day that it happened. It was nearly time to end the lesson when it came to her. It was almost intangible in the beginning, so slight and quiet that, at first, she doubted it was really there at all. Then it grew stronger. Gewey had once described it as a pulse, but to Kaylia it was a heartbeat. The heartbeat of the earth.

Her eyes popped open. "I felt it!"

Nehrutu smiled broadly. "That is good. And sooner than I expected."

"It was wonderful." She trembled with excitement. "It was as if I could feel the living earth all around me." She closed her eyes, but Nehrutu placed his hand on her shoulder.

"That is enough for tonight," he said.

"But..." she began to protest.

Nehrutu's stare silenced her. "Tomorrow will come soon enough," he said. "And I am weary."

The next three days were like nothing Kaylia could have imagined. Though she felt ready, Nehrutu warned her against actually drawing the flow inside.

"Only see it for now," said Nehrutu. "Hear it sing its song. Let your own heart beat with the same rhythm. Once you can do that, then you will be ready to go further."

By the end of the third week, she was ready. Drawing in only small amounts at first, little by little she increased this. Before long, her entire body was saturated with power. For the first time, Kaylia felt that she now fully understood what Gewey experienced, and the intoxicating effect it had on him.

By now, the field was rapidly filling with hundreds upon hundreds of elves, with many more yet to arrive. Bellows had been erected, and the sounds of the smith's hammer echoed all over the field. The smell of war filled the air. The pavilion had been taken down, and the rubble cleared away. The field was covered with tents and piles of provisions. By the time they were ready to march, their force numbered twenty-five hundred. *More than enough*, Kaylia thought, *to retake Valshara*; this was still barely a portion of what was to eventually come.

On the morning of their departure, Theopolou addressed the elves. He'd thought long on what to say. He had not spoken of war in five hundred years, and he knew that he must inspire.

"I have received word that the High Lady of Valshara has petitioned the King of Althetas to aid us," Theopolou announced. His voice was clear and forceful. "And he has agreed to do this. The city guard will be awaiting our forces north of the temple."

He looked out over the gathering. "This will be the first time in our history that we have fought alongside humans. But rest assured, until the Dark One in the North is defeated, it will not be the last. I know that many will resist this notion, but the time for old hatreds has passed. We fight for more than the possession of one human temple. We will show the powers that seek to divide and destroy us the peril they place themselves in when choosing to take what is not theirs. And we do not belong to Angräal. We will not believe their lies. We will not be played for fools. And we will not allow them to annihilate our people."

A chorus of enthusiastic cheers rose up. Theopolou waited for them to subside before continuing. "Though our brothers and sisters on the Steppes had been brought under the yoke of the Dark One, we will not suffer the same fate. So now we march."

He stood silent for a moment. The gentle breeze bent the tall grass, and the smell of oil and leather permeated the air. Theopolou's final two words then broke the silence, booming and echoing all over the field.

"To war!"

This time, the roar of cheers and war cries was deafening. Theopolou's heart raced. It had been five hundred years since he had spoken words of war, and though he'd hoped he would never have to do so again, the fire in his people's eyes told him that it was time. Time to live in the world once more. Time to fight for the right to survive. And, if good was truly destined to overcome evil, time for victory. It would all begin here.

In less than an hour, the elves had formed ranks. Unlike a human army, there were no wagons and horses. No banners fluttering in the breeze. No. An elf army was marching death—fast and efficient. Theopolou, Linis, and Kaylia stood at the head, with Nehrutu and Mohanisi close behind. The rest of the elders would march among their individual tribes.

Kaylia looked back on the field to where she and Gewey had spent their first night together truly bonded.

Nehrutu touched her shoulder. "Your love will return," he whispered.

She grasped his hand lightly. "As will yours."

Theopolou raised his hand high. "Forward!"

It was done. The elves now marched to meet their destiny.

CHAPTER 13

Gewey awoke to find Aaliyah sitting alongside and looking down at him with an expression of both curiosity and understanding. His dreams had been filled with visions of Kaylia, yet somehow he knew that Aaliyah could see his dreams. "Do you think about your unorem often?" he asked.

She smiled tenderly. "It was not he who occupied my thoughts. There was another, years later."

"What happened?" He propped himself up on his elbows.

She thought for a moment before replying. "It was best that we did not complete the bonding." She touched his cheek. "Sometimes, what is in your heart is not what is best."

"I don't agree," said Gewey. "My father taught me to follow my heart, and so far it has guided me well."

"Ah," Aaliyah replied. "But your years are still few—at least in this world. You are a leader of both human and elf. I think, in time, you will find that you must do what is best for those you care for rather than follow your own desires."

"I do that now," he asserted, ignoring the remark about his youth. "I think that if I follow my heart, I will do right by them."

"You think that now," she said, withdrawing her hand. "But you have yet to face the burdens of leadership. You have been the student, but the time will soon come when the whole world will look to you for hope and strength. When that day arrives, then you will understand."

The camp was already abuzz with activity. Gewey could see that their hosts were making preparations to leave. A small group of them were digging a large hole just beyond the perimeter of the camp.

"I wonder what that's for?" remarked Gewey.

"We bury anything we leave behind," said Pali as he strode up, a small pack slung across his back and a cloth bundle in his arms. "Here, these will be better for keeping you cool." He tossed the bundle to Gewey.

Inside, Gewey found two sets of clothes identical to those that Pali wore. He gave one set to Aaliyah, then found a private spot to change. The cloth felt cool on his skin and was far softer than it appeared. It was much like the elf clothing given to him by Theopolou.

By the time he and Aaliyah had changed, the rest of the camp was already gathering. Pali and his mother stood side by side on the edge of the oasis, speaking in hushed tones. Pali smiled when Gewey approached.

"Now you look civilized," Pali remarked approvingly. A moment later, Aaliyah appeared. She looked very much like a desert elf. "If you are ready, we have much ground to cover before sundown."

Weila embraced her son and bowed to Gewey and Aaliyah. "I pray you a safe journey. Listen to my son. He may not be a Sand Master, but he knows the desert. He will guide you well."

"I thank you for your aid and hospitality," said Aaliyah. "I hope we meet again."

Weila smiled and turned away, moving slowly toward the other elves. Pali waved a farewell to them all, which was boisterously returned with cheers and shouts. Pali pointed Gewey and Aaliyah north, and within minutes, they were around the dunes and out of sight.

"Where are the others going?" asked Gewey.

"They head east to join more of our people," Pali replied. "Our business here is done."

"And what was your business?" asked Aaliyah.

Pali unslung his pack and pulled out a thin, blue blanket. "This." He handed it to Gewey. "We trade with the humans in this area for spices and wool."

The blanket was as soft as silk and warm to the touch as if heated near a fire. "What is it made of?" Gewey asked, handing it back.

"The plant is called Trulu." He shoved it back into his pack. "It will keep you warm on the coldest night, though I still prefer a fire for comfort. Humans tend to be more sensitive to the cold. You will be happy I brought them come nightfall. With Soufis in the area, we cannot risk lighting a fire."

For the rest of the day, they wound their way between the high dunes, with Pali occasionally climbing to the top to take a look around. The sun was brutally hot, and Gewey's legs burned from trudging through the soft, deep sand. After only two hours, he drew in the flow to give himself enough strength to continue. To his great relief, Aaliyah caused a cool breeze to follow them, making the heat more bearable. This caused Pali to take notice.

"My mother would be very displeased," he remarked. "But I must admit, it is a useful skill." He glanced at Gewey. "I was unaware that humans could also steal life from the earth. Perhaps the humans of the desert have forgotten such things." Receiving no reply, and seeing Gewey's sudden unease, he shrugged. "It matters not."

They stopped only once to rest and did not eat. By sundown, even with using the flow, Gewey could still feel the tightness in his legs. He almost dreaded the evening when he would release it and the pain would set in. Once darkness began to fall, they found a high dune and climbed up onto it to make camp.

Pali distributed the blankets and some dried meat. "I know you may be accustomed to more frequent meals, but in the desert, a full stomach will cause your gut to knot." He smiled at Aaliyah. "Though, with such a soothing wind at our backs, perhaps tomorrow we will have a small midday meal."

Just as Gewey feared, the moment he released the flow, the pain in his legs struck hard. He moaned with discomfort.

Pali laughed. "It will take some time to build your strength."

Aaliyah leaned over and placed her hands on his aching legs. Gewey could feel the flow rushing in and the pain immediately subsided.

"Thank you," he said. For once, he did not feel shy at her touch. "My father told me stories as a child of terrible creatures that roam the desert. Some I can hardly believe."

Pali tilted his head and grinned. "There are all manner of beasts on the sands. But most will leave you alone, as long as you do the same."

"What about the giant lizards?" asked Gewey.

"Your father must have listened to an elf loremaster to have heard such stories," said Pali. "If they exist, they must be in the North West canyons where no human or elf roams. I have never seen such a creature here, and there are few places among the dunes I have not traveled."

Gewey couldn't help but be disappointed. "What about wolves?"

Pali nodded. "They are very real. Though not as perilous as people believe them to be. They will not trouble you as long as you have a companion with you, and even an elf does not wander the desert alone. Not even a Sand Master."

They stayed up and talked for another hour. Aaliyah kept quiet, preferring to listen. The wind brushed across the dune rhythmically, but Gewey found the blanket to be more than adequate for keeping out the cold. Soon he felt himself drift.

Even as his breathing grew deep and steady, he was woken again by a low grumble. He rose quickly to see Pali and Aaliyah already on their feet with weapons drawn. Reaching down, he freed his sword, at the same time filling himself with the flow.

"What is it?" Gewey whispered.

"Wolves," Pali replied in a low tone.

"I thought you said they didn't bother people," said Gewey. He closed his eyes and listened. At once, he sensed them. Six beasts, all as large as ponies, were slowly circling the dune. The feral growls rose, causing the hairs on the back of his neck to stand up.

"They don't," said Pali. "There's something wrong. I have never heard of them preying on anything but a lone traveler. And even that is rare."

"Do not fear," said Aaliyah. She drew in the power of the air. A small ball of flame burst to life above her head. "I have faced fierce beasts in my lands, yet I still live."

"They go for the throat," warned Pali. "Stay low."

No sooner had he spoken than all six rushed up the hill at once. Their speed made a Vrykol seem slow by comparison, and their immense paws appeared to glide effortlessly across the sand. The flame above Aaliyah flew away from her and exploded, engulfing the leading wolf in white-hot fire. It let out a high-pitched cry and tumbled back down the dune. Gewey caused the sands beneath another creature to heave skyward, but to his dismay, the wolf fell back, only stunned. Another jumped at his throat, and he only just managed to duck away in time. The wolf slid to a halt and turned, its teeth gnashing. Gewey quickly glanced over his shoulder.

One wolf lay dead at Pali's feet; he was keeping another at bay with his long scimitar.

A flash of light illuminated the dune and Gewey heard another wolf cry out. By then, the wolf attacking him had recovered. It didn't go for his throat as the first one had, instead choosing to run straight at him with cruel teeth gleaming. Gewey brought his blade down in a narrow arc, splitting its skull completely in two. Even so, its body slammed into him, knocking him from his feet. The other wolf was on him the moment he fell, bringing its deadly jaws down hard at Gewey's neck. He raised his sword and steel met fangs. He then pushed hard with the flow to send the wolf sprawling. It landed a few feet down the side of the dune, turned, stopped, and glared back hatefully.

Gewey struggled to his feet. Aaliyah and Pali were already next to him. Pali's left shoulder hung loosely at his side, his shirt soaked with blood that ran down his arm and poured off the end of his fingertips. As it continued to stare, the beast's black eyes suddenly glowed with an unnatural green light, then it slowly backed away and disappeared into the darkness.

Pali stumbled and collapsed. Gewey caught him, gently lowering him to the ground.

Aaliyah knelt down and ripped away Pali's shirt. Blood was still pumping from the vicious bite. The teeth had sunk deep, nearly tearing his shoulder away from its socket. She closed her eyes and directed her power at the wound.

Pali tried to push her away. "No," he protested. "You cannot."

Aaliyah did not yield. "I swore an oath to your mother that you would return unharmed. I intend to keep it." She looked up at Gewey. "You must help me."

Gewey placed his hands on top of Aaliyah's and their spirits combined. The flow rushed through him, and for the first time, he drew both air and earth together as she guided his energy. Pali struggled at first, then gasped, arching his back. Gewey could feel the wound close as the flow surrounded it. He had healed before, but Aaliyah's skill astounded him. In less than a minute, the wound had closed.

"We must help him to recover the blood he has lost," she whispered. She sent the power deep inside Pali's body. It expanded and pulsed, saturating him completely. Finally, she lifted her hands and smiled. "It is done."

Gewey stared at her in awe. He understood now just how much he still had to learn.

Pali sat up, his face twisted in anger. "What you did is forbidden. You had no right..."

"I had every right," snapped Aaliyah. "I made a promise to your mother. And even if I hadn't, I would not allow another elf to suffer death when I had the power to prevent it." She rose to her feet. "I need not justify myself to you. If you prefer death, seek it somewhere else. And if you must leave us, so be it."

Pali glared for a long moment, then closed his eyes and lowered his head. "I will not leave you. I made a promise as well." He looked up at Aaliyah and rose to his feet. "I will guide you. But we must leave this place before the scavengers catch the scent. They can be far deadlier than even the wolves."

The slain creatures were scattered across the top and sides of the dune, but it was the unnatural glow of the retreating wolf's eyes that still burned most in Gewey's mind as they moved on. Pali led them east for about an hour before bringing them atop another dune. Here, they all wrapped the blankets tightly around themselves and stared into the darkness. Gewey reached out with the flow, and, to his great relief, heard nothing.

"I am sorry I was angry," said Pali after a time. "You saved my life. But you must understand how we feel about such things."

"I do understand," said Aaliyah. "And had there been another way, I would not have gone against your wishes. But I will not return your dead body to your mother when I have the means to prevent it."

Pali smiled and chuckled softly. "No. If I were you, I suppose I wouldn't want to do that either. And if you knew her better, then that feeling would become even stronger."

"You said that you've never seen wolves attack like that," stated Gewey.

"No, I have not." He looked sideways at Gewey. "Nor have I seen their eyes glow green light before. Something evil has entered the sands." He pulled the blanket closer. "Perhaps the Creator had you save me to find out what it is—and destroy it."

"Perhaps," Aaliyah agreed. "Still, I will not have you go beyond the border of the Oasis. From there, we go on without you."

"I go where I please," said Pali. "Besides, it seems to me that it is unwise to camp alone. If the wolves will attack the three of us, they will certainly attack a single elf."

Aaliyah thought hard on this. "Perhaps you are right. But if what your mother says is true, the dangers within the Black Oasis may be far worse."

"Whatever dangers are out there," said Pali. "I would rather face them with friends at my side." He smiled at Gewey. "Even if those friends are human. Though I must admit, you fight like no human I've ever seen. I am certainly grateful that the Soufis are not as fierce as you."

"I was trained well," said Gewey.

The rest of the night was quiet, though none of them slept. They continued on their way an hour before dawn. As they walked, Gewey flooded himself with the flow, listening for any signs of danger.

"We will arrive at the Oasis by sundown," said Pali. "I suggest we wait until tomorrow before entering. I would not want to brave the Black Oasis at night."

"Agreed," said Aaliyah.

By late afternoon, Gewey was becoming increasingly and inexplicably anxious. It was as if an aloof presence lurked just beyond his senses. From time to time, he glanced over at Pali and Aaliyah. They seemed untroubled, although alert.

An hour before sundown the dunes began to flatten and Gewey noticed a jagged black stripe peaking over the horizon. It stretched for miles in either direction, and even in the waning sun, heat radiated above it, causing the air to ripple and twist. Gewey tried to use the flow to see it more clearly, but light reflected off the surface, distorting his vision.

"We're here," said Pali. "The Black Oasis."

"Indeed," remarked Aaliyah.

"It's enormous," said Gewey.

"Yes, it is," agreed Pali. "It is twice as deep as it is wide, and so thick with trees and brush, one can hardly move. A path exists, but we'll have to find it."

"We should stop here." Aaliyah eyed the Oasis warily. "This is as close as I want to be at night."

"Then we rest here and look for the path in the morning," said Pali.

That night, Gewey's sleep was troubled by a dark presence. Several times he awoke, reaching for his blade. Aaliyah did not sleep at all. She sat hugging her knees close to her chest, peering into the blackness. Only Pali slept properly, drifting off almost as soon as he lay down.

Finally, deciding that restful sleep was out of his grasp, Gewey sat down next to Aaliyah. The presence remained. "Do you feel it?" he asked.

"Yes," she replied. "Something resides there. Something ancient. Something with fury in its heart."

Gewey glanced over at the sleeping figure of Pali. "How can he sleep so near this place?"

She pulled the blanket tight around her. "It could be that he cannot feel it. Or..."

"Or what?" he asked.

"Or perhaps whatever lives there chooses not to trouble him."

She shuddered. "If that is so, then it knows we are here. Either way, I am pleased our guide will be rested. I feel we will need all of our wit and strength very soon."

CHAPTER 14

Theopolou led the army at a pace that would have astounded any human warlord or general. They paused briefly only once a day to rest and take a quick meal. At night they made camp alongside the roads and trails, sleeping for only a few hours, then marching on again before the sun had even broken the horizon.

Kaylia and Nehrutu continued with their lessons, though only for an hour each day. Still, she progressed rapidly, and by the third day of the march was able to allow the flow to pass through her with ease. By the end of the first week, she could move small amounts of earth, and use the power to heighten her senses far beyond that of even the most experienced seeker.

Scouts brought news of Valshara preparing for a siege, with sightings of at least a dozen Vrykol roaming the area surrounding the temple. A guard of twenty men blocked the path leading up to the gates, and bowmen patrolled the ramparts both day and night. Theopolou had hoped that they might be able to enter through the rear passageway, but the latest reports told him that this had now been completely blocked off.

The army turned north to avoid coming too close to Valshara before joining with the human forces. It added an extra day, but Theopolou felt it better to hide their numbers until the last moment. The terrain became rocky and jagged, causing them to twist and turn to avoid spots where they could be ambushed.

The day before they arrived, Theopolou called a council of the elders. Nehrutu and Mohanisi joined them, as did Linis and Kaylia. Theopolou had received word that the soldiers from Althetas awaited them twenty miles north of Valshara.

"This means they will be expecting an attack to come soon," said Chiron. "A human army is loud and easily spotted."

"It is likely they know we are coming as well," said Theopolou. "It is not the battle that will take them by surprise. It is the weapons we bring." He motioned to Nehrutu and Mohanisi, who stepped forward.

"We can break open the gates," said Nehrutu. "But from the way they are described, it may take both of our efforts. The approach is narrow and exposed, so we will need to dispose of the enemy archers."

"Our bowmen can give you the time you need," said Bellisia.

"I assumed so," Nehrutu continued. "But if the gates are held by these Vrykol, we may find ourselves faced with a different problem. If they can only be slain by removing their heads, then we will lose many elves before overcoming them. The narrow passage will make our superior numbers count for nothing."

"Let us not forget our human allies," Bellisia reminded. "Their city is close, and they may be well supplied with siege engines."

"I have not forgotten," said Theopolou. "But aside from petty border squabbles, they have not made war in five hundred years. The human armies of old were cunning and powerful, but I doubt a single soldier today has ever seen true battle." His eyes grew dark and distant. "And many of us have."

"Still," Linis interjected, "they are our allies, so perhaps we should wait until we meet with them before making any final decisions. Otherwise, they may take it as an insult."

"Linis speaks wisely," said Nehrutu. "Though it is clear that Mohanisi and I must breach the gates, you would be well served to include your new allies in your planning. And as Lady Bellisia has pointed out, they are near to their home. This may provide assets we cannot yet account for."

"Then we wait," said Theopolou. "We will join with the humans tomorrow."

The knowledge that they would soon be joining with humans had caused palpable tension among the elf army ranks. Many were still unsure, not having been present at the Chamber of the Maker. They accepted the word of the elders, but this did little to calm their unease. Large numbers had never even seen a human before, although all had grown up with the hatred.

That evening, they halted early and slept until dawn. Theopolou wanted his army rested when they arrived. By midday, they could hear the sounds of blacksmiths' hammers ringing out in the distance. The ground had now become level and far less rocky, with even a few trees struggling out of the barren soil. When the camp came into view, Theopolou and the other elders gathered in front and called for a halt.

Moments later, trumpets blew a loud fanfare. The sound of human commanders barking orders carried over the still air as the soldiers scurried to form ranks.

"I see elves among them," remarked Linis. "That is a good sign."

Theopolou only nodded.

The humans formed a long line of red shields and spears. A lone banner hung lifelessly, bearing the image of a great serpent coiled around a full moon. Having formed up, the humans now remained absolutely still. Soon, all was silent. Some of the elves among them stirred uneasily but did not approach. It was Theopolou who moved first, followed closely by Linis and Kaylia.

"The rest stay behind for the moment," said Theopolou over his shoulder.

When they were about one hundred yards away, the line parted and four figures appeared. Three of these Theopolou recognized immediately: the first as Selena, High Lady of Valshara, and then Haldrontis and Stintos, his escorts who had been sent back to Valshara. The fourth was a tall, lean man with a salt-and-pepper beard, deep olive skin, and piercing blue eyes. His face was wrinkled and cracked with age, but his strides were still as long and sure as a young man in his prime. He wore simple leather armor with a long sword on his belt, but atop his brow rested a thin gold crown.

"I am pleased to see you are well," said Theopolou to Haldrontis and Stintos.

"We have been well-tended," said Haldrontis.

Theopolou nodded. "Then return to your comrades. They will be glad to see you." They bowed and walked on toward the elves. He turned to Selena. "I am pleased to see you again, too."

Selena smiled warmly. "And I, you." She stepped aside to allow the man next her to step forward. "May I present King Lousis Maldiva, King and Protector of Althetas."

"I am honored to meet you, Lord Theopolou," said the king. His voice was coarse and gruff, though steady and commanding. "Lady Selena speaks highly of you." He held out his hand.

Theopolou paused a moment, then accepted, shaking hands firmly. "The honor is mine, Your Highness. I extend to you the friendship of my house, and the houses of all my kin."

The king smiled and gave Theopolou's hand one more solid shake. "My city has welcomed elves for some time now. We are glad to extend our hospitality to as many as care to take it."

"Sadly, we are in need of far more," said Theopolou. His somber expression wiped the smile from the king's face. "And I fear many lives may be lost before we see peace again."

"As do I," the king agreed. "But perhaps spilling our blood together will remedy old fears and hatreds. If that is the price we must pay, then I am willing to pay it."

Theopolou nodded. "Then let us begin here. Together, we shall rid Valshara of this plague that had besieged it."

"If what the High Lady tells me is true, then this is only the beginning." The king turned and ordered his men to break ranks. "Come, let our forces be as one. Tonight, we dine and celebrate our union. Tomorrow is for war."

"I would speak to your generals and captains as soon as it can be arranged," said Theopolou.

"They already await you," the king replied. "The High Lady has been mapping out the temple for us. Of course, we wanted to wait until your arrival before forming a plan of attack."

"I thank you." Theopolou bowed slightly. "We have assets that may save many lives, Your Highness."

He raised an eyebrow. "That's good news. We have been fearful of the approach to the gates. We hope that you have a way to lessen our enemy's advantage. I have five hundred swords and fifty horses. More could not be spared without leaving my city and territories defenseless." He held his arms wide. "But that can be discussed later. Your elves have traveled far. We don't have much in the way of comforts, but you are welcome to all that we do have."

"It is gratefully accepted," said Theopolou. He raised his hand high, and the elf army marched forward.

"It's good to see you again," said Selena to Linis and Kaylia. She moved in and hugged them both. "I notice that Gewey is not with you."

Kaylia paused, her eyes suddenly sad and distant at the mention of Gewey's name. "He will be joining us as soon as he is able."

Selena nodded with understanding. "I'm sure he will."

The elf army halted when only a few yards away. The campground the humans had chosen was easily large enough to accommodate them, but they remained still, uncertain what to do.

King Lousis stepped forward to address the elves. "You must feel welcome. We have brought food, water, and wine enough for you all. My soldiers have been instructed to provide you with whatever you may need."

After a nod from Theopolou, his army slowly made its way into the camp and spread out. Unlike the elves, the humans had brought dozens of wagons filled to the brim with provisions of all types. Three bellows had been erected at the north end away from the main group, and a large tent, surrounded by several smaller ones, had been placed in the camp center. Theopolou told the elders to gather here as soon as they could.

"If your elders require tents, it can be arranged," said Lousis. He led the group toward the large tent.

"That will not be necessary," said Theopolou.

The procession of Theopolou, Linis, Kaylia, Selena, and King Lousis attracted more than a few stares as they made their way through. Theopolou was thankful that this first encounter was with humans who'd had previous dealings with elves. Also, there were already elves among the king's men. The situation could have been far worse.

The large tent was guarded by two stocky, tough-looking soldiers, and was spacious enough for ten people to enter comfortably. The guards snapped to attention at the sight of the king. Inside, a small round table placed dead center was almost completely covered by a roughly drawn map. In the corner was a small wooden cot, together with a chest. A brass lantern hung in each corner, and two others directly above the table. In the far left corner, six chairs were arranged in a semi-circle around another small table.

King Lousis instructed the guard to bring his commanders, then offered Theopolou and the others a seat. "I must say, this has happened at just the right time." Lousis grabbed a bottle of wine from the chest and sat down with a grunt. "I fear that if we are left on our own, we shall come under the thumb of Angrääl."

The mention of Angrääl caused Theopolou to sit up. "Have they troubled you before?"

"I wouldn't say that," Lousis replied, after taking a long drink from the bottle. "In fact, they have made offers of friendship in the past. But I know an ultimatum when I hear one. They all but cut off our trade with Baltria when I refused to sign a trade agreement stating that we would only ship to cities allied to the Reborn King." He sighed. "But that is not what troubles me the most. They have made such trade bargains with many other cities all along the coast. You must understand, though my title is king, I only rule my city and the lands that surround it for fifty miles."

"And the other cities?" asked Theopolou.

"The same," Lousis replied. "There are twelve kings and queens from the north port of Lamitia to the Tarvansia Peninsula. We govern our territories absolutely, with no interference from the others. This has been the way of things since the Great War."

"And if something threatens you all?" asked Kaylia.

"Then a council of kings and queens is called," said Lousis. "Before the war, Althetas ruled the whole coast of the Western Abyss. After the war ended, the cities were in turmoil. Several leaders, mostly former governors of the territories, all wanted to seize control. But instead of descending into civil war, we eventually formed an alliance of city states."

"A wise decision," Theopolou remarked.

"It was," Lousis agreed. "The war was over, and no one desired more blood, so the council was forged. It has kept the peace for five hundred years. But now..."

His jaw tightened. "Now a snake has slithered its way into our midst. Men and women I once trusted are under the influence of a foreign power. That is why, for now, Althetas stands alone. Even the kings and queens, whom I still name as friends, and, in the past, would have called for aid, fear reprisal. None are as rich as Althetas, and they can ill afford to lose trade with Baltria."

"Why did you not sign the agreement?" asked Kaylia.

Lousis's back stiffened and his eyes narrowed. "Althetas trades with who it chooses. We do not bow to the will of some tyrant in the north who clearly seeks war and havoc. Our ports and markets have always been free. And while I live, they will remain so."

"I commend your resolve," said Theopolou. "I can only hope that your example will show others the right path."

"Cities in the southern region are far more vulnerable than those north of Althetas," said Lousis. "We use the roads as much as we do our ports. But I'm embarrassed to say ... your people hold the lands to the east of the southern cities, so they are fearful of traveling by land."

Theopolou nodded. "Rightly so. But those times are now in the past."

Lousis grinned. "That is good to hear. It will go a long way toward uniting the twelve cities when the time comes."

The tent flap opened and three armor-clad men entered, each bearing the crest of Althetas on their chest plate. The first was tall and lean, and though clean-shaven, had a weathered and worn look much like the king. The other two were considerably younger and far broader in the shoulders, though not quite as tall.

King Lousis stood. "Ah, good. This is Lord Maynard Windcomber, war master and commander of my forces. These are his captains, Lord Brasley Amnadon and Lord Jeffos Windermere." The commander and his captains bowed low. Theopolou and the others stood and returned the gesture.

Moments later, Nehrutu, Mohanisi, and Chiron entered. After Theopolou had made the necessary introductions, they all gathered around the table.

"The remaining elders have chosen to stay with the army," said Chiron, before Theopolou could ask. "Though the humans here have had experience with elves—alas, the opposite is not true. They want to be near to their people in case of any misunderstandings."

Theopolou nodded. "That is probably for the best. We can go over the plans with them later."

"To business then," said Lousis.

Lord Maynard leaned over the map. "I'm sure you are aware of the danger in approaching the gates. The way is narrow and protected by bowmen. Unfortunately, this is the only way in."

"We can fell the gates," said Nehrutu. "But not without exposing ourselves. The narrow approach makes it impossible to match their bowmen in number, and as skilled as elf archers are, our enemy need only shoot into the thick of our ranks."

"What about the rear entrance?" asked Linis. "We were told it has been blocked. Can it be cleared?"

"No," Lord Maynard replied. "It has been completely collapsed. But we face yet further danger." He pointed to the path leading to the gates. "We must defend the cliffs on either side of this path. Should the enemy control these, they can simply rain down death upon us. We'd be destroyed before we came close enough to even see the temple."

"Do you know their strength?" asked Theopolou.

"We haven't been able to get close enough yet to know their numbers," admitted Maynard. "They have already taken six of my scouting parties. Even so, if they have the number to protect the cliffs, then we'll need to take them first. That won't be easy. The terrain is rough and uneven. A skilled captain could make it difficult for us to dislodge them."

"And if they are not defending them, we waste our strength," said Linis. "We should send elves to scout first. I will lead them. No offense to the skill of your men, of course."

"There is no offense taken," said Maynard. "I have been told of elf seekers. But make no mistake. The men I sent were not without talent, and most were intercepted and likely killed." He placed his palms on the table and looked directly at Linis. "The elves that came with the High Lady told me of the Vrykol. I think it must be these creatures that watch the pass. If you go, you may not return."

Linis flashed a sinister grin. "I have dealt with the Vrykol before. If I encounter them again, there will be less for us to deal with later."

Maynard raised an eyebrow and smirked approvingly. "I like that. I like that, indeed." He turned to Theopolou. "You say you can smash the gates from bow range, as well as take out their archers?"

"Yes," said Theopolou. "Without a doubt."

"How will you do this?" asked Lousis. "I saw no siege engines with your army, and we brought none. And even if we had, the difficult approach would make them useless."

"My kinsmen and I have the means," said Nehrutu. "We possess skills you may not be able to understand. But rest assured, it can be done."

Lousis looked skeptical, scrutinizing the elf. "You back up this claim?" he asked Theopolou.

"I do," Theopolou replied. "But still, we are left with our archers being bunched up and exposed."

"I think I can help," said Maynard. "My men can protect them with shields until they are close enough to fire."

Chiron shook his head. "If you do that, then they will be first through the gates. Those behind must wait until they move forward. You will lose many men."

Maynard laughed loudly. "Then our foes will die at the hands of humans rather than the elves. We have not marched here to stay out of the fray."

"Then I suggest your soldiers meet with our archers as soon as possible," said Chiron.

Maynard glanced at his captains, who nodded in return. "My men will be at your disposal."

Other details of the battle plan were simple. Once the gates were down, they would then section off each area of the temple until it was completely secured. With the exception of the initial force of humans, the rest of the attack party would be entirely made up of elves, with the remainder of the Althetas soldiers protecting the rear. At first, Maynard protested, but eventually let go of his pride in favor of Theopolou's wisdom. If Vrykol were encountered, humans would be no match for them.

After the meeting, the group dispersed. Kaylia and Linis stayed with Theopolou and found a place among his kinsmen, while Nehrutu and Mohanisi found a spot far removed from the rest. At the same time, Theopolou and Chiron met with the other elders to explain the battle strategy. As a result of this, each tribe sent their best archers to meet with Lord Maynard just north of the camp to drill.

By late afternoon, barrels of wine were being unloaded from the wagons, and cooking fires burned everywhere. At first, the elves kept to themselves, but soon the humans intruded and forced their hospitality upon them. The elders and commanders made certain they were close at hand in case trouble broke out, but the so-called 'rebel elves' who, like Linis, had been living among humans for some time joined them. This went a long way toward easing tensions, and by the time the sun was beneath the horizon, the camp was completely integrated. And though the comfort level was not yet exactly one of warm friendship, it wasn't long before stories and songs began springing up from both human and elf.

Selena invited Kaylia to join her in her tent, pitched just beside the king's. When she arrived, Selena was sitting on a chair beside a small chest, atop which sat a cup of wine. She smiled and offered the chair beside her, then filled another cup and handed it to Kaylia.

"I could see your pain when I mentioned Gewey's name earlier," said Selena. "I thought you may wish to talk."

"There is nothing to say," Kaylia replied. "Gewey is on an important mission, and I worry. That is all."

Selena leaned forward and placed her hand tenderly on Kaylia's. "I'm no elf. But I am a woman and can tell when another woman needs help. Please..."

Selena's words and genuine concern struck home, bringing tears to Kaylia's eyes. She took a deep breath and recounted the events leading up to the march.

"I see," said Selena, in a half whisper. "And these elves from across the Abyss—you are certain they know what Gewey is?"

"Yes," she replied, wiping her eyes. "Though I know Gewey loves me, I still fear that she will convince him that she is the better choice." She lowered her eyes. "I should not despair, but the loss of our bond is driving me mad. If not for Nehrutu, I..."

"Gewey is your husband," Selena interrupted, "to use the human term. He is not hers and never will be. What I know of Gewey tells me that his heart is true. More importantly, that heart belongs to you. If you feel that learning these powers will benefit you, then by all means do so. But if you think you must compete for his love, please think again."

She shook her head, laughing, then squeezed Kaylia's hand fondly. "You are the one he chose. And you chose him. That is all you need to care about. And I assure you that when he returns, nothing will have changed between you."

Kaylia smiled. "Thank you. Your words have lifted my spirits."

The sounds of songs and laughter drifted in from the camp.

"Speaking of spirits," Selena remarked, "it seems as if the very first elf-human alliance is going better than expected."

"So it would seem," Kaylia agreed. "Though I wonder about the wisdom of wine and song on the eve of battle."

"I think it may bring the two peoples closer," said Selena. "Better to have an aching head and good allies than suspicions and mistrust."

Kaylia thought on this for a moment, then rose to her feet. "Perhaps we should join them." She held out her hand and helped Selena to her feet.

The chilly night was warmed by dozens of fires. The smell of meat and wine filled the air, mingling perfectly with the songs and laughter. By the time the meal was served, Kaylia stood in amazement at the sight of two armies—elf and human—laughing as if the Great War had never happened. Her heart filled with hope. And though her thoughts were ever on Gewey, she knew somehow that all would be well.

CHAPTER 15

The orange sky that came with the dawn brought with it an eerie glow that washed across the sand. Gewey thought it beautiful in a way that must be appreciated firsthand. Kaylia was the only person who would ever be capable of understanding what it looked like through his eyes—he could never describe it properly in words. Just then, his heart ached from the emptiness he felt without her voice inside him.

"Keep your thoughts here and now," scolded Aaliyah.

Pali stirred and stretched. "I see neither of you slept." He reached into his pack, retrieved some jerky and flatbread, and shared it with Gewey and Aaliyah.

Something caught Gewey's eye; a figure was approaching from the direction of the Black Oasis. As it neared, he could see that it was a human woman. Her dark blond hair was tangled and matted, and her tattered clothes were covered with dust and grime. She stumbled through the sands as if near to exhaustion until she was only a few yards away. Gewey and the others stood but did not approach her.

"Who are you?" the woman asked weakly. She didn't meet their eyes, instead staring submissively at the ground. Cuts and bruises on her face and arms told of abuse. "Why are you here?"

"A slave," whispered Pali. In a louder voice, he then asked: "Who is your master?"

"Why are you here?" she repeated.

"You need not fear us," said Aaliyah. "If you wish, we shall protect you."

Pali nodded approvingly. "Come forward."

She didn't move. "Please. Why are you here?"

Gewey could see the fear in the woman's eyes. He took a step forward, but she jumped back, wrapping her arms around herself.

"Slavers do this to them." Pali's face burned with fury and disgust. "They destroy their will, and torture them until they are nothing resembling what they once were." He looked hard at Aaliyah. "This is why we protect the humans." He turned to the woman. "Look at her. She is so afraid, she refuses to accept our offer of help. She fears what will happen to her if she tries to escape. I've seen this before—far too many times."

"Is this true?" Aaliyah asked the woman. "Will you not let us help you?"

Tears welled in the woman's eyes. "Please. I must obey my master. He wants to know why you're here." She anxiously gripped the sides of her long tan skirt. Her light blue blouse was caked with thick patches of dried blood and filth.

"Who is your master?" asked Gewey.

The woman shook her head nervously. "Please."

"Tell your master that our business is our own, and none of his affair," said Pali.

The woman bowed and scurried away.

"Poor wretch," Pali muttered sadly. "It seems we are expected. What do you suggest?"

"We have little choice," said Aaliyah. "We must continue. They may expect us, but I doubt they are prepared for us."

They watched the slave return to the Oasis, making a note of the point where she entered. Once she had disappeared, they cautiously followed. Gewey reached out, but his senses were deflected. The look on Aaliyah's face told him that she was faring no better.

As they neared, the blackness of the Oasis changed; enormous deep green and thick gray vines were now visible. Slick, round leaves beaded with the dense humidity hung low, some touching the moss-covered ground. Vines and thorns twisted their way through the branches, wrapping themselves from tree to tree in a never-ending web. Tiny blue flowers dotted the vines and low branches, their colors so deep and rich that one had to strain to notice them as they blended with the leaves. Each flower was cradled by a nest of blackberries no larger than the tip of a child's finger. High above the canopy, flocks of jet-black birds, the like of which Gewey had never seen before, darted and swirled, landing in the treetops for just a moment before taking flight again.

The air was full of clinging moisture. It was in stark contrast to the arid desert, and the scent of rotting foliage left a foul taste in Gewey's mouth. They checked the point where they had seen the slave woman enter but could see no trail or path. Pali slowly scanned the area, then with a satisfied smile, pushed his hand against a patch of brambles. It swung back as if on hinges. Gewey could make out a narrow trail that disappeared into the blackness.

"I will lead," said Aaliyah.

Gewey could feel her drawing in the flow and reaching out. Soon, her face began twisting in frustration; moments later, she drew both of her daggers. The trail was very narrow, making both Gewey's sword and Pali's scimitar all but useless at present. He pulled out his own small dagger and continued following Aaliyah into the dense gloom of the Black Oasis.

Though Aaliyah was only a few feet ahead, even with his heightened senses, he could still barely see her. Thankfully, the trail for the time being was straight and even. The ground was covered in thick moss that felt nearly as deep and difficult to walk on as the desert sand. The impenetrable trees and vines compounded the darkness, making it impossible to see more than a few inches on either side. Even the humidity was getting worse. Already his clothes were soaked and his hair hung limp. The few sounds to be heard were the drops of dew and creaking of trees, plus the occasional rustle of some small animal scuttling through the undergrowth.

Aaliyah stopped short, her back stiff and straight. "Something lurks," she whispered. The sound of her voice barely reached Gewey.

"What is it?" he asked.

"I do not know," she replied. "But I can feel something watching us."

Gewey looked around. He couldn't imagine from where someone might be able to spy on them. The foliage was far too thick for a man or even an elf to pass through. He closed his eyes, breathing deeply. Then, just like an itch in the small of his back where he couldn't reach, it was there—a presence—watching. It reminded him of when he was in the Spirit Hills with Dina.

"Some say, 'the Black Oasis is alive,'" remarked Pali. "And though I do not possess your skills, I too feel something odd."

They continued for another half mile. Both Gewey's and Aaliyah's frustrations grew as their senses faded; neither could now sense anything beyond a few feet ahead, regardless of how much of the flow they allowed to pass through them. Then they smelled it—smoke. Foul smoke. Ahead, they could see the trees thin and open into a small clearing. The closer they came, the more apparent it was that this was not a natural clearing. No, this had been carved out by hand. The perimeter smoldered and, in some spots, small fires still burned. The moss on the ground had been trampled flat, while at the far side, the ongoing trail had been sheered wider. Gewey and Pali put away their daggers and drew their swords.

"Whoever was here has clearly fled," said Pali.

"Yes," agreed Aaliyah. "But why?"

"I don't know," said Pali. "But I'd wager we'll find out."

Gewey listened for signs of people, but as before, his senses reflected back on him. "Well, whoever they are, there's only one way they could have gone."

"Don't be so sure," said Pali. "If they can survive this place, they may well have learned its secrets."

Aaliyah nodded in agreement before cautiously moving across the clearing. The smoke lingered just above the ground, reeking like rotting earth mingling with decaying flesh. Gewey nearly vomited. As they neared the ongoing trail, he spotted a dark lump spread across it a few yards further along. At first, he couldn't tell what it was, but then a cold chill ran through him when the blood-spattered face of the slave girl came into view.

"Monsters," he fumed.

"Indeed," said Pali.

They dragged the body into the clearing and covered her with a blanket.

"We must continue," said Aaliyah.

Gewey nodded and said a silent prayer for the poor creature.

The ground on the trail ahead had been stripped of all life, leaving only tightly packed black earth. The trees and vines on either side had been hacked away, making it wide enough for them to walk abreast.

Aaliyah slowed their pace to a near crawl, then, after about twenty yards, stopped altogether. She knelt down and examined a cut vine on the side of the trail. The second she touched it, she quickly withdrew her hand and shot to her feet.

"I think I understand," she whispered. "And if I am correct, the mystery has deepened."

"Correct about what?" asked Gewey.

"The Black Oasis is alive," she replied darkly.

"How do you mean?" Gewey bent down and looked at the vine. It pulsed and throbbed like an open wound.

"I mean that the presence we sensed was not those who reside here," she explained. "It was the Oasis itself." Her face tensed. "And whatever has cut it away like this must be strong enough to resist its wrath. This place is powerful—and angry." She turned to Pali. "You say that none who have ventured here have ever returned?"

"Not that I know of," he affirmed. "But then I know of no elf who has ever dared the Black Oasis. At least, none that have in my lifetime."

"If whoever is here is so strong, why did they flee?" asked Gewey.

"Perhaps they didn't," said Pali.

Aaliyah nodded in agreement. "I think you are right. I think we are being allowed to go deeper inside."

"Maybe we should go back to the clearing," Gewey suggested.

"I do not think that would help," said Aaliyah. "We can only go forward, or leave this place."

"Assuming we would be allowed to leave," muttered Pali.

They continued cautiously for another half mile. Ahead, a dense haze now obscured their vision. Gewey reached out with the flow in an attempt to move the fog aside but with no effect. Aaliyah tried as well, with the same lack of success.

As they entered the mist, Gewey immediately felt a presence wrap its spirit around him, pressing in on his mind. He was only just able to repel it and stumbled, gasping from the effort. Aaliyah placed one hand on his shoulder and wiped the beads of sweat from his forehead.

He held out his hand to steady himself. "I'm fine." He looked into Aaliyah's eyes. "Did it try to reach you as well?"

"No," she replied softly. "What did it feel like?"

Gewey thought about the first time Lee had entered his mind. "It was as if someone wanted to force its way inside me. I was barely able to keep it out."

Aaliyah furrowed her brow. "It is good you had the strength. Though it could be useful to know what is out there."

"Should I allow it in?" asked Gewey. The idea worried him.

"No," she replied. "The risk is too great. But let me know if it happens again."

At the start, the denseness of the fog only allowed them to see two or three feet ahead, and the air around them felt several degrees colder. However, to Gewey's great relief, after a few hundred yards it began to thin, though the chill remained even after the fog had cleared completely. The light that crept in from the widening of the trail now allowed Gewey to see the true color of the Oasis. In contrast to the dark, foreboding green of the exterior, the leaves here were a rich vibrant mixture of green, pale blue, and delicate lines of bright yellow. The trunks were smooth and without blemish as if polished by skilled hands. Even the vines and brambles were less sinister in appearance, flowing in an elegant weave of life and symmetry.

Further ahead they could now see a narrow black stone archway the height of two men. Symbols of the nine gods had been carved across the face and inlaid with pure gold. Just beyond the archway, the ground had been paved with smooth red marble, veined in green and blue, and polished to a mirror shine. The moment they passed beneath the arch, the forest on either side melted away like wax in a fire. In its place was a series of white marble columns the same height as the archway, all of them connected to each other by small arches of blood-red volcanic glass. To the left and right of these columns, the ground had been transformed into a meadow of soft turf scattered with tiny yellow and purple flowers. This colorful area extended for more than one hundred feet before the dense trees and vines once again reclaimed the terrain.

The sun beamed down, illuminating the glass arches and sending tiny rays of red light shooting out in every direction. At the end of the path stood a forty-foot pyramid of polished bronze. The sides were smooth as glass, and the top was crowned with a blue crystal. At its base, a shallow arched corridor of black marble led to a silver door with the nine gods etched in a circle at its center.

"What is this place?" gasped Pali.

"It is a temple built to house the tools of the gods," explained Aaliyah. "I have read of its existence, but had never thought I would see it for myself."

Gewey shifted uneasily. "We still haven't seen whoever is in here, and it looks as if this is as far as we can go. So where are they?"

"Perhaps they await us beyond the door," suggested Pali.

"Then I suppose there's only one thing to do," said Gewey. He strode down the path toward the door and turned the small silver knob. Aaliyah and Pali stood, weapons drawn, just behind him.

The door opened without a sound. Just inside, a narrow passage led to a stone staircase leading down into the earth. The walls were covered with bronze plates that gave off a faint light similar to the glowing globes of the elves. As Gewey moved on, the glow became brighter, extending all the way down the walls of the staircase. They descended for about thirty feet to another long hall before being faced with a dull gray stone wall.

"A dead end?" asked Pali.

Aaliyah examined it carefully. The stone was rough and uneven, in stark contrast to everything else there, and tiny quartz crystals were embedded throughout. She reached out and gently ran her index finger over the stone, then pressed her palm flat against it. She stood there, silent and still, for a full minute.

"There must be another way," said Gewey.

"Did you see one?" asked Aaliyah, irritably.

Gewey reached over her shoulder and touched the wall. Instantly, there was a bright flash of white light. When it was gone, so was the wall. In its place was another silver door. All three of them stood in amazement.

Aaliyah reached for the door, but Gewey grabbed her wrist. "Don't."

"What is it?" she asked.

Gewey put his back to the door. "It is meant for me only. I can't say how I know this. I just do." He placed his hand against the door, feeling the cold metal. The pulse of the flow was everywhere, calling to him. "Don't you feel it?"

Aaliyah touched his shoulder and let her spirit flow toward his. She could feel the power calling to Gewey. But it was different. It was not the abstract raw power she molded to her will. This had form and consciousness. His eyes shot wide as she snatched back her hand. "It knows you."

"Yes," Gewey affirmed. "I don't understand how, but it does. I can almost hear its thoughts."

"Hear whose thoughts?" asked Pali.

"The temple," Gewey replied. "It speaks to me. From here I must go alone. It won't allow you to enter."

Aaliyah took Gewey's hand. "Are you certain?"

Gewey smiled and nodded. "Yes. Don't worry. I don't sense the anger of the Oasis. But I do know that I must go on alone."

Aaliyah squeezed his hand and stepped back. "We will await you here."

Gewey turned and placed his hand on the doorknob. But the moment his fingers touched the metal, everything was plunged into darkness. Then came a great rumbling sound, as if the very earth was being shattered all around him. Aaliyah, Pali, and the hallway all vanished. For a moment, he was struck by fear and panic as the rumbling grew into a roar and a powerful wind rose up. It swirled around in a tempest, lifting him skyward. He let out a scream as he struggled vainly against the force. Then, as quickly as the wind had come, it disappeared again. He was beginning to fall back down. Faster and faster he fell. Unable to see through the darkness below, all he could do was grit his teeth and brace himself for the terrible crushing impact that he felt sure was to come. But the impact never arrived. Instead, amazingly, his feet landed gently on soft ground. Gewey knelt down, expecting to touch grass but was shocked to find what felt like polished marble. He pressed down with his finger. The surface gave way, sinking in, then reforming once he withdrew.

"This can't be real," he said. His words echoed repeatedly, then slowly faded away. "Am I alone?"

As if in response, a small ball of light appeared just in front of him. It grew brighter and brighter until he was forced to shield his eyes from the glare. Then it dimmed and there stood the figure of a man. He was as tall as Gewey, and just as broad. His raven hair fell carelessly in loose curls just above his shoulders. He was dressed in a long, silver robe, open at the front, revealing a loose-fitting white shirt and trousers beneath. His features were sharp and angular, with a perfect symmetry that was beautiful to behold. His flawless ivory skin bore no sign of age or blemishes and glowed with a soft radiance. He smiled as he met Gewey's eyes.

"I knew you would come," he said. His voice was deep and soothing.

"Who ... who are you?" Gewey stammered.

"You know me as Gerath," he replied.

"God of the Earth," Gewey whispered.

"Yes," he replied. "And no."

Gerath stretched out his arms. "What you see before you is merely an image. A piece of my essence left behind in this world. Left behind for you."

Gewey eyed him carefully. "Are you my father?"

Gerath laughed. "Indeed, I am. At least I am your father in the way you would understand it. I played my part in your creation."

"Then who is my mother?" he asked. The words of Felsafell echoed in his mind. This knowledge would drive him mad. Suddenly, he was afraid to hear the answer.

"I'm sorry," he replied. "But some answers I cannot give."

Gewey became irritated. "Then why are you here?"

"I am here to help you," Gerath turned around slowly and bowed his head. "Many mistakes have my kind made. And you must help us atone. You must redeem us."

"How am I to do that?"

"By mending what we have broken." He faced Gewey again. His face bore immeasurable sadness. "We had foreseen our imprisonment," he continued. "And we built this place. We built it so that you could one day find it. What resides within this temple will aid you and those whom you love ... should you choose to follow the path put before you. But I sense that your efforts will be hindered. Something evil now surrounds you. You must face it. You must drive it out."

"What is out there?" Gewey asked.

His eyes grew dark. "Creatures of pure hate and malice. They were sent by the one who imprisoned us. But do not fear them. You are stronger—far stronger than they can understand. Stronger than all in creation, save one." He stepped forward and placed his hand on Gewey's shoulder. "My son." His voice was filled with compassion and sorrow. "Of all the gods, you were chosen to right our wrongs. You are untainted by our sins and bound to this world. Your connection to this place binds your spirit to the very heart of the earth. Use that connection to attain your true power, and none can stand against you."

"How do I do that?" Gewey felt the touch of his father. Like love, it was a tangible thing he could see and taste. Only his bond with Kaylia could compare. "Can you teach me?"

"No one can teach you this." He withdrew his hand, reached inside his robe, and pulled out a small silver chain with a medallion the size of a gold piece attached. On it was carved the symbol of Gerath. "In a few moments, I will empty myself into this. From that moment on, I will cease to be, yet my power will remain. Wear it, and my strength will pass to you."

"What do you mean, 'you will cease to be'?" he asked.

"The part of me I left behind—its will and its mind—will be gone." He handed Gewey the medallion. A light flashed, and a table appeared beside him. On the table rested a bow, a dagger, and a staff, all gleaming white. "Take these. They are the tools of Vismal, crafted by my own hands. Give them to those whom you love and trust and your power will aid them. But choose carefully, for once given they will serve only that master." He smiled a sad smile. "I have little else to give you. Most of what I am has been trapped by the betrayer. What you see is a shadow. But the shadow of our kind carries great power. Use that power so that you may better understand what you must do."

"Why not just tell me?" Gewey cried. "Why not show me?"

"I cannot," he replied. "If I do so, all will have been for naught. You must discover your power on your own. I can only say that you have begun rightly. I sense mortal teachings within you. They can give you what we never could." He staggered back. Gewey reached out to catch his arm, but his hand passed through Gerath as though a mist. "My time is short. The moment you stepped within these walls,

I began to fade. My knowledge does not extend beyond the moment I was put here, and that slips away from me with each passing second."

"But I have so many questions," said Gewey. "Please, I must know more."

Gerath's form began to ripple and fade. "Know that you have your father's love, and that I await you even now." He gave Gewey one final loving smile. "I have only one more thing to give—your name."

"My name?" Gewey's mind raced.

"Yes," Gerath replied. "It is the name given to you by a father whose worst crime was to sacrifice you to a world of peril and hardship in order to undo what he cannot."

As he faded away completely, Gerath's final four words hung in the air.

"Your name is Darshan."

Gewey stood in stunned silence for several moments. "Darshan," he whispered.

He approached the table and examined the weapons. The dagger was sheathed in an ivory scabbard etched with the symbol of Gerath. The hilt was wrapped in white leather and crowned with a single diamond. The bow, short and impossibly thin, looked sure to break if drawn, though Gewey was certain it would not. The staff was as long as he was tall, with three snakes carved to coil their way up its length. No sooner had Gewey gathered these weapons in his arms than the table faded away and he found himself alone in a large, empty room. A glow radiated from bronze plates on the walls and he could see the silver door at the far end. Carefully cradling the weapons and holding tight to the medallion, he walked to the door and pulled it open. There stood Pali and Aaliyah.

Aaliyah beamed and threw her arms around him, nearly causing him to drop everything. "Thank the Creator. When you vanished, I feared the worst."

"We may be facing the worst," said Gewey. "If what I was told is true."

"What are those?" asked Pali, pointing at the weapons.

"Gifts," Gewey replied. "Gifts from Gerath." He recounted his experience, although he left out any mention that he was the son of Gerath. He could not be sure of how Pali would react to that.

"Darshan?" asked Aaliyah when he finished. "You are called Darshan?"

Gewey nodded. "I know you call me Shivis Mol. But have you heard this name before?"

"It means, 'The Bringer of Knowledge,'" Aaliyah replied. "Shivis Mol is more a title than a name, given to the one who will bring healing to the world."

Gewey shrugged. "I don't know about that. Right now, I'm more concerned about getting out of here. Gerath said that an evil resides here—one that will try to stop us."

Aaliyah nodded in agreement. "Yes. These matters can wait until we reach safety."

"I have heard of the legend of Darshan," Pali interjected with a curious stare. "But if that is who you are, then it can only mean that the gods walk among us." He looked Gewey up and down. "Is that what you are?"

Aaliyah stepped forward, but Gewey caught her arm and pulled her back. "I will not try to deceive you. Yes, I am a god. But I am not as you may think. I eat, I sleep, and I can be hurt, just like any other man. My spirit is no different than yours." He could feel Aaliyah's muscles tensing in his grasp.

"I ask that you do not reveal Darshan's presence," she said.

"You mustn't worry," said Pali, smiling broadly. "I will not betray you. And you need not fear my people. They bear the gods no hatred, though you may find it difficult to convince them that you speak the truth. I admit, had I not seen you vanish and then return bearing your gifts, I would have doubted it as well. Besides, if the legend is true—and it seems that it is—then this is joyous news. It is said that Darshan will cast out the evil that plagues the sands and bring everlasting prosperity to our people." He slapped Gewey on the shoulder. "But there will be time later to tell you of our legends. I will be coming with you when you return west."

"You cannot," objected Gewey.

"Oh, but I must," Pali countered. "If Darshan has come, then it means that the elves of the desert shall be reunited with our brethren in the west." He eyed Aaliyah. "I must see it done."

"I swore an oath to your mother," said Aaliyah sternly.

"I may be her child, but I am not a youth to be coddled," he challenged, meeting Aaliyah's gaze. "If you do not allow me to come with you, I shall make my own way west."

Pali and Aaliyah stared hard at one another for a full minute.

"Look," said Gewey, breaking the deadlock. "We can talk about it once we're out of here." He took a blanket from his pack and wrapped the staff, strapping both it and the bow across his back. The dagger he fastened to his belt.

"Are you going to wear the medallion?" asked Aaliyah.

Gewey held it in his hand for several seconds, tracing his finger over the engraving. Slowly, he draped the chain around his neck and took a deep breath.

"Well?" asked Pali.

Gewey reached down and lifted the medallion off his chest to examine it again. "Nothing." He rubbed it with his thumb. "I feel nothing at all."

"Perhaps you should draw power from the earth," suggested Aaliyah.

Gewey did as she suggested, but still nothing changed. "I don't understand."

A loud blast from a great horn rang out. Even when muffled by the walls of the temple, the sound was still strong enough to cause the corridor to tremble. Gewey drew his sword. The narrow hall would make it awkward, but he knew that the increased ability to use the flow would be needed. He looked down the hall, but no one came.

"They await us outside," said Aaliyah, after a few minutes. "We are trapped."

"Maybe they want to take us alive," offered Pali. A wicked grin crept across his face as he looked at Gewey. "But then, we have Darshan with us. I wonder if they are prepared for that?"

"My enemies know about me," said Gewey darkly. "If they choose to attack, they know who and what they face. And they know that I bleed just like you."

Gewey led them down the corridor and up the stairs to the door. It was still shut. The horn blasted once more, making Gewey wince. "Stay here," he commanded, before stepping outside the temple.

It took a moment for his eyes to adjust to the intense glare of the sunlight. When his vision had cleared, he saw a familiar black-cloaked figure, long curved blade in hand, standing twenty paces ahead.

"Do the Vrykol fear death?" Gewey shouted. The flow raged through him.

The Vrykol took a step forward, then pushed back his hood. "We do not."

Gewey gasped, and his eyes widened. It was not the burned, twisted features he had seen before. Instead, it was the face of an elf. His skin was lightly tanned, and his long black hair was tied in a tight braid. His face was narrow and angular, with closely set deep blue eyes that tried to stare straight through Gewey.

"You can't be..." said Gewey. "How?"

The Vrykol smiled, as though he had not a care in the world. "My master went to great trouble in my creation, young godling. I am the first of my kind, though not the last,

I assure you. I am here to offer you your life." He chuckled. "Though I already know what your answer will be."

"Then be gone," said Gewey. He strengthened his grip on his sword. "Allow us to pass."

"I'm afraid that is out of the question," he replied. "That is unless you surrender what was inside the temple to me. Do this, and I shall let you and your companions go free."

"If you attack us, I will have your head," warned Gewey.

"Perhaps," said the Vrykol. "You may be able to fight your way out of this place. I know you are powerful. But understand that I am not alone. Ten of my more brutish brothers and sisters are in the clearing, and fifty Soufis await you beyond the Oasis. Do you think your friends will be as fortunate as you? Are they gods as well? If so, then you should ignore my offer." He paused to pull the hood back over his head. "I await your answer in the clearing." He turned and disappeared down the path.

The door behind Gewey opened. Pali and Aaliyah stepped out.

"What was that abomination?" asked Pali, horrified.

"They're called Vrykol," said Gewey, still staring down the marble path to the trees. "I'm not sure what they really are, but they're fast, strong, and hard to kill. You must take off their heads to stop them."

"I have heard stories of the Vrykol," said Pali. "They were the assassins of the gods. But I never thought them to be anything more than a myth."

"This one is different from the others I've seen." Gewey looked hard at Aaliyah. "We may have no choice but to give them what they want."

"We will do no such thing," Aaliyah protested. "We have journeyed too far to simply give this creature what we came for."

"I agree," said Pali. "If these weapons are as powerful as you were told, you cannot let them fall into the hands of evil."

Gewey thought for a moment. "Gerath told me that I must give these things to those I love and trust. And once given, they only serve that master. Why then force me to give them up? They would be useless."

"They may not be aware of that fact," Pali suggested. "It seems that they were unable to enter the temple on their own, which is likely why they allowed us to enter unmolested. They may not have knowledge of what was kept there. And perhaps it is not the weapons he desires." He pointed to Gewey's medallion. "If that contains the essence of a god..."

"He's right," said Aaliyah. "You cannot let that fall into their hands. We must fight."

Gewey straightened his back and clenched his jaw tight. "Then you should know that Vrykol can block your ability to use the flow. At least, when used directly on them. But you can still affect things around them." He withdrew the Vismal dagger from his belt and held it out to Aaliyah. "Take this."

Aaliyah stared at it. Finally, she reached out and asked for confirmation. "Are you certain?"

Gewey nodded. She took it from his hand, but the moment her fingers touched the weapon, she cried out and fell to her knees. Gewey reached down to help her.

"Are you all right?" he asked, cradling her forearms.

Aaliyah smiled. "Yes. More than all right. You have no idea what you have given to me." She looked around wide-eyed as if seeing color for the first time. "It is beautiful." She rose lightly to her feet, holding the dagger to her breast. "Gerath was right. You must choose wisely to whom you give these."

Gewey turned to Pali, but the elf shook his head, knowing what Gewey was planning to do.

"Keep the rest and give them to those who will use them." Pali held his sword aloft. "I cannot steal life from the Creator, but with this, I can certainly take life from the wicked."

Gewey smiled. "Then let us meet our foes. They await an answer."

With Gewey leading the way, they headed down the path, past the columns, and into the wooded trail. The surge of power through both Gewey and Aaliyah was so great that the earth shook with each step and the air roared before them. As they approached the clearing, Gewey could see a line of black-cloaked figures wielding cruel jagged blades; they were standing just a few yards from the opening. He counted ten in total. Just as they entered the clearing, he spotted another Vrykol a few yards behind the others. Though cloaked, he assumed it was the one who had spoken to them outside the temple.

Gewey lowered his eyes and took a breath. "I see you hide behind the others."

"And I see your answer is what I expected," he shouted back. "A pity. Your friends will pay for your lack of wisdom." He spun around and held up his right hand. "Kill them," he ordered. With that, he disappeared down the path.

The Vrykol charged. A ball of flame burst to life, exploding at the feet of three, but they moved with tremendous speed, running straight through the flames. Gewey barely had time to react before two of the beasts were upon him. Four had rushed directly at Pali, and the others at Aaliyah. He knew he had to make quick work of these two or his friends would certainly be killed. He struck at the neck of the nearest foe, but it stopped just before it was in range of his sword. The other feinted and slashed, though only close enough to keep Gewey at bay.

He charged forward, but they only fell back, darting in and out to keep him off balance. He understood the tactic. They were planning to keep him busy until the others had defeated Pali and Aaliyah. Gewey glanced over to Pali. His sword was flashing in tight arcs as he danced and spun, avoiding blows. One Vrykol lay dead, but the others were pressing in, forcing his back to the trees and vines. Aaliyah was faring a little better. Two Vrykol were surrounded by flames, their black cloaks burning brightly. Another had already lost its head. The fourth was moving to her left, swinging wildly. Gewey tried to step right to help her, but the Vrykol cut him off, and the two that were on fire stepped in between, pressing Aaliyah back.

Gewey spun around and used the flow to upheave the earth behind him. Pali had cut the arm from another creature but was bleeding badly from his left leg. The two creatures at Gewey's back had already recovered by the time he'd rushed over to aid Pali. Gewey drove his blade through the chest of one of his friend's attackers, then, pulling it free, took the head of another. Pali grinned and pushed forward.

Gewey was only just able to duck and roll as the Vrykol at his back thrust their swords in unison. While still on his knees, he swung his sword and took both legs off of one, leaving it helpless on the ground. Pali was still fighting two. The one Gewey had skewered had moved in to Pali's right and its blade found his shoulder. Pali cried out, but he managed to move away and open up a wound across the chest of the beast to his left. He struck again and sent its head flying. Before he could turn to face the last, a blade shot through his chest. Pali gasped and staggered forward, the blade slipping out. Blood spewed forth as he dropped to his knees and Gewey could hear the soft hissing laugh of the Vrykol.

Gewey looked over just as Pali's body hit the ground. His heart filled with rage. He rolled, bringing his blade up between the legs of Pali's killer, spitting it completely in two. As the halves separated and fell to earth, thick, black blood sprayed out like a fountain.

Gewey's anger continued to rage, but he knew he couldn't allow this to cloud his mind. Aaliyah still faced three Vrykol, though two had slowed considerably as they burned. He leaped to his feet and took the heads off both flaming beasts with two quick strokes. Aaliyah ducked under the other's guard, and in a flash, its head rolled off its shoulders.

The final Vrykol paused. "This means nothing." Its rasping voice grated at Gewey's ears, fueling his anger even more. "You will not leave the desert alive." It charged.

Gewey snarled, and his sword took the creature's head quickly and cleanly. The instant it fell, Gewey decapitated the legless Vrykol and then rushed to Pali's body. He rolled him over, only to see dead eyes staring into nothingness. Gewey bowed his head and gently closed the elf's eyelids.

"Are you hurt?" he asked as Aaliyah knelt beside him.

"Thanks to your gift, no." She placed her hand on the back of his head. "You did your best to save him."

"He should not have been here," Gewey whispered. "We should never have brought him with us."

"He came of his own free will," said Aaliyah. "And he came as a gesture of friendship and kindness. We would not have made it here without him."

Even in the moment they were pausing briefly to consider this thought, a loud crackling sound, as if from a thousand campfires, suddenly filled their ears. They jumped up to see the bodies of all the Vrykol now turning hard and gray. Thousands of tiny cracks formed on their corpses, splintering like glass and then turning to dust. The ground shook and rumbled. A second later, the earth around Pali's body exploded and hundreds of thin roots shot upward before wrapping themselves over him. Before Gewey could even move, in front of his horrified eyes, the roots had pulled the elf's body right down into the earth. Gewey fell to the ground, digging furiously with his bare hands. Aaliyah stood back, staring in wonder at the spectacle. After a minute or two of fruitless work, Gewey pounded his fists in the dirt and screamed with rage.

"What is this? What is happening?" His anguished cries were met with silence. Slowly, he rose to his feet.

Aaliyah gasped and grabbed his arm, pointing a few feet away. "Look."

A soft ball of light hovered just above the ground, expanding until it took the form of a man. Its features were hazy and unrecognizable. Its feet didn't touch the earth, and its arms were held wide.

"Who are you?" Gewey demanded.

At first, there was nothing. The specter was silent and still. Then nine more figures appeared just behind it.

"We are the firstborn." The voice was distant and echoed as if within a great cavern. "We thank you for our freedom."

"I don't understand," said Gewey.

"The creatures which we were forced to become are now gone," it said. "We are free. And here ... we are safe."

"You mean you are the Vrykol?" asked Aaliyah.

"Yes, we were," it replied. "Our spirits were enslaved by the evil that holds the power of the gods. The spirits of the firstborn turned into abomination and darkness."

"I think I understand," said Gewey. "You are the spirits of Felsafell's people. That's what he meant at the Chamber when he said he had to free his kin."

At the mention of Felsafell, their lights grew brighter. "Yes. He is the last of us that walks with the living. It is good to know he has not forgotten us."

"What of Pali?" asked Aaliyah. "What of his spirit?"

"He is safe with us," it replied. "This place is special. The gods created it and gave it life. Now that you have driven out the sickness that has poisoned it, it can begin to heal. Your friend will stay here with us until the path to heaven is no longer barred by the one who seeks to destroy you. Only when he falls will the spirits of the dead be led to paradise. Only through his destruction can the world once again be set to rights."

The specter's lights began to fade.

"Wait, please!" Gewey implored. But they faded completely.

Aaliyah took Gewey's hand. "They are gone, and we should leave as well. If what the Vrykol said is true, fifty Soufis await..."

Her words stopped abruptly, replaced with a loud cry of pain as a tiny black dart struck her in the shoulder. Pulling it free, she threw it to the ground.

On the far side of the clearing, Gewey caught sight of a black cloak vanishing down the trail, harsh laughter trailing behind it. He began to race after the creature but had only covered a few yards when he heard Aaliyah's loud moan. He turned just in time to see her fall to her knees, her hand grasping at her wound. He rushed back to her side.

"Poison?" he asked.

She nodded, wincing.

Gewey pulled her hand away and touched the wound. It had already closed and was no larger than a pinprick. He reached into her body with the flow, seeking to expel the poison, but was forced back.

"I don't understand," said Gewey.

Aaliyah closed her eyes and breathed deeply. For a full minute, she knelt motionless. "Mandrista," she said weakly, opening her eyes. "I have been poisoned with sap from the mandrista tree. I cannot be cured using the powers of the earth and spirit alone."

"What can we do?" asked Gewey, desperation creeping into his voice.

"I must return to the ship," she replied. "I have the means to extract it there."

"Do we have time?" he asked, squeezing her hand tightly.

"The poison is slow." She struggled to her feet. "Three days. We may make it if we hurry."

Gewey's thoughts turned to the Soufis. He needed to deal with them quickly. "Wait here. I'll take care of the Soufis myself."

"You cannot do this alone," she protested. "I..."

"No," he said, fiercely. "Pali has died, and I'll not watch you die too." Fury burned in his eyes. "We'll see how brave the Soufis are when I blast them apart and then bury their bodies in their precious desert."

Before she could argue, Gewey tore off across the clearing and down the path. He covered the distance in only a few minutes, his legs fueled by the flow of both air and earth. The brush that lay in front of the entrance had already been pushed aside, and he could make out the figures of men twenty yards away. He slid to a halt a foot beyond the path, his blade tight in his hand. But he had no intention of cutting his way through fifty men.

The Soufis were lined up in two loose rows. They were wrapped in thick tan robes with white turbans covering their heads. The men in the front row held long curved blades, while those at the rear carried lengthy black bows. The Vrykol stood front and center, his hood thrown back revealing his elf features.

"Did your elf mistress enjoy my gift?" he asked, laughing.

"Laugh if you want," said Gewey. His eyes narrowed and his legs parted. "But if I were you, I'd be running."

The Vrykol smiled. "Excellent advice. But we'll meet again, Gewey Stedding. Or should I call you Darshan?" With that, he turned and disappeared behind the Soufis lines.

The moment he was out of sight, the Soufis bowmen notched their arrows and fired. Gewey raised his hand and a blast of wind halted the arrows in mid-flight, sending them falling harmlessly to the ground. The Soufis retreated a step, looking confused and murmuring with doubt and fear. Before they could decide on their next action, Gewey let loose a great ball of flame into the heart of their lines. Twenty men fell instantly, while several others rolled screaming in the sand, trying to put themselves out. This was enough to send the rest scattering. But Gewey was in no mood to be merciful. He sent another flame streaking across the ground. The sand crackled and popped as the flames surrounded the remaining Soufis. He tightened the circle, forcing them together. A few tried to run through the fire but were roasted alive before they reached the other side.

"Die!" Gewey roared and closed the circle.

Cries of pain and desperate pleas for mercy went unheard as the Soufis burned. The flames grew hotter and taller until they reached fifty feet in the air. The voices of the Soufis were silent. Only the roar of Gewey's anger could be heard.

As he allowed the flames to subside, Gewey scanned the area for the Vrykol, but he was already gone. The burned stumps of the Soufis dotted the sands, and the sickly sweet smell of charred flesh filled the air. A great circle of pale green glass had replaced the desert sand. It glittered splendidly in the desert sun, its beauty in sharp contrast to the carnage that its creative force had wrought.

Gewey turned away and ran back to Aaliyah. By the time he reached the clearing, she had already dressed her wound and sheathed her knife. Her face turned grim when she saw Gewey.

"They are gone?" she asked.

Gewey relaxed his muscles and nodded. "Yes. They're all … gone." He took her hand and led her from the clearing.

The image of the flames still remained fixed in his mind. As they approached the entrance to the Oasis, he hesitated. Gewey didn't want her to see what he had done. He almost held her back, but she moved past him and stepped out onto the sands. For a moment, she stood silently surveying the carnage. Timidly, he followed her out.

"All gone, indeed," she remarked.

"I was just…" Gewey paused. "I was just so angry."

"The wrath of a god is truly not to be taken lightly." She turned to him and smiled. Her face was awash with pity and understanding. "But you did what had to be done."

"I know," said Gewey. "This is not the first time I've killed. It's just that I never imagined unleashing such power." He held up the medallion around his neck and examined it. "Only the gods know what I can do when I learn to use this. I fear that it may be too much power for me to control."

"I doubt it," said Aaliyah. "The one you must vanquish wields more power than you can imagine. You will need this and more." She glanced a final time at the smoldering corpses. "We must go. My time grows short."

With that, they headed off in the direction of the shore, Gewey desperately hoping that they would make it in time to save Aaliyah's life. As they traveled, he swore an oath to kill the Vrykol who had poisoned her.

And before he killed it, he would make a special point of teaching it to fear death.

CHAPTER 16

Frost covered the bleak landscape as Lee and Jacob rose from their tent, shivering and rubbing their arms. The bitter cold of the far north was not something even a Hazrian Lord could ignore. Fires already burned around the camp, and the scent of bacon wafted on the frigid air. Darius was already up—something most uncharacteristic for the fat merchant. He was kneeling down by a fire, cradling a cup of hot coffee in his gloved hands. Lee and Jacob joined him.

"Are you sure about this?" asked Darius. "It seems foolish to me."

"I'm sure," Lee replied. He grabbed the tin kettle suspended over the fire and poured himself a cup. "If what I hear is true, we will gain passage north if we join the army. All new recruits are sent to Kratis for training and deployment. And that's where we need to go."

"I haven't asked you your true business," said Darius. "And I won't. But you seek the palace of the Reborn King, it would seem. If you do this, you will be caught, and you will die. You don't want to know the stories I've heard about what they do to spies."

"I can imagine," Lee said, soberly. The thought of his son suffering torture caused his stomach to knot. "Still, we must try."

"Well, if I cannot dissuade you," said Darius, "at least allow me to help you." He reached into his coat and pulled out a piece of folded parchment. "It's a letter of endorsement stating that you have been in my service for the past five years. I am known in these parts, so it will pass scrutiny."

Lee took it and smiled gratefully. "Yes. This will certainly help us."

They ate and then packed their gear. Fennio and three others were waiting for them by the road. Lee knew that he was taking a risk in traveling with these men. Should his and Jacob's cover story be questioned, any of them could say that they had only recently joined the caravan. If that happened, the endorsement letter would become a liability instead of a help.

Darius was also at the roadside, holding a number of small purses. "All right, lads," he said. "Don't ever say I'm not a fair man." He handed out the purses to the men. The jingle of coins sounded as they bounced them up and down. "Just don't go counting it yet. You've been paid already, so wait until I'm gone before complaining about how little extra is there."

"Thank you for all your help," said Lee. He shook the man's hand firmly and smiled.

Darius laughed heartily. "And thank you for saving my life." He waved his hand in a gesture of dismissal. "Now go. I have a business to run, and wine to drink." He turned away and strode back to his tent.

The recruiting station was three miles away at the Whiterun Pass garrison, just south of the city itself. It took them only an hour to arrive, but the town could be seen from more than a mile away. Tall buildings of burgundy stone rose from behind thick granite walls. Lee was impressed.

Cities and towns this far north were usually little more than trading posts. In fact, Hazrah was by far the largest city north of the Razor Edge Mountains, and that was small compared to Baltria or Althetas. Clearly, Angrääl had been hard at work.

The garrison was impressive as well. It resembled an ancient fortress, very similar to those shown in paintings Lee had hanging in his house back in Sharpstone. The twenty-foot high curtain walls were smooth and seamless, as if carved from a single block stretching out at least two hundred feet, left to right. In the center, an arched iron gatehouse door covered in vicious spikes was closed. At each corner of the walls, looming another twenty feet higher, were round towers with dozens of arrow slits for defending archers to fire through. Capping every tower was a domed turret manned by three watches. From what Lee could see, there were at least two dozen more archers and pikemen patrolling the length of the walls between each turret. Flapping in the strong north wind atop all four domes was the now familiar banner of Angrääl.

A long table had been set up just outside the gatehouse door. A soldier stood at each end, and a slightly built man in a red linen suit and thick wool coat was sat behind it, taking information from four new recruits. Lee, Jacob, and the others filed in behind them. Each recruit was told to wait a short distance away from the table after their information had been taken.

When it was Lee's turn, he handed the recruiter Darius's letter. The man examined it for a moment, then sighed.

"More sell-swords," he muttered. "Do you have any military experience?"

"No, sir," Lee replied. "But my nephew and I are both good with a blade. We're from…"

"I don't care where you're from." He glanced up and shook his head. "I'm sure you are both eager to join up, so we'll make this quick."

After registering both Lee and Jacob under the names given in Darius's letter, the recruiting officer wrote down what skills they listed. After he finished this, he had them sign a large parchment and instructed them to wait with the others. For hours, they just sat there huddled together, trying to fight off the cold as dozens more men came to join. By late afternoon, their numbers had swelled to nearly one hundred. No offer of food or drink had been made, so Lee and Jacob shared what little they had with Fennio and the rest of Darius's former guards, who had clearly not thought to bring anything for themselves.

An hour before sundown, the recruiter stood and announced that anyone else who wished to join must return tomorrow. With that, the two guards picked up the table and followed the man into the gatehouse. The sun was nearly gone, and the air was starting to turn even colder. It wasn't long before many of the new recruits became restless. Disgruntled whispers could be heard.

"Enough of this bloody nonsense," yelled a stocky, dark-haired fellow clad in thick leather mail. "I did not come here to freeze and starve." He began striding off in a southerly direction.

There was a whistle, followed by a thud as an arrow pierced the back of the man's neck. He fell to his knees, grasping desperately at the arrow before crumpling to the ground and gurgling his last breaths.

"In case you were wondering, you are not permitted to leave." A tall, lean man stepped from the gatehouse. He wore a shining metal breastplate with the broken scales of Angrääl etched in gold across it. His blond hair was cropped close, and even in the fading ligh,t his chiseled features and square jaw were evident. He was as broad as Lee in the shoulders and carried himself with supreme confidence. A thick, heavy broadsword hung from his belt, while in his hands was a short, curved bow. He dropped the bow to the ground and walked toward the men. "I am Captain Faris Lanmore. From the moment you signed your names, you were in the service of the Reborn King of Angrääl. And as you can see, we do not tolerate desertion."

He strolled casually in front of the men. When he reached Lee, he paused. "You have a hard look about you." His eyes went to Jacob for a moment. "Is this your son?"

"No, sir," replied Lee. "He is my nephew."

Captain Lanmore nodded, rubbing his chin. "Then that would make you..." He paused for a brief moment. "Barath. Yes, that's the name you gave. I noticed you and your nephew as you approached. You claim to be a mere sell-sword, here to do some soldiering?"

"Yes, sir." Lee tensed.

He pointed to Lee's sword. "That's quite a weapon for a sell-sword. Let me see it."

Lee unsheathed his blade and handed it to the captain.

"It's well-balanced," Lanmore remarked approvingly. "Superbly crafted. A true master's sword." He looked up at Lee and smiled. "Is that what you are? A sword master perhaps? By the way you walk, I doubt you're a mere sell-sword. I've been a soldier too long not to notice things like that." He handed Lee back his weapon.

Lee returned his sword to his scabbard and squared his shoulders.

"And you know when to be silent as well," remarked Lanmore. "Good. Very good. Well, whatever you run from, you need not fear it here. The Reborn King will give you a new life. Would you like that?"

"Yes, sir," Lee replied.

"I thought as much." He turned his attention to the rest of the men. "That goes for all of you. Whoever you were before, whatever wrongs you have committed, they are, as of this moment, forgiven. The Reborn King grants you pardon. Together, we shall forge a new world in his name. We shall sweep aside the liars and oppressors." His sword sang as he pulled it from his scabbard and stepped back. "But be warned. If any one of you seeks to betray us or fails in his duty, you will find the King's justice to be harsh and final." He turned to the gatehouse and whistled.

Ten men burst forth carrying sacks of food and blankets, which they distributed among the new recruits. Soon fires were lit and the scent of cooked meat permeated the air. Lee and Jacob sat with Fennio to eat.

"What do you think?" asked Fennio. "All sounds a bit crazy to me. Not to mention that Captain Lanmore fellow shooting that poor chap."

"If he hadn't, we'd still be sitting here hungry and cold," said Lee. "The point was to make an impression."

"Exactly," said a voice just behind Lee. It was Lanmore.

Lee and the others leaped to their feet and stood at attention.

"Come with me, Barath," ordered Lanmore.

Captain Lanmore led Lee through the gatehouse door and into the fortress. The flagstone path led to the inner yard where a few scattered soldiers were patrolling the area. The keep at the far end was a single-story structure with a gray slate roof. Barracks large enough to house two hundred men each were built just below the curtain walls on either side.

Halfway to the keep, Captain Lanmore halted and turned. "I've brought you here to see if my judgment has failed me."

A man broader and taller than Lee, clad in black fur, leather boots, and carrying a long, two-handed sword, stalked out of the barracks and made his way over to Lanmore's side. His head was shaved and scarred, and his dark eyes were fixed menacingly on Lee.

"This is Lars," said Lanmore. "He is by far our strongest warrior and one of the few we have here who is native to Angrääl. I want you to kill him—if you can."

Without a word, Lee drew his sword and prepared for Lars to charge. He didn't have to wait long. The hulking Northman sprang forward with surprising agility and speed, but Lee easily moved aside and brought his blade across the man's left arm, laying it open. The Northman roared with fury and swung his sword in a wide arc, but again, Lee stepped away. This time, he sliced open his opponent's right thigh. As Lars reached down, clutching at the wound, Lee smashed the hilt of his sword square between his opponent's eyes. Lars staggered, and Lee struck him again, this time sending him onto his back.

"Why are you toying with him?" asked Captain Lanmore. "Has he offended you?"

Lars struggled to rise, sword still in hand, but Lee brought his boot hard down on his fingers. The great blade fell free and Lee kicked it away.

"Your order stands?" asked Lee, the tip of his sword hovering at Lars's throat.

Lanmore said nothing. Lee nodded with understanding, then rammed the blade clean through Lars's exposed neck, burying the tip in the flagstone below. The Northman gurgled, clutching at the wound. After a minute, he moved no more. Lee cleaned his sword on his opponent's furs.

"I'm glad I didn't test your skills with my own blade," Lanmore remarked with a hint of amusement. "You are clearly one of the best-trained swordsmen who has come through here in some time. But then, you don't hide it as well as you might think. In fact, I think you could have taken Lars the moment he came at you. Why didn't you?"

"I may have been able to kill him more quickly," agreed Lee. "But I've learned to never underestimate an opponent. His first strike may have been a deception. As it was, he moved with great speed for one of his size. I saw no need to risk it."

"Wise," said Lanmore, smiling. He reached in his belt and pulled out a small red ribbon. He handed it to Lee. "You shall lead the recruits on the journey north. Do a good job and there may be more rewarding positions awaiting you." He spun on his heels and walked away toward the keep.

Lee cursed under his breath and walked to the gatehouse. Four men were already collecting the body of Lars. When he reached Jacob, he pulled him away from earshot. His face gave away his feelings.

"What's wrong?" asked Jacob.

"I have failed to go unnoticed," Lee replied. "Captain Lanmore is a very good judge of people. At least, from a soldiering standpoint. He saw my training in my movements. Now, I'm promoted."

"How is that bad?" Jacob laughed. "Won't that make things easier?"

"Don't be a fool," growled Lee. "As a simple soldier, I could move about without drawing attention. As an officer, not only will I be noticed, but sooner or later I'll be discovered for who I am." He thought for a moment. "If I am captured, they will figure out who you are as well. It may be better if you flee."

"You know I won't," shot Jacob.

"Yes." Lee reached out and squeezed his shoulder. "I know. But if I'm found out, you must try to escape. You must abandon your attempt to rescue your mother and head to Sharpstone. Millet will aid you." He met Jacob's eyes. "Swear it."

"But..." began Jacob.

"Swear it!" he repeated, this time much more forcefully.

Jacob bowed his head. "I swear. But only if rescue is impossible."

Lee wanted to embrace his son at that moment but resisted. He knew he must appear to others to be distant, and Lanmore may well be watching him. "I suppose that will suffice," he said. They rejoined the others and bedded down for the night.

The sunrise brought trumpets from the fortress walls. Captain Lanmore and six soldiers emerged from the gatehouse. Lee attached the ribbon to his coat and strode up to meet them.

"Good morning, Captain," he said.

Lanmore nodded curtly. "Get them ready, Barath. We march in ten minutes."

Lee spun around and jogged back to the recruits. "Form ranks!" The force of his voice snapped everyone to attention. At first, they just stood there, staring at him. "Now!" he barked. This was enough to get the men moving. In less than five minutes, all were packed and lined up along the road.

"You command men well," said Lanmore approvingly. "Not for the first time, I'd wager." He walked up and down the line. "We have an eight-day march to Kratis. We will do it in seven. Those who fall behind will be considered deserters. And I think you all know what happens to deserters." He looked at Lee. "Move them out."

Lee turned to the recruits and shouted out the command. "On my order! Move out!"

The line moved off with Lee in front, Captain Lanmore just behind him. The six soldiers positioned themselves, three on each side of the recruits.

"Push the pace, Barath," said Lanmore over Lee's shoulder. "I meant what I said about making it there in seven days."

Lee did as he was told, speeding his pace to a near jog. By midday, the recruits were panting and struggling with each step.

"Shall we halt for a meal, sir?" asked Lee.

"What do you think, Barath?" Lanmore replied. "Should we?"

"I do, sir," Lee replied. "If you intend for these men to maintain speed, they must also maintain strength. Twenty minutes to eat and rest still puts us in Kratis a day and a half ahead. And I would recommend a ten-minute respite every four hours."

"And why is that?"

Lee straightened his shoulders. "Because, sir, most of these men will not be able to keep this up for seven days without it; unless you intend to execute half of them before we arrive."

"Perhaps I want to weed out the weak," said Lanmore. "Or perhaps I simply don't care about how tired they get." He chuckled softly. "But as it happens, I agree. The King's army would not be served if I killed off half of the men."

Lee was relieved. "May I ask a question, sir?"

"You may," said Lanmore.

"Do you usually escort new recruits to Kratis?"

"No," said Lanmore, with a hint of irritation. "I've been summoned."

Lee knew better than to ask why. He joined Jacob and Fennio for the short meal, then moved the men out again.

"You will no longer eat among the recruits," said Lanmore. "You shall take your meals with us. If you wish, your nephew can join us as well."

"He should eat with the men," said Lee.

"Not wanting to show favor, I see. Or perhaps the two of you aren't close?"

"He is my sister's son," said Lee. "I am bound to protect him if I can. But no, we're not close."

Lanmore shrugged. "It's for the best. Gives a lad a chance to make his own mark."

On the first night, Lee set his bedroll a few feet away from the soldiers. They had put up a small tent in which

Captain Lanmore would bed down, but he chose to eat and talk with them for a short while before turning in. Away to one side, Lee could hear the recruits laughing and talking and wondered how Jacob was getting on. He shook his head, quietly laughing at himself. He was thinking as if Jacob were still a boy playing with other children. Fearing that their time together would soon end, he wished he could be with him now. Lee knew his chance for success was slim, and often on their journey, he'd wished he could turn Jacob away in order to keep him safe. It no longer mattered that his son had betrayed him. Lee had brought that on himself. His thoughts turned to that day with the Oracle, causing his anger to swell. How he wished he had ignored her. He should never have deserted his family.

Once this is finished, my part is done, he swore to himself. The world can end in fire for all I care. He would take his family far from this conflict. Even if that meant living in the remote desert.

Over the next few days, Lee kept the men moving at a near-unbearable pace. Even the hardened soldiers escorting them showed signs of fatigue. They passed dozens of companies of troops marching south.

"War comes," said Lanmore offhandedly on one occasion, as they were forced to make way for five full companies and their supply wagons. "Then we can march south and leave this icy land behind."

"When will it begin?" asked Lee.

Lanmore shrugged. "Soon, I hope. I hear there are things to take care of in the West first. But those are matters for kings and diplomats." He slapped Lee on the shoulder. "We're soldiers, you and I. Our job is to fight and die, yes?"

"Yes, sir," said Lee. He couldn't help but respect Captain Lanmore. He was a true leader and soldier. Ruthless and harsh, yet educated in the ways of men. Everything he did was calculated. Even the slaying of Lars had a purpose behind it. By then, rumors had been leaked about the incident—most likely at the direction of Lanmore, Lee suspected—and the recruits gave him a wide berth, accepting his orders without question.

On the fifth day, a light snow began to fall. The sky told Lee that it would soon be coming down in earnest. Normally, given how close they were to their destination, this wouldn't be a cause for concern. But he knew that the recruits, with just a few exceptions, were ill-prepared for such conditions. If a storm came, many would freeze to death. When Lee brought this to Lanmore's attention, he just laughed.

"The King hasn't allowed a blizzard for years," said Lanmore.

"Are you suggesting that he controls the weather?" asked Lee, feigning ignorance.

"When you meet him, you'll understand," Lanmore replied. "He likes to meet all of his new officers, from the grandest general to the lowliest lieutenant."

"That will be something," said Lee. The thought of meeting the Dark Knight of Angrääl sent his heart racing. He hoped to be away with his wife and son long before that happened.

"You have no idea," said Lanmore. Lee could hear unease in his voice. "To be in his presence is no small matter. You may have seen many battles, and slain many men, but nothing can prepare you for it. The Reborn King possesses the power of the gods." He rubbed his hands together nervously. "I felt like a naked child. To tell you the truth, I can't even remember where I was or what he looked like—just a feeling of being totally overwhelmed."

He cleared his throat and stiffened his back as if catching himself in an awkward state. "In any event, you have some time to go yet before you're worthy of such an audience. Now, go tend to your duties."

As Captain Lanmore had said, no storm came, though the temperature dropped to a point where even marching at a double quick pace did nothing to warm the men. On the last night of the march, they were all huddled so closely around the fire that several were actually singed. The only ones seemingly unaffected were Lanmore and Lee. Lee had looked in on Jacob a few times, and it became clear that his son had decided to stay close to Fennio and the other men from Daruis's guard.

"You deal with the cold well, for a southerner," remarked Lanmore as they took their meal.

"I am cold, sir," said Lee. "But there's no point in complaining. Besides, I have to set an example for the men."

"Quite right, Barath," he replied. "Quite right, indeed. You'll do well here. And don't worry. We'll be south soon enough." Lanmore alluded often to the coming war, but never once divulged anything useful. "Thanks to you, we're far ahead of schedule. It's a break in protocol, but you will stay with the officers when we arrive tomorrow. I think you'll find it more pleasant than the recruit barracks."

"Thank you, sir," said Lee. He stared deep into the campfire, pleased. Perhaps the officers would have information on his wife. And it would separate him from Jacob. Should things go badly, Jacob would need time to escape.

"If you wish to speak to your nephew," Lanmore added, "you should do so before we arrive. It's unlikely you'll see him again anytime soon. Officers and soldiers train separately."

"I'll do that tonight," Lee replied.

Lee went to seek out Jacob as soon as he'd finished his meal. He found him playing dice and passing around a small flask of brandy with several other recruits at the far end of the encampment. When they saw Lee, they all jumped to their feet and stood at attention.

"Jasper, come with me," Lee commanded.

Jacob nodded and followed Lee away from the camp.

"Did you find out where Mother is?" asked Jacob.

Lee shook his head. "Not yet. But I'll be staying in the officer's barracks when we get to Kratis. I hope to find out more then." He placed his hand on Jacob's shoulder. "If I'm discovered, I intend to bring all hell down upon Angrääl before I go. If that happens, you must run. Keep to the woods. Avoid towns until you are south of the Razor Edge Mountains, then make your way to the Goodbranch and take a riverboat to Sharpstone." He handed Jacob six gold coins. "Hide these. It's enough to get you to Millet." He saw a flash of defiance in Jacob's eyes. "There can be no debate. If things go wrong, it won't take them long to come after you. If I fail and they capture you, all is lost. You must survive."

"I will do as you say," said Jacob.

"I'm so very sorry," said Lee, forcing back a tear. "But I'm about to hit you."

Jacob stepped back. "What?"

"As we speak, Captain Lanmore watches. It must seem as if I don't care about you. It will keep his attention on me." Lee clenched his fist. "Are you ready?"

Jacob nodded.

Lee's fist connected with Jacob's jaw, sending him tumbling to the ground. He looked down at Jacob, using all his willpower not to rush to his side. "You're on your own, boy," he said, making sure his voice carried far enough for all to hear. He then marched back to his bedroll.

"Didn't go as well as you hoped?" Lanmore spoke not from amusement but from curiosity.

"It went as expected," said Lee. "As you said, they have to find their own way." His heart was aching. He glanced over his shoulder to see Jacob stumbling back to camp, holding his jaw.

Lee bedded down, trying to slow his mind. The pain of punching Jacob mingled with fears of his son being captured, making sleep impossible. At dawn, he mustered the men and had them ready to leave in short order. Every time he came close to where Jacob stood, shame washed over him. But at least hitting him seemed to have the desired effect. Twice as many recruits now ate with him during the noon respite, and Lanmore made no further mention of him at all.

As the afternoon wore on, Lee noticed more and more buildings and houses lining the road, most of them crafted from the small gray stones common to the region. There were a few farms here and there, but the fields were barren at this time of year. Lee reckoned Angrääl imported most of its food supply up the Goodbranch from Baltria.

An hour before dusk, six massive black spires broke the horizon and the city of Kratis came into view. Lee saw all six very clearly, even though the city walls were still five miles away. He stood in awe of the sheer scope of the city. Construction of such magnitude should have taken decades at the very least, not to mention skills thought lost to the master builders long ago. Not even the ruins of the forgotten kingdoms of old boasted buildings of such great height. The city of Kratis had indeed been the seat of power in Angrääl in the distant past, yet Lee had never imagined it as being much more than a place the size of Hazrah.

Captain Lanmore noticed Lee staring at the towers. "We'll not be going that far. Not just yet."

"I didn't know buildings of such scale were still possible," said Lee, unable to hide the fact that he was impressed.

"Kratis is being rebuilt," said Lanmore. "In the time of King Rätsterfel it was the greatest city in the world. The Reborn King has discovered the secrets of the ancients, or so I've been told, and will see it returned to its former glory."

"So it would seem," said Lee.

The garrison came into view minutes later and was nearly an exact copy of the one in Klinton, only four times the size. Lee guessed that it housed at least fifteen hundred men. Lanmore halted them at a narrow road leading east just before reaching the fort and ordered the soldiers to escort the recruits to their barracks. Lee was told these were a mile west of the main garrison. He knew this may present a problem if things went wrong, but there was little he could do about it.

"You will come with me," said Lanmore. "I need to present you to Lord Pollus, the garrison commander. He's a bit of a pompous ass, but a competent leader. Keep quiet and only speak when spoken to."

Lee followed Lanmore to the gatehouse. Two guards halted them.

"And you are?" asked the guard.

Lanmore stepped forward, bringing his face a mere inch from the guard's. "You know very well who I am. Are we to do this again?"

"I'm sure I don't know what you mean, sir," he replied with disdain. "I simply didn't recognize you at first."

Both guards smirked, then stepped aside, allowing Lanmore entry. But when Lee tried to follow, his path was barred.

"He's with me," said Lanmore. "Allow him to pass."

"Not until I get word from Lord Pollus—Captain." The guard stiffened his back. "Until then, he can wait here with us."

Lanmore glared at the guard before stalking off into the fort. Lee waited silently. The guards didn't seem interested in conversation and completely ignored him. After ten minutes, the captain returned. He shoved a piece of parchment firmly into the guard's chest and motioned for Lee to follow.

"They can't stand it when a commoner advances through the ranks," explained Lanmore as they passed through the gatehouse. "In their minds, only a lord should command."

Lee cracked a smile. "In my experience, if only lords commanded, it would take a year to march an army ten miles."

Lanmore threw his head back in laughter. "I wouldn't repeat that in the officers' barracks. Especially 'round those bloody Baltrian fools. Most will run straight to Lord Pollus to try and curry favor. And frankly, he isn't known for his humor."

"I'll keep that in mind." Hearing that Baltrian lords would be near did not ease Lee's mind. He hoped that they would be too young to recognize him.

The main yard was filled with soldiers, about three hundred in total, drilling and marching. The barracks were as high as the curtain walls, with two catapults placed on each of the flat roofs. The keep was much larger than that in the other fort as well, standing two stories high and covered with arrow slits capable of raining down terror inside the parade yard should the walls be breached. The clash of metal, stomping of boots, and shouting of orders combined to fill the air with a cacophony of noise. Lee marveled that the sound did not carry outside of the fort, or even through the gatehouse. The design must have held its own secrets. Even the catapults appeared sophisticated compared to others he'd seen. He saw only a single hand crank, and a long metal tube placed just above the arm. Lee guessed that this held the shot. If a single soldier could operate this weapon, instead of the usual four, it would be devastating. A lone platoon could wreak havoc.

The entrance to the keep was unguarded, but Lanmore still paused long enough to take a deep breath before flinging open the door. Lee followed him inside. The gray stone floor and walls were lined with weapon racks and maps. To his left were three rows of long tables, with a door at the far corner leading to the kitchens. To his right, where he expected there to be an officers' lounging area, were instead dozens of desks and small tables. Cotton and linen-clad bureaucrats sat busy at their duties, not even bothering to look up as Lee and Captain Lanmore passed by.

"Welcome to the heart of the kingdom," joked Lanmore.

"This is where we take our meals?" asked Lee.

Lanmore shook his head, chuckling softly. "No. I'm afraid the keep is reserved for the commander and these fine fellows. We take our meals in the barracks."

They entered a door directly ahead. Through this, a long hall ended in a flight of stairs leading to the second level. At the top, the hall split off into two directions, each with several doors along the walls.

"The bureaucrats stay in these rooms," said Lanmore. "They're quite comfortable compared to our quarters."

"A soldier has no need of comfort," said Lee.

They turned left for several yards, then right for a few more until reaching an elaborately carved mahogany door. Attached in the center of this was a polished silver carving of broken scales, the sigil of Angrääl. Only with great self-control did Lee manage to fight back the urge to smash it to pieces and to keep the feelings of disgust from showing on his face. Captain Lanmore knocked firmly before pushing the door open.

In the center of the room they entered was a round table on which rested various maps and charts, while at the far end was a large oak desk. A long rope hung from a small hole in the ceiling just behind the desk. To Lee's right, a plush, tan suede couch and four matching chairs with small brass end tables were arranged in a semi-circle facing a hearth that burned brightly. Three polished brass lanterns hung from the ceiling center, and two more protruded from each wall at ten-foot intervals. Behind the desk hung a mural depicting a gleaming champion on horseback leading a charge against an elf army. Between the lanterns on the left stood an oak bookcase that held beautifully leather-bound tomes along with a crystal decanter and glasses.

A man sat behind the desk dressed in a fine white shirt and a red jacket. His salt and pepper hair was oiled and combed back in regal fashion. His tan skin gleamed in the bright light, offsetting his fragile build and narrow features.

"Ah, Captain Lanmore," said the Commander. His voice was tinny and a bit feminine. "I see you have arrived ahead of schedule. And with a new officer."

Lanmore bowed his head sharply. "Yes, Commander. The message said to come with all speed."

"Indeed, it did," said Lord Pollus. "And yet you chose to travel with the recruits rather than on horseback." He rose to his feet. Though thin, he was quite tall—as tall as Lee—and walked with the effortless grace of a true noble. He sighed. "I suppose there is nothing to be done." He finally took notice of Lee, looking him up and down. "And you are?"

"I am Barath, My Lord," said Lee, bowing as Lanmore had done.

"Just Barath?" Pollus shook his head and frowned. "Yet another commoner." He turned and went back to his deck. "I suppose if Captain Lanmore deems you worthy, you will do." His eyes fell on the captain. "He is your responsibility and under your command. And please, if he doesn't have a last name, tell him to choose one. People will think he's one of those native Angrääl barbarians our gracious king has scattered among our ranks. Dreadful people."

"You will be pleased to know that Barath fought one of those before we set out," said Lanmore.

Pollus raised an eyebrow. "Is that so? And you survived. Impressive."

"He did more than survive," said Lanmore, puffing out his chest. "He defeated him as if fighting a child."

"Impressive, indeed." Lord Pollus opened his desk drawer, pulled out a piece of parchment, and scrawled something on it. After blowing the ink dry, he pushed it across the desk. "This is your commission—Barath. If for no other reason than ridding the world of an uncouth beast, I am happy to give it. I have left enough room for you to put in a proper name."

Lee took the parchment and bowed again. "Thank you, My Lord."

Lord Pollus reached behind him and pulled down on the rope. A moment later, a thin, blond boy in a dark blue tunic and trousers scurried in.

"Show this man downstairs," Pollus ordered. "He is to be given a commission under Captain Lanmore." He dismissed the boy with a wave. "As for you, captain, I will speak with you now."

Lanmore looked sideways at Lee. "I will join you as soon as I can." He then turned to the boy. "If I am not down in time, show him to the barracks when he's done."

Lee bowed one last time and followed the boy downstairs. He was taken to a desk where a scrawny wraith of a man was busy scribbling on one of the many pieces of parchment piled high on his desk. Lee held out his commission.

The man didn't look up, but opened the parchment and began writing notes. "What is your surname?"

"Drakis," Lee replied. Drakis was the name of a fiend in a story he'd heard as a child. He almost smirked at the thought, but it was the only thing he could think of at the time.

"You have an odd sense of humor," the man said off-handedly. "And before you ask, I know that tale as well. All men of the north do."

Lee sat quietly as the man spent the next half hour writing, checking, and then double-checking each note. Finally, he handed Lee a small round wooden token with the number one painted on either side.

"Give this to the quartermaster," He straightened the pile of papers on his desk. "He'll issue you with what equipment you'll need."

Lee stood up and turned to the door. The blond boy was standing just behind him, waiting patiently. Halfway to the barracks, Captain Lanmore caught up with them.

"I'll take it from here, boy," said Lanmore. Without a word, the boy ran back to the keep. "Did you pick a name?"

"I'll be known as Barath Drakis," Lee replied.

"A dire name to be sure," he said with obvious approval.

"Will it be possible to see my nephew?" asked Lee.

"I thought you weren't close," said Lanmore. "In fact, if I recall, you nearly took his head off the last time you spoke."

"I would not have it end as such between us," Lee explained. "Though I have no great affection for him, he is my sister's child."

Lanmore nodded. "I'll see what I can do. Until then, we need to get you settled in. We'll be here for three weeks."

"A short time for training," said Lee.

"Pollus likes you," said Lanmore. "Mostly because you killed Lars. But I also assured him that you understand military discipline and that I would personally train you." He stopped and faced Lee. "Do not disappoint me, Barath Drakis."

"I will not," said Lee. A tinge of guilt struck him. He knew that he would indeed soon be betraying the captain's trust. And even though he was the enemy, Lee was beginning to respect him.

"Good." Lanmore slapped Lee on the back. "I enjoy having officers without the arrogance of nobility draped about their shoulders."

The barracks was no more than a two-story warehouse with dozens and dozens of three-man bunks lining the walls and a series of long tables and benches in the center. A brazier, filled with hot coals, had been placed between the tables on either side of the entrance. A crude flight of wooden spiral stairs stood dead center. Only a few dozen men were scattered about. Some were sleeping, others playing cards and dice at the tables, and a few were reading over paperwork or going over maps. Most took notice as they entered, but none spoke.

"Officers of the Reborn King live the same as the common soldier," said Lanmore as they entered. "We're lucky to have arrived when we did. The day watch is on duty now, so we'll not have to spend the next hour on introductions. The night watch is mostly commoners like us. They don't care much about who comes and goes." He walked toward the stairs. "We'll be bunking on the second floor."

The upper floor was much like the lower, except for several casks of ale neatly stacked along the far left wall. Lanmore removed his pack, throwing it on an empty bed and motioning for Lee to do the same. He then escorted him back outside and around the side of the keep to the quartermaster's stores. In exchange for the wooden token, Lee was first of all handed a tunic embroidered with the sigil of Angrääl. Showing on the sleeves was one red star signifying his rank of lieutenant. Next, he was supplied with a set of studded leather armor. He was also offered a sword, but told the quartermaster that he would rather use his own weapon; the man looked down at it and nodded approvingly. A large, burlap bundle containing a commissioned man's coat, boots, and trousers contained the final items that would complete Lee's transformation into an officer.

"Anything else, you have to buy for yourself," said the quartermaster grumpily. "There are smiths and armorers in Kratis who can outfit you if you want something sturdier than plain leather. I'd also go there if you need your sword tended. I don't trust the garrison smithy."

Lee thanked the man and left.

It was nearly full dark by the time they returned to the barracks. The day watch was just beginning to file in, all of who took immediate notice of Lee and Lanmore. Hissing whispers of speculation could be heard throughout the room as servants busied themselves preparing the table for the evening meal.

"We needn't bother with this lot tonight unless you want to," said Lanmore. "I intend to take my meal in the bunk, then get a good night's sleep."

Lee knew he should at least try to gather information, but felt it may be better to speak with Lanmore in a more relaxed setting. "I think I will do the same."

Lanmore called over a servant and instructed him to have their meals brought up. The meal was a simple beef stew and salted bread, along with a cup of sweet wine. As simple as it was, Lee was grateful for the sustenance. After a servant retrieved their plates and cups, Lee stripped off his clothing and changed into a pair of heavy cotton pants and thick wool socks. He felt his muscles relax as he eased into his bunk. He had to fight the urge to fall asleep.

"May I ask you a question, sir?" Lee rolled over so he could see Lanmore.

"Ask," he replied, yawning.

"How did you end up in the service of the Reborn King?"

Lanmore smiled and slid down beneath his blanket. "At one time, I was captain of the Kaltinor city guard. I was accused of theft and treason by the city temples and forced to flee or face execution." He laughed softly. "I journeyed north to Hazrah and caught word that Angrääl was seeking soldiers. I heard that a man could remake himself there, no matter what burdens his past carried. It sounded like a good idea at the time, so off I went. The funny thing is, as it turned out, it was Angrääl that controlled the temples in Kaltinor, and probably gave the order to have me accused in the first place."

"If you know this, why not return?"

Lanmore closed his eyes. "I have pledged my fealty to the Reborn King. I couldn't return now, even if I wished to. You'll understand when you're in his presence. When that happens, there's no turning back—ever."

Having said that, he drifted off into a deep sleep.

Lee awoke abruptly a short time later and instinctively reached for his sword.

"Don't move!" yelled a harsh voice.

He looked up to see five soldiers, all of them pointing crossbows at him. He raised his hands.

"What is the meaning of this?" roared Captain Lanmore. "Answer me at once!"

From the stairs, Lord Pollus strode toward them, glaring at the captain. "It would seem, my dear captain, that you have brought a spy along with you." His gaze fell on Lee. "Don't bother with denials—Lord Nal'Thain."

Lanmore leaped from his bunk. "Barath?"

Lee's eyes never left Lord Pollus. "How did you find me out?"

Pollus laughed. "Your son, My Lord. How else?"

CHAPTER 17

L inis returned shortly before dawn, just as the armies were preparing to march. He and his scouts had found the cliffs unguarded, though they had seen Vrykol lurking there.

"The Vrykol fell back the moment we approached," Linis told Theopolou.

Theopolou nodded and left to inform the king. Linis joined Kaylia and Selena, both of who had been ordered to join the rear guard. Kaylia was clearly unhappy about this.

"I don't like being treated like I'm some helpless child in need of protection," she complained.

"We can't afford for you to be harmed," Linis told her. "If you are killed or captured, what would happen to Gewey?"

"Besides," Selena added, "you may not need protection, but I do. And I feel much better with you at my side." She smiled. "And didn't you promise your husband that you would stay safe until his return?"

Kaylia mumbled angrily but did not pursue the matter further.

Soon, the huge army set off. Marching at the head were Nehrutu, Mohanisi, the elf bowmen, and the human shield bearers. Theopolou, along with Chiron, led the vast mass of elf soldiers just behind this front line. The other elders were scattered among the elves, serving as captains. At the rear, led by King Lousis, the Althetans were just behind Kaylia, Selena, and Linis.

Selena was surrounded by what remained of the Valsharan guard, along with a few other knights who had arrived following the siege. Ertik had refused to let her out of his sight and spent most of his time seeing to her every need.

"How are you faring?" The boisterous voice came from behind. It was King Lousis, sat astride a great black warhorse.

"We are well," replied Selena. "And you?"

"I long for battle, High Lady." He leaped from his horse with the vigor of a much younger man. "I hope that the elves don't win the day before I arrive."

"I pray they do," said Selena. "I would not see you in peril. Your people need you. As do all free people of the world. In these times, a stout heart and firm resolve is in short supply."

"I think they need you far more than they need me, my Lady." His friendly smile was a welcome respite from the nervous tension of men and elves preparing for war. "Your name will become a battle cry after today, and Valshara, a symbol of hope for victory."

"Indeed, I hope not, Your Highness," said Selena. "I would not have men and women going to their deaths with my name on their lips. Though I fear it may be so."

The entrance to the road leading to Valshara was half a day's march away. Soon, the men began singing songs of victory and glory, and though the elves did not join in, it seemed to lift their spirits, nonetheless. Theopolou had earlier sent a small advance force to secure the road and paths leading to the cliffs, and reports now came back that the way was clear.

"Whatever they have planned, it is to wait until we are within the cliff walls," said Linis. "They know we come, yet refuse to guard an easily defensible road. Our numbers would count for nothing in that narrow passage."

"Are you worried?" asked Selena.

"I am," he replied. "You should stay near me at all times." He tapped Kaylia's shoulder. "You too. I will not explain to Gewey why I allowed you to be hurt."

"He knows full well that I can look after myself," Kaylia shot back. "If something happens to me, the fault will be mine."

"That will not matter to him." He looked up and saw the Stone of the Tower come into view. His face grew solemn. "Frankly, at this moment, I wish he were here with us."

All nodded in agreement.

Word came back that the advance force had secured all access points to the cliffs, and that the road was abandoned. The Temple, however, was not. From the cliffs, they spotted dozens of archers lining the battlements, and smoke billowing up from within.

Slowly, the huge army funneled into the narrow valley, guarded from above on each side by fifty elf archers. It took a full hour before the Althetan soldiers at the rear began to creep forward.

The king rode up, sword in hand, and clearly eager for battle. "I'd ask you to halt here and allow my men to pass," he said.

Kaylia opened her mouth to protest, but Selena held out her arm and bowed to signal her compliance. She and the others made their way over to the cliff face, allowing the soldiers the room they needed. Nearly half of them had entered the passage when a low horn blast sounded in the distance. Not from the temple, but from the north, behind the human lines. A second blast rang out.

"What is that?" asked Selena.

Linis drew his weapon. "I believe we are flanked, High Lady."

Orders were shouted by commanders as the Althetan army slowly turned. Another horn echoed against the cliffs, followed by a low rumble. Kaylia, Linis, and the Valsharan guard formed a protective line in front of the High Lady. The rumble grew to a roar as hundreds more frenzied voices joined in. The king rode up, fury in his eyes.

"We are out-maneuvered," he yelled. "Linis. Inform Theopolou."

Linis nodded and pushed his way through the soldiers into the narrow passage where more Althetans were still trying to turn and exit. Linis had to knock several to the ground in order to make passage. Once clear of the lines, he ran full speed to the elves, who were less than a quarter mile ahead. He grabbed the first elf he reached and ordered him to relate to Theopolou what had happened, then raced back to Selena and Kaylia. By the time he reached them, he could hear that the battle had already begun.

The king was shouting orders and waving his sword wildly. He tried to spur his horse forward, but a dozen men surrounded him, and would not allow him to move. Selena was still against the cliff face, clinging to Kaylia's sleeve.

"Are you all right?" asked Linis.

Selena nodded. "I'm..."

The hairs on the back of Linis's neck stood up. He spun around to see the sky streaked with incoming arrows. The guards quickly raised their small round shields and pushed back, hiding Selena and Kaylia. Kaylia squirmed and strug-gled, but Selena tightened her grip. Linis backed away. There was no room for him, and he carried no shield. The air was now filled with the high-pitched whining of arrows. Dozens of loud thuds and cracks sounded as they sank into the ground or smashed into shields. Linis darted to one side, only just in time to avoid being skewered. One guard fell screaming, the shaft of a black-feathered arrow protruding from his chest. Two other guards reached down and pulled the man to the rock face. Selena bent down and immediately began tending his wound, but her guarding knight dragged her back to her feet.

"How dare you!" she shouted.

"We will see to him," said the knight. "You must stay behind us." As she looked down, she realized it would be useless, anyway. The guard was slumped over, eyes closed, and with a trickle of blood coming from the corner of his mouth. The arrow had pierced his lung. There was no hope.

Linis could see that the Althetans were being forced back, though he was still unable to catch sight of the enemy. A tall soldier ran up, his breastplate covered in blood.

"High Lady," said the soldier, trying to catch his breath. "The king commands that you retreat into the passage. We are outmatched, and I fear that our line may soon collapse."

"How many are there?" asked Linis.

"Nearly a thousand," he replied. "They came from nowhere. We were only just able to form ranks when they reached our lines. They fight like men possessed."

"Hold fast," said Linis. "I've sent word to Theopolou. Help is coming."

No sooner had the words left his mouth when dozens of elves came pouring out of the passage, weapons drawn.

"What is your name, soldier?" asked Linis.

"Mitchis," he replied.

"Come with me," he ordered, then turned to Selena. "As soon as the elves clear the passage, you and Kaylia go inside." Without waiting for an answer, he and Mitchis ran to meet the elf warriors.

Bellisia's face was the first one Linis recognized. In each hand, she wielded a thin, short sword. When she saw Linis approaching, she rushed to meet him.

"What has happened?" she asked urgently.

Linis nodded to Mitchis, who explained the attack.

"Our left flank is nearly gone. If it collapses, we are undone," he said.

"Go tell them that help is on the way," said Bellisia. She pointed the sword in her left hand to an elf carrying a longbow and bearing the symbol of her tribe on his leather armor. He nodded with understanding and shouted for the other archers to form a line. Bellisia reached in her belt, pulled out a small silver horn, and blew. The high-pitched sound pierced the air like the cry of an eagle.

"The humans need us to reinforce their left flank." Her voice rose above the sound of the battle. "It is time to prove our worth." She pulled three elves aside. "See that the king is unharmed. Get him to pull back to the wall if you can." They bowed quickly and obeyed. Lousis was still atop his horse, urging his men forward while his personal guard continued with their struggle to keep him from riding to the front line.

Bellisia and Linis raced to catch up with the others. As Mitchis had said, the left flank was nearly demolished. Warriors in black mail with the symbol of broken scales in bright red across their chests were starting to push through. The bodies of the dead and dying littered the ground. The elves charged forward, cutting a path through the advance. In the face of this new onslaught, the enemy panicked and quickly fell back. The Althetan soldiers began to pursue, but their commanders wisely called them back and reformed the lines.

Linis looked to his right. The elves had arrived just in time to prevent the enemy from crushing the Althetan center as well. They met the forces of Angrääl with sustained fury as the clang and clatter of steel sang its deadly song.

For nearly an hour, the battle raged as more elf reinforcements arrived. On three separate occasions, it looked as if the Althetan center would break, but somehow they managed to hold on long enough for more elf support to arrive and push the Angrääl soldiers back. Linis had slain at least a dozen men, and Bellisia just as many. Linis was impressed with her fighting skill and smiled every time he caught sight of her.

By mid-morning, the Angrääl forces were in full retreat, with the men of Althetas hard on their heels. Nearly half of the elf force had come out of the passage to aid in the battle. Hundreds had died. The king's right leg was broken when his horse reared and threw him during the final surge forward, after which his personal guards were able to carry him to the cliffs and place him beside Selena and Kaylia.

Bellisia was cleaning her sword on the tunic of a dead enemy soldier when Linis approached.

"You fight well," he remarked. "As well as any seeker."

Bellisia smiled, looking prideful. "My father was a seeker. He trained me until I came of age and chose the life of a scholar and healer instead." Her smile vanished as she cast her gaze over the battlefield. "A skill I believe we will need at this moment."

Theopolou appeared from the passage with half a dozen elves. Linis waved his arm in greeting and went to meet him. Bellisia walked beside.

"What are your losses?" asked Theopolou.

"I cannot say," replied Bellisia. "Substantial, I would think. The enemy was well prepared."

Theopolou led them to where the king was being tended. Lousis smiled as they approached and sat up straight.

"Are you badly injured?" asked Theopolou.

"No." The king looked at his leg with disgust. "But my fighting is done for now. How about you? Were your elves assaulted in the passage?"

Theopolou shook his head. "No. I believe the enemy were counting on breaking through our rear and attacking us that way."

"If you hadn't sent your elves back to help, they would have," said Lousis. "I mourn the loss of those who died in our defense."

Theopolou bowed. "As I mourn the loss of your soldiers. They died bravely facing overwhelming numbers."

"What will we do now?" asked Linis.

"We will do what we came here to do," said Theopolou. Determination burned in his eyes. "Nehrutu and Mohanisi are with the archers and shield bearers, one thousand yards away from the gates. They await my return." He turned to Linis and placed a hand on his shoulder. "You should know that the bodies of three of your seekers hang from the walls."

Linis lowered his eyes and clenched his fists. "I will come with you."

Theopolou nodded. "What are your plans, Your Highness?"

King Lousis shifted uncomfortably, digging a rock from beneath his thigh and tossing it aside. "The wagons are being emptied to carry the wounded back to the city. Those that can't be moved will be cared for here." He looked out on the battlefield riddled with bodies. "I will have my men take care of the dead. Rest assured that the elves will be taken care of as well."

"Are there captives?" asked Bellisia.

"A few," the king replied. "I suppose I must see to them until this is over. I'm hoping that we can learn something useful from our prisoners."

Selena approached; blood from treating the wounded covered her clothes. Kaylia was at her side.

"I will remain with the High Lady and Kaylia," said Bellisia. "I believe my healing skills will be of greater use than my skills in battle."

"Your help is most welcome," said Selena.

"I will join you and Theopolou," said Kaylia.

"No," shot Linis. "My heart is full of vengeance. I am told that bodies of my kin hang from the walls of our enemy. I cannot promise to protect you, as my fury may blind me. You will stay here."

Kaylia could see from Linis's expression that would not be moved. Reluctantly, she stepped back.

Theopolou bowed to King Lousis and Selena. "We must hurry." He spun around and headed back to the passage. Linis and the guard followed close behind.

"It is done," said Selena.

"What is that, High Lady?" asked Kaylia.

Selena lowered her eyes. "Human and elf have bled together. Whatever our destiny may be, we will now meet it together."

She sighed. "I only wish that the cost of peace were not so high."

CHAPTER 18

The wind whipped between the tall cliff walls, blowing the banners tight. Linis and Theopolou pushed their way through the ranks until they reached the vanguard where Nehrutu and Mohanisi awaited. Linis fixed his eyes on the tall, thick walls of Valshara. Just as Theopolou had said, three bodies swung in the breeze just left of the main gate. He boiled with fury as he recognized Sitrisa, Prustos, and Santisos. Their faces were swollen, bruised, and caked with dried blood and grime—their clothes tattered and stained.

"They will pay for this dishonor." Linis drew his long knife and grabbed the blade tightly. His blood trickled down to the hilt. "I swear this."

"You must wait until the gates are down and we vanquish the archers before you charge," warned Nehrutu.

"My fury does not make me a fool," Linis snapped.

"Of course not," Nehrutu replied. "And you are not alone. The sight of my kin displayed with such malice and contempt fills me with rage as well." His eyes fixed on the mutilated bodies. "I swear that you will have vengeance. They will understand wrath and fear after this day."

"Then ready yourself to advance," commanded Theopolou. The shield bearers lined up in front of the archers, with Nehrutu and Mohanisi just behind them, weapons drawn.

"Attack!"

Slowly, the column inched forward. Trumpets blared from behind the wall. Men scrambled about behind the bowmen manning the battlements as orders were frantically shouted. Theopolou and Linis stood shoulder to shoulder, watching as their forces came within range of the enemy's arrows. The thwack of dozens of bowstrings rang out and streaks of death flew across the sky. The shields came up, and the elves crouched behind them. But the arrows never found a mark. Both Nehrutu and Mohanisi stood absolutely still, their arms outstretched. A blast of wind gusted up, forcing the oncoming arrows back. The clatter of wood on stone punctuated what had happened, bringing murmurs of shock and approval throughout the elf ranks. Soon this was followed by loud cheering. The humans on the wall merely stood in silent amazement and fear.

"Why would they need the shields?" wondered Linis.

"I think it is for when Nehrutu and Mohanisi bring down the gates," Theopolou answered. "It may be beyond their skill to do both things at once."

The elves drew closer until, finally, they were in range. The archers stood and fired, and all but one of them found his mark. Men on the battlements slumped and disappeared. Others fell screaming from the wall. This success brought another round of cheers from the elves. The defenders returned fire, but again, Nehrutu and Mohanisi sent their missiles back. After four more volleys from the elf archers, the wall was clear.

Nehrutu and Mohanisi remained where they were, their heads now facing down and arms folded. Then the earth began to shake violently. A moment later, the gates to Valshara burst into flames. The heat could be felt all the way back to where Theopolou and Linis were standing. In retaliation, several arrows flew from over the wall, but they were completely random and undirected. Only a few came close enough to strike the shields. The ground continued to shake until finally the gates burst into flaming splinters. The elf archers then crept forward, all the time keeping their eyes fixed on the ramparts.

"Forward!" cried Theopolou.

At a quick march, the army moved in behind the archers just as they reached the shattered gates. Smoldering pieces of wood littered the ground, but these were quickly stomped out by elf warriors. Smoke obscured their vision, making it impossible to see more than a few feet beyond the gate.

"To me!" roared Nehrutu, holding his sword high.

Black-cloaked figures appeared from out of the acrid, gray smoke. First, one, then another, until five stood in the entrance. Five more were standing just behind them. The elf archers fired in a volley. The arrows struck home but had no effect.

"Vrykol!" shouted Nehrutu. "You must take their heads!"

The archers dropped their bows and drew their long knives. The Vrykol were tall, menacing, and motionless. A thick ball of flame shot out from in front of Nehrutu and Mohanisi engulfing the beasts, but the flames died the moment they reached them. When the shield bearers were only a few feet away, the Vrykol stepped forward in unison. Their blades struck with tremendous force, shattering all but two shields and throwing the soldiers to the ground. The elves leaped over the fallen humans, hacking and slashing furiously. Two Vrykol were laid open across their chests. Foul, black ooze poured out of the wounds, but this did nothing to stop them.

The humans scrambled to their feet, but the elf line blocked their way, and they could only watch as the Vrykol cut the elves down, one by one. After the first wave of elves was slain, the Vrykol fell back to the gate to await another charge. Stumbling over the bodies of their fallen elf comrades, the Althetan soldiers attacked. It was a brave but futile gesture, and they were immediately cut to pieces.

Nehrutu and Mohanisi charged in together, followed by a dozen elf warriors. As they clashed with the Vrykol, a wave of air erupted, throwing the creatures back and slamming them into the other Vrykol standing at the rear. Nehrutu took three heads with unearthly speed, and Mohanisi two more. The Vrykol countered, killing three elf warriors and pushing them back past the threshold. A second blast of air then knocked two Vrykol off their feet. Nehrutu moved swiftly in to take another head. Ten elves were at his back, moving to engage the rest. Soon the Vrykol were overwhelmed—hacked to pieces by vengeful blades.

Beyond the gates, the center of the courtyard was empty. At the rear, just in front of the temple, a six-foot-high wooden wall had been erected. It spanned the entire breadth of the yard

Nehrutu held out his arms to halt the attack. "I need archers, now!" he called.

The words were barely out of his mouth when arrows flew from behind the wall in a low arc. Nehrutu and Mohanisi tried to deflect them by creating another blast of air, but their actions were too late. Only a few missiles were sent back, and three elves were struck, including Mohanisi.

"No time to wait," shouted Theopolou from behind. He forced his way past Nehrutu, followed by Linis and a long stream of screaming elves.

Nehrutu looked down at Mohanisi and saw a red-feathered arrow protruding from his belly. His anger boiled as he drew in the flow. Theopolou and the others were already halfway across the yard. He let loose all the power he could muster. A ten-foot section of the wooden wall heaved up and flew against the side of the temple, sending the men behind it scurrying back.

From both sides of the battlements, and atop the roof of the temple, more archers appeared, all eager and ready to rain down hell on the advancing elves.

Mohanisi struggled to his feet. Blood soaked his tunic and trousers. "Bring down the wall," he told Nehrutu. "I will handle the archers."

A tempest erupted directly above the heads of Theopolou, Linis, and the other attackers. Dozens of arrows that were only a heartbeat away from causing mass death and injury were thrown clear. At the same time, Nehrutu destroyed another section of the wall just as the elves were about to engage the enemy. The defending archers above now abandoned their positions on the wall, dropping their bows and unsheathing their swords.

"That's enough," Nehrutu said to Mohanisi. The tempest dissipated. He helped his friend to the wall and allowed him to gently slide down.

"I will be fine," said Mohanisi. "Attend to the more seriously injured." He looked up to see Linis and Theopolou already cutting a path through the human enemy.

Elves continued to pour in through the destroyed gate to join the fray. More soldiers came running out from the temple and down from the battlements to meet them.

"The temple will soon be ours," said Nehrutu. "I will need your help, my friend." He pulled the arrow from the wound. Mohanisi grimaced. "Be still." He placed his hands on Mohanisi's stomach. In moments, the bleeding had stopped.

"You can complete this once the battle is done," said Mohanisi, smiling. "You have done enough for now. Go aid Theopolou."

Nehrutu squeezed Mohanisi's shoulder and leaped to his feet. "I shall return as soon as I am able."

The battle continued to rage. By now, the Angrääl soldiers had formed a shield wall around the main entrance to the temple and had managed to stop the elf advance. Several elves fell to spears thrust from over the rims of the shields. Nehrutu drew in the flow and released a blast of air, pushing the humans back. He could have easily destroyed the line but dared not use more force with the elves so close at hand. Another blast pushed the soldiers further back, this time creating a small gap. It was all the opportunity Theopolou needed. He immediately ordered the elves in, and within seconds, the line was scattered. The sounds of clashing swords mingled with the cries of the dying.

Nehrutu held back as the elves finished off the remaining soldiers. Dozens simply threw down their weapons and fell to their knees once it became clear that the fight was lost. By the time the courtyard was secure, hundreds of soldiers lay dead, along with several dozen elves.

Without wasting a second, Theopolou ordered the courtyard cleared and began gathering the wounded. Several elves wanted to enter the temple, but he told them to wait. Linis climbed the wall and retrieved the bodies of his fallen comrades.

"The interior is vast," Theopolou said to Nehrutu as he helped carry a wounded elf. "There may be many more soldiers inside. And they will have had time to set traps and prepare a defense. It may take time to dislodge them."

"The rear of the temple is blocked," said Nehrutu. "There is no escape. Perhaps you should offer them their lives in exchange for surrender." He glanced at the prisoners, who had been herded against the north wall. "It would seem they have no intent to fight to the last man."

Theopolou nodded. "And for that, I am grateful. Too much blood has been spilled this day."

"What will you do with them?" asked Nehrutu.

Theopolou shrugged. "It is for the High Lady of Valshara to decide their fate. It was Amon Dähl that was attacked, and her people who were slaughtered when the temple was taken." He shook his head slowly. "I do not know if they will be shown any mercy."

Nehrutu looked up to see Linis several yards away, kneeling over the bodies of his seekers. "I am not certain they should be."

Theopolou tightened his jaw and walked over to where the prisoners were being held. He picked out one of the soldiers and had him brought to the main door of the temple.

"Tell any remaining inside that they are to throw down their arms and come out at once," Theopolou ordered. "If they do not, then the Temple of Valshara will become their tomb."

The soldier nodded and stepped inside the temple. More than an hour passed before he returned. By then Selena and Kaylia had joined Theopolou. Tears welled in Selena's eyes at the sight of so many dead.

"They will come out," said the soldier. "But you must promise that they will be spared."

"I promise to burn this place down around them if they don't come out at once," said Selena furiously. "You tell them that I will send their ashes back to Angrääl in a box."

The soldier lowered his eyes, clearly afraid. "Yes, my Lady." He turned and re-entered the temple.

A short while later, the door swung open again. Soldiers began to file out, unarmed, with their hands on their heads.

"What will you do with them?" asked Kaylia.

"Until my anger subsides—nothing," Selena replied. "I will not act until I am certain that my mind, and not my heart, speaks for me."

They watched as the soldiers were led to the north wall. Once they were all out, a small group of elves entered to check that the temple was indeed empty. A few minutes later, the door flew open, and a woman was shoved through. An elf held a long blade at her back. Kaylia recognized her at once.

"Salmitaya," she whispered, drawing her knife.

Salmitaya stood there, defiant and proud. She was dressed in a long black robe, with a silver cord tied at the waist. Her light brown hair was pulled back and interlaced with white and gold, bound together at the back by white silk.

"I knew I would fall to an elf blade," said Salmitaya, glaring at Kaylia. "But I would not have it happen by your hand."

Selena stepped in front of Kaylia. "You may yet save your wretched skin. I have heard your name before—Salmitaya. And I have known of your evil works longer than you think." She grabbed Salmitaya's chin and forced her to look into her eyes. "I also know that you are high in the council of the Reborn King."

Salmitaya jerked her head free of Selena's grasp. "You know nothing, fool." She shut her eyes. "Kill me and be done with it."

Selena scrutinized Salmitaya for a full minute. "I may. Or perhaps I should send you back to Angrääl."

Salmitaya's eyes opened wide with fear.

"Yes. That's what I'll do." Selena stepped back and smiled.

"Please," cried Salmitaya. "You can't..."

"I can, and I will," said Selena. Her tone was low and dangerous. "Or do you wish to remain here?"

"I wish you to kill me," she replied.

"I say we give her what she wants," said Kaylia, still holding her knife.

Linis approached. He snatched Salmitaya by the arm and shook her violently. "Who had the elves hung from the walls?"

Salmitaya said nothing.

"Answer him," Selena commanded. "Or I swear I will send you back."

"Yanti," Salmitaya answered after a pause.

"Who is Yanti?" asked Selena. "Was it he who ordered the taking of Valshara?"

"You will find out soon enough." Salmitaya shook her head. "But understand that I know nothing of value to you. I am disgraced in the eyes of my lord. If you intend to question me, you will get nothing, for I know nothing. If you set me free, I must continue to fight you. That is ... if I'm allowed to live. So you have to kill me."

"It appears you fear returning to your master more than you fear death," said Selena. She looked up at the elf who had brought Salmitaya out. "Put her with the other prisoners for now. We have wounded to attend. I will decide her fate later."

Linis glared at Salmitaya, then released her.

"Do you think she will tell us anything?" asked Theopolou, once Salmitaya had been led away.

"I don't think she knows anything," Selena replied.

"Then why keep her alive?" asked Kaylia.

Selena bowed her head. "As I said, I will not decide anything until my anger lessens. Whoever Yanti is, it is clear he escaped before we arrived."

"He may be among the prisoners," offered Theopolou. "If not, they may know where he has gone. I will have them questioned."

Selena nodded in agreement. "Thank you. Let me know what you discover."

The rest of the day was spent tending to the wounded. Once Nehrutu had cared for Mohanisi, he and Kaylia began treating the most severe injuries. Mohanisi was too weak to assist, so was taken inside the temple and given a bed. Selena ordered that the wounded from the first battle be brought in, and soon the entire courtyard was filled. King Lousis refused further treatment until all the men and elves had been seen to first. By nightfall, Nehrutu and Kaylia were exhausted, stumbling from person to person as if in a daze. Finally, Selena decided to intervene.

"You must rest," Selena said to Kaylia. "We have other healers among us. You have already saved the most critically wounded."

"I will rest when Nehrutu does the same," said Kaylia.

"Then that time is now," came the voice of Mohanisi from behind her. "I am now well enough to continue what you have started. I will take over until morning." He strode off to relieve Nehrutu.

While a small group of elves led by Linis were gathering the bodies of their fallen kin and preparing them for the funeral rites, King Lousis ordered that his slain soldiers should be taken back to Althetas. The bodies of the enemy were to be burned and buried near the passage entrance, along with their weapons and armor.

With the exception of Salmitaya's clothing and a few extra books, Selena found that her chambers were pretty much as she had left them. She ordered the bed clothing to be burned and replaced, after which she had all of Salmitaya's belongings packed away. After washing and changing into a plain cotton dress and suede moccasins, she settled into her plush chair. Closing her eyes, she tried to push the visions of battle from her mind. She was still sitting like this when a light rap sounded at her door. King Lousis entered, along with a guard helping him to walk on his broken leg. He was followed inside by Theopolou, Linis, and Nehrutu.

"It is good to see you back where you belong," said Linis, smiling.

Selena rose from her chair. "As soon as possible, I want the injured in the courtyard brought inside the temple."

"We are already clearing out the rooms," said Theopolou. "I can have the beds ready within the hour. Though, I am not certain what to do about the prisoners. We cannot keep them here indefinitely."

"I will decide what is to be done with them in the morning," said Selena. "Keep them under guard until then."

"And Salmitaya?" asked Linis.

"I will speak with her again shortly," Selena replied. "She will be kept apart from the soldiers. We have a small holding area in the west wing."

"I would like to be with you," said Linis.

"No," Selena replied. "I will speak to her alone."

"Should you decide to spare the soldiers," said Lousis, "I can have my men construct cages in a small compound outside Althetas."

"I will keep that in mind," said Selena. "How many did we lose in battle?"

"More than three hundred men and elves," answered Lousis. "But our enemy lost three times as many. Angrääl will think twice before moving against us now."

"This was nothing," said Theopolou. "A skirmish, at best. When the Dark Knight sends his armies south, we must be ready. This defeat may only serve to anger him. And it may cause him to march sooner than he had originally planned."

Lousis furrowed his brow. "Are you saying we should have held off our attack?"

"Not at all," Theopolou replied. "This victory has solidified the bond between elf and human. And it will show potential allies that our defeat is anything but certain."

"It will go a long way toward helping our cause when I assemble the kings and queens," said Lousis. "That must be my first priority. I shall leave tomorrow."

"Are you well enough to travel?" asked Selena.

Lousis held his head high and smiled broadly. "The king of Althetas will not be laid low by a broken leg, High Lady."

Nehrutu leaned over with his hands outstretched to Lousis's injured leg. "With your permission."

The king nodded. "If you are well enough."

Nehrutu touched the leg, eyes closed. Lousis gasped, reached for Nehrutu's shoulder, and cried out in pain. The king's guard rushed to his side, but by then, it was over. Nehrutu straightened his back and heaved a sigh.

"It is done," he said.

Lousis tenuously put his weight on the injured leg. A low chuckle turned into a full-on belly laugh as he began stomping his feet hard. "If only my people possessed such power."

Nehrutu smiled weakly. "Perhaps one day they will. I cannot say with certainty that such abilities are beyond your kind."

Lousis slapped Nehrutu on the shoulder. "What a wondrous notion." He turned to Selena. "I must beg your leave. Thanks to our elf ally, I can now see to my men as a king should. Unless you object, I will be leaving fifty soldiers here to give you aid. I will also send more men and materials to repair damage done during the battle."

"Your help is well received, Your Highness," said Selena.

The king bowed low and left, his guard struggling to keep pace.

"A strong leader," remarked Linis with an approving nod. "We could use many more like him."

"Indeed," Theopolou agreed. "And his haste is warranted. We must decide our next course of action."

"I intend to join Millet and Dina in Sharpstone," said Linis. "Angrääl will certainly move its armies down the Goodbranch River. If they secure that, they will have a supply line leading all the way to Baltria."

"I agree," said Theopolou. "But we must remember that elf and human are not united there. Your presence may be disruptive."

"I can ask Lord Ganflin for assistance," said Linis. "And Lord Broin as well. The sight of human lords alongside elves may ease fears."

"Then you should depart with King Lousis," said Theopolou.

"I will send what is left of the Knights of Amon Dähl with you," Selena added. "Dina sent out a general request for aid, but in light of the attack, I doubt that many responded. I would not have her mounting a defense with nothing but sell-swords. I can send instructions ahead of your arrival by messenger flock."

"That will be wise," said Linis. "Even if Broin and Ganflin are able to help, it may still take time for them to assemble men and supplies. Millet and Dina should be made aware of the situation as soon as possible."

"And what will you do?" Selena asked Theopolou.

"I must see to the situation with my kin from the Steppes," he replied mournfully. "I cannot allow Angrääl to divide us further, and I am certain that once the elves have served the Reborn King's purpose, they will be disposed of."

"How do you intend to accomplish this?" asked Linis. "Will our people even accept them now that they have spilled elf blood?"

"I have spilled elf blood, Linis," said Theopolou. "During the first split, I led thousands to their death against our own kind. I will not sentence our brothers and sisters to death for sins I have committed myself unless all hope of redemption is exhausted."

"So you will go to the Steppes yourself?" Linis's face was dark with worry. "Then you should see if Mohanisi or Nehrutu will travel with you as well."

"I cannot," said Nehrutu. "I must await Aaliyah and Gewey. But I agree that one of us should go. I will speak to Mohanisi tonight."

"And what shall you do, Kaylia?" asked Selena.

"I will wait here for Gewey," she replied. "If you will allow it, High Lady."

Selena smiled. "You are now a part of this temple and can stay as long as you wish. And I could certainly use your help in the coming days. At least until Gewey's return."

"With your approval, I would like to leave some of my own people here in addition to the king's," said Theopolou. "The elders will be returning to their homes to organize a defense of their lands, and to help other elves understand our cause. There will still be much resistance to these new ideas. Though considering what has happened here today, I doubt that resistance will persist for long."

Selena nodded. "Your people are welcome to stay, and their help is also welcome. But now I must rest. I have much to think about. Kaylia, would you find Ertik and have him bring Salmitaya here in two hours?"

"Yes, High Lady," replied Kaylia.

The party bowed and left. Selena walked the floor of her chambers, looking closely at each and every object. She was loath to touch anything until it had been cleaned. The mere idea of the beasts who'd slaughtered her people pawing through her possessions made her skin crawl. She wasn't sure what to do about Salmitaya—or the enemy soldiers, for that matter. The screams of her people echoing through the halls of Valshara were still fresh in her mind, and she knew this was not the time for rash choices. She must still her anger first.

As she slipped into her bed and closed her eyes, fatigue took over. Though feeling a bit guilty for resting while others were still laboring, she could feel that she was spent. She hoped a couple of hours' rest would be sufficient to clear her mind and rejuvenate her body. The soft bed cradled her, pulling her into a deep slumber. And though much blood had been spilled, she couldn't help but feel happy to be back in her bed and in the temple she loved.

I shall restore this place, was her final thought before consciousness faded.

CHAPTER 19

Selena was shaken out of her slumber. As her vision cleared, she saw Ertik standing over her, his face awash with worry.

"I'm sorry, High Lady," he said. "But you ordered the woman Salmitaya brought to you in two hours."

Selena stretched and rubbed the back of her neck. She was not exactly rejuvenated but felt more like herself than before. "Give me a moment to change, then bring her in."

Ertik bowed and left.

Selena searched her wardrobe and found a long, blue linen dress with the symbols of the Nine Gods embroidered in white on the front. She doubted that Salmitaya would have chosen to wear such a thing, but still, Selena wished she had brought other attire with her. She pulled her hair back, tied it in a loose ponytail, and looked at herself in the mirror. The lines of worry and age were carved deeper than ever before. She sighed, scolding herself for her vanity.

"Bring her," she called out firmly. The door opened and in walked Salmitaya, hands bound in front of her, Ertik scowling behind.

"Cut her bonds."

Ertik hesitated for just a moment before drawing his dagger and cutting the rope.

Selena sat in her chair and motioned for Salmitaya to sit across from her. "Please, leave us," she told Ertik. Once he had reluctantly departed, she took a deep breath. The anger still boiled in her breasts.

"What do you want from me?" Salmitaya demanded, as defiant as ever.

"I'm not sure," Selena replied. "Perhaps nothing. Maybe just to look at the face that had my temple captured and its people slaughtered."

Salmitaya sneered. "Then you will be disappointed—High Lady. When I arrived, Valshara was already taken."

"Is that so?" She looked into Salmitaya's eyes. The woman masked her fear well. "If that is true, then why not plead for mercy? Why wish for death? You speak as if you would prefer it, rather than being returned to your master."

"If you don't kill me now, I shall die soon enough." She shifted in her seat. "If you imprison me, then I will languish in squalor until Angrääl returns and destroys this place. Then die I surely will, and very slowly as punishment for my failure."

"If you are so certain your master will kill you, why return? Why not flee?"

Salmitaya sneered. "You know nothing. Don't you think I've tried to run away? You imagine I would be under the lash of someone like Yanti if there were any other way? If it were possible, of course, I would disappear. But I can't. And even if I could elude Yanti, I've been in the presence of the Reborn King. I've heard his true name. I am bound to serve him until I die. There is no other way." Her lips trembled at the mention of her true master. "And when he comes—when he has you put in chains and brought before him, you will give yourself to him too."

"I think you underestimate me," said Selena.

Salmitaya laughed. "It is you who have underestimated him. Do you think this petty victory means anything? Do you think allying yourself with the elves will save you? Nothing you can do will stop what is coming. He possesses the power of the gods. By his will, he has imprisoned them. Such a man will not be defeated by the pitiful force you have gathered. And when the time comes, not even your godling will be able to save you. No. Soon, even Gewey Stedding will be his as well, along with everything and everyone else in this cursed world."

"If you know what Gewey is, then you can't possibly think that your king can gain power over him," Selena scoffed. "He is powerful, yes. But he is still just a man."

"That may be, but the Reborn King has laid low the gods of this world in one fell stroke." She cocked her head. "They are nine—he is one. Gewey will either serve or die. As for me, you waste your time speaking to me. I know nothing of value. And you gain nothing by keeping me alive."

"That is for me to decide," said Selena. "For now, I give you your life. But you need not fear. I will kill you myself before I allow Yanti, or your king, to take you." Selena called for Ertik. "We will speak again very soon."

Selena returned to bed. She knew what she must do next. She had known from the beginning. The captured soldiers could not be released. They must die. But such things could wait until morning. One night more without being the instrument of death was all she asked for—and she would have it.

The next morning, the temple was a beehive of activity. Selena ran into Ertik on her way to the kitchen. He had already prepared her breakfast and was bringing it to her room.

"Thank you, but I'd rather eat in the dining hall," she explained. "Could you find Theopolou and King Lousis and ask them to join me?"

Ertik bowed and ran down the hallway, the tray of food still in his hands. When Selena entered, the east dining hall was filled nearly to capacity. Elves and humans dined together, talking and laughing over their meals. Selena smiled at the sight. She had only walked a few steps when cheers broke out. Mugs began banging on tables. Loud, boisterous voices calling: "Hail the High Lady of Valshara—Hail Amon Dähl," carried throughout the hall. Selena held up her hands to quiet the crowd.

"Please," she said in a clear, strong voice. "It is you who deserves all the praise. If not for you and your bravery, this holy place would still be under the control of Angrääl. Through your ability to set aside old hatreds and misgivings, you have found kinship and solidarity. It is I who applaud you." This set off another round of loud cheers.

Selena smiled graciously and sat down. She had barely begun to eat her breakfast when King Lousis and Theopolou entered.

"How go things this morning?" she asked after they were seated.

"Well," Lousis replied. "The courtyard is now clear, apart from the prisoners. The elves have made preparation for funeral rites a few miles beyond the passage. Also, I have chosen the men to remain behind. Ertik has already taken it upon himself to organize them."

"I have also chosen fifty of my people to remain," added Theopolou. "Once the funeral rites are complete, most of us will return to our lands to gather our full force. Lousis has asked me to delay my journey to the Steppes until after his council meets, and I have reluctantly agreed."

Selena nodded, pleased. "That is good. I think your presence at the council may be of great help." Her face turned grim. "And now I must tell you what is to be done with the prisoners." She lowered her eyes and breathed deeply. "They are each to be questioned—and then hanged."

"High Lady," said Lousis. "I know they have wronged you, but one does not simply execute prisoners of war."

"You said you would abide by my decision in this matter," she countered.

"I will, but..." He stopped as Selena held up her hand.

"They are not prisoners of war," she continued. "They did not march across a field and do battle. They did not sack the city of a nation with whom they were at war. No!" She rose to her feet. "They broke into my house and slaughtered my family. They are brigands and thieves, nothing more. Should a murderer of the innocent be allowed to return to his home, stained with the blood of his victims? Would you allow it in your city, King Lousis?"

The entire hall was silent. The King stared at Selena for a moment before answering. "I would not." He sighed. "But I fear this choice may haunt you."

"It haunts me even now," she replied. Her eyes turned to Theopolou, who was sitting quietly with his hands folded in front of him. "And what say you?"

"I agree," he said, after a long pause. "They are not prisoners of war. And if you look upon them as criminals, they should be treated as such. But I think that is not why you do this."

Selena stiffened. "I beg your pardon?"

"You need to show Angrääl that you are as ruthless and determined as they," said Theopolou. "You know this to be a minor victory. Since this campaign began, I have thought it odd that the Dark Knight should show his hand so soon. There was no reason to take Valshara now. Not unless he was certain he could keep it. And if that was his plan, it was a blunder. You must see to it that he is understanding of this."

He drew a deep breath before continuing. "You are correct in your actions, High Lady. And though I cannot say I would do likewise, I will not criticize your decision. You have chosen to keep the woman Salmitaya alive, and I think you do this to somehow ease your conscience. However, whatever you do, from this moment to the last, I do not feel it serves you to be in denial. You said you held off your decision until it could be made without anger, so to claim indignation now is false. And though your actions are harsh, they are justified."

Selena sat back down. "You are correct, of course. And though I hear your words, my mind is not swayed. I stand by this decision."

Theopolou nodded.

"I will order gallows built at once," said Lousis. He leaned forward and cleared his throat.

"You have something else to say?" asked Selena.

Lousis nodded hesitantly. "We found the bodies of your people. They had been piled up and burned in one of the basement rooms. I have had my men gather the ashes and the few personal possessions that remained."

Tears welled in Selena's eyes. "Thank you ... I..." She quickly wiped away the moisture. "I will see to the remains personally."

"Very well," said Louis. "Do you wish for me to arrange the executions?"

"No, Your Highness," Selena replied. "It is my decision that sends them to their death. So it must be I who will see it done. I only ask that you leave me skilled interrogators."

"I have seen to that, and they have already begun the questioning," said the king. "But I have another question. I would wish you at the council when it convenes. Will you be able to come?"

Selena shook her head. "Sadly, no. There is too much for me to do here. Sister Celandine is in Sharpstone with Millet. They are gathering the few remaining knights of Amon Dähl there to establish a foothold along the Goodbranch River. Linis is to join them, and I must see to it they have all that is required. Also, I must make contact with the other temples throughout the land. We must know who is with us, and who has been compromised." She looked at Theopolou. "Keeping

Salmitaya alive serves more than to ease my conscience." She leaned back and rubbed the bridge of her nose. "I will be sending out some of the people you leave with me into great peril. You should be aware of this."

"My men are at your command," said Lousis. "I would not leave them otherwise."

"As are the elves who are remaining," added Theopolou.

"Good," she said, smiling. "So, when do you depart?"

"I have already sent word to gather the kings and queens together," Lousis replied. "I only have a few more things to attend to, then we will be away."

"I would ask you one last favor," said Selena. "Though I cannot attend, I would like Ertik to witness the council and represent me in all matters. Unless there is some protocol that will not allow this, of course."

"Actually, I think that is wise," said Lousis. "Your presence carries weight and will be much missed. But as you cannot attend in person, your proxy should suffice. I will ensure that all there are aware he speaks on your behalf, and that he is afforded the due respect and courtesy."

"Thank you." Selena pushed her food away. "I have no appetite any longer. So, if there is nothing further?"

Theopolou and King Lousis excused themselves, leaving Selena to sit for a minute longer staring at her unfinished plate. She knew Ertik would resist the idea of leaving her side and was not looking forward to informing him of his mission.

She spent the rest of the morning walking about the halls, seeing that everything was in order. Though with Ertik about, this was a fairly pointless exercise and only served to keep her distracted. He had been busier than she thought any man was capable of. When she eventually cornered him and told him he would be leaving with King Lousis, he very nearly broke down in tears, begging her not to send him away. It was only after she promised to have an elf guard with her at all times that he reluctantly accepted the situation.

Kaylia had also made it clear that she intended to remain close to her side, having chased away several Althetan soldiers awed to be stood in the presence of the High Lady of Valshara, leader of the legendary order of Amon Dähl. At first, these admirers didn't trouble Selena, but soon questions about the Dark Knight and his time within the Order arose. These were subjects that she didn't care to discuss, and Kaylia had become adept at knowing when it was time to tell the soldiers to move on.

At midday, Selena and Kaylia sat quietly in the High Lady's chamber. A light meal of fruit and bread had been brought in. As they ate, Selena could tell that Kaylia had something on her mind. But whatever it was, something was preventing her from speaking about it.

"Kaylia," Selena began. Her voice was calm and reassuring. "You must not think me frail. If you wish to speak your mind, you must do so."

Kaylia sat her plate on the small table beside her chair. "I do not think you frail. Nor am I afraid to speak. I simply do not wish to cause you more grief so soon after all the tragedy and bloodshed that has passed." She fixed her eyes on Selena's. "I cannot help but wonder why you do not speak of the Dark Knight's time in Amon Dähl. Surely, this knowledge could be valuable to our cause."

Selena nodded. "It would, without doubt. But sadly, I know very little. When the Dark Knight first came to power, he all but destroyed this order, including all records of who he really was. Those who might have known him cannot remember anything specific about him—even those who were among us at the time of the betrayal." Her face was grave. "You must understand that the Sword of Truth wields a power beyond your imagination. My guess is that he used it to mask his true identity from the minds of those within the order who knew him."

Selena sighed. "During my early days with the order, I heard of a great knight with unparalleled strength and valor who aspired to be the protector of the Sword. But his efforts failed, and another was chosen in his place. Enraged, he abandoned his vows and sought out the Sword's resting place." She rose wearily to her feet. "That is the limit of my knowledge. The rest you already know."

"Then why not tell people this?" asked Kaylia.

Selena sighed sadly. "You ask me to speak of what has brought Amon Dähl its greatest shame. For thousands of years, we were guardians and protectors. Now..."

"I understand," said Kaylia. "I will not ask you again."

When it was time for the king and the others to depart, Selena and Kaylia, along with the majority of those who would be remaining behind in Valshara, gathered in the courtyard to see them off. Selena's eyes wandered repeatedly to the prisoners against the wall. She wanted not to hate them. She wanted to believe that her decision was the right one, and not simply made out of vengeance.

"Do not heed my earlier words," said Theopolou. Clearly, he could see her self-doubt. "I spoke from the perspective of my longing for peace. This is war, and I would do as you are. You cannot afford to second-guess yourself in these times. You will act wisely. Have faith in that."

King Lousis took Selena's hands and kissed them fondly. "I will eagerly await our next meeting, High Lady."

Selena blushed. "As do I, Your Highness."

Once the farewells were said, she watched as the party departed. Cheers erupted from both humans and elves as they passed through the shattered gates. Ertik looked back at least four times before disappearing out of sight. Theopolou's words still echoed in her mind.

She called to Lord Jeffos Windermere, the officer left behind in charge of the Althetan forces. "I want you to have your men take the prisoners to the temple basement. There, you will find an empty wine cellar. It hasn't been used in many years, and is large enough to house them for the time being." Windermere threw his fist to his chest in salute and marched away.

"I must not doubt," she whispered softly.

CHAPTER 20

The reflection of the sun on the desert sands made navigation increasingly difficult as Gewey and Aaliyah made their way back to the shore. Each dune looked much the same as the last, and Aaliyah could no longer sense the direction of her ship. Though their pace started fast and determined, signs of the poison working its way through her system began to show after only a few hours. Gewey did his best to keep the air around them cool with the flow, but each time Aaliyah stumbled or paused, he found it difficult to concentrate. On more than one occasion, a blast of hot air washed over them, making it nearly impossible to breathe. He couldn't imagine living in such a hellish place.

By mid-afternoon, their pace had decreased to a slow walk. Beads of sweat formed on Aaliyah's brow; her skin was pale, and her breathing shallow and quick. Gewey took her arm, but she pushed him away.

"No need for that," she said weakly. "It would seem the poison is stronger than I anticipated. I think I will rest for a moment." She eased herself onto the sand. "If you would just keep the air cool, I think I will be all right in a few minutes."

Gewey could tell she was lying. He tried yet again to heal her, but as before, his flow was thrown back. He clenched his fists in frustration. "There must be something I can do."

"There is nothing, I'm afraid." She reached into her pack, pulled out a blanket, and used it to cushion her head as she lay down. "I just need to rest." She closed her eyes.

"You must fight it," Gewey pleaded. "You must stay with me."

She reached up and touched his cheek. "I have fought, and it would appear I have lost. But do not be sad. I am content to have lived to be a part of your story. I have seen our kin reunited, and for all of this, I am thankful."

"Don't talk like that," said Gewey fiercely. "I will carry you if I must."

"There is no time," she said. "I will be gone in a few moments. I can feel it."

"Please." Gewey's voice cracked. "I can't let you die."

Aaliyah smiled sweetly. "This is beyond your power." She closed her eyes. "Tell Nehrutu that I am sorry. Tell him I only did what I had to do. Tell him ... I..."

Gewey lifted her head and cradled it in his arms, tears flowing freely down his face. Her body grew limp as life slipped away. Throwing his head back, he let out a primal scream. The sand all around them exploded, and the earth trembled.

As the ground settled, Gewey closed his eyes and allowed his spirit to drift to her. The light inside Aaliyah was dimming, and the warmth of her spirit growing colder. He could not bear to see her fade away in such a manner. Without consciously willing it, he suddenly found that he was drifting skyward. From above, he could now see himself holding her limp body in his arms. It was the first time he had ever viewed his human form in such a way. The scene threatened to shatter his heart. He could see his own life force burning brightly, while hers flickered and finally vanished.

Then, as if from far away, he heard the sound of a child's laughter. At first, there was only one, but then another and another joined in until he could hear dozens of mirthful infant voices all laughing at once. Not in a clamor of incoherent sound, but in the purest of harmony. Gentle at first, they grew louder and stronger until the sound surrounded him with magnificent wonder. In between each sweet voice, the tinkling of tiny bells increased the harmony. A wave of joy washed over Gewey, causing his heart to swell with unmeasured happiness. It was as though bliss were tangible—a treasure that one could possess.

He gazed back down at his body still holding Aaliyah's. He appeared the same, but her body was now surrounded by a million tiny points of light twinkling and swirling in rhythm with the laughter. The lights moved closer and closer together until they began to take form. At first, it wasn't clear, then slowly he realized it was the figure of Aaliyah. She glowed and shimmered with the light of a thousand stars. Her face beamed at him as she drifted away from her body.

Gewey reached out. It was then he felt a burning on his breast. He looked down and could see only a specter of Gerath's medallion still hanging around his neck. Heat upon heat burned into his spiritual flesh until he thought he could bear it no longer. He tried to scream, but no sound came from his lips. He could see Aaliyah above him, drifting further away. Her spirit was fading. He called to her. At the sound of his voice, she stopped.

In that instant, he understood.

He concentrated on nothing but the sounds of laughter. Within moments, they started to take on a physical form, appearing as a shimmering mist that surrounded everything. It was everywhere. Gewey could not believe he had never seen this before. He knew this was the spirit of the flow. The very soul of the earth.

Reaching out to Aaliyah's spirit, he shepherded it carefully back into her body. He then drifted down into his own. As he did so, the laughter grew distant and finally faded away altogether. He looked down at Aaliyah. Almost imperceptibly at first, her chest moved up and down as life returned. He reached into her with the flow, and this time there was no resistance. The poison was gone. He allowed his energy to run through her, slowly at first, then more and more, until he could feel her strength returning.

"That is enough, Gewey."

Her voice shocked him back into reality. She was smiling up at him, gently stroking his arm.

"How do you feel?" he asked, brushing her hair away from her face.

"Thanks to you, I feel alive," she replied. "But weary, all the same. I should rest until morning, I think." She squeezed him tight, then nestled her head in the blanket. "You felt it, didn't you?" she whispered. "The spirit of the earth."

"Yes," said Gewey. "It was beautiful. Like nothing I could have ever imagined."

"I wish I could have seen it." She sighed and promptly fell into a deep, restful sleep.

Gewey watched over her until the dawn broke, keeping the chill night air around them warm. When she awoke, the sun was just peeking over the horizon. She looked at him and scowled.

"You have not slept," she scolded, though not convincingly.

Reaching into his pack, Gewey took out his flask and a piece of flatbread. He gave these to her. "I'm fine. I've lived with less sleep before. And after traveling a swifter pace." He was remembering his journey from Valshara to the house of Theopolou.

"Still, what you did for me could not have been easy," she countered.

"Actually, it was." He tore off a piece of bread. "Though I'm not sure I could do it again." He remembered the medallion and reached to his breast. It was gone. "The gift I received from Gerath showed me how."

Aaliyah touched his chest where it had once hung. "Such a sacrifice."

Gewey smiled. "Not really. I don't need it anymore. The power that was in the medallion now lives inside of me. I can feel it there."

"That's amazing. How does it feel?"

He shrugged. "It's hard to explain. It's not much different from when I touch the spirit of another person, just many times more intense. It lacks the negative emotion and uncertainty of the mortal spirit. When your spirit left your body—in a way—I could kind of see you joining with it. Do you remember?"

"No," she said sadly. "I truly wish I could. I remember fading as if falling asleep. Then waking up in your arms. I knew you had found a way to save me."

Her words brought a blush to Gewey's cheeks. But barely had Aaliyah spoken them when she jumped to her feet, listening intensely. Gewey heard it too. Footfalls, barely audible in the sand even to Gewey's heightened senses, were just about to crest a nearby dune.

"An elf," Aaliyah whispered.

"Better than the Soufis," said Gewey, relieved.

Then, from over the top of the dune, Weila appeared.

"Perhaps not," said Aaliyah.

As Weila descended the sandy slope, Gewey could see the intensity in her expression.

"Where is my son?" she demanded before she was even half the way down.

Gewey opened his mouth to speak, but Aaliyah cut him off.

"He fell in the Dark Oasis," she said, lowering her head.

Weila's hand slid toward the knife on her belt and hovered just above it. "He was not to enter that evil place. You swore an oath to me!"

Aaliyah told her about the wolves and Pali's reason for continuing with them.

Weila spun around, clenching her fists. "Did he die well?"

"He died bravely, expelling the evil from the Black Oasis," said Aaliyah in a reverent tone. "Because of his courage, your people need not fear entering that place ever again. It is there that his spirit rests, kept safe by the life force that dwells within."

"And how do you know this?" she asked, her voice wavering. "Did you see it?"

Aaliyah told her of their battle with the Vrykol, and what their spirit had told them. "He is safe. This I swear."

"You swear nothing," she spat angrily. "You swore to protect my son, and yet his body is rotting in the jungle of the Black Oasis. Keep your oaths to yourself."

"It's not her fault," said Gewey. "It's mine. I was unable to protect him. I tried, but I couldn't reach him in time."

She sneered at Gewey. "Arrogant human. What could you have done? A weak member of a weak race who..." Her words trailed off. She closed her tear-filled eyes. "I am sorry. I should not have said that. I did not mean it."

"No need to apologize," said Gewey. "I understand your pain. I have lost those close to me as well."

"Unless you have lost a child of your own, you cannot ever understand." Her tears fell freely onto the sand. "I do not know how to bear such pain." She rocked back and forth, weeping.

"You could journey to the Black Oasis," said Aaliyah gently, once Weila's sobs had lessened. "You can see for yourself where his spirit resides. Now that the evil is gone, it is safe."

Weila wiped her eyes. "I may, in time. But for now, I must ignore my pain and do what I came here to do. You are to accompany me to see the Amal Molidova. She has sent me to retrieve you."

"I am sorry," said Aaliyah. "But we are in need of haste. Our people await us."

"You will not leave the desert unless she allows it," said Weila coldly. "Your presence is not an option. The Soufis are gathering in vast numbers, and she will see what role you have played in all of this."

"We have nothing to do with it," Gewey protested.

"Perhaps," said Weila. "That will be for Lyrial to decide. Do not try to run. You will be cut down before you reach the shore." She motioned for them to follow. "And don't think your powers will save you. I know what you did to the Soufis, Aaliyah. Their burned corpses are a testament to what you are capable of."

Gewey started to correct her, but a stern glance from Aaliyah silenced him.

"We will comply," said Aaliyah. "How far must we travel?"

"It is an eight-day journey," Weila replied. "But we will get there much faster."

"How?" asked Gewey. The idea of more than two weeks' delay did not sit well.

"You shall see." Without another word, Weila headed west. Gewey and Aaliyah looked at each other, then followed her.

The heat of the day was nearly unbearable, but Aaliyah thought it best not to use the power of the flow to cool the air. Weila was in pain at the loss of Pali, and she certainly didn't want to make matters worse by offending the woman's beliefs.

By midday, they had nearly exhausted their water, though Weila had not even opened her flask, and her pace was steadily increasing. A few hours later, they saw a small rock formation at the base of a large dune. As they neared it, they could make out an opening just big enough for a single person to pass through.

"We are here," said Weila. Just inside the opening was a steep staircase leading into the dark depths of the earth. "Mind your feet. These stairs are treacherous."

Gewey had to duck to enter the opening and quickly found his feet hanging awkwardly over the edge of each step. Within seconds, the light from the entrance was gone; total darkness surrounded them. The air was stale and dusty, and the corridor was barely wide enough for Gewey to squeeze through. They descended for several hundred yards before the stairs finally ended, bringing them into a narrow hallway. This twisted and turned for nearly half a mile. Eventually, Gewey could see a soft light ahead.

As they drew closer, he realized that the light was coming from the walls of a rough, rounded, natural enclosure around twenty feet in both height and diameter. At either end of this, a tunnel disappeared into the distance. Thousands of tiny blue crystals were embedded into the rock, each giving off a faint light to illuminate the cavern. The floor was smooth and polished, clearly made so by the hands of skilled craftsmen, although right through the middle of this smooth surface was a trail of gritty sand that spanned the cavern and disappeared into the entrance of both tunnels. The closer Gewey looked, the more this sand appeared to move and ripple.

"That is how we will travel," said Weila. She moved to the far right end of the cavern where a number of curved disks, roughly four-feet in diameter, were leaning against the wall. She grabbed three and gave one each to Gewey and Aaliyah.

"I don't understand," said Gewey.

Weila reached in her belt, pulled out a copper, and tossed it on top of the sandy trail. At once, it came to life, flowing like a swift river into the tunnel. "This is the Blood of the Desert. We will ride it to the Waters of Shajir."

Gewey and Aaliyah stared in wonder as the sand settled. Gewey bent down to feel it, but Weila quickly snatched him back.

"Do not touch it," she warned sternly. "It will pull you in and drag you down into the depths of the earth." She placed her disk on the floor just beside the sand. "This is a slithas. We will ride atop them." She motioned for them to place their disks beside hers.

Gewey closed his eyes. He could feel the flow raging all around him. He was tempted to let it in but resisted. "This place, did your people build it?" he asked.

"It was here when we arrived," Weila replied. She took some leather strips from her belt and lashed the slithas together through tiny holes along the edge. "There are many such as this scattered throughout the desert, though only a few are safe to use."

"And the ones that aren't?" asked Gewey.

Weila pushed the slithas into the Blood of the Desert. Again, it came to life. "They lead to a great vortex in the center of the desert. If you go there, you will not return." She put one foot atop the lead slithas. "Now be ready."

Gewey took the center, and Aaliyah, the rear. Weila nodded sharply, and they all jumped aboard. They barely had time to sit before the sands grabbed the slithas, flinging them forward. Such was the force the staff and bow strapped to Gewey's pack jammed into his kidney, sending a shockwave of pain through his body.

Almost immediately they were through the tunnel and the glow of the crystals was replaced by darkness. After Gewey's eyes had adjusted, he turned to Aaliyah. She was sitting, legs crossed and eyes closed.

"Have you ever heard of a place like this?" he asked.

"No." She folded her arms and sighed. "But it is truly wonderful. I can feel the power of the earth here like in no other place I have ever been. Even the jungles of my home seem dead and dreary by comparison."

"This is where the power that you steal comes from," said Weila with a tinge of disgust. "The desert is filled with such wonders. If my heart were not so heavy, I would tell you about them." She covered her face with her hands and shuddered. A moment later, she heaved a sigh and wiped her eyes. "I know that it was not your fault that my son perished, Aaliyah. You made the only choice you could. If the wolves attacked, then it was due to dark forces. They are not evil creatures by nature. I would not have had Pali left alone in the desert."

"I thank you for your understanding," said Aaliyah. "And I hope you will journey to the Black Oasis. I believe seeing what has become of it will help to heal your heart."

"Perhaps. But for now, I must mourn." She noticed the bow and staff Gewey carried. "You did not have those when we first met. Is that what you were after?"

"It was," Aaliyah affirmed. "The Oasis guarded these things. They were what drew the evil there. It wished to possess them."

"Is that why the Black Oasis is now safe?" she asked. "Because it no longer has anything to protect?"

"Yes," Aaliyah replied. "At least in part."

"Then Pali died for a worthy cause." More tears fell from Weila's eyes.

"Your son died fighting at our side," said Gewey. "He could have stayed within the temple but chose to face the evil that had invaded your land. To me, that alone is worthy of pride."

"You are wise for one so young," said Weila. A smile crept upon her lips. "To die fighting alongside one's friend is worthy. But to face evil when it is easier to hide—that is even more so." She touched Gewey's arm. "Your words are a comfort to me when I thought none could be found."

Hours passed as the slithas sped along, twisting and winding through the bowels of the desert. The disks appeared to guide themselves, with no actions required from Weila. Gewey had never spent so much time beneath the surface, and soon he'd lost all track of time and direction.

As they continued, he noticed the air changing from time to time. It would grow warm and dry, then later cool and moist. Gewey tried to imagine what lay above them that would cause this. Occasionally, they passed through a section of tunnel with the glowing blue crystals dotting the walls. It was then that he could feel the flow really intensify.

There is so much I don't know, he thought. *So many mysteries.*

As if reading his thoughts, Aaliyah said: "I could spend a lifetime learning about this place."

"You could spend many lifetimes and never learn all the wonders of the desert," remarked Weila.

Finally, Gewey looked ahead and saw the glow of another cavern rapidly approaching. Weila crouched on her slithas; Gewey and Aaliyah did the same.

"We are traveling faster than you may realize," said Weila. "You will have only one chance to get off. If you miss it, you will end up in the vortex. Just jump when I do and you will live."

Unnerved by the idea of being swallowed by a vortex of sand, Gewey allowed the flow to enter. The world slowed and his heartbeat calmed. When they reached the cavern, Weila jumped. Gewey and Aaliyah followed just in time. Even with the power of the flow raging through him, he still very nearly lost his footing as his boots struck rock.

Much to Gewey's relief, the passageway leading to the surface was a gentle, upward slope. Hours of sitting had caused his legs to cramp and twinge. But what the passage lacked in depth, it more than made up for in length. He guessed that they walked for at least a mile before reaching the surface. As they emerged, he could see the stars of the night sky shining in the heavens.

The landscape had changed from endless dunes to flat, tightly packed sand, with patches of coarse, brown grass and thorny bushes scattered about. On the horizon, the silhouette of jagged mountains blackened the sky. Gewey had seen his father's map of the desert when he was a child. He would bring it out when he told him stories of the fire lizards.

He gasped out loud in amazement. "We're at the other end of the desert. How...?" During their passage, it didn't seem as if they had traveled anything long enough, or fast enough, to have come this far.

Weila cracked a smile. "I told you. The desert is full of wonders."

She led them east along a well-trodden trail. Only a few miles ahead, they could see a bright blue light, the same hue as the crystals in the caverns, cutting away the darkness.

"When we arrive, you must be silent until I speak with Lyrial," said Weila. "She will take the death of Pali no better than I."

"Why is that?" asked Gewey.

Her face was hard and dark. "In human terms, she was his wife."

A cold chill shot down Gewey's spine. "I see."

"What is she exactly?" asked Aaliyah. "What authority does she possess?"

"She is the Amal Molidova," Weila replied reverently. "She is the spiritual leader of my people. In times when a single voice must guide us, we have chosen for it to be hers."

"And the sand masters?" asked Gewey. He had assumed they were the leaders of the desert elves.

Weila held her head high. "We concern ourselves with matters of the desert. Our task is the well-being of our people as they journey through the dunes. Once our folk are safely home, our responsibility ends. War and turmoil are rare, so we do not often need a single voice to guide us. But things have changed. The Soufis are forming an army. This has never happened until you arrived."

Gewey felt Aaliyah's unease. Since he had returned her spirit to her body, he could increasingly share what she was feeling. It was similar to the bond he had with Kaylia, only more subtle.

The light ahead quickly grew brighter and brighter until the surrounding area was awash with blue illumination. Gewey could feel the flow growing ever more powerful with each step. The light seemed to be rising from the ground, and soon an immense, fifty-foot-high statue came into view. At first, he was unable to make out what it depicted because of the light dancing playfully across its surface. But as they drew closer, the image cleared. It was of an elf woman in a flowing gown, face upturned and holding aloft a silver urn. The urn was tilted forward, allowing a constant stream of shining blue liquid to spill out.

When they were only a few yards away, the ground changed from sand to polished white marble. Gewey realized that this was part of a massive round platform. In its center was a pool more than one hundred yards in diameter, filled with the blue liquid that poured from the statue. The white marble reflected the light from the water, giving off an eerie yet calming glow that made Gewey think of being within a dream. The flow was so strong that it very nearly entered him before he could stop it.

"Wait here," Weila ordered. She walked around the edge of the pool and disappeared behind the statue.

Gewey and Aaliyah waited in silence, gazing into the water. Nearly an hour passed before Weila returned carrying a small, tan reed basket. Beside her walked a tall, thin elf woman with golden hair falling loosely about her shoulders and all the way down to the back of her knees. Her alabaster skin was made more pronounced by her penetrating, dark green eyes. She wore a blue satin robe that was tied at the waist by a silver cloth and embroidered with hundreds of tiny, intricate silver swirls that interlaced to form one large pattern. Her ageless features were thin and delicate, yet bore the seriousness of authority. Her bare feet made no sound as they touched the cold marble. Just before she reached them, Gewey could smell a salty, sweet fragrance that reminded him of the wildflowers after a spring rain.

"I am Lyrial." Her voice was feminine and soft, yet commanding. "Weila has brought news that Pali fell in the Black Oasis, fighting at your side."

Gewey wasn't sure if he was to speak, so he just nodded.

Aaliyah stepped forward and bowed. "I am…"

"I know who you are," she interrupted. "And you know who I am. You are here so I can determine if your arrival has anything to do with the recent gathering of a Soufis army. Once I have found the truth of the matter, then we will discuss Pali."

"I can assure you, we do not have anything to do with the Soufis," said Aaliyah.

Lyrial's expression gave nothing away. "We shall see. But I am not a discourteous host. You shall eat and rest. Then we will talk. Weila will see to your needs." Turning, she made her way back to the statue and sat cross-legged beside it.

Weila opened the basket and pulled out two thin blankets, a loaf of bread, some dried fruit, and a bottle of wine. "You will have a few hours before she will speak with you. I suggest you rest until then. I will return shortly before sunrise." She turned to leave, then paused. "Don't worry about the cold. The Waters of Shajir will keep you warm enough."

Once Weila was gone, Gewey and Aaliyah laid out their blankets and ate their meal. The bread was plain and tough, but the fruit was sweeter than expected. The wine wasn't as good as some he'd had in the past, but it went down well enough.

"What should we do?" asked Gewey, leaning back on his elbows.

"What can we do?" Aaliyah lay down and closed her eyes. "If we run, we will either be killed or forced to kill those who are not our enemy. We will rest while we can, and then speak to Lyrial. Hopefully, we will be able to convince her that we have nothing to do with the Soufis."

"I may be forced to tell them what I am, you know."

Aaliyah opened her eyes and looked at Gewey. "That is for you to decide."

Gewey lay down and allowed himself to drift off to sleep. Aaliyah was right. What else could they do but rest and see what the dawn brought?

CHAPTER 21

Gewey and Aaliyah were woken by Weila. She offered them both a cup of clear, sweet-smelling juice, which they gratefully accepted. However, its fragrance did not prepare Gewey for the sour taste that followed. His face twisted, and he nearly spat it out.

Weila laughed. "It is from the fruit of the ganhi bush. It is sour, but very good for you."

"Is Lyrial ready to see us?" asked Aaliyah.

Weila nodded and pointed to the far end of the pool near the statue. "Go to her. I will wait here."

"You're not coming?" asked Gewey.

"As I said, this is a matter for the Amal Molidova, not a sand master," she explained. "Do not worry. We have spoken of Pali, and she does not hold you to blame any more than I."

Gewey and Aaliyah finished their juice, then made their way around the pool to where Lyrial sat waiting. Two flat round cushions had been placed in front of her. She motioned for them to sit. She wore a pair of loose-fitting, cream, linen trousers and a matching blouse. Her platinum blond hair was now in a tight braid that fell all the way down her back and wound around her waist, ending up in her lap. As she looked at them, her bright green eyes twinkled in the blue light rising from the water. Her face had the same timeless quality Gewey had come to know in elves, yet he knew she must be quite old.

Lyrial's eyes darted back and forth from Gewey to Aaliyah. "I do not think you are in league with the Soufis. So do not fear."

"That is good," said Aaliyah. "And know that we come in friendship."

Lyrial raised an eyebrow. "Is that so? It is hard to imagine that those who exiled my people so long ago have suddenly had a change of heart. No. I believe that if you desire friendship, it is out of necessity. Whatever the troubles are in the west, I think you have brought them with you."

"First, I would say that it was not my people who exiled you," said Aaliyah, her tone forceful and steady. "My people are from across what you know as the Western Abyss. But do not think that is a reflection on the other elves of this land. I do not believe they even remember you exist. Certainly those living today had no part in your exile."

Lyrial shook her head and let out a huff. "It would stand to reason that their arrogance and folly would shorten their memories."

"Your kin do not seem to share your attitude," said Aaliyah. "Those we spoke with seemed pleased that the elves of the west would come."

"It is for them to live and die, free in the sands," she shot back. "It is for me to protect that freedom. Their hearts are not as burdened as mine. They do not read the ancient lore." She paused and sighed. "Still, I am not unwilling to welcome others if my people truly wish it. And stories of the elves from across the Abyss have been told long before we came here. But if your people have returned after all this time, then perhaps it is you who have brought war."

"I can only tell you we have not," Aaliyah retorted. "We have been unable to return until now."

Lyrial sighed. "Very well then. Tell me your tale."

Aaliyah told her story, beginning with their arrival, and ending when they left for the desert. All she left out was Gewey's identity as a god. "I know that Weila told you why we came, and that we had intended to leave your desert in peace," she concluded.

"She told me what you allowed her to know," Lyrial replied. "But you have not revealed all. What is it you fear me to learn, I wonder?"

Aaliyah stiffened. "I have told you all that you need to understand—that we are guiltless regarding the Soufis. Anything else is our affair."

Lyrial placed her finger to her chin and met Aaliyah's gaze. "Is that so? You may not have caused the Soufis to gather yourself, but I'll wager that whatever it is you fight most surely can be held responsible. Soufis are wretched slavers that plague the sands. They may be cunning and fierce, but they would never gather in such great numbers on their own. They raid and flee."

"I will say nothing more on the matter," said Aaliyah.

Lyrial and Aaliyah stared into each other's eyes, neither one blinking.

"What she hasn't revealed is me," Gewey interjected. "I am what she will not tell you of."

Aaliyah stiffened, then folded her hands.

Lyrial was unable to prevent herself from laughing. "You? And what could she possibly reveal about you?"

"We came here to retrieve what was guarded within the Black Oasis," he said. "They were gifts. Gifts left for me by my father—Gerath."

Lyrial burst out laughing again. "You think a half-man is something new to us? You think us ignorant fools?"

"I am not a half-man," Gewey asserted. "And it was not Aaliyah who burned the Soufis. I did."

"I see." Lyrial stood. "So you claim to be a god and not a half-man? That would be something indeed—if it were true. Of course, such an outrageous claim can be settled easily enough."

She held out her hand. Gewey took it, and she led him to the edge of the Waters of Shajir. "Do not move," she instructed. In a flash, she drew a dagger from her sleeve and cut the back of his hand.

Gewey winced, more out of surprise than anything else, as his blood trickled into the shimmering liquid. The effect was instant. The second the blood touched the surface of the water, the ground began to rumble. Beneath the waters, a billowing red cloud boiled up, rapidly covering the entire pool. Suddenly, a thunderous boom knocked them both off their feet. Fire erupted from the urn atop the great statue, shooting hundreds of feet into the air. The flames fanned out, then fell quickly back down again before disappearing in a blinding flash just a few feet above the ground.

Gradually the earth stopped shaking and the blood red water transformed back into its original blue color. Lyrial remained where she was, eyes wide and mouth agape. Gewey got up and offered her his hand. She gazed at him in awe. Only after a long moment did she allow him to help her to her feet and lead her back to where they had left Aaliyah. Lyrial still looked stunned, unable to speak.

Just then, Weila ran over. "What happened?"

Lyrial finally found her voice. She motioned for them all to sit. "It seems that this concerns all elves, Weila. You should stay." She leaned forward and stared into Gewey's eyes. "How is this possible? Can the end times be here at last?"

"I don't know anything about that," said Gewey. "But if you will allow me, I'll tell you my story as well."

Lyrial nodded. "Of course. Yes, please."

Gewey recounted the events of his life, beginning with the death of his father. Several times he had to stop and backtrack as he remembered details. Lyrial and Weila took a special interest when he told of his bonding with Kaylia, asking him three times to repeat the details of this.

More than two hours passed before he'd finished. By then, the light of the morning sun had painted the sky red and purple. Gewey got to his feet, rubbed his neck, and stretched his arms.

"Then it has come to pass," Lyrial whispered to herself. "Your name—Darshan. We have heard this before. It is the name of the one who will herald the end times. It is said that your coming precedes the reunion of the elves, and the upheaval of the world. The waging of a great war that will remake creation and reveal a new destiny for the elves."

"I have no desire to involve your people in any war," said Gewey. "I came here only for the gifts of Gerath. Now that I have them, I intend to leave you in peace."

Lyrial shook her head and smiled benignly, as a mother speaking to an ignorant child. "The Soufis have gathered for war. The one you call the Dark Knight is clearly behind this. He either intends to make war on us or to march them from the desert and make war on you. Either way, we cannot allow it. If the Soufis attack us, then it will be their doom, but if they leave the sands..."

Her jaw tightened. "I will not allow the filth of the desert to visit their horrors on the rest of the world. And if this Dark Knight would call on such people to fight for him, he has revealed to us his true nature."

"What will you do?" asked Aaliyah.

"We have already begun to gather our forces," said Lyrial. "And our scouts are watching every move the Soufis make."

"Then you should take care to watch for the Vrykol," said Gewey. "They are powerful and deadly. It was a Vrykol that killed Pali, and nearly killed Aaliyah. If they are with the

Soufis, you must be careful. They can only die if you remove their heads."

"I will inform my people of this," said Weila grimly.

"If the Soufis attempt to leave the desert, we will stop them," stated Lyrial. "Once they are dealt with, we will go west for the first time in many generations." She got to her feet and looked at the statue, her arms across her chest. "And though this may be our end, we will not be idle while evil floods the world."

"How many are you?" asked Aaliyah.

Lyrial turned back to face Gewey, her chest swelling with pride. "We can raise an army of twenty-thousand in a short time. Twice that, if needed. But it would take longer."

"And how many are the Soufis?" he asked.

"They have three times our number at least." Lyrial smiled viciously. "But they could have ten times that, and still they could not hope to defeat us. It is long past time, we dealt with them once and for all. The atrocities they have visited on the people of this land will finally be avenged."

"I would hear more of your people," said Aaliyah. "Your desert is filled with wonders I have never dreamed of. The scholars of my land could spend generations studying the Blood of the Desert alone. And this." She pointed to the statue. "Who built it?"

Lyrial sat and crossed her legs. "It was here long before we arrived. The legends say it was built by the gods. And as far as our tales go, it will be a pleasure to tell you of the desert. For all my people's merits, they care little for my stories."

"That's not true," Weila protested jokingly. "I have listened to you ramble on for six-hundred years and never complained."

Both Aaliyah and Gewey's eyes grew wide.

"How old are you?" asked Aaliyah.

Lyrial smiled. "I am seven-hundred and four. But Weila is far older." She could see the confusion in their expressions. "This surprises you?"

"Indeed," said Aaliyah. "I am nearly three hundred. The elders of my land rarely see six. How is it that you live so long?"

Lyrial thought for a moment. "Perhaps it is that we do not steal life from the earth. Perhaps that power shortens your life."

Aaliyah looked closely at both Lyrial and Weila. "That may be. Or perhaps it is the desert itself that extends your life."

Lyrial nodded. "That could also be. It is said that the power of the Creator first gave life to the world here. And that it was here that the gods were born. It is quite possible that our legends are more than just stories."

"If it is the desert that extends your life," said Aliyah, "then I fear what will happen if you try to leave it."

Lyrial pondered this for a moment then said: "I cannot allow this to concern me. My people will not be trapped by our own mortality. We will know soon enough if what you suggest is true."

"But..." began Gewey. Lyrial held up her hand, silencing him.

"There is nothing to discuss," she asserted. "Our course is set. I will not dwell on it. Now, if you still would like to hear stories of my people?"

"Of course," said Gewey.

For the next few hours, Lyrial told them of how her people were exiled for protesting over the enslavement of humans, and how they came to live in the desert. She spun tales of adventure, tragedy and joy. She told them of their fight with the Soufis, and their protection of the humans from slavery. Weila looked bored and began dozing.

"Your people have lived a noble life," Aaliyah remarked once Lyrial had finished. "That you were exiled for objecting to the subjugation of humans connects with our own history."

"A story you can tell me another time," said Lyrial, rising to her feet. "I will not delay your mission any longer." Weila handed her a small silver flask. Lyrial walked to the pool and filled it. "Take this," she said, handing the flask to Gewey. "The Waters of Shajir are powerful. Their healing properties are unmatched. A single drop will heal the deepest wound."

"Thank you," said Gewey, bowing low. "It will serve as a reminder of your kindness."

Lyrial bowed in return. "Once we have defeated the Soufis, I will march my people to the western edge of the desert. There we will await word from you. For now, Weila will take you to the shore." She smiled at Aaliyah. "I look forward to our next meeting. Please tell our kin that were are overjoyed to reunite with them."

Aaliyah nodded. "I will. And I know they will feel the same. Your friendship will be of great value in the days to come."

Lyrial took one final lingering look at Gewey before smiling and walking away. Gewey's eyes followed her as she departed.

"Come, Darshan," said Weila. "If we hurry, I can have you back to the shore by nightfall tomorrow."

"I wish we had more time," said Gewey.

"I agree," said Aaliyah. "We should send an envoy here as soon as possible."

"But what if you're right?" Gewey couldn't help but think about what might happen if the desert elves were to leave their home. "What if it is the desert that lets them live for so long?"

Weila stopped in her tracks. "My people will not sacrifice their honor for a long life. Do not think on it any further."

"How long do you live?" asked Gewey.

"Our elders see nine hundred years or more," she replied. "But think on this. I listened to your story. You have lived more in your short life than any elf that walks the sands. I would give all of my years to live a life of substance, however short it may be. If we step off the sand and perish, it would still be better than to have hidden ourselves away in fear and dishonor."

Weila led them for ten miles before reaching a rock formation similar to the one they had seen on their journey to the Waters of Shajir. Once again they descended deep underground.

This time their trip riding a slithas on the Blood of the Desert seemed to pass by much more quickly. Weila regaled them with tales of her homeland with ceaseless energy.

Finally, she turned to Aaliyah. "I noticed that during your recount of events you spoke very little of your own home. Surely there is much to tell."

"There is," she replied. "More than could be told in the time we have."

"Then tell me of your village," said Weila.

Aaliyah laughed. "Well, my village is actually a city of more than one-hundred thousand elves."

Gewey cocked his head. "Then that's something I'd like to hear about too."

"Very well," she said, laughing softly. "My city is called Parylon. It is on the shores of what you know as the Western Abyss, though on the other end and many leagues away." Her voice became distant. "To put is simply, Parylon is beautiful. Tall silver spires that glimmer majestically in the sunlight, dwarfing the redwood forest that border it to the east. Between the spires are lavish homes and stunning gardens. Halls of learning and meditation are built from the finest marble, and adorned with sculptures and reliefs lovingly carved by the greatest artisans the world has ever seen. One could spend a hundred years wandering the city and never see them all.

"The streets are paved with polished green slate that reflects the light of the noonday sun, making the whole city look as if it were an extension to the Creator's grace. In winter, when the sea churns and foams, the spires cast a green shadow, transforming the coast into an emerald field of waves and sand.

"Each afternoon the city fills with music and laughter. We boast six schools where the finest musicians study, teach, and compose. Each afternoon, the students take to the streets so that the world can listen to what they have learned. In the evening, the masters give concerts in the city square. As a young girl I would wait for hours and hours for the song masters to arrive, and listen until my mother would find me and take me home.

"At night, a million lights shine more brilliantly than the stars in the heavens. During the spring, the moss of the listorlia grows on rooftops in never-ending intricate swirling patterns. In the light of the full moon it glows softly and releases its snow white spores into the air, covering the streets in a blanket of sweet smelling wonder."

She paused and sighed sadly. "I do miss it."

"How could anyone leave such a place?" asked Weila. "Why would your people have come here to begin with, when such magic exists in their homeland?"

Aaliyah smiled. "I look at your desert home and see far more magic. For all our accomplishments, we have nothing like the Blood of the Desert or the Waters of Shajir. And our life is not without peril. I tell you of the best we have to offer. These are the things I love, yet not all there is. Beyond our borders lives a brutish race of foul creatures. We call them the Morzhash. Though only the Creator knows what they call themselves."

"What are they?" asked Gewey.

"We do not know for certain," she replied. "They are twice the size of any human, stronger than any elf, and covered in thick black hair. Their faces are twisted and flat with a swine like nose and narrow red eyes."

"Are they intelligent?" asked Weila.

"They are cunning to be sure," said Aaliyah. "And deadly. Though, it seems they possess nothing more sophisticated than clubs and spears. They do not work metal and live in makeshift huts as they hunt and scavenge the forests and jungles. Occasionally we find what remains of a camp, but have never yet found any permanent settlements. As far as we know, they live a nomadic life."

"It wouldn't seem like they could trouble your people too much," said Gewey.

"For thousands of years they have been little more than a nuisance," she replied. "They raid a village or attack a traveler. We have captured a few but have never been able to decipher their crude language. In fact, until the time of my grandmother, we had no idea they even had a language."

Gewey tried to picture the creatures in his mind. "You say they raid your villages. Why?"

Aaliyah shrugged. "There is no apparent reason. They take nothing. They simply kill and destroy."

"Why not hunt them down?" asked Weila.

"We have tried," she replied. "For all their size and girth, they move through the forest with amazing speed. And they disappear long before we can track them."

"Still, it seems like a minor problem," said Gewey.

"Until the past few years, it has been," she said. "But lately their raids have become more brazen. They have begun to invade deeper into our land than ever before."

"You think it is because of what's happening here?" asked Gewey.

"It may be linked somehow," Aaliyah replied. "The Morzhash would certainly make formidable allies should the Dark Knight find a way to control them."

The thought of these massive savage beasts fighting on the side of the Dark Knight sent chills down Gewey's spine. The Vrykol were bad enough, but should these creatures reach their shores, they could cause fear and panic across the land. "We must hope the two things are not related," he said.

Weila laughed, shocking Gewey out of his morbid thoughts. "Beasts or no beasts, I intend to see your city, Aaliyah. And may the Creator help any pig-nosed oaf that tries to stop me."

Aaliyah smiled. "I would not worry. My city is one of three and by far the oldest. The lands around us would burn to cinders before we let it fall. Though we did not come in great numbers to these shores, should the Dark Knight think to extend his grasp to my home, he will find that only the humans of this land could raise a larger army."

"Your words give me hope," said Weila. "I must admit, the elves of the desert have been alone for too long. Your arrival, Darshan, has brought us the hope of kinship." She folded her hands and bowed her head. "Yes, I think that perhaps your arrival has saved us. A people cannot live without moving forward. We have become too set in our ways."

Gewey reached out and touched her shoulder. "Darshan is a name given to me by a god. And yes, I am his son. But my father was a human. He raised me and taught me to be the man I am. He named me for his father—Gewey."

Weila's face twisted as she tried not to laugh. "Gewey is a silly name for a savior."

"Gewey is a human name," he countered. "And it will be the human in me that fights the Dark Knight. I will either defeat him or be destroyed myself. And should I win that battle—if I somehow find a way—nothing will change. Your people will still be in the desert." His gaze shot to Aaliyah.

His passion swelled. "Your people will still be across the sea. The world will still be the world. Humans, elves, and even the Morzhash. Nothing will change. Once there is victory—what then? What will you do with the world you are given?" The flow was raging through him as his voice roared. He closed his eyes, but his frustration and anger grew. He reached out desperately. Aaliyah was there. His spirit had flown straight to her.

"Calm your storm," she whispered. "I am here."

Gewey shot an accusing glance. "You... I..." His eyes fell. "I don't know why I said that. I suddenly felt angry. I am sorry."

A tear spilled down Aaliyah's cheek. "There is no need to apologize. I could feel your passion. Your true nature is beginning to assert itself."

"What do you mean?" he asked.

"You are what your nature has made you," she explained. "Your human side is only one part of you. The gods are the most powerful beings ever created. And their feelings are equally powerful."

"This is true," agreed Weila. "Even in our stories, the anger, love, hate, and desires of the gods are far beyond those of mortals."

"Are you saying I am becoming more ... more god?" The idea frightened him.

"Perhaps," Aaliyah replied. "I cannot say for certain. But I feel that you are changing."

"How do you mean, you feel it?" asked Gewey.

"When you saved me, it created a bond between us," said Aaliyah, smiling sweetly. She touched his cheek. "I knew it at once. I am surprised you did not."

"But ... but..." Gewey stammered. "What of Nehrutu? And what of Kaylia?"

"What we share is different," she explained. "When you touched the essence of my spirit, I became a part of you."

She could see Gewey's discomfort. "Do not fret. As far as I can tell it has not interfered with your connection to Kaylia. And as far as Nehrutu is concerned, that time between us has passed." The mention of Nehrutu brought sadness to her voice.

This did little to ease Gewey's mind. "Please release your hold on my bond with her," he said.

"You could do this on your own, I suspect." She sighed and nodded. "But very well. I will do as you ask."

Suddenly, Gewey could feel the barrier being lifted. Instinctively, he reached out for Kaylia. She was there. Joy and rapture rushed through him as they became one. The longing was over. He was with her.

Aaliyah was barely able to shake him out of his communion before they arrived at their destination. Weila led them back to the surface. As they emerged, the sun was just going down and Gewey could taste the salty sea air. Three hours later they were back to where they had left their small boat tied up on the beach. Gewey and Aaliyah said a heartfelt farewell to Weila, then made their way back to the ship. The crew cheered wildly as they climbed on deck.

"Tales will have to wait until tomorrow," announced Aaliyah. "We are both weary from travel."

That night Gewey washed and slid into bed, still excited that he could contact Kaylia once again.

"I envy her good fortune," said Aaliyah as she lay down and pulled the blanket tightly around her.

Gewey looked over. "I am the fortunate one. And not only because of Kaylia."

CHAPTER 22

Kaylia ran through the halls of Valshara, nearly knocking over several people as she raced past. On reaching the healing chamber, she threw open the door. Nehrutu was treating a wounded soldier who had been hurt building the gallows.

"You look happy," he remarked. "Has something happened?"

"Aaliyah has released her hold on Gewey," she replied, speaking and laughing at the same time.

"That is good," said Nehrutu. "Were they successful?"

"They were," she replied. "They are returning as we speak. Better still, Aaliyah has given up her quest for Gewey's heart."

Nehrutu nodded. "Then you have won. You should be pleased."

"I am." She knelt beside Nehrutu. "But this also means you can be with Aaliyah again."

"Perhaps," he replied skeptically. "First, I would first like to know what happened to sway her. She does not give up easily. That she abandoned her aspirations for Gewey does not necessarily mean she wishes to return to me."

The door opened and Selena entered. Her face was dark with worry. "I have received a message from the one called Yanti."

"What does it say?" asked Kaylia.

"He is demanding the release of his soldiers," she replied. "He says that he rightfully occupied Valshara by order of King Halmara. Halmara claims that Valshara rests within the borders of his kingdom, and not those of King Lousis."

"Do you think there is any truth to this?" asked Nehrutu.

"I don't know," she replied. "But if there is, King Lousis may be in danger. We must warn him. The council will be meeting any day now."

"Yanti may be trying to draw you out into the open," Nehrutu suggested. "If you leave these walls, you will be vulnerable."

"I agree." She furrowed her brow. "I have already sent a messenger. But if what Salmitaya says is true, Yanti is powerful. If he defeated my son, he will certainly be able to stop a messenger from getting through easily enough."

"There is nothing to do but wait and see," said Nehrutu.

The door flew open and Matrus, one of Selena's personal guards, entered. He looked pale and anxious. "High Lady. There is someone requesting your presence at the gate. He says his name is Yanti."

Selena's eyes widened in surprise. "I want archers on the wall at once," she ordered. "Tell them to not let him out of their sight."

"A bold move," Nehrutu mused. "Or he does not fear us. Will you speak to him?"

Selena thought for a moment. "I will."

"But High Lady..." objected Matrus.

"Don't worry," said Selena, smiling. "If this Yanti fellow makes a move to harm me, it will be his last. No, I think if assassination was his goal, he would not simply walk up to the gates."

"Still," Nehrutu said, "you should keep your distance. I will accompany you."

"As will I," added Kaylia, thumbing her knife.

"Now go," Selena said to Matrus. "I want archers on the wall in five minutes."

Matrus turned quickly and sped off.

Selena allowed sufficient time for the archers to get into position before making her way to the front gate. Yanti stood a few yards away from the entrance. He was dressed in an elegant red shirt, black trousers, and a black satin jacket with polished gold buttons. A red leather belt held a beautifully crafted gold-hilted rapier. His brown curly hair was oiled and pushed back in true noble fashion. He flashed a broad smile and bowed low as they approached.

"Thank you for seeing me, High Lady," he said.

"What is it you want, Yanti?" asked Selena, trying to contain her anger.

"As my message said," he replied, "I want my men. Oh, and Salmitaya as well, if you please." He spoke her name as if it were an afterthought.

"Your men are to be hanged," said Selena. "And you will never see Salmitaya again."

Yanti laughed and wagged his finger. "There is no reason to hang my men. They are not criminals. And as for dear, sweet Salmitaya—what possible use would you have for her? She has no information useful to you."

"Your men are criminals," she shot back. "They broke into my home and slaughtered my people. That was the act of thugs, not soldiers. And they will be treated as such."

"They acted on orders given by the lord of this land, my love," said Yanti. "Your temple's very existence is in clear violation of the laws of King Halmara and the city of Skalhalis. I simply carried out the will of a trusted ally. Your quarrel is with him. Not me; not my men; and certainly not poor

Salmitaya. If you release them to me, then we can all put this unpleasant business behind us."

"You waste your breath," barked Selena. "And my time. You think you can come here after what you have done and dictate to me what I must do?"

Yanti sighed and shook his head. "I think you would want to prevent further bloodshed, my love. I shudder to think what King Halmara will do when he learns what has happened here. Especially if you were to execute my men." He glanced up at the archers on the wall. "And please, do not think to harm me. Should that happen, the consequences to King Lousis would be most severe." His smiled widened. "And you should know that your message to the king was not received, though I assure you that your messenger is unharmed—for now."

Selena's face turned red with fury. "If you harm him..."

Yanti held up his hand. "Fear not, my love. I am not an animal. I only take life when I must. After all, I did choose to leave your beloved son alive, did I not? I'm sure Salmitaya has told you of our little scuffle."

It was all Selena could do not to order the archers to fill Yanti with arrows. "You should be most glad that you did. Or I swear your false king would hear your screams all the way in Angrääl."

"I admire your passion," said Yanti. "It is a shame you have chosen to be an enemy of the Reborn King. Your fall will cause me great sadness."

"We shall see who falls," she said, clenching her jaw. "If there is nothing more to say, you should leave now, before I decide to do something rash."

"I will leave when the matter of my men is settled," said Yanti. "Release them by sundown and I will send word to Althetas to allow King Lousis to live. Do it not, and he will surely die." He bowed again. "I will await your favorable reply." He turned and strode off.

"Do you think he is telling the truth?" asked Kaylia. "Do you think he really has the means to assassinate the king?"

Selena watched as Yanti disappeared around a bend. "I don't know. But I'm not sure I can afford to take that risk."

"And what of Salmitaya?" asked Nehrutu.

"No matter what happens, she will remain here," Selena replied firmly. "I gave my word that she would not be returned to that brute, and I will keep it."

Her next words seemed to stick in her throat. She knew what must be done, though it stabbed at her heart. "Prepare the prisoners for release," she said. "But see to it they leave with nothing more than their underclothes. Pile their possessions in the center of the yard and burn them."

Selena went to her quarters and sent for Salmitaya. A few minutes passed before a guard arrived with Salmitaya in shackles.

"You can remove those," Selena ordered.

Salmitaya sat across from Selena, her face expressionless, hands folded in her lap.

Selena told her about Yanti. "I promised you I would not allow you to be taken, and I will keep my word. But I need to know..."

"You need to know if he has someone near King Lousis," Salmitaya cut in. "I would think he does. In fact, I'm certain of it. And if he says he is allied with King Halmara, I would think that is true as well. Yanti lies, but he mixes lies with truth. I also know that if you do not do as he requests, he will make good on his threats."

"I will release his men," said Selena sternly. "But I will not turn you over."

Salmitaya shook head and chuckled softly. "If you do not, he will make good his threat. Lousis will die."

"He may do that regardless," Selena countered.

"No," said Salmitaya, "He will hold to his agreement. At least until his men are away. By then, you may be able to warn the king."

"Why would Yanti care about a few hundred soldiers?" she asked.

"Who knows?" Salmitaya bowed her head. "But it is not out of a sense of responsibility to them, that much is certain. Whatever the reason, he is not one to bluff. If he says he will kill Lousis, you can count on it."

Selena stood up and poured two cups of wine. Offering one to Salmitaya, she stared thoughtfully into the woman's eyes.

Salmitaya held the glass under her nose, savoring the sweet scent. She closed her eyes as the wine passed over her tongue. "I remember when I was a novice," she said softly. "I would sneak away to the tavern to drink wine and listen to the musicians with my friends. We were always so afraid we'd get caught but that just made it even more fun." Her body now felt totally relaxed. She could almost hear the songs and laughter of her fellow novices. "Things were so much simpler then," she added, her voice now a mere whisper. Her eyes were growing heavier and heavier. The wine glass slipped from her fingers, but the sound of it breaking as it struck the floor seemed distant. So very far away. Yes, that's what she wanted. To be far away.

Selena called the guard. "Have her body wrapped in linen and given to the captives when they are released." She leaned down and pushed the hair away from Salmitaya's face.

"I'm sorry," she said.

CHAPTER 23

For six days, the kings and queens of the twelve city states had been arriving. Only King Halmara was still absent. The presence of elves had caused more than a few nervous stares, especially as King Lousis made a point of greeting each new arrival with Theopolou and Ertik at his side. Co-existence with elves was common in most of the twelve cities, but only in certain areas—and never as welcome guests in the house of the king. But even the elves didn't cause so much of a stir as Ertik's presence. As a representative from the High Lady of Valshara, speculation ran wild as to his reason for attending.

Theopolou spent his time exploring the king's library and reading about the history of the twelve cities. Mohanisi spent most of his time with Linis, who was busy preparing to journey to Sharpstone. From time to time, Theopolou would be approached by the kings and queens and asked about the goings on of the elves. Word had already spread about the battle in Valshara. Most could scarcely believe that human and elf had fought side by side. Theopolou politely answered their questions.

By the seventh day, it was decided to proceed without King Halmara. That evening there would be a banquet, and in the morning the council would meet.

A few hours before the banquet, Theopolou returned to his quarters. The flood of questions had steadily increased until the very thought of another conversation caused him to cringe. As he settled into a plush chair and opened a book, there was a soft rap at the door.

He sighed and closed the book. "Come."

It was Linis. "I want to speak to you before I leave for Sharpstone. Mohanisi is still exploring the city and says he will not be joining you for the banquet."

"Your company is welcome," said Theopolou, smiling. "I wish my presence at the banquet was also not required, for I would gladly join Mohanisi." He raised an eyebrow. "Have you spoken to Lord Ganflin?"

"I have," he replied, taking a seat beside Theopolou. "He is providing me with two dozen men and ten thousand in gold coin to aid Millet and Dina. He has already sent word to Lord Broin, and I hope to get his help as well."

Theopolou nodded approvingly. "That is good. You should have enough to raise a sizable force."

"I hope to send for elves soon," said Linis. "But I think it best to prepare the people of Sharpstone first. Most people along the Goodbranch have never seen an elf and have only stories of the Great War to form their opinions."

"I am certain you can ease their fears," said Theopolou. "Let me know when the time comes, and I will send as many as can be spared." He could see Linis's expression darken. "What is it?"

Linis sat. "I have heard some disturbing news. The human woman, Maybell, has just arrived in the Temple of Ayliazarah here in Althetas. She was a priestess in Kaltinor and traveled with Gewey and Lee when I first met them. I am told she was accompanied by Malstisos."

"I know of him," said Theopolou. "His father and I fought together in the Great War."

"He has left Althetas to go north to the Steppes." Linis paused. "To face judgment."

"For what purpose?" he asked, taken aback.

"I do not have enough information to say for certain," said Linis. "But I think you should speak to Maybell."

"I will send for her after the council meets." Theopolou stood. "And you should not delay any longer, my friend."

Linis got to his feet and sighed. "It seems I am ever traveling. But you are right. Every moment is precious. Farewell, Theopolou. May the Creator bless you."

"And you," he replied, smiling.

Once Linis left, Theopolou sat back down and tried to clear his mind. He felt age gathering upon him as he thumbed through the pages of his book. His journey to the Steppes weighed heavily on his mind, and the fact that Malstisos had gone there to face his judgment could well complicate matters. He put the book down and slipped into bed. A bit of sleep would do him good.

A few hours later, he rose and dressed for the banquet. The king's manor was vast, with a dining hall large enough to seat more than two hundred guests. Originally built just after the Great War, the building stood three stories high and was constructed from the hard black stone quarried in the lands just south of the Steppes. Though the décor was not elaborate, it suited the personality of Althetas and its people. Tapestries of great warships and valiant warriors hung on the walls of the larger rooms alongside huge paintings. There were also sculptures of various lords and heroes. The furniture was diverse, as one would expect from a port city; examples of styles from all over the world could be seen in every room. Theopolou even spotted a few tables and chairs of elf make. He had seen paintings of the original building, and knew that it was much smaller than what presently stood.

He'd been told that each new king had added a little bit more to the manor during his reign.

The grounds were well tended and included dozens of small flower gardens. These were filled mostly with local flora, but here and there a flower from a distant land could be seen. A tall, wrought iron gate provided an imposing entrance, while matching railings with a manicured hedge running just inside of this surrounded the entire manor and grounds.

Theopolou contemplated the idea of skipping the banquet. Every moment he spent in idle conversation with the nobility of the Western Abyss made him anxious to depart for the Steppes. He wandered for a time, admiring the tapestries and sculptures, and though these were not as fine as those in his own home, he was nonetheless impressed at the talent of human hands.

He sighed. Attend he must.

When he finally arrived in the banquet hall, the polished oak double doors were open wide and the room was already filled to capacity. Six long tables had been placed end to end and ran very nearly the full one-hundred-foot length of the room. To his left, a harpist played softly; the music carried over the voices, filling the hall. Three crystal chandeliers hung from the tall ceiling, while dozens of silver lanterns lined the walls. At the opposite end of the room, a raised platform held another table that spanned the hall's width. There, King Lousis, Ertik, and the other nobles were seated. He saw a few elves that had taken seats at the far right table, along with Lord Brasley Amnadon. Theopolou had only taken a few steps when a trumpet rang out.

"Lord Theopolou, Your Highness," cried a herald stationed beside the door.

The room became silent as all eyes fell on him. He paused for a moment, then made his way to the king's table, where an empty seat at the monarch's right side awaited him.

Everyone rose and bowed. Theopolou returned the gesture before taking his seat.

"Our kitchen has been preparing a few elf dishes just for you and your people," said Lousis cheerfully. "Though from what I've heard, The Frog's Wishbone may far outshine what I have to offer. Lord Ganflin prides himself on his elf cuisine."

"Yes," said Theopolou. "Linis has mentioned it. If ever I have the time, I would like very much to explore your city."

Just then, a servant approached and whispered in the king's ear.

"It would seem that King Halmara has arrived," announced Lousis, a look of concern on his face. "Along with a representative from Angrääl."

"Will you receive this representative?" asked Theopolou.

"If he travels with King Halmara, then I have little choice," Lousis replied angrily. "To deny him entrance would be seen as an insult. Skalhalis is an important port, and nearly as large as Althetas. And King Halmara carries much influence within the council."

"Prepare them a seat," Lousis ordered the servant. "And show them in. Then have quarters prepared."

The servant scurried off.

"So it would seem Angrääl is making no secret of their intent," said Theopolou.

"It could be worse than you think," said Lousis. "Valshara is within King Halmara's borders. If he took part in the siege, then this council meeting may well be a useless gesture. The cities to the south will certainly side with Skalhalis, leaving the coast split in two. Then we will be caught between the elves of the Steppes and Skalhalis."

"I hope to sway the elves there from their present course once my business here is concluded," said Theopolou. "If I am successful, then the situation will not be as dire."

"And if you fail..." Lousis's words faded as two figures stepped inside the hall.

The first was dressed in a fine blue silk shirt, open at the neck with silver ruffles, matching trousers, and polished black leather boots. A golden scabbard hung from a black belt. The hilt of the sword was interlaced with gold and ivory and crowned with a blue sapphire. His short, sandy blond hair was oiled and combed back neatly. Though clearly a man of some years, his tan skin and stout build gave him a somewhat youthful appearance.

At his side was a short, thin man dressed in a plain, black cotton robe tied in at the waist with a slender, white rope. Theopolou guessed him to be in his early thirties, yet his jet-black hair was already thinning. Though not strong in stature, his piercing blue eyes were striking, even from across the room. This, together with his confident strides, gave him a commanding presence. He followed close behind as they approached the table.

King Lousis stood up and bowed. "King Halmara. I welcome you."

Halmara smiled. "Thank you, my old friend. I have missed your company." He stepped aside and motioned toward his companion. "I present Lord Sialo Magrifal, Ambassador of Angrääl and servant of the Reborn King."

"You dress oddly for a lord," remarked Lousis. "Do you not?"

"If my attire offends your highness, I will change," said Sialo, bowing low.

"Not at all," Lousis replied. "Please, be welcome. A place has been set for you both. My home is at your disposal."

They bowed and took their seats at the far left end of the table.

"I think I will be glad to have you in the council tomorrow," said Lousis quietly to his right. "Your support will be crucial."

"Naturally, I will help if I can," Theopolou replied. "Though my experience of dealing with humans is quite limited, I am still well-versed in the nuances of diplomacy."

Lousis lifted his cup. "A skill I will need in abundance. As for me, I have never enjoyed the subterfuge and misdirection of the nobles. My father was the politician. I am far too plain-spoken for my own good."

Theopolou laughed quietly. "I regard that as an admirable trait. I may speak the language of politics, but I prefer the simple truth."

Lousis chuckled. "I doubt we'll hear much of that tomorrow."

After another hour had passed, Theopolou excused himself from the banquet. He could feel the eyes of Sialo Magrifal following him as he walked out of the hall. Two elves immediately jumped up and accompanied him to his room, insisting that they guard his door. At first, he'd protested, but seeing their determination, eventually relented. They wished for this business to be done. With every day that passed, the Dark Knight's grip on his kin would strengthen.

The darkness closed in as Theopolou allowed himself to drift into a dreamless slumber. His final thoughts were of Sialo Magrifal.

He knew beyond doubt that the man's arrival was a bad omen.

CHAPTER 24

Theopolou was wakened at dawn by Mohanisi arriving at his door.

"What did you think of the city?" asked Theopolou.

"Humans have come a long way," he said approvingly. "Their skills at building are more advanced than I would have guessed. In fact, many of the temples are quite stunning."

"And the people?" he asked.

"Not what I expected." He took a seat. "Though some are clearly not accepting of us, in large they are very hospitable and kind, particularly Lord Ganflin. Have you met him?"

Theopolou shook his head. "Not yet. Though I am sure I will soon enough."

"I heard from the others that a representative of Angrääl has arrived," said Mohanisi. "How do you think this will affect the council?"

"Not well. We may be fighting on two fronts if my mission to the Steppes fails. King Lousis believes the cities south of Skalhalis will rally to King Halmara's banner. And it is quite possible that he was involved in the siege of Valshara."

There was a knock at the door and a young servant boy entered.

"King Lousis summons you to the council, Lord Theopolou," said the boy timidly.

"Very well," said Theopolou. "Wait for me outside."

He rose to his feet. "Go to the Temple of Ayliazarah," he told Mohanisi. "There you will find a woman named Maybell. I need you to bring her here. Tell her you are a friend of Linis and she will come."

Mohanisi nodded. "I will do as you request. I wish you fortune today."

Mohanisi left, and Theopolou got dressed. The servant boy then led him through the labyrinth of corridors to the east end of the manor, where they came to a broad oak door guarded by two soldiers. The soldiers snapped to attention as Theopolou opened the door and entered the room. He glanced around. The council chamber was a fifty-foot square hall. The walls on both left and right were covered with carved reliefs of various ships and sea creatures. At the far end stood a dozen pedestals with marble busts, each bearing a gold crown. The center of the room was dominated by a round table with fifteen chairs evenly spaced around it. The kings and queens had already arrived. Ertik was seated at the left-hand side of King Lousis and Theopolou's chair stood empty at his right.

"Ah, Lord Theopolou," called Lousis. "Now we can begin."

Theopolou took his seat and looked out over the table.

Lousis stood. "My lords and ladies, this is Lord Theopolou. As many of you know, he is here to represent the elf nations. You have been introduced to Ertik, representing the Order of Amon Dähl." He raised his arm in a grand sweeping motion. "These are the rulers of the western kingdoms. Starting to my right, King Stanis of Calderia, King Tredford of Yuledan, Queen Lilian of Farthing, King Brääl of Maiden Shore, Queen Fasheil of Lamitia, King Halmara of Skalhalis,

Lord Sialo Magrifal, ambassador of Angrääl, King Victis of Tarvansia, Prince Loniel of Sieren Bay, King Jeris of Wisterton, Queen Illirial of the Saraf's Jewel, and King Tranton of Red Cliff. On behalf of all the kings and queens of the twelve cities, we bid you welcome." He took his seat. "I think you all know by now why I have called this council."

"I hope it's to explain why your soldiers have invaded my land and taken possession of what is rightfully mine," said King Halmara.

Ertik stiffened and turned red with anger, but a glance from Lousis kept him silent.

"Surely, you do not refer to the liberation of Valshara?" Lousis countered. "We merely came to the aid of a friend in need. A friend who had been set upon by the forces of Angrääl. Forces who marched on your borders long before my men arrived."

"Then perhaps this has all been big a mistake," Sialo Magrifal interjected. "We were asked by our dear friend and ally, King Halmara, to expel those residing illegally in Valshara. According to King Halmara, they were in clear violation of his law."

This was more than Ertik could stand. He shot up out of his seat. "You lie! Our temple has stood for thousands of years unmolested. You murdered my people out of revenge. Revenge your master could not exact after he was expelled from Amon Dähl for his betrayal."

Lousis grabbed Ertik's arm and pulled him back into his seat.

"This is who the High Lady sends to speak on her behalf?" mocked Sialo. "You should learn to govern your passion when in the presence of your betters."

"Ertik may have spoken out of turn," said Lousis. "But he speaks the truth. And I would remind Lord Sialo that no question has been posed to him, yet he chose to speak—in the presence of his betters." This brought a round of soft laughter.

Sialo showed no signs of anger. He merely nodded and folded his hands.

"The fact remains that I was well within my rights to take Valshara," said Halmara. "It should not matter that I enlisted the aid of Angrääl to do so."

Queen Fasheil spoke. "You believe it none of our affair that a foreign force is allowed to enter our domain?"

Halmara curled his lip. "And what of the elf army that slaughtered the Angrääl soldiers when King Lousis marched his men into my land? Is that not a foreign force?"

King Stanis of Calderia, King Tredford of Yuledan, Queen Illirial of the Saraf's Jewel, and King Victis of Tarvansia all nodded in agreement.

"The elves have as much right to be here as we," said Lousis. "They have been here far longer, and have lived among us in peace. The presence of Angrääl is of great concern to them as well."

King Stanis spoke. "Is your memory so short? There are elves still living today who fought our people in the Great War. You may be liberal in your thinking, King Lousis, but for those of us in the south, we cannot ignore that elves have been a constant threat to our way of life. They have never been able to forgive humans for their defeat—and I doubt they ever will."

"What say you to this, Lord Theopolou?" asked Queen Fasheil.

Theopolou looked over the council. "King Stanis is correct. In fact, I fought in the Great War." This brought gasps and whispers. "Until recently, I was opposed to a human-elf alliance, as were most of our elders. But that has changed. We face a threat that none of us can overcome alone. We must leave behind mistrust and hatred in order to survive."

"And what threat is that?" asked Halmara, contempt plain in his voice. "The only threat I see here is you."

"You know well the threat I speak of," Theopolou replied calmly. "That you have aligned yourself with the power you believe will be victorious will not save you in the end. Should the elves fall and the armies of Angrääl sweep across this land, do you think your people will remain free?"

"If I may?" said Sialo. Lousis nodded his consent. "The Reborn King has no intention of making war on this or any other land. He only seeks to strengthen friendships and create prosperity for all. Lord Theopolou speaks of unity, yet his own people from the Steppes assault him. He would have you believe that his people will protect you from the wrath of a kingdom that has done nothing to offend you. We have not invaded your land, nor will we ever. It is the elves that seek protection. And what is worse, they seek protection from their own kind. It is they who would need you."

Theopolou smiled. "Very well put. I can see why your master sent you. And I must admit, you are not entirely wrong. We do need an alliance with humans to survive. Our numbers are few compared to the vast armies in the north. But if your king has no intention of making war, then why raise a force so immense as to rival the armies of the Great War? Such an army can have only one purpose. Conquest."

"You exaggerate, My Lord," said Sialo, smiling back. "We have been beset with requests for aid from all corners of the world. We only raised the forces necessary to accommodate our ally's needs."

"I see," said Theopolou. "Then you should be willing to allow the kings and queens of this land to send envoys to Angrääl to seek the truth of the matter—am I correct? Certainly, they would report that tens of thousands of soldiers are not massing for war, and that their neighboring kingdoms are not under the yoke of Angrääl. In fact, I could send an elf envoy along with them. It would certainly ease the minds of my people. If they departed right away, they could be there and back before spring. Of course, you would remain here to ensure complete objectivity."

Sialo glared at Theopolou.

"What say you, Lord Sialo?" asked Lousis, clearly amused at the man's anger. "You could remain as my guest until then."

"I, naturally, would have no objection," Sialo replied, regaining his composure. "But you would have to allow me to send word of their coming."

"I think not," said Lousis. "That may cause doubt about their findings."

"I must insist," Sialo retorted. "I would not want there to be any misunderstandings."

"You could write a letter of safe passage," offered Lousis. "Certainly, that should clear up any potential misunderstandings that might occur."

Sialo shifted uneasily in his seat.

"Enough of this distraction," roared King Halmara. His voice echoed through the hall. "I came here to resolve the matter of the invasion of my land, not listen to my guest have his honor insulted."

"Indeed," Lousis agreed. "Though I do not see where anyone has given insult. The fact is that foreign forces invaded and killed those within your rightful borders."

Halmara leaned forward menacingly. "And as I said, they were acting on my behest."

Lousis cocked his head and furrowed his brow. "I'm confused. What crime did these people commit to warrant their slaughter?" He leaned back. "Surely, if some crime was committed, they should be brought to justice, not put to the sword without trial."

This brought murmurs of agreement, even from the southern rulers.

"You say that Valshara existed in violation of your laws," Lousis continued. "I know your laws well, Your Highness.

They were written at the same council as ours here in Althetas, along with all the other kingdoms. Since when is a temple considered an outlaw state? When is a temple looked upon in the same manner as a brigand or bandit?"

"Valshara hid their existence from us," argued Halmara. "They have never sworn allegiance to my rule. Moreover, they support a military branch of their order. You expect me to sit idly by while this so-called temple builds its own army beneath my very nose?"

Lousis nodded in the direction of Ertik, who by now had managed to calm himself.

"The Order of Amon Dähl has never had an army," Ertik began. "Any who would say differently knows nothing. For thousands of years, we have been the guardians of heaven and the keepers of history. Our knights have fought to protect all that is sacred, and have served the gods since the ancient kingdoms were young. All this is well known to the Reborn King. He betrayed our order and seized the Sword of Truth, which we had protected for generations."

He stood up and looked over the council. "You need not go to Angrääl to see the Dark Knight's treachery. Temples throughout the land have been desecrated, their priests and priestesses murdered. In Baltria, the king has become little more than a puppet. In Hazrah, there are entire battalions garrisoned and ready to march. Do you really think that the people of Hazrah need so many for protection?

"Most of you will have heard tales about my order. But can any one of you say that you have heard stories of our armed conquests? Of course not! We have remained hidden for so long simply because of what we guarded. The Sword of Truth has the power to unravel the entire world should it fall into the wrong hands. Well, that terrible thing has now happened. The master Lord Sialo serves possesses a power beyond any of your imaginings. Do you think he has no intention of using it?" With a final contemptuous glare at Sialo, Ertik sat back down.

There was a long pause before Sialo got to his feet, his eyes never leaving Ertik's. With a loud sneer, he pushed back his chair and stormed from the hall. King Halmara quickly stood and followed.

In the wake of their departure, the hall remained absolutely silent for more than a minute. Finally, King Lousis stood and addressed the council. "I believe we should adjourn for an hour."

The council rose and filed out. Only Theopolou, Ertik, and Lousis remained. A servant brought them cups of wine.

"I hope that what I said made a difference," said Ertik. His hands trembled as he held his cup.

Lousis slapped Ertik on the shoulder. "I think it did. If we can sway enough of the southern rulers to our side, the rest will abandon King Halmara." He drained his cup. "If our fortune holds, we may yet turn the tide in our favor."

"What will happen if we cannot?" asked Theopolou.

Lousis shook his head and sighed. "In all probability, civil war. Halmara will rally the southern cities, and we will be forced to respond in kind."

"That would be a tragedy," said Theopolou. "Let us hope we can avoid it."

Barely had he finished speaking when a sudden, violent change came over Lousis. The king's eyes narrowed, and he clutched at his throat. A moment later, he slid from his chair, head thrown back, gasping for air.

Theopolou rushed to his side. He looked back to tell the servant to get help, but the boy was already gone. "The king is poisoned," he said. "The wine!"

Ertik looked at his cup and flung it to the ground.

"Are you all right?" Theopolou asked.

Ertik could only nod.

Theopolou swept the table clear. "Help me get him up, then go find Mohanisi. If he is not in the manor, he may be at the Temple of Ayliazarah."

They lifted Lousis up onto the table. Theopolou placed his hands on the king's chest and closed his eyes. Ertik bolted from the room, yelling for the guards. Theopolou could feel Lousis's life gradually draining away as he used the flow to slow the poison coursing through his veins. Whatever the assassin had used, it was powerful. All he could do was strive to keep the king alive long enough for Mohanisi to take over.

Six guards burst in, swords drawn.

"Find the servant who was just in here," Theopolou commanded. "And let no one leave the manor. Two of you stay and guard the door."

The guards obeyed at once.

Lousis slipped further away as Theopolou continued with his struggle. "Stay with me," he whispered. "You are still needed."

CHAPTER 25

Together with a dozen guards, both elf and human, Theopolou and Ertik waited anxiously just outside King Lousis's chambers. The other kings and queens had by now all been secured in their quarters and the manor sealed. The king was on the very brink of death by the time Mohanisi arrived; Theopolou could only pray that he wasn't too late.

One of Lousis's personal guards approached, fury in his eyes. "The servant has been found dead in his quarters, but King Halmara and Lord Sialo are no longer in the manor. It seems they have fled the city. I'm sending men to pursue them."

"No," said Theopolou. "There is no need. They will see justice soon enough."

"But My Lord," protested the guard, "the king is poisoned, and the culprits are within our reach."

"I doubt that very much," said Theopolou. "Someone like Sialo will have planned his escape well." He placed his hand on the guard's shoulder. "If you wish to serve your king, send more men to the city gates and scout the surrounding area."

The guard heaved a sigh of frustration. "It will be done, My Lord."

The door to the king's chambers opened and Mohanisi stepped out. "The king will live," he announced. "Though it may be a few days before he is fully recovered. He was moments from death, and even my skill has limits."

This news brought cries of relief from the guards.

"Say nothing to anyone," ordered Theopolou. "Tell the council I wish to speak to them. I will await them in the council chambers in one hour."

"Not to offend, My Lord," said an older guard. "But the council may not honor your request. They are a prideful bunch, and not all of them care much for elves."

Theopolou smiled. "If they refuse, then threaten to drag them to the chamber by the scruff of their necks." He could see the look of fear in the guard's eyes. Clearly, the idea of threatening royalty disturbed him. "The king nearly died, and it is very possible that one of the other kings and queens had a hand in it. I swear you will not be punished if you are forced to become insistent."

The guard smiled devilishly, then marched down the hall.

"Do you really think one of them had something to do with this?" asked Ertik.

"No," Theopolou replied. "But I am well aware that the allies of King Halmara fear such an accusation. I cannot undo what has been done to the king. But I can use it to our advantage."

"How do you propose to do that?" asked Mohanisi.

"With your assistance," Theopolou replied. "We must show them our strength. And most of all, we must help them to unite."

One hour later, the council filed into the chamber. Mohanisi stood behind Theopolou as they watched the kings and queens take their seats. Many wore looks of both anger and concern.

King Victis of Tarvansia spoke first. "What right have you to summon us?"

"You ask me this after what has happened?" said Theopolou, not hiding an accusing tone.

"What are you suggesting?" King Victis's nostrils flared.

"I suggest nothing," Theopolou replied. "Only that King Lousis is poisoned, and someone is responsible."

"It's obvious who is responsible," said Victis. "King Halmara is the only one absent."

"That is true," Theopolou agreed. "But it begs the question—did he act alone?"

"You think to call us here to accuse us?" Victis shouted. "How dare you! You are not a ruler of these lands. What right does an elf have to be so bold?"

Prince Loniel spoke. "King Victis, perhaps you should ask if King Lousis still lives. That is the first question I would have asked, and what weighs most heavily on my heart."

"And if he does not?" asked Theopolou. "Will you march under the banner of King Halmara?"

Prince Loniel leveled his gaze. "My father has long been a friend to King Lousis. Were it not for his ill health, he would be here himself, and his first question would be about the well-being of his dear friend. But to answer your question. If King Lousis dies, we may have no choice. We are not blind to the strength of Angrääl, nor are we the fools you may think us to be. Without Althetas, how can we resist such an enemy?"

He took a deep breath before pressing on. "King Lousis has no heir. His passing will throw the city into chaos. If the Reborn King would have our lands, would not that be the time to take them? Who will stand against him? What resistance could we offer? We have no standing armies. Will the elves save us, as you claim? With how many swords will you do this? Ten thousand?" He laughed sarcastically. "By the words of your own ally, we would need a hundred times that."

"There is more to war than swords," said Theopolou. "And victory is claimed by those who have the will to take it. If Angräal marches on this land, it will not find simpering cowards, but a free people fighting to protect the things that they love. If the King of Althetas has died, will you simply hand over your freedom? The king has been poisoned. Do you really think those who poisoned him will not take what is yours by force?"

He motioned for Mohanisi to step forward. "But you are right that we must possess the weapons to combat such a foe. And I tell you that we possess strength the armies of Angräal has yet to account for."

Mohanisi held his palms out flat. A ball of flame appeared a few inches above them, gradually growing in size as the heat became more and more intense. The spectacle immediately caused panic. The members of the council leaped from their seats and bolted for the door. The flame shot out from Mohanisi's hand, barring their way.

"You have nothing to fear," said Theopolou. "Please be calm."

Mohanisi allowed the flame to die.

The council returned to their seats. They all stared fearfully and Mohanisi.

Prince Loniel was the only one who seemed undaunted by the display. "And will this one elf defeat these vast armies?" he asked.

Theopolou smiled. He liked the young prince. "No. Not alone. But know you are not without great power on your side."

Queen Illirial spoke. "I, too, have been a friend to King Lousis. And I certainly do not wish to be under the thumb of King Halmara. But if Lousis dies, the most powerful of all the twelve city states is still left without a monarch. The Althetan people will not accept any of us here to rule in his place, and they certainly won't follow an elf ruler."

"Then you must form an alliance now," said Theopolou. "Your unity will galvanize the people of Althetas. Should the king die, there are worthy lords who could take up the mantle. You could lend your strength to this city. You could give hope to those who would otherwise despair."

"And what role will the elves play in all this?" asked Loniel.

"We defend our homes, our lives, and our children," Theopolou replied. "We have lived among you for more generations than can be counted. And though we have been separated by fear and hatred, we intend for that to end. Already elf and man have spilled blood together. We have fought side by side and faced death as brothers. Understand that I was against this before your grandmothers were children. If I can change, then so can you. Elf and human live in this world together, so we will rise or fall together. You ask what our role will be. Our role is to create a new world—together." He rose to his feet. "Those of you who will join me in this cause ... stand with me now. Those who will not..."

He paused and held his hand to the door. "Your presence is no longer required."

One by one, the kings and queens stood up.

"Then I leave you to your plans," said Theopolou.

"Will you not stay?" asked Queen Illirial.

"I cannot," he replied. "But until our elders arrive, Ertik speaks for my people."

Ertik looked at Theopolou, shocked. "My Lord..."

Theopolou turned to face him and took his hands. "You have my confidence, Ertik. If I am to stand by what I say, I must trust in my own words. You are to be the voice of the elves whilst I am away." He smiled warmly. "If you need aid, there are elves here who can assist you until Lord Chiron or one of the others arrive."

Ertik stared, stunned. Finally, he bowed his head and returned to his chair.

"Before you leave," said Queen Illirial, "I wonder, did you intend to tell us that King Lousis still lives?" Her face slowly twisted into a smile.

"As you were able to discover this on your own," replied Theopolou, "that would now appear to be unnecessary."

Theopolou bowed and left, Mohanisi just behind him.

"I noticed you did not mention Shivis Mol," said Mohanisi.

"That is not for me," said Theopolou, "and I think it would have done more harm than good. These people fear for their lands and family. It is enough that a vast army intends to wreak havoc. Should I tell them that their very souls are at stake as well?"

Mohanisi nodded with understanding. "The woman, Maybell, is here."

"Good," said Theopolou. "Gather the men. We leave as soon as I have spoken to her."

Mohanisi led him through the manor to where Maybell waited, sitting on the edge of a bed. She had dimmed the lanterns and allowed the dark to surround her.

"You are Maybell?" Theopolou's voice was deep and soothing.

"Yes," she replied weakly. "And you want to hear my story. You want to know what happened to Malstisos."

"I do," he replied, sitting down next to her. "My name is Theopolou. I am..."

"I know who you are," she cut in. "And I know why you're here. But I don't know if what I can tell you will be of any help."

"Whatever it is, I need to know," said Theopolou

"You know, when I watched two brothers—real brothers, mind you—fight to the death, I thought I had seen enough to break my heart in two." The light from the crack in the door silhouetted Theopolou. "But when I saw someone as noble and kind as Malstisos slowly becoming dark and diseased..." A tear fell down her cheek. "I can't explain what happened."

"Do your best," said Theopolou.

Maybell recounted the events up to and including the duel between Grentos and Vadnaltis. "Once that happened, Malstisos withdrew," she continued. "His mind and spirit grew darker with each day. At first, I thought he was agonizing over what had happened, but soon it was clear to me there was more to it than that. He began muttering to himself, almost like he was arguing with some inner demon. I tried talking to him, but he either ignored me or became angry."

"Do you think he went mad?" asked Theopolou.

"I did at first," she replied. "But then strange things started to happen. Wherever we went, I could see dark figures lurking about. Then Malstisos began disappearing for hours at a time. I thought he was only scouting or hunting until one night when we were camping just outside a small farm village. That's when I saw him hiding behind a clump of bushes while talking to a black-cloaked figure. When I asked him about this, he became angry—shouting and flailing his arms, he was. I swear, I thought he was going to hurt me."

Theopolou rubbed his chin thoughtfully. "This cloaked figure. Could you hear what it was saying?"

"No," she replied. "I could only hear whispers. But after that, I didn't question where he went."

"Did he say or do anything else that would explain what was happening to him?"

She shook her head. "By the time we reached Althetas he had stopped talking to me altogether. But whatever is happening, I pray you can help him." She covered her face and wept. "He was so good and kind."

Theopolou placed his hand gently on her head. "If I can help him, I will. That he kept his word and delivered you safely means there may still be hope."

"I'm sorry." She choked back her sobs. "I wish I could tell you more."

"You have told me enough." He stood up. "If you wish, I can have you escorted to Valshara. Kaylia is there."

"I would like that. Thank you." Maybell stood and walked with Theopolou to the door. "May the gods keep you."

Theopolou smiled and left.

Mohanisi was waiting outside. "Was she helpful?"

"I do not know," he admitted. "What she said was strange. From what I know of him, Malstisos was strong-willed and noble. I cannot imagine what may have affected him in such a manner. But I intend to find out. Ready yourself to depart and meet me in my quarters in one hour."

Alone, Theopolou pondered on what Maybell had said. Perhaps whatever corrupted the mind of Malstisos had affected the elves of the Steppes as well. If that were true, he would have to find a way to overcome it.

If he could not, this may very well be his final journey.

CHAPTER 26

For over three hours, the council had been debating on what to do about King Halmara. Most of the southern rulers, with the exception of King Tredford, thought it would be best to negotiate rather than go to war. The others argued that the attempted assassination of King Lousis left them with no other choice. Ertik was to the point of utter frustration when the door flew open and King Lousis entered, assisted on either arm by a guard. His face was pale as he struggled to take each step, but the fire in his eyes said he was determined.

There was a moment of silence, then the hall erupted in applause and cheers. As Lousis took his seat, he held up his hand to quiet the council.

"By the gods, we are grateful that you live, Your Highness," said Prince Loniel.

This prompted another round of cheers.

"I'm grateful as well, Prince Loniel," he replied, his voice matching the fire in his eyes. "I am told King Halmara and the snake Lord Sialo have fled. Also, that you have seen the wisdom of alliance against Angrääl. Though I wish it hadn't taken an attempt on my life to accomplish this."

King Victis spoke. "We are all overjoyed that you have survived. And clearly, Angrääl cannot be trusted. But many of us feel that King Halmara might have been deceived into doing you harm—if indeed it was even King Halmara at all. Is it possible that Sialo was acting alone? We would know the truth before we consider war against one of our own."

"The truth is that he has fled," said Lousis sternly. "The truth is that he allowed the murder of all the men and women in Valshara. That is enough for me to go to war. Those who do not have the stomach for it—well, then, you have chosen your side."

Queen Illirial spoke. "But Your Highness, surely you would rather not see us at war with each other? Would not a peaceful resolution with King Halmara be preferable?"

"While you contemplate peaceful solutions, Angrääl may be already moving against us," Lousis countered. "I understand that the southern cities are dependent on trade with Skalhalis as well as Baltria, and the idea of losing that trade worries you. But King Halmara is not fit to rule. And either by his action, or inaction, he has made his intentions known. I will not allow him to sit on the throne after what he has done. He has brought shame to his house and his kingdom." Lousis struggled to his feet. "Those who are willing, you should begin to muster your armies."

"What do you intend to do?" asked Prince Loniel.

"I intend to defeat King Halmara," He sat back down. "Then I will do the same to this so-called Reborn King." He looked to Ertik. "I am informed that you speak for both Valshara and the elves."

"This is true," Ertik replied. "Lord Theopolou gave me that honor. He heads north with Mohanisi to speak to the elves of the Steppes."

"Then I will need you to send word to Valshara," said Lousis. "We will need all the help that Theopolou's people can give."

"I will go there myself as soon as possible," said Ertik. "You will have whatever support you require."

Lousis looked over the council carefully. "I will return to my chambers now. In one hour, those who are with me may join me there. Those who are not—you are free to leave my home."

King Stanis spoke. "And should we not join you, will you make war on us as well?"

Lousis smiled. "I will not. Unless you provide support to King Halmara, you will remain unmolested by me. But know this. When Angrääl comes—and they certainly will—you stand alone." He struggled to his feet, and the guards rushed to his side. "You have one hour to discuss it. Ertik, as your mind is already set, I would have you join me now."

Ertik followed as the king carefully made his way from the chamber. They could hear the room erupt as the door slammed shut behind them.

"What do you think they will do?" asked Ertik.

"Most will not suffer Halmara to sit on the throne," he replied. "They would eventually come to that conclusion anyway, without my help. Of course, it would take them many weeks to do so. And if Halmara is bold enough to make an attempt on my life, then he obviously feels there is nothing the rest of them can do about it, and that he has the strength to keep them in line. It may also mean he is ready for war."

"You think Angrääl has already sent an army?" asked Ertik.

The king shrugged. "I don't know. But if they haven't, they will soon enough. We must be ready."

They wound their way back to the king's bedchambers. Ertik was surprised to see how humbly the man lived. The walls were covered with paintings of past rulers of Althetas, each with an engraved gold placard fastened below stating their name and years they had ruled. The large mahogany bed was well made and comfortable, but simple in its design. A small, round glass-topped table and four chairs sat beside a picture window overlooking a well-tended garden. At the opposite end, a tall sturdy bookcase housed dozens of leather-bound tomes. A door on either side of the bed hung ajar, one revealing a shower, the other a closet filled with the king's clothing.

Lousis dismissed the guards and walked carefully over to the table. He eased into a chair. Ertik took the seat opposite him.

"The southern rulers are not as bad as they seem," said Lousis. "They fear for their people should trade cease. None would admit to it, but the Reborn King has already forced many of them to trade exclusively with Angrääl. His stranglehold on Baltria has forced them into it."

"If that is the case, then what will you do?" asked Ertik.

"First, I will deal with Halmara. Then I will see to Baltria."

"You intend to make war with Baltria?" asked Ertik.

"I hope not," he replied. "But it may very well come to that. This war may begin here, but it will soon spread to all nations. We must find other allies. Baltria may not be as lost as we think. My understanding is that Angrääl has influenced the nobles and merchants there. If we can break that hold, then war will not be necessary. Of course, if Baltria is already under military control, then we will be forced to liberate it."

"Do you have enough men?" asked Ertik.

"Alas, no," admitted Lousis. "Even with all twelve kingdoms united, we would be hard-pressed. The elves will be of great help, but we will need even more."

"Then let us hope there are more rulers, such as you, who are not afraid to stand against the Reborn King."

Lousis smiled. "Make no mistake, I am afraid. But I fear even more what would happen to my people should we fail."

There was a knock at the door, and Prince Loniel entered.

"I hope Your Highness doesn't mind," said the Prince. "I grew tired of listening to the nobles bicker. My mind was set the moment you were poisoned."

Lousis offered him a seat, which he gratefully accepted.

"How are things faring?" asked Lousis.

"As one might expect," he replied with a shrug. "They speak of peaceful resolutions and are in fear of war. But I think most are more afraid of standing alone. And in light of recent events, they are now also in fear of what Angrääl may do to them."

"So you think they will side with Althetas?" asked Ertik.

"I do," Loniel replied. "At least, they will give what support they can. Most cities do not have the wealth of Althetas, and could raise no more than a few thousand soldiers at best."

"It will be enough," said Lousis. "It will have to be."

A short time later, the other kings and queens began entering in ones and twos. With only a few minutes to go until the stated hour was up, only King Victis had not yet arrived.

"It will be a blow to lose the Tarvansia Peninsula," remarked Loniel.

"Being that it has the most direct route to Baltria, it will make things far more difficult," agreed Lousis.

Just then, the door opened and an unhappy-looking King Victis entered. "I am loathed to use force against King Halmara," he stated. "But as the will of the council is against me..."

Queen Illirial spoke. "King Lousis. As you know, none of our kingdoms possess the wealth of Althetas, and this shall cut off our trade with Baltria. What can you do to ensure our people don't starve?"

"If I must, I will empty my treasury," Lousis replied, allowing his gaze to meet each one of them in turn. "There are already lords and ladies in my city who are struggling against this growing threat. We will enlist their help as well. Once we deal with Halmara, then we will address Baltria."

"So, you will expand this war to include Baltria?" asked Victis, scowling.

"Naturally, I will try other means first," said Lousis. "But we cannot allow a port of that size to be under Angrääl's control." He waved a dismissive hand. "However, that is a matter to be discussed once we have settled with Halmara. In the meantime, we must discover what is happening in Skalhalis. I will ask Ertik to send elf scouts there to see if they have armed for war."

"I will do so at once," said Ertik. "And I would suggest that you send more men to Valshara. One hundred can hold off a siege for a long time but not indefinitely."

"I agree," said Lousis. "I intend to make Valshara our staging point." He got to his feet. "I know that some of you do not have many soldiers to offer. That being so, all cities south of Althetas should retain whatever numbers are required to keep order in their own lands, and send the rest to Tarvansia. If Angrääl moves forces from Baltria, that is where they will strike first. The rest will join my forces in Valshara. Agreed?"

Gradually, all nodded in agreement.

For the next several hours, they mapped out plans for troops and supplies. It was late in the afternoon before they decided to adjourn for the day. Lousis asked Victis to remain in his chambers once the others had left.

"Thank you, my friend," said Lousis. "I know how difficult it was for you to make this decision."

"King Halmara is my cousin," Victis replied. "But in the end, there is no denying that you are right. He is not fit to rule. I have worried about the future of my land for some time, and I am not blind to what Angrääl has done. I can see what will become of us. But I still do not think we can prevail."

"Then why did you join us?" asked Lousis.

Victis held his head high. "Because I am King of Tarvansia. My people will remain free for as long as I draw breath." He moved to the door. "But I am tired, and I believe we have several more days of planning ahead of us." Just as he was on the point of leaving, he paused. "I thank you for excluding me from the campaign against my cousin."

Lousis smiled as the door closed. He changed into his night robe and slipped into bed. His body ached, and his head was swimming. The battle of Valshara entered his thoughts. The sights and sounds of the dead and dying were still fresh in his memory. This would get worse. Much worse. He looked up at the portrait of his father, King Hersal, hanging on the wall close by. Hersal had ruled for fifty-two years. In all those years, there had been only one border dispute and a few bands of marauding raiders that needed to be run out of the kingdom.

"What I would give to trade places," he muttered before allowing himself to drift off to sleep.

CHAPTER 27

For six days, Lee had been chained, hands above his head, to a cold stone wall. At least, that's how long he thought it had been. Not a morsel of food or drop of water had been offered during that time, and even with the strength of Saraf running through his veins, he was now beginning to weaken. Occasionally, he would hear someone enter the small cell he was held in, but a blindfold had been kept over his eyes throughout, so he could not tell who it might be. He did his best to concentrate on what was going on nearby, but the only sounds he heard were of various rodents scurrying about and the stomping of hard boots on stone floors.

His mind wandered to thoughts of Jacob. He refused to believe that he had been betrayed, though his captors had clearly wanted him to believe so. He would not fall prey to doubt and despair. In all probability, his life would end soon, and he would need more than innuendo for his last moments to be filled with anger.

The door opened, and this time the footfalls were light and graceful, not the clumsy, plodding of a soldier. The scent of lilacs filled the air.

"So, they have sent a woman to attend to me," said Lee. His mouth was so dry that every word was painful. "You can tell your master that his efforts to break me will fail. It is just as well that he kill me now and be done with it."

He felt a cup touching his dry, cracked lips. The water poured down his throat. He moaned with relief in spite of himself.

"So, what is it you intend to do?" he asked contemptuously. "Keep me alive so you can watch me suffer?" There was no response. "You fear to speak? It's just as well. Your words would only be lies."

"I don't know what to say." The voice was a soft whisper.

"Then say nothing," he shot back. "Better next time they send a mute fool."

There was a long silence, then he felt a cool rag gently cleaning the grime from his face.

He shook his head violently. "Do not touch me. Not unless it is a blade you carry."

"Are you so anxious to die?" she asked.

The voice was familiar. Another trick, he told himself.

"Yes, my love." She spoke as if she could read his thoughts. "It is me." She lifted the cup to his lips again, but Lee turned his head away.

"Then remove my blindfold," he commanded.

"I am forbidden," she replied. "It was the only way they would allow me to see you."

"I know you are lying. Penelope would not act with such cruelty."

"I will remove your blindfold," she offered. "But know that if I do, I will be taken from here at once and not be allowed to return. Yes, you will have learned I speak the truth, but we will not see each other again—ever."

Lee's heart ached. "Then leave me blind. But know I will tell you nothing the Dark Knight may want to know."

"That is best," she said. "There is much that has happened of which you are unaware."

"And Jacob," he asked. "What has happened to him?"

"He has escaped," she replied. "He did not betray you, Lee. He was recognized by a recruit from Hazrah."

"That is good to hear," he replied. He felt a great weight lifting from his heart. "But if the Dark Knight intends to break me, why tell me this?"

She continued to clean his face. "The Reborn King does not need to leave you in despair to break you, my love. You will understand this once you are in his presence."

"He may find it more difficult than he imagines."

"He is aware of your strength," she said. "That is why he has waited. He wishes you intact. Should he force his will upon you, your spirit could shatter."

"And how is it that you know all this?" asked Lee.

"I have been in the presence of the Reborn King," she replied sadly. "I have witnessed his power. No one can resist him. Not even you, my love."

"Did you come here to warn me, or prepare me?" he asked angrily. "Penelope would never say these things."

"I only tell you the truth," she replied. "I wish things were different. I am Penelope Nal'Thain, but no longer the woman you knew. The King has changed me."

"Then help me," said Lee. "I will undo what he has done."

"If only that were possible." Her voice was filled with sorrow and longing. "But I am lost. Even if I helped you to escape, I would betray you eventually. I wouldn't be able to help myself. You can't know what it means to be under the King's power."

He could hear her weeping softly. "Please. I can help you. I swear it. I can break the hold he has over you."

"I must go." She lifted the cup to his lips once more. "I will try to return tomorrow. Soon you will be brought before the King." Lee heard the door creak open. "I would speak to you again before you become his."

The door slammed shut. A tear fell down his cheek. He didn't want to believe that this woman was really Penelope, but he knew in his heart it was. Rage and frustration swelled in his chest. He jerked the chains around his wrists with all his might, but even with his immense strength, they were far too thick to break.

He knew he must escape—somehow. He would find a way to free Penelope and take her away from this wretched place. His thoughts turned to Jacob. He had escaped. But would he run? He doubted it. Jacob had too much of his father in him, which meant he would most likely end up being killed or captured. There had to be a way of escaping before it was too late. If what Penelope had told him was true, and the Dark Knight really did have the power to break him, then soon he may be powerless to do anything at all. How he wished he could have seen her, if only for a moment.

He thought back to the last time they were together. Her eyes had been filled with tears, but her voice was hot with anger. She'd cursed him for leaving his family.

The door opened again. His heart jumped, but the sound of boots told him that it was not Penelope returning. The disappointment over this had only just formed when a fist slammed into his abdomen, causing him to gasp out loud.

"You know what you cost me, Starfinder?" It was Captain Lanmore. "Because of your deception, I have lost everything."

"And you expect me to feel guilt?" Lee scoffed. "You are the servant of my enemy, and the enemy of all free people." A fist crashed into his jaw. The taste of blood filled his mouth, but he spat it out defiantly. "I'm surprised they even allowed you to live after realizing your stupidity and incompetence."

Lanmore moved close to whisper in Lee's ear. "I should kill you now. But perhaps I'll kill your son instead while you watch. Yes. He's stupid enough to think he can rescue you. When he's caught, I'll skin him alive."

Lee laughed. "Those are the words I would expect from a coward. You are truly bold when faced with a man in chains. Were I free, you would run like the scared dog that you are."

"You think me a fool?" He grabbed Lee's face and squeezed. "I am not ignorant to what you are, Lee Nal'Thain, Starfinder, or whatever you call yourself—son of Saraf. Do you imagine my king sends us to war ill-informed? I know what you are capable of. So, if you think to goad me into releasing you, then you waste your breath."

"Then I suggest you finish your business and leave," said Lee.

"I'm finished," said Lanmore. "And soon, you will be, too."

The door slammed hard. Lee couldn't help but feel pity for the captain. A commoner in a world of nobles, clawing his way through the ranks, was admirable. He had felt a genuine kinship with the man. But he was the enemy, nonetheless. Lee had not really imagined he could anger Lanmore sufficiently to release him. But it had been worth a try. Still, there must be another way.

He slid down the wall, allowing the chain to support him. He needed to rest. He needed to stay strong. When the moment arrived, he would be ready. He fell asleep, his determination as strong as ever.

The sound of a creaking door shocked him out of his slumber. It was the light footfalls of Penelope but mixed with the clinking of metal and scraping of leather. He felt thin, delicate fingers pulling the blindfold from his eyes. At first, he squinted painfully at the light from the torches, but as his eyes focused, he saw her.

Her long, straight, raven hair fell around her shoulders and down her back, framing her sweet features. Her ivory skin and deep blue eyes were staring lovingly at him. She smiled a warm, sad smile as she stepped back. Even in the blue nightgown she wore, she looked graceful. Age had not touched her. She was every inch the woman he remembered.

"It is you," he cried, tears forming.

In her right hand, she held a large iron key. A moment later, she had unshackled him. Lee nearly collapsed. Struggling to steady himself, he threw his arms around his wife and embraced her tightly.

"I am here, my love," she whispered. She pulled back slightly and met his eyes.

Lee was now weeping openly. He kissed Penelope long and deep, crushing her to his chest. "I prayed for this. Come. We will find Jacob, and I will get you away from here."

She pointed to a guard's uniform and sword piled next to the door. "Quickly. Change into this."

Lee beamed and quickly donned the uniform. "Are you ready?" he asked.

Penelope smiled a sad smile before kissing Lee once again. "I cannot go with you."

"What do you mean?" he exclaimed. "Of course you can. They will not stop us. If I have to, I will cut my way through every soldier in Angrääl."

Penelope suddenly grasped her stomach and doubled over. Lee rushed to her side, supporting her as she slid to the floor.

"What is wrong?" His voice was desperate.

"I am saving you the only way I can," she said weakly. "I told you. I belong to the King now. He has enslaved my spirit. I could only resist him for a short time. But it will be long enough..."

She winced in pain as she reached inside her robe to pull out a small, empty vial.

Lee recognized the faint odor of venil root immediately. "Please, no!" he sobbed. "Not this way!"

"It was the only way I would not betray you," she explained, smiling. "I could not bear for you to fall under the same curse that now possesses me. The Reborn King is more powerful than you can imagine. He must be stopped. His plans go far beyond the coming war. He wants to watch the world burn. And once he has conquered all, he will destroy the earth— and heaven along with it. Nothing will remain."

She tried to push Lee away, but he held her fast. "Now go," she pleaded. "Jacob has been spotted three miles south of the garrison. Find him before they do. Please ... save our son." Her eyes closed, and with one final gasp, she went limp.

His tears continued to fall freely as he pulled her body close. How long he held her like this, he couldn't say. Then, like an echo in his mind, her last words came back to him.

Save our son.

He laid her gently on the floor and kissed her lips. "Goodbye, my love," he said softly. After one final tender look, he wiped his eyes dry. Dark sadness began to boil over into blinding rage.

He opened the door to his cell; two guards lay dead just outside, one wearing nothing but his underclothes. He dragged the bodies inside and closed the door. Lee thought about the layout of the garrison, hoping that the uniform disguise would be enough to allow him to pass through unnoticed. *That was why Penelope had cleaned his face,* he thought. She must have known all along what she intended to do. The memory stabbed at him. No. He must push aside despair for now. He recalled how he had been brought there. They had not blindfolded him until after he was put in chains. Their mistake.

He made his way through the stone corridors of the keep until he reached the main hall leading to the front entrance. His muscles tensed as two guards walked by, but to his relief, they didn't even bother to look at him. The bureaucrats had left their desks for the evening, so the path to the door was open.

Hoping it was now dark, he opened the door and stepped into the yard. Torches burned around the perimeter and along the slate path leading to the gatehouse. The frigid night air swept under his clothes. He shivered for a split second, then walked at a steady pace toward the gate. Two guards were stationed there, but they scarcely seemed to notice his passing.

The road south was empty. He looked north to Kratis. The city glowed brightly against the background of the dark night sky, its towers looming ominously. The thought of the Dark Knight being so close redoubled his rage. But this was not the right time for such thoughts. Forcing this anger down, he headed south. Once out of sight from the garrison, he left the road, darting in and out from behind trees and brushes, stopping every few yards to listen for signs of Jacob. Just as Penelope had said, after three miles, he heard him.

Lee crept silently until he was only a few yards away from a felled tree. Jacob was crouched behind it, ready to spring.

"Jacob," whispered Lee. "Come out."

Jacob stayed perfectly still. Lee called out again. This time, he cautiously climbed over the tree and walked to where his father waited. Lee embraced his son.

"How did you escape?" asked Jacob.

The pain of Penelope's death cut deep once again. "We must flee."

"But what about mother?" he pressed.

Before Lee could respond, he heard several men approaching from the road. He spun around, but heard more men coming from the other direction.

"Don't try to run," called out the voice of Captain Lanmore. "There is no escape."

Lee and Jacob drew their swords.

"Come closer if you long for death," responded Lee.

The men halted their approach.

"There is no need for this," Lanmore told him from a few yards away. "My master wishes you returned to him unharmed. You ... and your son."

"If I return to your master, it will be to end his life," roared Lee.

Lanmore laughed. "Even your dear wife knew that was impossible. Why do you think she helped you to escape?"

Jacob shot Lee an accusing glance.

"And for that, she paid with her life," Lee replied, hatred spewing from his lips. "My wife lies dead because of your master's evil. If you imagine, even for one second, that I will simply return with you, then you're a far bigger fool than I thought."

"Do you really think the Reborn King would allow such a noble lady to die?" Lanmore asked. "She could not escape his grasp so easily. No, Lord Nal'Thain. Your wife still lives."

"You lie!" he shouted. "I saw her die. I held her in my arms."

"I'm sure you did. But the King is powerful. Those whom he wishes to live will do so." Taking a step forward, Lanmore sheathed his sword. "He knew she would help you to escape, and he knew she would try to take her own life to ensure that she could not betray you. Ask yourself this. How did you escape so easily? How did you manage to walk straight through the front gate? He knew you would try to find your son. Should we have tried to capture him, he would have resisted. And the King does not want his blood. Return with me now, and you can be with your family again."

"When I run, you follow," Lee whispered to Jacob.

"But mother..." he protested.

"Your mother is dead," Lee snapped. "And you will not follow her."

Lee burst into a dead run heading southeast, Jacob hard on his heels. Both of them shot past the soldiers before they had time to fully react. They gave chase, but Lee and Jacob were much too fast for them.

Soon they had disappeared completely into the darkness.

The soldiers returned to Captain Lanmore, scraped, bruised, and out of breath. After ordering them back to the garrison, he remained where he was, staring into the shadows of the forest. He could feel a presence just behind him. Its raw power nearly sent him falling to his knees, but he did not dare to turn around.

"Such a pity," said a voice. It was close to a whisper, yet it carried a power that gave the sound an almost physical form.

"Forgive me, Master," he said. Fear pierced his heart. "They escaped. My men weren't fast enough."

"If I had wanted them captured, I would have sent the Vrykol," the voice said. It sounded amused. "But it matters not. I have already foreseen the fate of Lee Starfinder."

The presence vanished. Lanmore fell to the ground and wept.

CHAPTER 28

Gewey stared over the bow of the ship. Aaliyah had continued with his training, but as they drew closer to their destination, he noticed that she would frequently lose focus. After a week, she had taken to sleeping on deck. Gewey offered to give her their room to herself, but she told him that she preferred to sleep under the stars and enjoy the scent of ocean air.

He tried on several occasions to speak with her, hoping to lift her spirits, but she withdrew even further. After the ship rounded the Tarvansia Peninsula, Aaliyah informed him that he would be spending his remaining time on board studying with Drasalisia, the navigator. He tried to object, but Aaliyah would not be swayed and seemed most relieved when the navigator reluctantly agreed.

From the onset of the lessons, it was clear that Drasalisia intended to be a strict taskmaster. On the very first day he joined her at the bow of the ship, she simply looked at him sideways and handed him a small cup of water. She then had him sit cross-legged on the deck a few feet behind her.

"You can join me when you learn control," she said. She held out her hand. Almost immediately, a small droplet of water floated up from the cup and hovered in mid-air a few inches above it. The drop then floated down onto the cup's edge, where it rolled around a few times before sliding back inside.

She stood up and stared down at Gewey for a moment. "When you can do this, you are ready to continue," she said. Then, with a huff, she returned to the bow.

Gewey closed his eyes and allowed the flow of the air to surround the tiny cup, but with no success whatsoever. Time after time, the cup simply spilled over. On every occasion he returned with more water, the navigator shot him a disapproving glance. After three hours, he leaped to his feet and let out a frustrated scream.

"What good is this?!" he shouted. "How does this help me?"

The navigator strode over and picked up the cup. "Hold this in your palm."

Without enthusiasm, he obeyed. He watched as another tiny droplet of water floated out and drifted toward the navigator.

"Not everything requires brute force," she said quietly.

Without warning, the droplet flew forward at blinding speed, striking the cup in his hand and shattering it into a hundred pieces. Water and fragments fell to the deck. Gewey stared in amazement.

"Such a thing could be quite useful, wouldn't you say?" Drasalisia remarked. As she returned to her duties, she glanced over her shoulder. "You will need another cup, I think."

Excited by what he had seen, Gewey very nearly broke into a run. For six straight hours, he continued to try, but was still unsuccessful. The sun was setting, and the navigator had just been relieved from duty when she walked over and sat next to him.

"Show me what you are doing," she said in her typical, emotionless way. She took hold of Gewey's hand and brought her spirit close to his.

Gewey tried once again, and once again failed. He forced the water over the side. The moment it touched the deck, he felt the navigator seize the flow and return it into the cup.

"You must understand the way this power works," she explained. "Earth, air and water are not different. At least, not in essence. They are all pieces of the same world. But you try to dig and lift the water with air, as a shovel to earth. Or you throw it, as a bale of hay into a wagon." She reached out and touched the flow of the water, surrounding a tiny drop and pressing it in. "You transition it from one to the other. It is as the left hand touching the right." The air stirred almost imperceptibly, blending with the droplet. In unison, they rose; the droplet carried on a tiny cushion of air. "Do you see?" The droplet sank gently back into the cup.

"I understand." His words were a gasp.

"Good," she said, now with a hint of satisfaction. "Return tomorrow and try again. You have done enough for today."

In spite of his desire to continue, he knew it was useless to argue. He spent the evening with the crew, learning about the ship and listening to their tales. Aaliyah joined him for dinner, but apart from this brief interlude, she remained alone in their cabin until going up on deck to sleep.

This time, however, Gewey was determined to find out what was on her mind. He brought his blanket and pillow and lay down next to her.

"I know you think you can help me," said Aaliyah. "But there is really nothing you can do."

"If I can't help, would you at least tell me what is troubling you?"

She sighed and closed her eyes. "I am trying to still my heart. Soon I must see Nehrutu again."

Gewey raised an eyebrow and smiled. "I would think you'd be happy about that."

"I am uncertain how I feel," she replied. "There is no doubt I will be pleased to see him, but I am unsure as to what to say. Through your communication with Kaylia, he will be aware of your decision—and my failure."

Gewey chuckled. "That should make him happy."

She looked over at Gewey. "If Kaylia left you in pursuit of another, would you be happy when she returned?"

"If it meant we would be together, I might," he replied. "But you left Nehrutu out of a sense of duty, not because you stopped loving him. I'm sure he understands that."

"He does. But I cannot help but wonder how I would feel if the situation were reversed. Would I be so willing to return to the one who spurned me?" She smiled. "I am acting as a child. But matters of the heart make children of us all. Even the most wise."

"Have you reached out with your spirit?" he asked. "I'm sure it will ease your mind if you do."

"I have more knowledge than you, Gewey," she replied. "But I am not as strong. I cannot span such great distances."

"I could help," he offered.

In spite of herself, Aaliyah could not hold back a laugh. "I am afraid such a meeting would be too personal. But I thank you, regardless." She closed her eyes. "Now, if you intend to stay under the stars with me, you must allow me to rest."

Gewey squeezed her hand and rolled over. The sound of the ocean swells lapping against the ship's hull was sweet music, singing him to sleep. As he drifted, he thought of Kaylia. He considered reaching out to her, but the motion of the ship pulled him down too fast. Within seconds, his breathing was deep and steady.

The morning brought the sound of gulls and the spirited voices of the crew hard at work. Aaliyah was already busy with the running of the ship, and now appeared to be in much better spirits. After breakfast, Gewey returned to the navigator carrying his cup of water. Taking his place on the deck, he continued the exercise. This time, after only two attempts, he did it. A small droplet of water floated from the cup. Gewey was elated. He moved it around, making it rise, fall, and travel in tight circles. He allowed the flow to swell and concentrate within him. He removed another droplet, then another, until there were ten in all. He formed them into a ring and pushed them above the navigator's head. Then, one by one, allowed them to drop.

The navigator turned slowly; her expression unmoved. "That is enough for today."

Gewey tried to suppress a laugh. "Don't you have a sense of humor?"

She turned back around, saying nothing. Gewey frowned and headed toward the cabin. After only a few steps toward the door, a large ball of water splashed down over his head, soaking him to the skin. The elves on deck burst into laughter. Gewey looked back at the navigator, who was still facing forward.

"There is nothing wrong with my sense of humor," she said.

Gewey couldn't help but smile. He used the flow to dry his clothes, then went in search of Aaliyah. He found her in her quarters, poring over a large map that covered the entire desk. He told her what the navigator had taught him—and what she had done in response to his joke.

"She must like you," she noted.

"You'd never know it by the way she looks at me," Gewey replied.

"I've known Drasalisia for seventy years and never once seen her be playful." Aaliyah leaned back in her chair and grinned. "We should arrive just north of the city of Skalhalis in two days' time. From there we will cut across country and arrive in Valshara the following day."

Just then, a bell sounded repeatedly from on deck. Aaliyah jumped up and flew from the cabin, Gewey following close behind. As they made their way up, he could feel the ship slowing.

"What is it?" asked Aaliyah, while making her way to the bow.

"A fleet of ships just beyond the horizon," said the navigator. "At least fifty."

"Can we avoid them?"

"We can," she replied. "But you may wish to go ashore further north. From their course, it looks as if they are heading for Skalhalis."

Aaliyah thought for a moment. "No. I want you to plot a course that has us arriving under the cover of darkness. Once Gewey and I are away, take the ship as far offshore as possible, while still close enough to be contacted."

"There is more." The navigator's countenance betrayed her worry. She took Aaliyah's hand and together they closed their eyes. After a few minutes, she let go and lowered her head as if fatigued. "Is that what attacked you in the desert?"

"It was," replied Aaliyah. She turned to Gewey. "It would seem Angrääl has sent more forces. Vrykol are aboard ships bound for Skalhalis. They will arrive just as we get to Valshara. You must warn Kaylia."

Gewey nodded sharply and ran to his quarters. Sitting in front of the desk, he reached out for Kaylia, but her thoughts were presently turned to matters of the flow. *Nehrutu must be giving her another lesson,* he thought. He pressed his spirit in even harder. This time, he managed to reach her. He explained what Aaliyah had told him, but the moment he'd finished, she broke contact.

Aaliyah entered a moment later. "Did you succeed?"

The shock of Kaylia pulling away so suddenly had made him feel dizzy. "Yes. I'm sure of it," he said.

Aaliyah walked over to the desk and stared down at the map. "We will come very close to the ships when we land, and we still may be seen from the shore if an army is mustering for war."

"Then they will not live to tell of our passing," said Gewey. A small fire was building in his heart. The rage returned. It felt good. He smiled fiendishly and looked sideways at Aaliyah. "I guess the war has truly begun."

She placed her hand on his shoulder. "It would seem so."

He spent the rest of the day with the crew, trying to calm himself and keep his mind as far away as possible from war. By now, he had learned quite a lot about the workings of the ship, and offered to lend a hand wherever he could. This was well received by the crew, who in short order were teaching him elven seafarer's songs and telling old tales passed down aboard ships for thousands of years. Most were about sea monsters and adventure, but a few dealt with the gods. Gewey tried to pretend not to be interested in these, but couldn't help wondering how much truth was hidden within the fiction. After seeing what secrets the desert held, he thought that the sea stories might hold more truth than anyone ever imagined.

In spite of all his efforts, his mind still kept wandering to the coming battle. The force that had marched on Valshara would certainly not be enough to defeat fifty ships filled with soldiers. And he had no idea of how many men might have already landed before these new arrivals. There could be a hundred-thousand troops ready to sweep across the land for all he knew. If that were so, then the war would be over almost before it had begun.

By nightfall, he was dreading what dreams might come. He knew Kaylia would be making preparations, and that meant he would most likely be unable to contact her. Aaliyah could tell he was troubled and stayed in her quarters with him.

"Should you need me, I am here," she said as they both slipped into bed.

"Thank you," he replied. He rolled over and closed his eyes. "I'll be fine."

"Do not fear the strength your feelings bring," she said. "They are a part of you. It was that strength that saved my life."

He sat up and pushed his back to the wall. "I know. And when it happens, I don't mind. But afterward—it's as if I lose who I am. I feel that it's changing me."

"It is changing you," she replied. "I told you that before. But that should not upset you. You are just becoming what you were always meant to be."

"And tell me, what is that exactly?" he asked, his concern clear. "I mean, I feel it most when I'm angry. What if that's how I eventually become—an angry, vengeful god? Will the world be any better off once the Dark Knight is gone if I remain?"

Aaliyah scowled. "You will not become evil, if that is what you're suggesting. Powerful—yes. Dangerous—absolutely. But dangerous to whom is the question? I think not to those who you love and protect."

"I hope not." Gewey slid back down and wrapped himself in his blanket. "Each time I feel it stronger than the last. The name Darshan is becoming more and more natural to me. I'm just afraid I'll lose the part of me that is Gewey."

"You will not," she said, her tone reassuring. "I swear it."

His dreams that night were troubled, filled with visions of hopeless despair and suffering. Human and elf huddled together, bleeding and crying. The whole world was trapped in an inferno of chaos and death. And he was stood alone in the midst of it all, powerless, unable to change anything. The morning was the only thing that brought him welcome relief.

They were due to arrive at sunset, so Gewey spent the morning gathering supplies and checking his gear. He then rested in the cabin until the early afternoon. He wanted to be as strong as possible when they landed, so only left the cabin twice to take his meals. When he finally went up on deck, he took his pack, the bow, and staff along with him. These he stowed near to the landing craft.

Aaliyah was already there and ready to depart.

"I see you are excited to get underway," she remarked.

He shrugged and leaned over the port railing to look at the setting sun. The cloudless, azure sky was beginning to reveal the night stars as daylight slowly faded. There would be no moon tonight. He was grateful for that.

As he waited to depart, the crew came one by one to bid him farewell. As night fell and the ship slowed to a halt, the navigator joined him.

"You will return once your task is done," said Drasalisia. "I still have much to teach you."

Gewey thought he almost saw her smile, but couldn't be certain. "I would like that," he said. He watched her for a second as she walked away. Then, as his gaze returned to the sea, he felt something strike the top of his head. The next instant, water was pouring all down his back. He spun around just in time to see the navigator entering the cabin.

Aaliyah approached, pack in hand. She smiled. "Of all the wonders I have seen, that was the most amazing. Were you an elf, you would certainly be doomed to be her apprentice."

Gewey laughed, at the same time running fingers through his saturated hair. "So, it's time to go?"

Aaliyah nodded, then led him to the boat. The crew lowered it into the water and they climbed down. As they moved away, Gewey looked back to see the crew gathered all along the starboard rail, waving. He waved back, as did Aaliyah.

He drew his sword and let the flow of the air rage through him. Soon he could make out the shoreline. The sea was calm, with small waves lapping against the sand. The moment the boat touched shore, they dragged it into some nearby brush and covered it with branches. He reached out to see if anyone was about. Approximately three hundred yards due east, where the beach turned into a thin forest, twenty men were moving north.

"I sense them, too," whispered Aaliyah. "And twenty more, a quarter mile south of their position."

"If they stay bunched together like that, we should be able to slip between them," said Gewey. "Kaylia taught me to move in the shadows unseen."

"A useful skill," she replied. "Let us hope it serves us tonight."

They crept forward until they were only a hundred yards from the patrol. He could see their armor reflecting in the light of the torches they carried. One soldier turned toward them, revealing the broken scales insignia of Angrääl across his chest plate.

They paused, crouching behind a clump of sand tails as the patrol slowly moved away. Just as Gewey and Aaliyah entered the tree line, they sensed an all-too-familiar foulness coming toward them from the east.

"Vrykol," Gewey hissed. "Only one though."

"But it's enough to raise the alarm," said Aaliyah. "If that happens, use the earth. Fire will draw even more down upon us. We should try to avoid that if possible."

Gewey allowed the flow of the earth to replace the air. It felt odd, yet invigorating. The earth was so much more physical and raw. "If it hears us, I'll knock him over. Soon as I do, we'll rush it. Hopefully, it won't have time to call out."

They moved south, then east. At first, it looked like the Vrykol wouldn't sniff them out. Then, just as they were parallel to it, the creature halted and began walking swiftly toward them. As it came into view, Gewey could see that it held a curved blade in one hand, and a small, bone horn in the other. Gewey was just about to fling a fallen log at the beast when it stopped and raised the horn to lips hidden beneath the black hood. The sound rang out, and the beast backed away.

"I guess they are becoming more cunning," observed Gewey. He remembered the elven Vrykol from the Black Oasis and the anger raged. He grinned maliciously at Aaliyah before charging forward. Aaliyah drew her dagger and followed.

The Vrykol waited for them. But instead of a sword, the twang of a bowstring sounded. The arrow whizzed through the air, seeking Gewey's heart. At the very last instant, he managed to twist and dive sideways. Only his incredible speed saved him from being skewered.

Aaliyah ran straight ahead, slashing at the Vrykol's neck. The creature was barely able to drop the bow and draw its sword in time. The sound of metal on metal rang out. Aaliyah pressed the attack, forcing the beast back.

Gewey scurried to his feet and charged in. The Vrykol slashed hard at Aaliyah and then reached inside its cloak. Just as Gewey was close to striking distance, the creature threw something to the ground just in front of him. The earth burst into flames, bringing Gewey sliding to a halt. He heard soldiers approaching from either side. Quickly, he threw the earth beneath the fire upward and to his left, then leaped over the small crater now left in the ground. Aaliyah was being pushed back as the Vrykol attacked furiously. Gewey slashed at its leg, cutting deep and sending it stumbling backward. Aaliyah slashed at its neck, but it lifted its sword to deflect the blade. In a flash, it then brought its fist crashing into Aaliyah's jaw. She fell heavily.

The Vrykol turned to Gewey, thrusting its blade at his gullet. Gewey twisted and countered, opening the Vrykol's chest. It fell back, stabbing wildly.

Just then, the first patrol of soldiers arrived. Aaliyah recovered her feet in time to bring her knife across the leading soldier's neck. She spun around, gutting another.

A blast of wind forced the center of the patrol backward as she set about attacking their left side, cutting down two men with a single stroke.

Gewey pressed the Vrykol hard. The flow swelling inside him was made even stronger by his sword. With all his strength, he swung the blade at the beast's neck. The Vrykol tried to block the blow, but its blade shattered under the massive impact. Still following through with the same devastating sweep, Gewey's sword sent the creature's head rolling from its shoulders. Rapidly, he then turned to see Aaliyah blasting the soldiers back with bolts of air as she carved her way through their ranks.

He could hear more soldiers approaching from the south. The flames from the Vrykol attack were beginning to spread to the dry leaves and twigs lining the forest floor. Hiding was no longer an option. He created a wall of flame, splitting the soldiers' ranks and pushing them back. Only two men now remained on the far side of the flames to face Aaliyah. Fear quickly overcame them. Dropping their weapons, they fled.

Gewey had already surrounded the others with flames. He tightened the ring, as he had done to the Soufis. The soldiers began to scream and cry.

"Kill them or let them go," yelled Aaliyah.

The wall of fire was still creeping slowly in, squeezing the men ever closer together. With a rush of self-awareness, Gewey realized that his spirit had become full of hatred and anger. He wanted them dead. He wanted to watch them burn. It took a huge effort of willpower for him to allow the flames to die. He shouted out to the panic-stricken men.

"Run, if you want to live!"

The soldiers needed no second telling. Dropping their swords, they ran as fast as they could. But by now, the second group of soldiers were coming into view. As Gewey turned to face them, a column of fire burst to life directly above his head, jagging back and forth menacingly at the new arrivals, daring them to take even a single step closer. It was enough. Shouts of terror filled the air as the second patrol also chose the far safer option of fleeing rather than fighting.

"Your powers are growing," said Aaliyah. "You could have easily bested ten times as many."

Gewey glanced down at the dead Vrykol. *Not powerful enough,* he thought. *Not yet.*

The pair of them ran off into the night at a full run. The flow raged, but it felt different. More intense. He smiled as he sped his way through the forest.

The name Darshan echoed loud in his mind.

CHAPTER 29

King Halmara paced in front of the jeweled throne of his forefathers, glancing angrily at the door every time he turned. The rarely used throne room was cold and empty. For generations, the well-being of his kingdom had been administered from the king's office and the council chambers. This room was for receiving honored guests and nothing more. The walls bore the banners of the twelve kingdoms, with the eagle and fish symbol of Skalhalis hanging proudly above the throne. His family had ruled for more than a thousand years. Now folly could end everything. Lord Sialo was sat in a plush chair to the right side of the throne, watching the King carefully.

"You should relax, Your Highness," said Sialo. "Things are going according to plan."

Halmara stopped and turned on Sialo. "Is that so? In what way was the poisoning of King Lousis part of the plan?"

"I told you before, I had nothing to do with that," said Sialo. "It was Yanti who gave the order."

"Then Yanti is a fool," he roared. "And when I see him…"

The door flew open. Yanti strode confidently in. "You will do what?" He laughed. "My good king, nothing has been done that wasn't according to my design."

Halmara snarled. "Your idiocy has ensured that the other kingdoms will surely align against me. They probably gather as we speak."

Yanti stopped. His eyes grew dark and threatening. "Mind your tongue, Highness, or you may find your long reign becomes a fleeting moment. I have enough soldiers to crush Althetas. They cannot muster enough of a force in time to stop us."

"I will not be intimidated by you," Halmara said. But his voice wavered.

"I do not try to intimidate," said Yanti. "I only want you to know your situation. You are a vassal of Angräal and will bend to the will of the Reborn King. And his will is what I tell you it is." He leveled his eyes. "Are we clear about this, Your Highness?"

Halmara felt as if his breath had been taken away. He slumped down onto his throne, defeated. "I still think it was a mistake to poison King Lousis."

"I'm truly sorry, but that had to be done," Yanti explained. "After poisoning my poor dear Salmitaya, it was imperative."

A messenger burst through the door and bowed low. "I bring news, Your Highness." He handed the king a rolled-up piece of parchment. The boy bowed again and hurried away.

Halmara unrolled the parchment and read it carefully. "It would seem your attempt on King Lousis's life has failed."

Yanti smiled and waved his hand carelessly. "It matters not. Once the army is assembled and ready, then we will see to him." He turned to Sialo. "How go the preparations?"

"On schedule," he replied. "Will you be staying?"

"Of course," said Yanti. "I have learned not to leave these events unattended. Now, if you will pardon me, I desire a wash and a fresh set of clothing. Please tell me this place is civilized enough to possess a shower."

The king didn't bother to respond. He instead rose, led Yanti to the door, and instructed the guard to show him to his chambers.

"You should be careful, Your Highness," warned Sialo. "The Reborn King puts a great deal of faith in Yanti's judgment. You should maintain a pleasant relationship with him."

King Halmara returned to his throne. He rubbed his finger along the cushioned chair arms and wondered how much longer he would be allowed to sit here.

King Lousis had been right. But it was too late now.

CHAPTER 30

Kaylia wandered the halls anxiously. Ever since Gewey had told her of the ships bound for Skalhalis, Valshara had been in a panic. Elf and human soldiers had been arriving for over a week, but so far there were only fifteen thousand in total, not nearly as many as they needed. The rest would not arrive for several more weeks.

Selena was distraught when she heard of the attempt on King Lousis's life. She knew it was because of Salmitaya. That the king survived was the only thing that kept her from flying into a rage.

Riders and fauna birds came three times every day, bearing news from the elf and human nations. The elf elders had succeeded in galvanizing their people and they were ready to fight, but many of these were far away. Assembling their armies would take up much valuable time.

Nehrutu ordered his ship to patrol the coast, but stay far out of sight, and to only observe and report. Should enemy ships attempt to invade the Althetan harbor, they would face skilled navigators more than capable of running their ships aground.

Maybell had been escorted to Valshara two days prior. She was no longer the unyielding yet witty woman Kaylia remembered, and after hearing what had become of Malstisos, Kaylia could understand why. The thought of such a noble elf falling prey to evil made her want to weep. Selena had taken Maybell under her charge and kept her close. Kaylia hoped that in time it would help Maybell become her old self again.

Ertik was also recently arrived. When he told her that Theopolou had left him behind in Althetas to speak for the elves, Kaylia had burst out laughing. Only a short time ago, he'd been totally opposed to any kind of contact with humans, and yet now he was actually allowing a human to speak on behalf of his people. Kaylia wished she could have seen her uncle one last time before he went north. She feared that he may never return.

While trying to find things to occupy herself with, Kaylia heard cheers coming from the courtyard. She hurried to see what all the fuss was about. Just as she neared the front entrance, the door flew open and standing there—dusty, hair tangled, and smiling widely—was Gewey. Aaliyah was just behind him. Kaylia was still trying to recover from the overwhelming joy and surprise of his appearance when Gewey dropped his pack and ran to her. He lifted her up, crushing her to his chest. Her heart surged with happiness. It was a moment she never wanted to end.

Gewey looked into her eyes. "I missed you so much." He kissed her with desperate intensity, as if he were trying to make up for their time apart in a single moment.

When their lips parted, she was temporarily unable to speak. Instead, she grabbed his head roughly and pulled him back close, kissing him again.

Eventually, she released her hold and smiled at him. "I have a surprise for you," she said, holding out her palm. A tiny ball of flame came to life. It hovered there for a second before she closed her hand, snuffing it out.

"Nehrutu has been a good teacher," said Gewey, unable to take his eyes off her. "Speaking of Nehrutu, where is he?"

"I am here, Shivis Mol." Nehrutu was standing in the doorway just behind Aaliyah.

Aaliyah spun around. "It is ... good to see you."

Nehrutu smiled. "It is good to see you as well." He stepped closer. "We have much to teach these people, Aaliyah. But there are also things I have learned from them." He grabbed Aaliyah and pulled her close. For a moment, he gazed into her eyes, then kissed her with tender intimacy.

Gewey smiled, suppressing the urge to laugh.

Aaliyah looked to Gewey and Kaylia, then back to Nehrutu. "Then we shall face the world as they do. Together as one." She pulled away from Nehrutu and walked up to Kaylia. "Please forgive me. I only acted out of a sense of duty. But Darshan has shown me that I was mistaken. You are his true mate, and I will never doubt that again."

Kaylia took her hands. "There is nothing to forgive. You were trying to protect your people. I might have done the same."

She then cocked her head to one side as the realization struck her. "Darshan?"

"I will tell you all about it," said Gewey. "There is much for us to talk about. But right now, I need to bathe and change."

Selena approached from the far end of the hall. "It is good to see the two of you safe. And not a moment too soon." She hugged Gewey before turning to Nehrutu. "Please have Ertik gather everyone together in the receiving hall in two hours." She glanced at Gewey and Kaylia, smiling. "No, make that four hours. You will forgive me, but I have things to attend to. I am excited to hear your tale." She bounded off.

"That is as happy as I have seen her in some time," remarked Kaylia. "But all this for later. For now, come..."

She led Gewey to her chambers.

The room was simple, yet comfortable. A large oak bed was pushed against the wall in the far left corner, with a small desk positioned opposite. Just beside the door stood a polished maple wardrobe, together with a small round dressing table and mirror. One unique aspect Gewey noticed was that, instead of the usual lanterns seen elsewhere in Valshara, here there were elf orbs hanging from the ceiling in each corner of the room.

Keeping hold of the bow given to him by Gerath, Gewey set the rest of his gear next to the wardrobe and took a seat on the bed. He laid the precious bow beside him.

"The wash water will take some time," Kaylia said. "You can tell me more about your journey until it comes."

Gewey grinned happily. Ever since Aaliyah had lifted the block on their bond, he had been so elated that he'd scarcely told her anything of his journey during their contacts. Now he picked up the bow and carefully handed it to her.

The moment she touched it, amazement showed on her face. She stood up, staring at the weapon in awe. "This is what you found in the desert?" she asked.

"Yes," he replied. "Along with some other things. And now that I've given it to you, only you can use it."

"I know," she whispered. "I can feel it."

"I wanted to give the staff to Theopolou," said Gewey. "Where is he?"

"Perhaps you can save your tale for when the others have gathered," she suggested. "Much has happened since you've been away." She recounted the events of the past few weeks. She had just finished telling him about the poisoning of King Lousis when two servants arrived carrying a brass basin filled with hot water.

Smiling and giggling impishly at them, the servants left. Kaylia stood and offered Gewey her hand. He took it and allowed her to help him to his feet.

"Enough talk for now." Her voice was soft and seductive. "I have missed my husband."

Gewey's heart raced as Kaylia dimmed the lights. No one would disturb them for some time. He now felt as he had done on their first night together. He stripped off his travel-worn clothes and tossed them into the corner. Dust flew as they landed on the flagstone floor.

Gewey smiled. "I'm filthy."

Kaylia retrieved a washrag from the wardrobe. "Not for long, my love."

CHAPTER 31

As they lay in bed, Gewey felt utterly content, his mind far
away from the obstacles he had already overcome and the
troubles he had yet to face. Kaylia smiled sweetly as she lay
with her arm draped over his chest.

"I never want to leave this room," said Gewey.

As if the fates had been challenged, there was a knock at
the door. "The High Lady sends word that it is nearly time,"
came a shy voice.

Gewey groaned, then called out loud enough for whoever
was on the other side to hear. "Very well."

Climbing out of bed, he rummaged around inside his
pack for the elf clothes Theopolou had given to him. He held
them up and frowned. They were wrinkled and stained. In
fact, all his clothes were in the same condition.

"I have clothes here for you," said Kaylia. "I would not
have you looking like a vagabond." She went to the wardrobe and pulled out a black silk shirt and matching trousers.

Gewey held up the shirt and cocked his head. "I'll miss
the comfort of my elf clothes," he remarked.

Kaylia laughed. "I'm sure we can find you some more. But this must suffice for now." She took out a pair of leather boots and a silver belt. "Do not worry. You will be covered with dirt again soon enough." She grabbed his arm and had him sit on a chair in front of the dressing table mirror.

He looked at himself in horror. His beard had grown to nearly an inch long and his hair was a tangled mess. "I can't believe you can bear to look at me."

"Don't worry," she said, kissing his neck. "I will see to it that you are presentable. Get dressed. I will return shortly."

She donned a cotton robe together with a pair of silk slippers and left the room. A few minutes later, she returned with a young girl dressed in a plain, green tunic and skirt.

"Go with her," said Kaylia. "She will see to your *grooming*." Her last word came out with a light titter.

Gewey gave himself one final look in the mirror and sighed. "Not exactly inspiring, am I?"

"We'll change that, My Lord," said the girl, with a perky bounce.

She led him to an unused chamber and set to work. Soon he was shaved and groomed. Just as the girl was finishing, a guard came in to tell him that Kaylia awaited him in the receiving hall.

The guard escorted Gewey to the hall. Just outside the doors, he saw Chiron speaking quietly to Bellisia.

Chiron beamed as Gewey approached. "Ah, now you are a welcome sight."

Gewey bowed to them both. "When did you arrive?"

"Just now," he replied. "Mine and Bellisia's lands are closer than the others. The remaining elf nations will be here within the month."

"Is it true that Angrääl has taken the city of Skalhalis?" asked Bellisia.

"It would appear so," Gewey replied. "It looks like time has run out. War is come."

"I hear that dear Theopolou left Ertik of Valshara to speak for the elves in Althetas," said Chiron. "How times are changing."

"For the better, I pray," added Bellisia. "The idea of elf and human living together is still unsettling to many of my people. But they are coming to accept it as inevitable, as I have."

"There is much you will hear that will surprise you, Lady Bellisia," said Gewey. "Aaliyah and I made many discoveries in the eastern desert."

"What could possibly be discovered in such a barren waste?" she asked, looking doubtful.

"I am sure Gewey will tell us everything once we are inside," said Chiron. He reached out and opened the door. "Shall we?"

Inside the receiving hall, a large oval table had been placed in the very center of the room. Most of the chairs were already filled with finely dressed men and women, some with obvious military insignia on their attire. Of the elves present, Gewey recognized several from the Chamber of the Maker. Aaliyah and Nehrutu were sat together near the far end. Aaliyah had changed into a deep blue dress with emerald embroidery, and her black hair was now decorated with tiny white flowers.

At the very far end sat Selena, dressed in the ceremonial robes of Amon Dähl. Ertik was to her left, and Maybell to her right. Maybell smiled when she saw Gewey; he waved and smiled in return. Kaylia was at the other end, next to an empty chair directly opposite Selena.

The room went silent as Gewey made his way to his seat. Kaylia touched his hand gently. Chiron and Bellisia found a seat near to Ertik. Chiron whispered something into Ertik's ear that brought a pleased look to his face.

Selena stood and addressed the room. "We all know why we are here. War has come sooner than expected. Angrääl has landed ships in the city of Skalhalis, and will surely march on the attack any day now. We must decide how to act. I know that most of our force is still gathering, but we have already gathered soldiers from Queen Lilian of Farthing and Prince Loniel of Sieren Bay, along with ten thousand elf warriors. King Lousis will have more men here by morning." She sat back down.

A tall, grizzled-looking man with silver hair and rough features got to his feet. "I am General Keise Halman of Farthing. Do we know the numbers we will face, or shall we march blindly into battle?"

"We are trying to find out how many Angrääl has sent," Selena replied. "But as of this moment, we do not know their exact number."

Prince Loniel spoke. "I think it is more important to know if they march on Valshara, or do they look to Althetas."

"We do not know for certain," said Selena.

"What, if anything, do we know?" asked General Halman.

Gewey stood. "We know that if we don't move quickly, this war will be over before it even begins." His large frame loomed tall and commanding over the gathering. "On my way back from the eastern desert, we spotted fifty ships bound for Skalhalis. Angrääl is moving to end this war here and now. It doesn't matter what we do not know. What we *do know* is that we must attack now, or all is lost."

General Halman sneered. "From the looks of you, boy, I wouldn't think you know much at all of battle and strategy. Perhaps you should join the rank and file, and leave the planning to the soldiers among us."

Kaylia very nearly leaped up from her chair, but Gewey held her in place with quick glance.

"And what experience do you have, General Halman?" asked Chiron. "Border disputes? Roving bandits? Before you embarrass yourself any further, perhaps Gewey should take a moment to tell us of what he found in the desert. Those of us who know him would most certainly like to hear of this. And those in this hall who do not yet know him—well, they may benefit as well."

Gewey nodded and went on to recount in detail his adventures in the eastern desert. As he finished, some of the generals and captains in attendance snickered and laughed. Only the elves nodded their heads with understanding.

"And what proof do you have of these outlandish claims?" asked General Halman, looking amused. "I mean, if you can kill fifty men, and are truly a god, then surely you can offer up some sort of proof."

"Gewey is what he says he is," said Bellisia. "And I do not doubt his tale. He need not prove himself to you."

"Clearly, this boy has made fools of you all," said Halman. "Can't you see that? What does a god need with armies? Could he not vanquish our foes with a wave of his hand?"

Without another word, Gewey waved not one hand, but both. Flames shot out from each, racing in opposite directions all around the walls of the hall until meeting just behind the general's head and exploding with a thunderous boom. Halman lurched forward, crying out in fear and scurrying onto the table.

Gewey met the general's eyes. "We do not have time for debate and bickering. So tell me, General Halman, is there anything more I can do to ease you mind?"

General Halman crawled down from the table and took his seat. His hands trembled as he shook his head.

"We will crush Angrääl regardless of how many soldiers they have sent," stated Gewey. His voice boomed and echoed off the walls of the chamber. "I will lay waste to the forces of the Dark Knight. I shall march with you to Skalhalis and burn them to cinders. And now we have new allies in the east to aid us."

Anger and hatred swelled inside him. His power grew. Kaylia reached out and touched his mind. He could feel her concern. He looked down at her and whispered: "I'm fine."

"And what would you have us do?" asked Prince Loniel.

"Gather your soldiers," said Gewey. "In two days, we march on Skalhalis. And when we arrive, Angrääl will know firsthand what it means to face a god." The ground shook for a moment, then subsided. The *flow* of the spirit raged through him, bursting forth and spreading everywhere at once. He could see it touching the entire gathering. It passed into each one, washing over them like a torrent.

Everyone at the table jumped to their feet. The name Darshan was spoken. First by a few, then more and more, until all but Kaylia and Selena, were shouting out his name. Throughout this commotion, the two women continued to look warily at him.

Gewey spun around and left the room, Kaylia following close behind. She stopped him a few feet outside the door and took his face in her hands. "What happened there? I have never felt such rage in you before."

"I am changing," Gewey replied. "Becoming more powerful. I have run so far. I have lived in fear for so long. It is time for that to stop. In two days, I will show the Dark Knight the true meaning of fear."

She looked deep into his eyes. "Am I speaking to Gewey or Darshan?"

Gewey took hold of her hands and pressed them to his heart. He kissed her gently and watched as a single tear spilled down her cheek.

"Now—I am both," he told her.

End Book Three

BOOK CLUB
QUESTIONS

1. Who is your favorite character? Why? And what about them make them enjoyable to read about? Has your favorite character changed since the last book?

2. How well does the author follow the formula of the hero's journey while making the story unique in its own right? Has the journey held true from book to book?

3. How well developed do you feel the character arcs are? And how do you think they develop throughout the book and series?

4. Do you feel Gewey will be the savior he is prophesied to be or will he succumb to the temptations of power? Have your feelings on this changed since the last book?

ACKNOWLEDGMENTS

Jonathan and Eleni Anderson, George Panagos, Vincentine Williams, Gerald and Donna Anderson, Hunter and Sarah Anderson, Bobby and Bobbie Anderson, the Ramos family, the DiBatista family, the Gnyp family, Jen Frith-Couch, Alex Harris, Jaocb and Elizabeth Bunton, Jenny Bunton, HCCS teachers and staff in Brooklyn and everyone who has supported me. I love you all!

ABOUT THE AUTHORS

Brian D. Anderson was born in 1971 and grew up in the small town of Spanish Fort, AL. He attended Fairhope High, then later Springhill College, where his love for fantasy grew into a lifelong obsession. His hobbies include chess, history, and spending time with his son.

Jonathan Anderson was born in March 2003. His creative spirit became evident by the age of three when he told his first original story. In 2010, he came up with the concept for The Godling Chronicles. It grew into an exciting collaboration between father and son. Jonathan enjoys sports, chess, music, games, and, of course, telling stories.

Discover more at
4HorsemenPublications.com

10% off using HORSEMEN10